A DEADLY GAME

The Game Master regretted that it had been impossible to remove Tracy's body from the scene. A single finger hardly qualified as a trophy of...of... He chewed his lower lip thoughtfully. Ah, yes, a trophy of *the sophomore.*

Poor little sophomore, a mere pawn sacrificed in a larger game, that of his next quarry, *the professor.* He had great hopes for her. "Yes." The Game Master smiled. "With a little assistance, the professor might prove my finest and most satisfying adversary."

The third crab pot lay some distance away. He'd saved the best for last, and anticipation made his hands tremble as he pulled up the wire cage containing *Number Thirty-six*'s skull.

"Ah," he crooned as the water drained away, leaving his prize gleaming ivory in the mist. "So many of you waiting for me... So many women, and all I have to do is collect them."

Other *Leisure* books by Judith E. French:

THE BARBARIAN
THE CONQUEROR

AT RISK

JUDITH E. FRENCH

LEISURE BOOKS NEW YORK CITY

*For my brother, Paul F. Donahue, Lt.,
Delaware State Police, retired, with love and
thanks for answering my endless questions and
for your unfailing support through the years.*

A LEISURE BOOK®

June 2005

Published by

Dorchester Publishing Co., Inc.
200 Madison Avenue
New York, NY 10016

ISBN 0-8439-5394-2

The name "Leisure Books" and the stylized "L" with design are trademarks of Dorchester Publishing Co., Inc.

Printed in the United States of America.

Visit us on the web at www.dorchesterpub.com.

AT RISK

Prologue

Somerville College, Dover, Delaware

Tracy Fleming stopped outside of her history professor's office and glanced at her watch. She was a few minutes early for her seven-o'clock appointment, but the door was open several inches. Hesitantly, she knocked.

"Good morning," called a muffled voice. "Come in."

Tracy pushed open the door and blinked. No lights were on, and the blinds were closed, making the room dim after the brightly lit hallway. "Thanks for seeing me on such short notice." She stepped inside and shifted her load of library books to one hip. "It's important, or I wouldn't bother you."

"Back here."

Thinking the professor must be using the copy machine in an alcove in the far corner of the office, Tracy moved past the desk. "It's about my research

1

paper," she said. "I know it's due on Friday, but I've got this jerk ex-boyfriend, and—"

The tall figure rose out of the shadows like a malevolent ghost.

Tracy opened her mouth to scream, but a fist slammed into her midsection, knocking the air out of her, making it impossible to utter more than a strangled whimper. She would have fallen from the force of the blow, but her attacker lunged past and seized her from behind.

One hard hand clamped over her mouth, and he leaned close to whisper in her ear. "Game's over, Sophomore. You lose."

Terror lent her strength. She drove an elbow into his ribs and tried to wrench free, but he arched her neck back and slashed once across her throat. Tracy felt an odd sensation of cold against her bared flesh as pinwheels of light exploded in her brain. A tide of blackness flooded her head, and then the wave receded, leaving nothing at all.

He released her, thrusting the body away so that it tumbled forward onto the carpet. Thin ribbons of light seeping between the blinds revealed a splash of liquid on his glove. For an instant, he regarded the crimson color like another man might a rare jewel. Then he smiled, lowered his head, and licked the drops from the back of his hand.

The blood was warm and slightly salty.

He liked the taste.

Chapter One

Somerville College, Dover, Delaware

Liz Clarke glanced at her watch as she hurried down the hall toward her office in Jacobs Hall. Her early class began at eight on Mondays, but she was already forty minutes late for her seven-o'clock appointment with a student in her popular Heroines of the American Revolution course.

Liz hated being late for anything. She'd deliberately set her alarm an hour early so she'd be on time for Tracy's appointment. Why had her car picked this morning to refuse to start?

Shifting her briefcase and purse to her left hand, Liz stopped to find her office key before realizing that her door was slightly ajar. Puzzled, she stepped inside and flicked the switch. The room remained dark. The only light came filtered through the closed blinds.

"Tracy?" A faint sense of unease made Liz cautious. "Is anyone here?" The room had an unpleasant, almost sweet odor. She hesitated, letting her eyes adjust to the gloom before she dropped her briefcase on the nearest chair and walked to the desk.

Glancing at the floor, Liz stopped short as she saw the dark, wet pool on the carpet. Water . . . No, not water, something thicker and darker. A chill washed over her as she took one more step and saw a slender hand. Blood? Liz rushed forward, took in the sprawled body of Tracy Fleming, throat slashed from ear to ear, and screamed.

Trembling, Liz dropped to her knees beside the young woman. She seized the girl's limp wrist, desperately seeking a pulse.

A man burst into the room. "Liz? What's wrong? I heard you—holy shit!"

Normally, Cameron would have been the last person she'd have wanted in her office. Now, even the grad student's face was a relief.

He froze, his handsome features nearly as bloodless as Tracy's. "Oh, God," he babbled. "Who? God, there's blood everywhere! Her throat . . . Holy shit! Is that Fleming?"

"I can't find a pulse." Liz gripped the girl's hand. "Call 911. Get security." Her voice came out in a rasp. Liz felt the wet carpet through her linen slacks and realized that she was kneeling in blood. She supposed the thought should have sickened her, but she was too numb to care.

"What are you doing? Don't touch her!" Cameron admonished with macabre fascination as he dialed from her desk phone. "You're contaminating a crime scene. The authorities—hello, yes. I'd like to report a murder. You heard me correctly. A murder."

Dazed, Liz sat on the floor beside Tracy's lifeless

body as Cameron calmly spoke with the 911 operator and then dialed campus security. Liz hadn't
known that a body so delicate could contain so much
blood. Or that Tracy could be such an unnatural
shade of white and yet still warm to the touch.

She lifted the girl's head to her lap and felt again
for a pulse, this time in the hollow below her ear, just
above her bloody throat. Nothing. Liz had taken advanced CPR classes, but this was beyond her ability.
She could do nothing but hold Tracy and wait.

She had no conception of time passing.

"Elizabeth?"

Michael's voice cut through Liz's stupor. She
glanced at the open doorway and sighed in relief.

"Elizabeth? Are you hurt?"

"No." Liz smoothed a clump of Tracy's stained
and matted hair. "But I think she's dead."

"I told Liz she wasn't supposed to touch the evidence." Cameron raised both palms and backed
away from the desk, as if distancing himself from
her ignorant blunder.

Michael didn't break eye contact with her as he
rolled his wheelchair into the dim room. "Did you
find her just like this?"

The knot in Liz's throat made it hard to speak. She
nodded, gently lowering the girl's head to the sticky,
wet carpet, turning Tracy's face so that her blond
hair hid the gaping slash across her throat.

"And you're all right?" Michael asked.

"She's dead, isn't she?" Liz stood up and swayed,
suddenly feeling as though she'd had too much to
drink.

"Of course she's dead." Cameron's voice was
scathing as he ventured out of the corner. "Any fool

can see the girl's dead. Her throat's been cut. Oh, shit. Her left hand. Where's her finger?"

Liz couldn't stop herself from looking. Someone had hacked off the ring finger of Tracy's left hand.

"I should have been here." Her words tumbled out . . . only half coherent as she stumbled to Michael's chair. "I was late. My car wouldn't start. Amelia had to drive me . . ." She heard a high-pitched buzzing as the room began to spin. "If I'd been here on time . . ."

"This isn't your fault," Michael insisted firmly, his tone calming.

"She had no business touching the body. I told her—"

"Whitaker," Michael cut Cameron off. "We don't need you here. Go out into the hall and keep everyone away until the police arrive."

"Security's doing that. What do you think, Captain? Attempted rape?"

Michael's gaze hardened. "Go to the front entrance and direct the responding officers to this wing. And stay close. They may want to question you."

"Yes, but—"

"Now, Whitaker."

Cameron vanished.

"She's beyond your help." Michael clasped Liz's blood-smeared hand. "You look faint. Maybe you should sit down."

She swallowed, trying to dissolve the constriction in her throat, hoping the floor would stop swaying under her feet. "I'm okay," she murmured, more to convince herself than him. "I'm all right."

"Nobody ever gets used to seeing this sort of thing." Michael's grip was reassuring. Despite his handicap, his commanding presence made her feel better.

"Tracy and I . . . we had an appointment," she explained, needing to talk. "I was late. My car wouldn't start. Amelia had to give me a ride." She knew she was rambling, repeating herself, but she couldn't help it. "When I got here . . ."

An ambulance wailed in the distance, the jarring sound as grating as a dentist's drill. "I locked my office yesterday," Liz said. "I know I did. I always do. Maybe maintenance—"

"No one's blaming you, Elizabeth." Michael pointed up at the darkened fluorescent fixture overhead. "That out when you arrived?"

"Yes. I tried the switch, but the light wouldn't come on." She pulled away, grabbed a fast-food napkin from her desk, and wiped her hands.

"What else did you touch in the room?"

"Nothing. The door was open. I came in, laid my briefcase on the chair, and . . ." Her voice seemed to fail her.

"There's a bench in the hall. It's better if we talk out there."

The antique church pew was only a few yards from her office. When they reached it, Michael motioned her to sit. Liz was vaguely aware of an assistant dean and other faculty members staring at her, but security had already begun to block off the area with yellow tape. Gooseflesh rose on her arms, and she began to shiver.

Michael took her hand again. "Look at me, Elizabeth. Don't pay any attention to them. Think. Did you see anything unusual on your way in? Hear anything?"

"Nobody. The hall was empty." She swallowed. Did he think she would have strolled calmly past a madman waving a bloody knife without alerting anyone?

"Did you see anyone outside? Electricians? Delivery vans?"

She shook her head.

"You entered where?"

"The double doors that open onto faculty parking. I told you," she said. "My car wouldn't start this morning. You'd already left, so I called Amelia to drive me to school."

"And you saw nothing out of the ordinary? No one you don't see on a regular basis?"

"No. Wait, yes," Liz corrected. "As we were turning into the parking lot, there was a motorcycle. A Harley. The driver was leaving in a hurry, and Amelia had to stop to avoid flying gravel. She drives that red BMW, and she didn't want dings in the paint. He was wearing a helmet, so I couldn't see a face, but he was in a hurry."

"He? You know it was a man?"

She shook her head. "No, I just assumed. He was wearing leather and looked too big for a woman." The sirens grew louder. "You don't think he—"

"I don't think anything." Michael took the bloody napkin she was shredding, balled it up, and thrust it into his pocket. "At this point, we ask questions, we don't conclude. Have you seen the Harley around campus before? Could it be a student?"

"It's possible. But that's the faculty lot. Students don't have the blue stickers. You know Ernie tows the kids' cars on the slightest excuse."

"But you don't remember seeing the bike here before?"

8

She shook her head. "I'd remember it."

"Can you describe the motorcycle?"

"Big. Black and silver." She shrugged. "It was loud and . . ." She broke off as two tall and booted state troopers came around the corner.

Michael squeezed her hand. "They'll take over. Tell them what you told me."

"I'm terrified," she whispered, watching the troopers approach.

"You'll be okay, Elizabeth. You're tough."

"Stay with me?"

His rugged features softened, and his vivid blue eyes clouded with compassion. "Absolutely," he promised. "All the way."

Hours later, after she'd finished the seemingly endless questioning and had a chance to shower and change into clean clothing at the school wellness center, Liz leaned back against the headrest of Michael's van and closed her eyes.

"Headache?" he asked.

"Worse. I think my skull's about to explode." Gravel crunched under the wide tires as Michael slowed for the right turn off onto Clarke's Purchase Road, the narrow blacktop that threaded around the edge of the marsh and cut through thick stands of oak and maple that had stood untouched for over a century. "I appreciate this," she said.

"Anything for a friend."

"This is what you did . . . when you were with the state police. Did you ever get used to it?"

"Death?" He exhaled softly. "Never did. Never wanted to."

Liz opened her eyes, glad for the dark glasses that

cut some of the afternoon glare, and stared out at the waves of reeds and grass that stretched toward the bay as far as the eye could see. To her right, a great blue heron rose gracefully above a glistening eddy of black water. Far overhead, a marsh hawk hovered almost motionless against a cloudless sky. "How could any human being do that to another?" She blinked back tears.

"They can't. Murderers aren't human."

"But who would want to hurt Tracy Fleming? She was the sweetest girl. One of our full scholarship students. Shy. Everyone seemed to like her."

"Not everybody, apparently."

"Could it have been a random mugging? Something to do with drugs?"

Liz avoided Michael's eyes, looking instead at his broad hands on the steering wheel. Michael was over six foot two and muscular. He was tanned from the sun, and he worked out regularly. No one who passed them on the road would guess that Michael Hubbard's legs were useless, courtesy of a drunk driver who'd skidded off the road one rainy night and hit the off-duty detective who'd stopped to help a stranded motorist.

"I can't believe someone murdered her in my office."

"You said you had an appointment with Tracy. How late were you?"

"I looked at my watch on my way down the hall and it was seven-forty. We were supposed to meet at seven because Tracy works—worked in the snack bar from eight until ten, three mornings a week." She swallowed, trying to dissolve the block of concrete in her throat. "If only my car had started this morning. If I'd been there—"

"If you'd been there, you'd probably be dead and on the way to the medical examiner's office instead of my place. It's not your fault, Elizabeth."

Liz took off her glasses and rubbed her eyes as she tried to erase the image of Tracy's hand with the missing finger . . . of blood everywhere. "Am I a suspect?"

He gave an amused grunt. "No more than me or that overaged grad student. Is Whitaker still making your life miserable?"

"I changed my phone number. And the new one's unlisted. I meant to give it to you earlier this week. Cameron's a jerk, but he's hardly a killer."

"Was Tracy Fleming married? If she was, chances are that the husband did it. Or a boyfriend. Most victims know their murderers." Michael eased off on the gas as the van rattled across the one-lane wooden bridge.

The abandoned and crumbling 19th-century farmhouse on the left was the last structure on Clarke's Purchase Road before they reached Michael's home. Her house lay another mile and a half beyond his place, surrounded by swamp and woods. On the far side of her farm were a wildlife preserve, more wetlands, and several potato farms, leaving the stretch of road without another inhabited dwelling for miles.

"I don't know if Tracy had a husband," Liz said, answering Michael's question. "I never saw her except in class. Once she came in with a black eye. She'd tried to cover the bruising with makeup, but I know what to look for. I counseled abused women at

11

my last college. When I asked her about the injuries, she had a logical excuse. They usually do."

"Did she ask for the appointment?"

"Yes, but I don't know why. Tracy's grades weren't outstanding, but she wasn't in danger of failing. She even turned in her last paper early, and I gave her a 97 percent—the best mark she's ever gotten." Liz put her glasses back on. "I didn't tell anyone but Amelia that Tracy would be there this morning. And that wasn't until I called her for a ride."

Michael shook his head. "That doesn't mean Tracy didn't tell someone." He seemed to consider his last words before stating, "You're telling me that your office door isn't normally unlocked?"

"No—of course it's locked. You don't think the murderer was looking for me, do you?"

"If he or she was, there was no reason to kill Tracy. I'm betting that someone followed her into your office. And my guess would be that it was personal, a crime of passion."

"Not some psycho targeting young women at our college?"

"Don't look for the worst scenario. I'm not. I did suggest that they double the security at school until we know what's what."

Michael worked part time as a special security consultant, and he'd been instrumental in installing the new video surveillance system for the college. "The cameras weren't running in the new wing yet, were they?" she asked.

"A glitch in the program when they were installed. Ernie already called the company, and they promised to have it fixed immediately."

Michael turned into his driveway, and Liz made

no protest. She didn't want to go home just yet. She was afraid that if she were alone, she'd start crying and wouldn't be able to stop.

"How does an early supper sound? I can toss up a salad and throw a couple of steaks on the grill," he offered.

"Thanks. I do want to come in for a while, but I couldn't eat. I don't think I'll ever be hungry again."

"You will, trust me. This is a lot for anyone to deal with. You're a strong woman. You'll get through it."

Michael's two German shepherds, Heidi and Otto, bounded down the lane to greet the van. Trained guard dogs, the animals were highly intelligent. Michael had raised them both from pups, and he was as devoted to them as any parent could be to his offspring. The dogs returned the love tenfold. Now, neither animal barked, but their obvious joy at their master's return was evident in their every stride.

"Don't get out yet," Michael warned.

"I know, I know."

He slipped a silent dog whistle off the rearview mirror, put down his window, and signaled the dogs that they were off duty. "Okay."

Liz waited as Michael made his way to the back of the vehicle, strapped himself into his chair, and used the electric lift to lower himself onto the concrete driveway. She followed him and the dogs up the ramp to the side door of the spacious ranch house and watched as he punched in the code to deactivate the alarm system.

"With Otto and Heidi, I don't know why you need that protection," Liz said. She put a bag of groceries on the counter and checked the dog bowls to see if they had clean water. Heidi was sitting in front of Michael's chair, offering him her paw to be shaken, and her mate was wriggling all over, as excited as any pup to share in the attention.

"Sixteen years on the job," Michael replied, stroking Heidi's sleek head with genuine affection. "I've seen enough to make me cautious."

"In other words, you're paranoid?"

"All cops are. At least the live ones," he said. "Lots of crazies out there. Some may figure that a cripple's a pushover. I don't intend to be anyone's easy mark." He rolled over to the counter, took down a container of dog treats, and gave one to each animal. "No more biscuits," he cautioned. "You'll get fat."

"Stop calling yourself a cripple." It was an argument they'd had often, and one she'd never won. "So your legs don't work. That doesn't make you less of a man."

"I hear you. Make yourself at home," he replied, changing the subject. "Time for an oil change." He flashed her a boyish grin. "I'd appreciate it if you'd check the suet feeders. Those woodpeckers go through them as though they grew on trees. I think both pairs of Downies are feeding chicks."

Heidi trotted after him as he rolled the chair toward his bedroom wing and the bathroom. Otto stretched out on the kitchen tile and gazed at Liz through half-closed eyes as she put milk, butter, and a dozen eggs in the fridge.

As always, Michael's house was neat and orderly, despite his varied interests. Two cameras with telescopic lenses and a stack of bird books lay on the dining-room table beside an opened sketchbook and a set of professional artist's charcoal pencils. A telescope and binoculars rested on the bench in the breakfast area beside the floor-to-ceiling bay window that offered a spectacular view of the marsh. Candid photographs of Michael's deceased wife, Barbara, were scattered in the various rooms, and Liz knew that a large studio portrait of Barbara held the place of honor over the family-room fireplace.

This was clearly a man's house, but not austere. Liz had felt at home here the first day she was invited in, two years ago, soon after she'd returned to Kent County. She still felt comfortable here. There was something very appealing about Michael Hubbard. She suspected she cared a lot more for him than she wanted to admit. "Want a beer?" she called.

"No, thanks. You have one, if you want," he shouted back.

"Iced tea will do." She wanted a double Scotch, but drinking alone wasn't a luxury she allowed herself. Neither was drinking alcohol on a workday. Not even today.

She put ice in two glasses and filled them with tea from a pitcher in the refrigerator. Then she hurried outside to check the bird feeders, glad to have something ordinary to do on a day that was far from normal. But as she slipped a fresh cake of nut and berry suet into a wire basket, she wondered if any day would ever be routine again.

Ten minutes later, Michael joined her in the kitchen. His shirt and tie were gone, replaced with an Eddie Bauer T-shirt over the tan cords he'd worn to work. "I bought a new game," he said, waving toward the computer workstation set up in one corner of the dining room. "Swords, dragons, and monsters. You'll love it."

"Maybe." Liz perched on a stool and gazed down at her hands. "I'm not a flake, but I keep expecting to see blood."

"You're right, you're not a flake."

Michael pulled salad greens, tomatoes, cucumber, and green pepper from the refrigerator, piled them on the counter, and looked directly into her eyes. "You know you're welcome to spend the night here, Elizabeth. I've got two extra bedrooms. I can't vouch for how comfortable the beds are, but I've never had any complaints."

"I'll be fine, but I may need you to give me a lift in the morning. That is, if you're planning to go in tomorrow."

Michael nodded. "Sure. I'll be there all week. But if you're nervous staying alone after what happened—"

"I'm used to being alone." She opened the utensils drawer, looking for a paring knife. "And I grew up . . . God, Michael!" She snatched her hand back. "Do you have handguns hidden in every drawer in this house?"

"Never know when you'll need one in a hurry."

She scowled at him. "I suppose it's loaded."

"Not much use if it isn't."

Liz removed a knife and slammed the drawer shut. "Don't you worry about children?"

"No kids ever in here but your Katie. And she's what? Nineteen? Old enough to respect firearms."

Liz began to peel a cucumber. "You know my opinion of handguns."

"I keep trying to talk sense to you."

"I'm not afraid of staying by myself. I grew up on

16

Clarke's Purchase. Daddy always said that if you lived this far out in the country, the bad guys couldn't find you. Besides, I've got good locks on the doors, and a cell phone as well as a house phone. If I need help, I'll call the police."

"Fair enough. Just remember, I'm a lot closer."

Liz didn't feel quite so sure of herself when she stood at her front window watching the taillights of Michael's van grow smaller and smaller until they disappeared around the bend in her long gravel lane. Maybe Michael was right. Maybe she should consider getting a dog, as much for companionship as for protection.

The old Dutch farmhouse seemed twice as large since Katie had gone away to school. Sometimes Liz could swear she heard her father's voice calling, "Rise and shine, porcupines! Time to get up!"

So many memories here . . . some happy, others best forgotten. And among them, those of her father were always the strongest. She'd read somewhere that the Chinese believed a house soaked up the events that had transpired there, that wood and brick and stone retained emotion. She'd never seen the ghosts that were supposed to haunt the brick farmhouse on Clark's Purchase, but she'd often felt them around her.

"What do you think, Muffin?" she asked her cat. "Are you willing to share your quarters with the canine species?" Muffin closed her eyes, obviously unwilling to be drawn into a discussion that involved dogs.

Suddenly Liz needed to hear her daughter's voice,

to make certain that Katie was alive and safe. She was only nineteen, just a baby. The same age as Tracy Fleming.

Gooseflesh rose on Liz's arms as she remembered Tracy's eyes, wide and lifeless, empty of all expression. So what if it was the middle of the night in Dublin? Hadn't Katie gotten her out of bed enough times? What else were mothers for if not to make their kids' lives miserable? Liz hurried back to the kitchen. There wasn't any need to look up the number. It was written in red marker on every page of her calendar.

Quickly she punched in Katie's number, and after what seemed like an unusually long wait, the phone began to ring. Once. Twice. "Pick up, kiddo," Liz urged.

After the sixth ring, there was a metallic click and Katie's cheerful voice proclaimed, "Linda and Katie aren't here. This is our day to have tea with the leprechauns. Leave a message and we'll get back to you. Ta-ta."

Liz replaced the handset with enough force to send a pen rolling to the floor. It was after nine p.m. here. That made it two in the morning in Ireland. Two a.m. on a school night and Katie wasn't in bed. She hoped her daughter would have a good excuse. Studying at the library wouldn't fly.

The irrational thought that something might have happened to Katie sent a chill through her. God, how she loved that kid. Her daughter was the only good thing she'd gotten out of four years of marriage to Russell Montgomery.

She'd been furious with Russell for suggesting Katie leave her tuition-free place at Somerville to go abroad and study. Now, despite her foolish fears, she was glad Katie was far away from Dover, where college sophomores who kept appointments with their professors ended up dead.

Too agitated to sleep, Liz made herself a cup of caffeine-free herbal tea and went upstairs to shower for the third time that day. She'd just stepped out of the tub when she heard the phone ring. Grabbing a towel, she wrapped it around her and darted into the bedroom. She snatched up the receiver but was too late. Whoever had called had hung up.

"Damn it." She dropped the towel and rifled through a drawer for her phone book before dialing Katie's number again. When the answering machine at her daughter's flat clicked on, Liz said, "It's Mom, Katie-Bird. Call me when you get in. I don't care what time it is. Phone home, E.T."

Something furry brushed against Liz's leg. She jumped, and then saw it was only Muffin. "Are you trying to give me a heart attack, cat?" She groaned and dropped onto the bed. If she wasn't careful, she'd end up as paranoid as Michael.

Muffin's tail was fluffed to a bottle-brush, and her ears were flattened against her head. She leaped up into Liz's lap, and her back claws dug into Liz's bare thighs.

"Ouch! Get down! What's wrong with you?" Liz switched out the light and went to the window.

Without the lamp to blind her, stark moonlight illuminated the backyard, dock, and marsh. Liz stared out, taking in the familiar objects: trees, the overturned boat that she'd been painting, and the stand of cedars near the lane. Reeds and cattails swayed soundlessly beyond the bull's-eye window glass, and ghostly clouds scudded across a pale lemon moon.

No wonder I'm jumpy, she thought. It was on nights like this that she and her sister used to scare each other witless with tales of headless apparitions and long-dead pirates. She'd been born in this house, the same as her father and grandfather, and his grandfather before him. There had been Clarkes living on this spot since the first Robert Clarke had traded a seaman's sewing kit and a French musket to a Lenape Indian named Dancing Otter for his daughter and three hundred acres of swamp and woods.

Since she'd been a small child, Liz had been accustomed to staying alone. Few days or nights at Clarke's Purchase had ever made her uneasy, but tonight was an exception. What was it that Michael had said? "When you get used to seeing violent death, that's when you need to worry."

She'd never get used to it.

A movement outside caught her attention. Something that could have been the figure of a man loomed at the edge of the cedar grove. Liz's mouth went dry. Were her eyes playing tricks on her? She watched for a space of time without seeing anything suspicious, before turning away from the window.

"See what you've done?" she said to the cat. "Maybe I should give up history and teach creative writing. I've got the imagination for it. Next I'll be seeing swamp angels."

Resolutely she returned to the bathroom, but before she could turn on the water, the phone rang again. "Katie? Is that you?" Liz asked when she picked up the receiver. "Hello?" The crackling hum lasted for another thirty seconds, and she could have sworn she heard someone breathing before the connection broke.

"Son of a bitch!" Liz wondered if she should call Michael. Was she overreacting, or was it possible that Tracy's killer had her unlisted number? Impossible, she thought. She hadn't even given it to Michael yet. She reached for the phone.

The ring startled her, and she snatched her hand back. Heart pounding, she snatched it up.

"Lizzy?"

"Who is this?" The voice on the other end of the line was hauntingly familiar.

"I know it's been a while, but—"

"Jack?" She stared at the receiver in disbelief. It couldn't be Jack, and yet she knew his voice as well as she knew her own. "Is that you?"

"Guilty."

She exhaled with relief that just as quickly became irritation. "I thought you were in prison."

Chapter Two

"I got out a month ago."

"How did you get this number?"

"I heard Tracy Fleming is dead. Is it true?" Jack's deep voice sliced away the years.

Liz felt her insides clench. "Somebody murdered her."

Jack swore.

"Was Tracy a friend of yours?" she asked.

"Hell, she lived down the street."

"She's half your age."

"Damn it, Lizzie, I've known Tracy since she was in third grade. What happened?"

Liz shuddered at the memory. "Somebody cut her throat. In my office at the college."

"Somebody, hell! It was that friggin' little shit, Wayne."

"Who?" Liz asked. Goose bumps prickled the nape of her neck.

"Wayne Boyd. Her ex-boyfriend."

"What makes you think he would kill her? Was he abusing her?"

"If you call beating her black and blue, and breaking her wrist, abuse. Yeah, he did his best. Six weeks ago, Tracy threw the bastard out, and he's been harassing her ever since. Last week, she found her tires slashed."

"You should be telling the police this, not me."

"Right." Jack's tone got deeper, his words more deliberate. With the Rafferty temper, when a Rafferty stopped shouting, it signaled trouble. "Tracy had a protection order against Wayne. It didn't mean shit."

"This is a matter for the authorities."

"A little late, don't you think?"

"Don't do anything stupid," she said.

"See you around."

"Jack. Wait!" There was a soft click as he hung up the receiver.

Liz curled up on the bed and hugged the feather pillow. She didn't know if she could deal with Jack Rafferty on top of Tracy's murder. Jack was a part of her life that she'd thought she'd put behind her. He was the reason she'd almost refused the position at Somerville, and it was because of Jack that she and her only sister ignored each other except for cheery cards on holidays.

The Raffertys were watermen, commercial crabbers and fishermen. When Liz's dad had been sober, he had captained a boat for Jack's father. The families had been friends and enemies for as long as Liz could remember. But when she'd become a teenager, her dad had threatened to shoot Jack and his brother

George if they came near his daughters. He always said that the pair of them would end up dead or in jail, and he wasn't far from wrong. George was doing ten to fifteen for running cocaine up the Delaware Bay on one of the Rafferty fishing boats, and Jack had just gotten out of jail.

Jack calling her . . . after all these years.

She and Jack had been an item the summer she'd turned seventeen. They'd been hot for each other until the romance came to an end when he dumped her for her sister Crystal. God, had it been that long since she'd spoken to him?

The first haze of a migraine flashed a rainbow of colors in her head. She thought longingly of the bottle of Scotch gathering dust in the kitchen cupboard. A drink might be what she needed to stave off the headache, she thought as she padded down the back stairs to the kitchen in her T-shirt and Jockey hi-cuts. Considering what she'd been through in the last twenty-four hours, maybe she deserved a double.

She had her foot on the first rung of the stepstool and was reaching for the cupboard's wooden latch when common sense took over. Rule #1: Never drink alone. Rule #2: Never drink because you need one. Rule #3: Alcohol is a waste of calories that could be used for chocolate.

Muttering under her breath, Liz shoved the stool back in front of the fireplace and fished two Excedrin Migraines out of the bottle in the cupboard. She was washing the tablets down with a glass of chocolate milk when the phone rang again.

Liz answered with trepidation, but this time she was rewarded by her daughter's voice. "Hi, Moms! What's up? Don't tell me you've got a boyfriend."

"No such luck." Liz licked the chocolate off her upper lip and sank into the cushions of an oversized rocking chair.

"Is anything wrong?"

Liz wondered where to start.

"Moms?"

"No, I'm good." Darkening Katie's world with the horror of Tracy's murder seemed as foolish as trying to dilute her own worries in a glass of Scotch. "Just missing you." That, at least, was the truth.

"You sound a little weird."

"I'm fine." Lying to Katie had to be better than scaring her half to death. And she couldn't bear to go over the gruesome details again tonight.

"Got another headache?"

"I wanted to hear your voice," Liz said. "Is that a crime?"

"Not checking up on me, are you? I'm an adult."

"Nineteen or not, I'm still your mother, and I'm paying the bills. Isn't this a little late to be getting in? Don't you have an early class?"

"S.U.C., Moms. Situation under control. I was at the pub with Niall and Liam."

"Pubs close at eleven."

"We went to Niall's to study." Katie rattled on, full of gossip about new friends, a pair of Italian sandals she'd found at half price, and a rock concert in Glasgow that Niall had bought tickets for. They ended up talking for the better part of an hour, and finally said their good-byes so that Katie could get some sleep before her first class.

"Be careful," Liz said. "When you go to Scotland, stay with Niall and don't wander off with strangers."

"Not unless he's six feet tall, gorgeous, and wearing a kilt. I've always wanted to see what they wore underneath." Katie giggled. "Not to worry. I can take care of myself. Give Michael a hug. Love you much."

Liz checked all the doors and windows to make certain they were securely locked, then turned on both the front and backyard lights before going upstairs. "Next I'll be jumping at shadows," she said to the cat, who trailed after her. Muffin meowed softly in agreement.

What Jack had suggested made her feel better. If the boyfriend, this Wayne something or other, had killed poor Tracy, other girls at school weren't in danger. Hadn't Michael said that the murder was probably a crime of passion? Certainly, *she* had nothing to worry about. Who would want her?

Still, she mused, it wouldn't hurt to get caller ID. And spending money on a security system might be a good investment. There was no telling when Katie might be here alone some night. She decided to ask Michael's advice on the best one to buy without annihilating her budget.

Budget. Liz grimaced. That was a sore subject. Putting a new roof on this house had cost double what she'd expected, and she'd been forced to have the whole place rewired. Painting, fixing the occasional leaky pipe, even a little carpentry, she could do. But electrical wiring was different, and hiring dependable servicemen who would come when they said they would was almost impossible. "I should have majored in electrical engineering instead of American history," she muttered to the cat. "Then we'd all be living in the lap of luxury."

What was wrong with her? Was she so insensitive that she could worry about finances when Tracy lay in a drawer at the county morgue?

Liz folded back the coverlet on her double bed before sliding between the sheets. She knew it was late, but she refused to look at the clock as she burrowed under the pillow. She had to get some rest tonight. She hoped she could do it without reliving the image of Tracy's body sprawled in dark pools of blood on her office floor.

Eventually, Liz drifted off, but memories of Jack and Tracy tangled her fitful dreams. She woke more than once in a cold sweat, listening to the creaking and shifting of the old wood in the house and the hoot of a great horned owl from the grove of trees outside. Sometime after four, the phone rang again, but when she picked up, an intoxicated woman demanded to speak to J.D. "You have the wrong number," Liz said sleepily.

"You tell him to get his sorry ass home, or else."

"You have the wrong number," Liz repeated. "There's no J.D. here."

The woman cursed her and slammed down the receiver.

"Great start to another cheerful day," Liz said to the cat. Pulling on a pair of jeans, she went downstairs to brew a pot of coffee.

It was too late to go to bed and too early to go to school. She sat in front of the window and watched the sun come up over the marsh. The big, old house was quiet but peaceful, without any of the creepy emptiness she'd felt when Michael had dropped her off the night before.

Michael had suggested she might want to take a

few days off from school, and the dean had agreed. But Liz knew that if she didn't go back to her office right away, she'd never be able to set foot in there again. Maybe she'd rearrange the furniture after the carpet was replaced and the walls repainted, she thought. Whatever she did, she wasn't going to be frightened away.

Donald Clarke had had a lot of weaknesses, but cowardice wasn't one of them. "Whatever scares you is what you need to face head on, kiddo," her dad had always said. "Otherwise fear grabs you by the throat and chokes the life out of you. You wake up one morning hiding from shadows."

"Okay, Daddy," she murmured into the empty room. "I'm here, aren't I? What more do you want from me?"

On a whim, Liz decided to see if her car would start before she called the garage. She didn't know jack about automobile engines, but the last time she'd called a tow truck, she actually hadn't needed a mechanic. She'd flooded the engine. At $125 a pop, she couldn't afford to make too many mistakes like that.

Apparently, her luck had changed. When she turned the key, the engine started. She called Michael to tell him she wouldn't need a ride, got ready, and drove to the college, arriving there by seven-thirty.

Somerville was a relatively new school, established only ten years ago, but Liz thought that the architects had done a marvelous job of blending the two-story, whitewashed brick buildings with the eighteenth-century mansion that had once been the heart of a colonial plantation.

Massive oak trees, stone walls, and boxwood

hedges graced the rolling green lawns adorned with marble fountains and wrought-iron benches. If she hadn't remembered the dairy farms that had been on either side of the crossroads before the land was purchased for the college, Liz might have assumed that Somerville had been offering a quality liberal arts education to upper-class students for more than a century.

This was the last place she'd expect a murder.

The school was a private institution, with tuition comparable to Penn State, but Somerville had already received national acclaim for the high priority of academics over sports. Liz knew how lucky she was to hold a full professorship here, even if she'd been forced to face old demons and memories of Jack Rafferty to accept the position.

She mulled over how lucky she was to have a position in such a respected school as she pulled into the parking area. Gritting her teeth, she steeled herself to enter Jacobs Hall and walk down the corridor—a simple act that had been routine until yesterday.

"Get a hold of yourself," she muttered. "You can do this."

The morning was sunny, so she chose a parking space under a big pin oak. As she was getting out of the car, she heard the roar of a motorcycle, and quickly turned to see a black and silver Harley coming toward her. It looked like the same bike she'd seen yesterday.

Liz hesitated, uncertain. Should she wait to see who the rider was or be cautious and go inside? Curiosity won out. She was pretending to check her door lock as the driver braked and tugged off his helmet.

"Morning, Lizzy."

"Jack?" She turned and stared at him, her throat dry, tongue frozen to the roof of her mouth.

Jack Rafferty was trouble in tight jeans. His dark hair was frosted with streaks of gray, but the years had only honed his roguish looks and air of danger. *Pirates,* her dad had called the Rafferty brothers. No description could have fitted Jack better. Give the man a cutlass, and he could have stepped off the set of a Johnny Depp movie.

Liz felt a chill as she realized that Jack had been the stranger she'd seen driving away yesterday morning. He'd called her in the middle of the night to ask about Tracy's murder. And he'd never explained exactly how he'd gotten her unlisted phone number.

"What are you doing here?" she asked. The years had been good to him. His craggy features were a little more weathered, but it was the same old Jack. Liz experienced the breathless sensation of leaping blindfolded into an abyss.

"I was looking for you," Jack said. "I went by your place, but you'd already left."

"You went to my house?"

"It's not like I don't know the way."

"I'm not sure how to take that."

"We're not exactly strangers, Lizzy."

"I saw you in this lot yesterday morning."

"Dropping Tracy off. She told me she had an appointment with you."

"She did." Liz glanced around. Ernie Baker, one of the security staff, was coming around the corner of the building. "Why did you bring her to school?" she asked Jack.

"I told you. Somebody slashed her tires. She asked for a ride."

"The weather was good. Why weren't you out on the bay fishing?"

"What is this? Twenty questions? You think I killed Tracy?"

"Hold it, buddy!" Ernie shouted, waving and breaking into a trot. "I want to talk to you."

Jack ignored him. "I went by Wayne's this morning. The trailer was empty. His truck's gone."

The guard was breathing hard. He slowed to a walk. Sweat glistened on his broad face. "Let's see some I.D. The police have some questions for you."

"See you around." Jack nodded to Liz.

"Jack," she insisted. "The state police—"

"The cops never had trouble finding me before." He wheeled his motorcycle in a tight circle and gunned it.

Ernie punched in numbers on his cell phone, presumably to summon help, but Liz knew the Harley would be gone long before the first security vehicle appeared. "You all right, Dr. Clarke?" Ernie's gaze dropped to the swell of her breasts above the modest vee neck of her blue angora sweater.

"Fine." Ernie had a habit of ogling students and female staff alike. It made Liz uncomfortable. "Don't let me keep you from your work."

"Yeah, uh . . ." He made a show of pulling out a crumpled pad. "I've got to make a report of this," he said with feigned importance. "You can corroborate my story, Dr. Clarke, that the trespasser was uncooperative."

"He wasn't trespassing," she said, suddenly feeling protective of Jack. "His name is Jack Rafferty, and he was here to see me."

Ernie scowled, licked his full lips, and hurried toward the beige van marked *Somerville College Security* that was pulling into the lot. The driver, a young Asian man Liz knew only as Barry, pulled the vehicle to the curb and rolled down the passenger window.

As the two men talked, Liz went in search of Michael. She had another appointment with a police detective Wednesday morning, but she couldn't wait to tell Michael about Jack. She might even mention those hang-up calls she'd received earlier in the night.

"Rafferty may have something," Michael said, ushering Liz to a seat in the security office on the far side of the campus. Maneuvering his wheelchair to the counter, he poured her a cup of coffee. "Just a little milk, right?"

She nodded. "It's annoying that Jack was able to get my unlisted number, but he's no murderer."

Michael opened the refrigerator and frowned. "Looks like Ernie forgot to pick up milk this morning. All we've got is that powdery white stuff. That okay?"

"Fine." She poured cream substitute into her coffee and stirred it with a clean stirrer. The coffee was strong and hot. It steadied her nerves and pushed back the gathering migraine. "Jack told me that he brought Tracy to school on his motorcycle yesterday. He was the man Amelia and I saw leaving the parking lot."

"She saw him too?"

32

"Yes—remember I told you that Amelia came to a full stop because his bike threw up gravel when he pulled out?"

"You did tell me that. And you went directly to your office when you arrived?"

"Yes."

"Wonder why he wasn't gone by then. You said you were forty minutes late for the appointment. What was Jack doing all that time?"

"I have no idea."

Michael frowned. "You say he thinks that this Wayne Boyd could have killed her?"

"Jack said that Tracy had a protection order out against Wayne—that he'd vandalized her car."

"If she had papers on Boyd, there'll be a record of it. I imagine those questions are already being asked." Michael's gaze met hers. "You realize that you shouldn't be talking about this to anyone but the police. Jack Rafferty could be a killer, and you'd be putting your life on the line as well as clouding a murder investigation."

"You're saying that I shouldn't be discussing this with you either?"

Michael nodded. "We're friends, Elizabeth. I care about you, and I'd do anything to protect you. But there's a right way and a wrong way to proceed. What you're doing is understandable but dangerous."

She sighed. "You're right. I wasn't thinking clearly last night."

"You told me that Rafferty just got out of jail. What was he in for?"

"Assault and attempted murder." Even in California, a world away, Liz had heard the story. Her sister had sent a clipping from the *Delaware State News.* Headlines had read "Local Waterman Convicted in Four-Day Trial."

"I think I remember that one," Michael said. "A dispute over crab traps, wasn't it?"

She nodded.

"Rafferty. Rafferty." Michael looked thoughtful. "Wasn't he involved in a drug-running operation on the bay? Something about picking up shipments of cocaine from Colombian vessels off the coast and—"

"That was George, Jack's brother."

"No, I'm certain it was two of them. And I think a Rafferty boat was confiscated."

"George was convicted. The drug charges against Jack were dropped."

"That doesn't mean he's innocent." Michael took a sip of coffee and shrugged. "It means the D.A. didn't think he had enough evidence to convict. Jack's conviction on the assault and attempted murder proves he's capable of violence."

"He's a waterman, Michael. They take robbing traps seriously."

"Dead seriously, apparently. Don't make excuses for him. He's gone to a lot of trouble to cast blame on Tracy's boyfriend. You're in deep water, Elizabeth."

"But why would Jack want to kill Tracy? And why do it here, at the school?"

"Don't put words in my mouth. There were no prints found in your office. We're not dealing with a stupid criminal. Most of them are idiots. But not this one."

Liz forced herself to speak lightly. "Now you're jumping to conclusions, aren't you? You said *he.* How do we know Tracy's murderer wasn't a woman?"

34

"If she was, she would have had to be an unusually powerful female. A wound such as Tracy suffered was delivered from behind, one quick slash. And from the angle of the cut, her assailant would have had to be close to six feet tall."

The coffee lost its flavor, and Liz placed the cup on Michael's desk. "How concerned should we be that the killer may be on the prowl for another victim?"

"There's no way to tell. Until he's safely behind bars, we have to assume that any woman could be the killer's next target." Michael shut down his laptop and closed the cover. "Could you take a few weeks off, fly to Dublin, and spend time with Katie?"

For a few seconds Liz considered the possibility. Seeing her daughter would be a joy. Getting away from all this would be heaven. "No, it's not possible." She shook her head. "Too close to end of term. I have a commitment to my students."

"Think about it."

"Why would I? There's no logical reason to think I'm in any danger. And if I leave, I may not have a job to come back to."

"I thought that was what you'd say. If you won't go, the least you can do is to take steps to protect yourself. Let me teach you to use a gun. I saw just what you need at the gun shop, a K-22 Smith & Wesson Revolver. Minimal noise and minimal recoil, with the same weight and feel as a .38."

"Absolutely not." Liz shuddered. "You know how I hate handguns."

"Is it easier to see yourself lying on the floor in a pool of your own blood? Tracy Fleming never had a chance against her killer."

"I'll think about it," she agreed reluctantly, "but I warn you, I'm a tough sell."

"Think hard, Elizabeth. It might be the most important decision you ever make."

"They found the murder weapon," Cameron said, taking the chair across from Liz's in the cafeteria. "It was right there under the body."

Liz looked up from her untouched lunch tray. "The weapon? Where? I didn't see—"

"Under Tracy's body." Cameron sniffed his egg salad sandwich, took a bite, and chewed with gusto.

Liz glanced away, wondering why she'd ever been even remotely attracted to the jerk. Too long without getting laid, she thought. But as much as she despised him now that she'd gotten to know him, she had to admit there was nothing wrong with the way the thirty-year-old grad student looked.

Cameron Whitaker was over six foot with a swimmer's sleek body and short-cropped blond hair. His features were in perfect proportion: straight nose, square jaw, and full lips almost feminine in their sensuality. Contacts tinted hazel eyes a stunning blue-green, and one tanned cheek dimpled charmingly when he smiled.

Cameron was smiling now, model-perfect teeth gleaming white. "I saw it—the weapon," he said. "An oyster knife." He took another bite of his sandwich, washed it down with a half glass of apple juice.

Liz rubbed her eyes, trying to ease the pain of her headache, wishing Cameron would go away. The morning had been bad. The kids were too stressed out to talk about anything but Tracy's murder. She'd canceled the test she'd planned to give, and instead they'd taken turns reading aloud from the journal of Minnie Talbot, a freed black woman who'd accompanied her husband to Valley Forge and later, as a widow, had served Washington's army for two years as a sutler.

Liz had another class after lunch, Women and the Oregon Trail, but she couldn't even go home after that. There was a meeting with the dean at three p.m., essays to grade, and after school she'd promised to help organize a memorial service for Tracy.

"The blade was honed to a razor's edge," Cameron said. "Are you listening?"

"What? Oh, yes." She stirred a blue packet of sweetener into her iced tea. "You . . . you seem to be well-informed."

He leaned over the table, resting his elbows on an illustrated edition of Rowe and Wright's *Bible of Etruscan Pottery* and lowered his voice. "I have my sources."

Cameron's breath smelled of spearmint. "I don't mean to be rude," she said, "but I'd rather not discuss the murder. Michael said—"

"Captain Hubbard? I wouldn't put too much faith in him, if I were you. His security expertise didn't work too well for Tracy, did it?"

"You'll have to excuse me," Liz said, rising to her feet. "I have to prepare for my next class."

"How did you sleep last night? Creepy out there in the boonies, isn't it? Any night you want company, I could come—"

"Thank you, but no thanks."

"You're missing a good thing."

"I doubt it." She turned deliberately and walked

away to deposit her tray, tea and all, at the return window.

Cameron was insufferable and, from what the students said, the worst grad student at Somerville. Yet Professor Steiner, his superior, positively doted on him. Since the new history wing had opened, Nancy Steiner's ancient history classes and Cameron Whitaker were directly across the hall from Liz's office and lecture hall. Liz couldn't avoid crossing his path a half-dozen times a day. She tried to remain civil, but it wasn't always an option. Cameron was as thick-skinned as a rhinoceros.

As she left the cafeteria, Liz couldn't get Jack out of her mind. Was it a coincidence that he should show up only hours after Tracy's death? Why was he still in the parking lot forty minutes after he claimed to have dropped Tracy off at school? Had Jack been involved in George's drug running? And if he had—how far was dealing in illegal drugs from murder?

The next twenty-four hours were as bad as Liz imagined they would be. After a terrible night's sleep, she kept her Wednesday morning appointment with State Police Detective Nathan Tarkington. He'd asked her to explain exactly what she'd seen and done when she discovered Tracy's body, and then he'd spent the next forty-five minutes questioning her on every detail of her story. Liz thought she had her emotions under control, but by the time she left the Troop 3, she was close to tears.

Somehow she got through the rest of the day, and when she returned for the rally and candlelight vigil that evening, the streets around the school were choked with students, parents, and the media.

After someone pointed her car out to a photographer, Liz had to call Michael on her cell phone and ask for his help in dodging television crews who were shooting film for the eleven-o'clock news. Cameron Whitaker had no such misgivings about speaking to the press. She saw him talking animatedly to a reporter and guessed that Cameron's handsome face would be plastered on the front page of the *News Journal* as well as the *State News*.

Later, when she joined friends and fellow staff members Amelia and Sydney in the school auditorium for the service, Cameron appeared, well pleased with himself. He slid into a seat just behind her during the opening prayer and leaned forward to talk to her.

"You missed the excitement, Liz. See that woman in the front row, the one with the bad dye job and the black dress? That's Charlene Cook, Tracy's aunt. I got a whiff of her on the way in, and she smells like a brewery. She's so smashed, she can hardly walk."

"Shh," Liz whispered. The memorial program showed the face of a younger and heavier Tracy Fleming smiling shyly in a high school graduation photo. It was all Liz could do to hold back tears.

"No sign of the boyfriend." Cameron raised his voice. "Wonder why?"

Amelia turned to glare at him. "Do you mind?"

Ignoring her, he nudged Liz's shoulder. "There, in the third row, on the far end. See the fat woman?"

Liz tried to give her full attention to the chaplain.

"That's the boyfriend's mother," Cameron said. "Mabel Frank. She's another piece of work, a real redneck."

Charlene Cook began to sob.

Liz felt Cameron's breath on her neck. "The aunt and the boyfriend's mother got into a swearing match in the parking lot. Charlene accused the boyfriend of being a murderer. I thought the fat lady was going to deck her."

"Will you please be quiet?" Liz whispered. "You're embarrassing us."

That silenced him until the end of the service, but when Liz rose to leave, he caught her arm. "You shouldn't be out there in that swamp alone," he said. "Certain you don't want me to drive you home?"

"Absolutely certain. Now, if you'll excuse us, we have dinner reservations."

"I haven't eaten either," he replied. "I could—"

"No," Amelia said. "That's not possible."

"Good night, Cameron." Liz peeled his hand from her arm and followed Sydney and Amelia through the throng into the hall. "I want to offer my condolences to Tracy's aunt," she told her friends. "Go ahead, and I'll meet you at the car."

Amelia pursed her lips. "I admire your patience. It was all I could do not to call for security to escort Whitaker out of the service."

"He's an obnoxious prick," Sydney said. "I don't know how Nancy tolerates him."

"I believe it's his prick that got him the position," Amelia murmured. "And helps him keep it. It certainly isn't his teaching skills."

Liz grimaced. "Gross. With that personality, he'd have to be good in bed."

"I've known Nancy for years," Amelia said. "She likes younger men, but she never stays with the same one long. She'll tire of Mr. Whitaker soon enough."

"Not soon enough for me," Liz added. "Somerville would be a lot more pleasant without him."

Liz spent the next few hours with Sydney and Amelia in a quiet corner of the Blue Goose Inn, talking and drinking decaf iced tea while they sipped white wine. Liz would have loved a glass, but she refused to allow herself the pleasure tonight because she was still too shaken by Tracy's murder. She was very cautious when and where she drank. As the child of an alcoholic, she felt the threat of addiction hanging over her head like some proverbial sword of Damocles.

She still had no appetite and barely touched her dinner. She knew she was poor company tonight, but being with friends was better than sitting alone at home facing a wilted salad.

It was after ten when they finally called it a night, and the other two dropped her off in the faculty parking lot. Liz looked in the backseat before unlocking her car and getting in. Sydney waved, and Amelia backed up and waited until she started her engine.

"See you tomorrow," Sydney called as they pulled away.

Liz was about halfway home when she noticed that the vehicle several car lengths behind her had made the same last three turns as she had. She sped up, but the headlights maintained the same distance. When a commercial van traveling in the opposite direction passed her, Liz glanced in her rearview mirror to try to see whether the object of her concern was a car or a truck, but she couldn't tell.

"Great," she muttered as a chill ran through her. "Now you're letting your imagination run wild." But when she reached the next stop sign, she barely slowed, turned the wheel hard in the opposite direction from home, and stamped hard on the gas. The speedometer hit seventy before she glanced back. The road behind her was dark.

Feeling foolish, she turned west and drove back toward Route 13, the main highway running the length of Delaware. She made a five-mile detour, driving past the mall, Atlantic Book Warehouse, and the Dover Downs Slots and Racetrack before heading back toward the bay and home.

Michael's lights were still on when she passed his house. She wanted to stop, but it was late, and she had an early morning class. She slowed, made the turn onto her gravel drive, and pulled gratefully up to the back door of the old brick house.

"Shit." The floodlight in the yard was out, but the kitchen lights were on. Odd, she thought. She'd been certain she'd left the outside one on as well, but after a day like this, she was lucky to remember her own name. For a few moments she sat there, uncertain what to do. Lowering the window, she listened. Other than the usual chorus of frogs, everything was quiet. "Fools rush in," she muttered.

Cautiously, with pepper spray in one hand and keys in the other, Liz got out. She knew that her car lights would remain on long enough for her to unlock the back door and get inside. She hurried up the worn brick walk and unlatched the gate before she noticed something lying on the porch by her back door.

Hair rose on the back of Liz's neck. It looked like ... It was. "A damned trap!" She climbed the wooden steps and grimaced as she looked down at a rusty iron trap containing the mangled carcass of a muskrat. "How the hell ..."

Maybe a stray dog dragged the muskrat up, she thought. But where had the trap come from? She wondered if somebody was illegally trapping on Clarke's Purchase. Her dad had never permitted the ugly practice when he was alive, and she had no intention of allowing anyone to do so now.

Still fuming, she started to unlock the back door. But when she put her hand on the knob, the door swung open. Liz froze, and her eyes widened in surprise. Muddy boot tracks trailed across her clean kitchen floor.

She opened her mouth to scream, but nothing came out. For an instant she could smell the stench of rotting flesh as the years receded and the image of a man materialized in her mind.

... One eye was blanketed with a ghastly white scum. The other, faded blue and rheumy, bulging with madness, stared at her. He grinned, revealing ruined blackened teeth and spilling tobacco juice down an unshaven, pustulated chin ...

"No!" Liz cried. "No!"

In seconds, she was back inside her car, trembling as she punched 911 on her cell phone. She gave the emergency dispatch operator her name, address, and cell number, and told the woman she would wait for the police at the end of the lane.

"It wasn't real," she mumbled aloud as she jammed the key in the ignition. Her breath came in quick, hard gasps. Her heart thudded against her ribs. "In my head . . . just something better forgotten." She fought to get control of her emotions. "You're okay, girl, it was nothing. Just a bad dream." Still, she locked her car doors and kept the motor running as she waited.

Within half an hour, a state policeman arrived, vehicle lights flashing. Officer Weeks didn't look much older than Katie, Liz thought, and he wasn't nearly as tall or as imposing as the troopers who had responded the morning of Tracy's murder. What had happened to law enforcement? If an intruder was hiding in her house, did they expect this teenager to protect her?

After Trooper Weeks confirmed the information she'd given the dispatcher, he went inside, presumably to search for a suspect. When he found nothing more alarming than the muddy footprints, he asked Liz to come in and determine whether anything of value was missing.

"Nothing that I can see," she replied after a quick inspection. The twenty-dollar bill she always left on the fireplace mantel was lying in plain sight, untouched. It was one security suggestion of Michael's that she'd taken months ago. He'd told her that if she ever came home and found the twenty missing, she should run because it meant that someone had broken into the house.

"I noticed the cash lying on the mantel," Officer Weeks said. "Anyone bent on robbery would have snatched that. I don't believe we're dealing with a criminal. My guess would be that you left the back door unlocked, and some trapper or fisherman wandered in. Either he was lost or he had boat or car trouble. Nobody was home, so he went in and used your telephone."

"And that's legal?"

"No, not legal, but understandable."

"And the muskrat trap on my porch? That's as easily explained?"

"A stray dog. Half my calls are dogs running loose."

"There's something more," she said. "I think someone followed me home from the school tonight."

He made a few notes on a report as she told him about the suspicious vehicle. "But you can't be certain that you both weren't going in the same direction?"

"No," she answered reluctantly. "I thought—"

"If you were followed, that person or persons couldn't get here ahead of you and track up the floor, could they?"

"No, I suppose not."

He frowned. "And no one else has a key?"

"Only my daughter Katie, but she's in Ireland."

"Have you thought that Katie might have lent her key to a boyfriend?"

"No. I can assure you that she didn't."

"Are you positive that you did lock up when you left this morning, Ms. Clarke?" The officer's tone was patronizing.

"Positive," she answered. "And it's Dr. Clarke."

"You're a physician?" He glanced at his clipboard.

"No, I'm a history professor at Somerville."

"I see."

It was plain to Liz that Trooper Weeks didn't see at all, that he'd already decided she was a fruitcake with nothing better to do than waste his time.

"Honestly, I don't believe you have anything to worry about. This could be a prank by one of your students." He handed her the clipboard. "Sign here, please. And don't hesitate to call if there are any more suspicious incidents." He removed his hat and slid behind the wheel of his police car. "And it never hurts to double check when you leave the house."

Tight-lipped, Liz watched as the officer turned his vehicle around and drove out of her yard. Maybe he was right. Maybe she'd only imagined that someone was following her tonight, but she hadn't forgotten to lock her back door. She'd done that religiously since she was nine years old.

If this was someone's idea of a joke, it was a sick one. And the only person she could think of who was capable of such behavior was that ass Cameron. Still seething, she went inside, turned the deadbolt, and prepared to scrub the muddy footprints off her clean brick floor.

Chapter Three

Clouds held sway over the salt marsh, blocking out the thin moonlight, locking the mist-shrouded stretch of grass and water in a timeless prism of shifting images and surreal sounds. Primeval sighing was interspersed with the rustle of reeds and an occasional splash that echoed hollowly through the phragmites.

The electric motor was nearly silent. Birds fluttered restlessly and frogs leaped as the small boat slid past, but the gray fox crouching on a spit of land barely pricked his ears as the Game Master appeared and then vanished in the fog along the course of the narrow, mud-choked channel.

The maze of salt marsh was home to a myriad species of birds and wildlife. Few humans ventured here, and fewer still at night, but the Game Master needed neither compass nor artificial light to find his way to the exact spot where he'd dropped three commercial crab pots a month earlier.

He cut his motor and drifted the last few yards to

the clump of marsh grass that concealed a long wooden stake. Running strong fingers down the slick pole, he found the chain and began to retrieve the first trap. The rectangular wire-and-frame cage was surprisingly light as he pulled it up. A six-inch jimmy clung to the grass inside, but the Game Master hadn't come for crabs tonight. Gently he extracted the crustacean and released it into the muddy current.

"Enjoy your swim, *Number Thirty-six*?" He lifted a slim ulna from the pot, thrilling to the texture of the slick, clean surface. The bone didn't answer, but he hadn't expected it to. His ladies rarely had anything to say after a period of submersion. The Game Master chuckled. When dead women started talking to him, he'd know he'd lost it. After all, he wasn't a madman.

No, he didn't expect conversation, but it would have been an intriguing variation on what had become the dullest part of the game. He'd have to think of a more creative way to dispose of the remains, some method that offered greater challenge. Letting the crabs eat flesh and hair off the butchered carcasses had become routine, and if there was one thing that bored him, it was routine.

He sucked a gummy scrap of residue off a cracked rib and tossed the bone into the water. The marsh would soon reduce that bit of offal to crumbling shreds, indistinguishable from the layers of muck that formed the floor of the ancient salt marsh. He tucked the remaining ribs into the gunnysack on the floor of the boat before tending his second trap.

Most of the phalanges and the metacarpals were missing from *the nurse's* right hand, but that was to be expected. This specimen had been short and petite, nothing like the supersized stockbroker last fall. Three traps had sufficed for *thirty-six*. He remembered her name, but she was a discarded game piece, too insignificant to bother addressing formally.

He frowned. *The nurse* had been a definite disappointment, not nearly as quick or crude as his first planned kill, *the waterman*, or as messy as *thirty-seven*, foolish Tracy, whose death had been hardly fulfilling.

The Game Master regretted that it had been impossible to remove Tracy's body from the scene. A single finger hardly qualified as a trophy of . . . of . . . He chewed his lower lip thoughtfully. Ah, yes, a trophy of *the sophomore*. Silly Tracy would be "*the sophomore*." Not a particularly original classification, he supposed, but then she hadn't been anything out of the ordinary. She'd been hardly worth the trouble it had taken to plan and carry out her execution.

Poor little sophomore, a mere pawn sacrificed in a larger game, that of his next quarry, *the professor*. He had great hopes for her. "Yes." The Game Master smiled. "With a little assistance, the professor might prove my finest and most satisfying adversary."

The third pot lay some distance away. He'd saved the best for last, and anticipation made his hands tremble as he pulled up the wire cage containing *Number Thirty-six's* skull. Her hair had been long and blond. He hoped a few strands remained. Skulls proved such interesting diversions—all those delightfully shaped holes—and those with hair were always the best.

"Ah," he crooned as the water drained away, leaving his prize gleaming ivory in the mist. "So many of you waiting for me . . . So many women, and all I have to do is collect them."

Liz's night had passed without further incident. She got up minutes before the alarm went off and followed her normal morning routine for a workday. She filled Muffin's water dish and had started for the door, briefcase and sweater in hand, when the phone rang. She almost didn't answer. It was getting late, and she had a class. But then curiosity got the best of her, and she picked up.

"Liz! Good, I caught you."

Damn. "Russell." Liz grimaced at the sound of her ex-husband's voice. "What an unexpected pleasure."

"How are you?"

"Russell, I can't talk now. I'm due at—"

"At school. I know. But I was talking to Katie, and she's worried about you. She asked me to call."

"I'm fine." She shifted impatiently from one foot to the other. "There's nothing wrong with me."

"I read about the incident in the papers. Awful. A terrible thing—terrible for you."

"Worse for Tracy Fleming."

"It's too early in the morning for sarcasm," he said. "Don't tell me you're still pissed about Katie going to school in Dublin. It's the experience of a lifetime. She's having a ball."

"That's what I'm afraid of." Liz glanced at her watch. "Did you want anything, Russell? Have you had a change of heart and suddenly decided to contribute toward her tuition?"

"Are you going to start bitching about money again?"

"Why not? Who's paying for our daughter's education? I am. You've never given me a dime of child support."

"It wasn't because I didn't want to. You know the bankruptcy wasn't my fault. My partner—"

"Your financial problems didn't stop you from re-marrying. Twice. Or from fathering other children."

"That comment's beneath you. You've been fortu-nate. You've always had enough income to provide for Katie's needs. And now you've inherited the fam-ily farm and—"

"*Bought* the farm," she answered. "Bought, as in an exchange of money. All I inherited were past-due taxes, a leaking roof, and debts."

"There were good reasons why I couldn't help out more when Katie was small."

"You were broke because you gambled away every cent you could get your hands on." She sounded like a shrew, but then, she could always count on Russell to bring out the worst in her.

"That was years ago. Dr. Elliott says I—"

"You don't need your shrink's excuses. You have an endless supply of your own."

"I didn't call you to argue."

"No? That's a surprise." She was annoyed and not about to let him weasel away from the subject. "Katie had a full family scholarship at Somerville," she re-minded him.

"Apparently, she wasn't happy there."

"She was happy enough until you filled her head with dreams of castles and shamrocks."

"That's unfair, Liz, and you know it. Katie has al-ways wanted to study abroad. With my cousin living in Ireland, it seemed the perfect solution."

"I'm hanging up, Russell."

"I'm worried about you. You never used to be so bitter."

"I don't think I'm bitter enough," she answered. "Contribute to her education fund, or Katie's coming home at the end of the semester. And give my love to Danielle and all the little Montgomerys."

"Liz—"

"Go to hell, Russell," she said before placing the handset gently on the receiver. "Damn." She'd forgotten to warn Katie not to give the new number to her father. And now that he had it, he'd probably buy billboard space and advertise it to the world. It was going to be another world-class morning.

She wasn't deceived by her ex-husband's apparent concern. He wanted something. A loan? Russell Montgomery never bothered being charming without a reason. Unfortunately, it had taken her four years of marriage to discover that.

"Experience is the best teacher," her father had always said. "A man learns more by living than he can get from books." She supposed that counted for women as well. She knew that being married to Russell had given her quite an education.

She paused long enough to gather Muffin in her arms and give the cat a quick hug. "At least I can depend on you," she murmured. Muffin was a superb mouser, and if she could just train her to drop the little rodent bodies in the trash instead of carrying them up to deposit on her bed, life would be that much calmer.

Liz was halfway to her car when she noticed a small boat approaching her landing. The operator stood and waved. Liz got into her car and drove across the lawn to the dock.

Jack Rafferty cut his motor, allowed his boat to drift against the mooring post, and leaped ashore. "Morning, Lizzy," he called.

Uncertainty made her voice sharper than she intended. "What are you doing here?"

He paused and gazed at the house. "You've cleaned the old place up," he said. "Looks good."

"Jack, I've got to go to work. If you stopped by to reminisce about old times—"

"No, I didn't. Come with me. There's something I want you to see."

"Why would I go anywhere with you? I have a class this morning."

He strode toward her, and the years fell away until she was seventeen again, standing on this spot and watching him come up the dock. Jack had added muscle since then, but the Rafferty eyes were the same intense hue, and he still moved with grace and purpose.

"What's happened to you, Lizzy? Lost your nerve? You didn't mind missing school in the old days."

"I was a stupid kid, Jack. I'm not that anymore."

He stopped. "No, guess you're not, *Doctor Clarke*." He shrugged. "But this has to do with you and probably with Tracy's murder."

"Can't you just tell me?" She knew the answer.

"Showing's easier."

He'd told her the same thing the time she'd asked him if he cared about her. Jack had never said the words she'd longed to hear. Instead, he'd pushed her down on the deck of his father's fishing boat and kissed her. No boy had ever kissed her that way before, and if she shut her eyes, she knew she'd feel the sun-heated planks beneath her bare back again and taste the salt on Jack's skin.

Oh, Lord, Jack Rafferty was her weak spot.

"Come on, unless you've gotten too high and mighty to take a ride with an ex-jailbird."

Common sense told her to turn the car around and drive to school, but Jack had always known how to make her break the rules. "Give me a minute to change into jeans and call to let the school know I'm not coming in."

He nodded, and she hurried to the house. She took the stairs at a run, located clean jeans, boat shoes, and a T-shirt, and pulled them on. Using a pad and ballpoint pen from a drawer in her night-stand, she left a note on her pillow. *Gone for a boat ride with Jack Rafferty.* If she disappeared, at least someone would know whom she'd been with last.

Liz wondered if she was getting paranoid. This was Jack, for God's sake. She ran a hand through her short hair, then picked up the note and crumpled it into a ball. She was about to toss the paper into the trashcan when she hesitated, unsure if she was be-having irrationally or not. Hadn't she just found a dead girl in her office? That wasn't normal. Maybe she had good reason to be paranoid. She threw the message on her bed and hurried downstairs.

Twenty minutes later, she was seated in the bow of Jack's boat as he steered a course out of the river and into the Delaware Bay. He turned south and headed down the coast. The tide was low, and Jack kept the small craft far enough from the beach to keep the motor from hitting bottom.

It had been too long since Liz had been on the open water. Another day, she would have reveled in the sound of the waves and the feel of salt spray hitting her face. But being with Jack, under these circumstances, kept her from fully enjoying the experience.

She twisted to look at him. One bronzed hand was on the tiller; the other rested on his left knee. His shirtsleeves were rolled up, and he had a baseball cap pulled low on his forehead. He looked as though he hadn't bothered to shave this morning. "Where are we going?" she asked.

"What?"

She raised her voice, trying to make herself heard above the wind and tide. "Where are we going?"

"You'll see."

At forty-four, Jack was as infuriating as he'd been at twenty. He revealed what he was thinking when he wanted to or not at all. The habit annoyed her no end, and she knew that he was aware of it.

They passed a lone fisherman anchored in the shallows in an aluminum pram and an older couple heading north in a twenty-four-foot Grady White. Gradually, Liz felt herself relaxing. She didn't know why she was here, but she felt better than she had since she'd found Tracy's body. She found herself caught up in the familiar sights and sounds of the bay: flocks of migrating shore birds wheeling in formation overhead before descending to the beach in search of horseshoe-crab eggs, a black and white osprey carrying twigs to her nest atop a channel marker, and the wind-blown shrieks of laughing gulls.

Maybe she was crazy, but she'd always seen beauty here. For all of California's balmy weather, white sand, and blue water, the West Coast had never stolen her heart as the Delaware Bay did. "Bay water in your blood," Daddy had said.

At Bowers Beach, Jack turned right and headed up the Murderkill River, past the public boat ramps and docks. An old man throwing bread to the ducks looked up and waved, and Liz waved back. The commercial fishing boats were all out on the bay. Private craft bobbed against their moorings on the South Bowers side, but Jack didn't let up on the throttle. He continued on past the houses and businesses lining the waterway.

"Where are we going?" she asked again.

"Not far."

They rounded a bend, and he pointed toward a boat ramp ahead on the left. An ambulance, an aging fire truck that read *South Bowers* in white letters painted on the side, and three police cars were drawn up at the landing. At the water's edge, a crowd gathered around a large wrecker in the process of winching a blue Ford truck out of the river. Several divers in wet suits waited nearby.

Jack steered the boat in a slow circle, then aimed the bow back toward the bay. "Wayne Boyd's truck," he said. "I heard they found it this morning."

"Tracy's boyfriend?"

He nodded. "Cops never caught up with him."

"Suicide?"

Jack shrugged. "He wasn't launching a boat. Apparently, somebody drove straight off the dock at a high rate of speed."

Stunned, she stared back at the truck. "Did they find a body?"

"Not yet. If they had, the divers wouldn't be going back in the water."

"You think Wayne deliberately drove the truck off the ramp?"

"No loss if he did. Wayne was a shit."

"But why kill Tracy and then himself? It doesn't make sense."

"Shits don't always make sense."

She was quiet as they motored past the restaurant and rows of pilings lined with squawking seagulls. "If Wayne did it, then it's over, isn't it? The other kids at Somerville are safe?" *I'm safe.*

Jack didn't answer.

That had always been his habit, as well. He didn't believe in stating the obvious. Liz shut her eyes and tried to imagine what it would be like to stop jumping at shadows.

Once they were out in the bay again, Jack turned the boat north. "I heard you have a kid in college," he said. "Just the one daughter?"

"Yes," she answered, grateful to be talking about Katie. "She's living in Dublin—Ireland. She—"

"I know where Dublin is, Lizzy. I may not have a doctorate, but I did manage a few years at Del State."

"I'm sorry," she answered. "I didn't mean—"

He grinned at her. "I'm a waterman. It's in my blood, like it's in yours. I'm not cut out for classrooms or a nine-to-five job. But that doesn't make me Jed Clampett, either."

Emotion made her voice husky. "Twenty years is a long time, Jack. I didn't know what you were doing."

"Didn't you?" He pushed the throttle to full. "I heard when you got your divorce."

She wanted to ask how he'd found out. Instead, she gripped the side of the boat and fixed her gaze on an osprey's nest atop a buoy. After several minutes, she asked, "Do you have any children?"

"Divorced. No kids."

"Significant other?"

He shook his head.

"Tracy?"

He scowled. "I told you, she was a friend. She lived down the street. Tracy didn't have much in the way of family. No father. Mother's in jail someplace down South. Texas or Arkansas. There's Aunt Charlene, but she never did much for Tracy except spend the kid's welfare allotment on beer, cigarettes, and the slots. My mom used to buy Tracy school clothes and shoes."

"She had ambition."

"She wanted something more out of life than she had. And she was sweet. Too sweet to be with a guy like Wayne."

"Did the police question you about her death?"

"Nope. Never found me."

"Why were you still in the parking lot when Amelia and I arrived? I was late. Tracy was murdered—"

"Earlier," he finished for her. "She was probably killed while I was sitting there waiting for her."

"Why would you wait for forty, forty-five minutes?"

"Tracy told me she had this important appointment with her history professor. She wanted to keep it, but she didn't plan to stay at school that day. She was scared of Wayne, and she wanted to move out of her trailer. After I dropped her off, she asked me to wait and take her home."

"But you were leaving when I arrived. Why did you go without her, if you thought she—"

"Look, Lizzy, either you believe me or you don't.

58

Tracy said that she'd see if you'd give her an extension on a paper that was due. She thought it wouldn't take more than twenty minutes. If she wasn't back in half an hour, she said for me to just go. There was another guy who had an early class and then nothing until after lunch. She thought he'd give her a ride home."

"So you waited how long?"

"Half an hour. Then another ten, maybe fifteen minutes, before I took off. I'm not sure. I wasn't expecting to provide an alibi. Hell, I didn't expect her to end up dead."

She took a deep breath. "Did you have anything to do with that truck in the river?"

"If I did, would I be stupid enough to tell you?"

Liz felt suddenly chilled despite the warmth of the morning. "No, I suppose you wouldn't."

His gaze locked with hers for what seemed an eternity. "I didn't do anything to Tracy or to Wayne. If I had found him, I wouldn't finish it that way."

Was he telling the truth? She thought he was. She'd never known Jack to lie to her, not even when he knew that his words would tear her world in two. On the other hand, he had a temper, and he was capable of violence. She'd always known that.

She remembered an afternoon in August hot enough to scorch the soles of her bare feet on the sandy Bowers Beach streets. She must have been seven, eight at the most. She and Crystal had been waiting outside of Casey's for their dad when they'd heard yelling in the vacant lot behind the bar. Running to find the cause of the excitement, Liz had discovered Jack and a taller boy, Sonny Shahan, rolling on the ground locked in bloody combat.

Fists, knees, and curses flew. Hooting local kids egged the pair on, but they needed no encouragement. Both opponents were already bruised and bleeding. Liz had started backing away when her sister grabbed her shirt and yanked her sideways. "Look out, stupid!" Crystal had warned.

Startled, she'd stared down at what she'd nearly stepped on. In the flattened grass lay the crushed and mutilated remains of a nest of newly hatched mallard ducklings. Later, when older heads and harder hands had separated them, Jack and Sonny had each blamed the other for the atrocity, but she had been too ashamed to pay much attention to the outcome of the fight. In full view of the jeering onlookers, she'd crouched in the gravel beside the weathered building and vomited up the moon pie and the grape soft drink she'd had for lunch.

Liz still couldn't abide the smell or taste of grape soda.

"Go ahead. Say it."

Jack's words jerked her back to the present. "What?" she asked.

"Say what you're thinking."

"I . . . wasn't," she stammered. "Not what you . . ."

"No?" His eyes narrowed. "You weren't going to remind me that I just spent over three years in jail for assault and attempted murder? That I tried to kill Randy and Daryll Hurd and damn near succeeded?"

"No, I wasn't going to say that," she insisted. "You've got the Rafferty temper, but I don't think you're a murderer." She shook her head. "But it wouldn't be the first time you decided to take justice into your own hands."

"Defender of stray pups and wronged women, that's me."

"Cut it out," she said. "We've known each other too long to play games."

"Have we? Games are what people do, aren't they? At least, most men and women."

"Take me home."

"All right."

Jack steered the boat in silence for a quarter of an hour before saying, "I heard Tracy's funeral is Saturday. What time?"

"When did you start attending funerals?"

"Some things have changed in twenty-odd years. You were away a long time, Lizzy. I'd given up expecting you to come back."

"Don't call me that," she said. "It's Liz now. Or Elizabeth."

"Or Doctor Clarke."

"Don't, Jack. We don't need to fight."

"We didn't part on the best of terms."

"That was a long time ago. I'm not the same person I was then," she said. "I don't want to be."

"No more Donald Clarke's girl?"

"Or Crystal Clarke's sister. I've worked hard for what I have, for what I've made of myself. For the life I've made for my daughter."

"And I haven't?"

"I didn't mean that."

"Believe what you want. I had nothing to do with George's business. He knew how I felt, and he made sure that . . ." Jack exhaled softly. "Hell. I'd be lying if I didn't say I had my suspicions. But George is my brother, and Raffertys—"

"Stick together?" she offered. "Did your father know?"

"Pop?" He shook his head. "If George was running whiskey, Pop would have laughed and told tales about the old days. Not drugs. Pop's old school. George was lucky that it was the Feds that caught him. Pop would have put a bullet through his head if he'd caught him running that shit on one of our boats."

"You lost the boat, didn't you?"

"The boat. Not the bank note. Pop had to sell off the *Nellie IV* to make up the difference while I was upstate. We've got seven boats left. Two crabbers, one still commercial fishing. Pop runs the *Sea Sprite* as a headboat, and the rest I manage as charters. We hire captains and crews for the other boats."

"I know the fishing is much worse than it used to be. It's not easy for a waterman to make a living today."

"When was it? In your dad's time?" He scoffed. "You'll have to come see sometime. I live on the *Dolphin III*. It's corporate office and home sweet home all wrapped up in one. We've gone high tech, state-of-the-art computers."

She looked at his scarred hands. "It's hard to imagine you at a keyboard."

"I told you I put in a couple of years at Del State, and they have quite a decent computer lab at the prison. Sorry if it damages my image as *good old boy*."

"What next? Your own website?"

"*www.fishcap'njack.com.*"

Liz chuckled. "Things have changed a lot, haven't they?"

Neither said much for the remainder of the return

trip up the twisting creek and through the marsh to her landing. When they reached the dock, Liz tossed the looped bowline over a mooring post and eased the boat in.

"What was it like?" she asked him. "Prison."

"Not open for discussion."

"I can't imagine—"

"No. You can't. And you don't want to."

"Jack . . . I'm sorry if I—"

"It's over." He signaled for her to sit tight while he stepped up onto the wooden platform. Crouching down on the salt-treated planks, he offered her his hand and helped her up.

"Thanks," she began. "I—"

He cut her words off as he pulled her against his chest and ground his mouth against hers.

Chapter Four

To hold Liz in his arms felt better than Jack's wildest fantasies. She clung to him, wrapping her arms around his neck, seemingly as hot for him as he was for her. Her mouth never left his as they discarded a trail of clothing along the dock and up the bank into the yard. Although he had the best of intentions, it soon became clear that neither of them could wait until they reached the house.

Instead, he stripped off Liz's jeans and lifted her onto the edge of an oak picnic table. Amid a haze of searing kisses, he managed to extract a condom from his wallet and fit it over his erection before completely discarding his cutoffs. Liz reached for him, wrapped her legs around him, and drew his rigid member deep inside. Her eager cries and the sensation of her nails digging into his bare back intensified his need to possess her completely. Groaning, he thrust harder.

From the trees a few hundred feet away, Cameron Whitaker watched the couple intently, conscious of his own stiffening cock. "Bitch," he said. "Cold-hearted bitch." The professor was getting it on, all right. His breathing quickened as he saw her partner nuzzle Liz's naked breast, then draw the nipple deep into his mouth. "Yes," he urged. "Yes, stick it to her. Hammer her!"

Cameron lowered the binoculars and wiped his mouth. Damn, he could almost taste her. Much more of this and . . . Hastily, he fumbled with his zipper, pulled himself free of his boxers, and began to jerk off.

When he trained the glasses on the pair again, he felt his hands slick with his own juices. Liz lay back on the tabletop with the bastard on top of her, and her lover was playing with a lock of her hair.

Cameron fine-tuned his Leicas. The binoculars were 10×50, state of the art, and they magnified every inch of Liz's long legs and luscious ass. He could even make out one well-formed breast and the dark smudge of a nipple. "Roll over, you cock-sucker," he muttered. "Stop blocking the view." He wanted to see her thatch.

Jack pushed himself up on one elbow. "Sweet heaven." He groaned. "That takes twenty years off my life."

Liz smiled at him. "Some things are worth waiting for."

He leaned close and kissed her bruised mouth tenderly. She moistened her lips with the tip of her tongue. He remembered her doing just that a long time ago, and something dangerous stirred in the pit of his stomach. He sat up. "Brrr—getting a little damp out here, isn't it?"

"I hadn't noticed." She looked at him with amusement. "Good thing I don't have close neighbors."

He motioned toward the house with his chin. "I could use a cup of coffee."

"What? No cigarette? Winstons, wasn't it?"

"Gave them up fifteen years and three months ago."

"And you still want one?"

"Like a man in hell wants ice water."

She laughed. "I've missed you, Jack." Liz located her bra, slid down off the table, and found her jeans and what was left of her silk panties. "I'll put in a claim for these," she said, holding up the torn garment. "$14.99. Victoria's Secret."

"You sure? They look like Wal-Mart's 99¢ special to me." He grinned at her, exposing even white teeth and a dimple in one stubbly cheek. "I'll buy you a dozen pairs, if you want."

Liz shook her head. "Don't waste your charm on me. No strings."

"I didn't think—"

Her eyes narrowed. "You said it yourself. We only go around once. Enjoy it while you can."

"You have changed."

"I'm not seventeen anymore."

"Lizzy, about what happened with your sister—"

"That's over. It happened a long time ago."

"I'm sorry. I never wanted to—"

She held up her hands, palms out. "We're not going to have this conversation. You did me a favor. Subject closed." Her features brightened. "But you're welcome to come in for that coffee—better yet, a beer. And I still make a mean grilled cheese and tomato sandwich."

"Hmm. Tomato soup go with the offer?" How many afternoons had they spent alone in her house? Her dad didn't always pay his light or phone bill, but he kept the cupboards stocked with canned goods. One thing about Donald Clarke—no matter how drunk he got, he never let his girls go hungry.

She chuckled. "Tomato soup and oyster crackers."

"It's a deal." Jack stepped into his jeans and zipped them up. "You're a hell of a woman, Lizzy Clarke. Kent County just hasn't been the same without you."

On Saturday afternoon, the Game Master went to *the sophomore's* funeral. It was a rare treat, one he didn't usually allow himself. It was such a false cliché—the serial murderer always attends services for the dead. The fools. What did the authorities know of him and his kind?

He saw them in the crowd, some in uniform, others poorly disguised as grieving friends or merely curious onlookers. A few faces he recognized, but he didn't have to know them by name to label them—like they would pin labels on him, if they could catch him.

The thought was amusing, and he almost made the mistake of smiling. That wouldn't do, wouldn't do at all. He must look properly sorrowful, living the lie that this school of poor fish was enacting—pretending that the dead thing in the box was worth shedding tears over.

It was nothing now, worse than nothing. *The sophomore* had provided a little amusement, a brief relief from monotony. The Game Master could still taste her blood on his tongue.

He glanced at his watch, wondering how long this farce would go on. He had business to attend to, files to update. A sense of uncertainty loomed. This was always a dangerous period. Flushed with the excitement of victory, he had to set up the board for the next match. He couldn't make the same moves twice, and he needed to take great care not to frighten the professor so badly that she ran away.

She had to die. Twice before, he'd selected women and then changed his mind, letting them live without their ever knowing of his interest. The professor would have no such luck. She was already too deeply into the game to survive. She was his, and she was special. Smart. Tough. The greatest prize yet. He'd waited so long for her, and his reward would be all the sweeter when he added her to his collection.

He closed his eyes, taking advantage of the strains of funeral music that echoed through the church. For an instant, *the hitchhiker* came to mind. So long ago, and he could remember her face as if it were yesterday.

It had been raining that night, and he was driving down from Delaware City along Route 9. It was late, close to two in the morning, and he hadn't seen a car on the road for the last ten minutes. He was driving fast. He liked speed, the sight of wet blacktop flashing past, the rhythmic swish of the wipers, and the exhilarating gusts of wind and rain hitting the car.

Occasionally, he'd catch glimpses of the bay on his left. There was a riptide. Nothing beat being on the water on a night like that. The waves would be building to ten feet, and the powerful gale would drop an atheist to his knees and make him pray for mercy.

Waves of pleasure engulfed him as the memories of that night flooded back.

He'd nearly missed seeing the hitchhiker on the narrow bridge. The girl had worn dark clothing, and every scrap had been plastered to her skin by the pounding rain. She'd thrown up a hand to shield her face from the glare of his lights, and then waved frantically to try to stop him.

He'd braked a few hundred feet later, considering whether or not she was worth the risk. She was only his third premeditated victim, and he was still cautious, feeling his way in the game. But he hadn't been able to resist. He'd pulled into an abandoned farm lane and turned the car around. She stepped farther onto the roadway as he drove back. Her thin face was chalk white against the black of her hair, her eyes wide with distress. She couldn't have been more than sixteen.

She was smiling with relief as he slowed the vehicle. He'd waited, savoring the moment, before stomping the accelerator. The thud of steel colliding with flesh and bone is unique, thrilling on a basic level. He remembered how her slight body soared like a seagull, up and over the railing, into the black water below.

Quick but efficient, he thought. And far too easy.

The Game Master swallowed. Ah, for the innocence of his early days of experimentation. There was satisfaction in primitive emotion, but he was long past such simple pleasures. There were rules to follow for one on his level, and paramount was the preliminary preparation of his new object, the lady-in-waiting, as it were. He covered his mouth with a hand to conceal his smile.

It was time to begin *the daughter's* harvest.

* * *

Liz, Amelia, and Sydney attended Tracy's funeral together. Most of the Somerville staff was present at the Methodist church, including Cameron Whitaker, Ernie Baker, and two other security guards from the school. The small frame house of worship was filled to overflowing, and a crowd of mourners gathered by the entrance. Tracy's Aunt Charlene, garbed all in black, hung weeping on the arm of a red-faced and ponytailed man with a bad complexion and a protruding beer belly.

After the service, Liz, Amelia, and Sydney waited until Charlotte's escort led her out of the church before rising to continue on to the interment. They were nearing the door when Liz noticed Michael's wheelchair in the back of the church. He waved, and she whispered to Amelia that she'd meet them at the cemetery.

"It's a big turnout," Liz said when she reached Michael's side.

He nodded. "Some come out of respect. Others out of ghoulish curiosity."

Liz had never seen Michael in a suit and tie before, and he looked positively handsome. He'd polished his black shoes to a glass finish, and the creases in his steel-gray trousers were impeccable.

"I'm surprised that the funeral wasn't delayed," he said. "What with the murder investigation, an autopsy usually takes longer."

"The dean is a personal friend of the governor," Liz said. "At least that's what Sydney heard. For the sake of the family and for the school, they wanted the funeral to take place as soon as possible. Bad publicity for Somerville."

"Figures. It's not what you know, it's who you

know." Michael glanced at a couple near the rear door. The man, who appeared to be in his thirties, held a fussy toddler in his arms. "Do you know them?" Michael asked.

"No," Liz replied.

"The woman is Tracy's cousin, the baby's Tracy's."

A wave of compassion washed through Liz. "Oh. I didn't know she had a child," she murmured with a catch in her voice. "Is the father—"

"Wayne Boyd. At least she claimed he was the father. A buddy of mine on the force told me that she was suing Boyd for child support."

"And now the baby's orphaned. How tragic."

"The cousin's applied for custody. Been married five years, no kids of their own. She drives a school bus. Her husband works for the City of Dover."

"It's good there are relatives willing to take the child."

"Better than going into a foster home or being adopted out. The state's supposed to weed out the crazies, but they're no better at that than keeping drunks off the road," Michael said. "Lots of kids are worse off in state care than they were to begin with."

Liz nodded. Michael had told her that he'd spent most of his childhood in foster homes. He'd never elaborated, but she had gotten the impression that his memories were unhappy ones.

"You heard about Boyd's truck?"

"Yes." She didn't tell him that she'd seen the rescue squad pulling the vehicle out of the Murderkill River. If she did that, she'd have to tell Michael whom she'd been with, and she knew he wouldn't approve.

"No body yet, but if it washed out into the bay, they may never find it. Lot of water out there."

"You think Wayne murdered Tracy and then committed suicide?"

"Maybe. Or maybe he's on the run and wants police to think he drowned." He glanced around to see that no one was close enough to hear. "A warrant's been issued for his arrest. Forensics is still examining the oyster knife for fingerprints."

He took hold of her hand and squeezed it. "I'm making crab cakes for supper if you'd like to stop by about six. I caught a few decent-sized jimmies at the end of my dock."

"I may take you up on that. Can I bring dessert?"

"As long as it's ice cream. Any Cookies and Cream in your freezer?"

"No, but I'll stop and pick some up on the way home. Are you coming outside for—"

He shook his head. "I want to stop by the school and run through the tapes of the security videos again. I know that they weren't working in your wing, but we have tape of the main entrance. The police couldn't find anything unusual, but I'll feel better if I check myself." He smiled at her. "Besides, graveyards aren't the best surface for these treads." He indicated the wheels on his chair.

"I'd be glad to push," she offered.

"No, thanks. Six o'clock. With ice cream."

For a fraction of a second, she thought she saw pain in his eyes, but then his tough-guy mask slipped into place. She'd insulted his pride by offering to help with his chair, and she was sorry. "Six," she agreed as she bent to hug him. "Love you, Michael."

His eyes twinkled. "Love you, Elizabeth."

Jack was waiting just outside. He took a puff on a

cigarette and dropped it to the ground. After stamping on the half-smoked butt, he picked it up and shoved it in his pants pocket.

"I thought you'd given that up," she said.

"Me too." He fell into step beside her. "You didn't call me yesterday."

"I know."

"I offered to call you, but you didn't want that."

"No." She avoided his gaze.

"Was I that much of a disappointment?"

"You know better than that."

"They're having a spread at the fire hall for Tracy's friends and family," Jack said. "Mom will kill me if I don't show my face. Would you like to come with—"

She shook her head. "No, thanks. I'll just go home after this is over at the cemetery."

"Lots of funeral ham and potato salad."

"Tempting, but no thanks."

"Can I come by later?"

"Not tonight. I have plans with a friend. Call me in a day or two." What had happened between them was too new. It had been good, better than good, the best sex she'd ever had. She needed time to decide whether she wanted it to happen again, and if he came to the house, she knew they'd end up in bed. Jack was as complicated as he'd ever been—and she was still putty in his hands.

"You know where to find me, Lizzy."

She could tell he was hurt by the look in his eyes. "Jack—"

"Later."

He strode away and joined two other men that Liz recognized as watermen. She hurried to catch up with Sydney and Amelia.

"Who was that you were talking to?" Amelia asked as they picked their way through the tombstones.

"Just someone I used to know," Liz replied.

"That's right—you grew up around here, didn't you?" Sydney said. "You must know half of Kent County."

Amelia chuckled. "If she's anything like these other Delawareans, she knows all the natives, and two-thirds are relatives."

"Pay her no attention," Liz said. "From what I understand, her DeLaurier in-laws are related to everyone in Baton Rouge and the four surrounding counties."

"Amen to that," Amelia said. "I thought I had a lot of relatives until I married into my husband's family. Thomas has at least five aunties on his mother's side, and only God knows how many uncles. He has twenty-some cousins. One cousin has seven children, and another has six. It's pandemonium at holidays."

After a second brief service at the gravesite, Liz said her good-byes and started home. She felt another headache coming on. The base of her skull felt as though someone were driving a spike into it. She almost wished she hadn't agreed to have dinner with Michael that evening.

He was her best friend, and being with him was always enjoyable, but she needed time alone. It wasn't that she regretted having sex with Jack so much as she felt she needed time to consider what she was getting into. Becoming involved with Jack again wasn't high on her list of good choices.

He was trouble. He always had been. The last thing she needed now was complication in her life. And Jack Rafferty had a way of getting to her that no other man—including her ex-husband—had ever done.

She supposed she had only herself to blame. It had been months since she'd been on a date, let alone been intimate with a man . . . unless you could count her time with Michael. And they hadn't done it.

Yet.

She lowered the driver's window and took a deep breath of the warm May air.

There it was—the question she'd kept pushing to the back of her mind. Did she and Michael have something more than friendship between them? Was she seriously considering something more permanent? And if she was—why was she letting Jack ruin it?

Michael Hubbard was solid and respectable, perfectly suitable for a professor's life partner. He was smart and funny and sexy. They shared a love of books, music, and the outdoors. God knew, he doted on Katie. Showered her with gifts. And Katie liked him well enough to call him Uncle Mike. He'd make a terrific stepfather.

Not that Michael had ever asked her to move in with him in a *significant other* situation. His pride wouldn't let him. But if she showed up at his door with a suitcase, there was no doubt in her mind that she could stay forever.

She swore and tightened her fingers on the steering wheel. There was no justice in the world. How could a sweet girl like Tracy Fleming end up with her throat cut, and a good guy like Michael have his world come crashing down around him? First a drunk driver had left him unable to walk, and then he'd lost a wife he loved and cherished in another senseless accident.

She thought for a moment how it must have been for Michael—returning home to find Barbara face-down on their bed, tangled in a down comforter and suffocated during an epileptic seizure. Life was so damned unfair.

Liz was so engrossed in her thoughts that she drove past the entrance to the supermarket. As she moved into the turn lane to go back, she decided to call the phone company about Caller ID and voice-mail service. She'd always been opposed to voice mail in her home, but since Katie had left for Dublin, she'd reconsidered.

Jack Rafferty was waiting for her at the end of her driveway. Liz felt herself tense when she sighted the motorcycle and the black-helmeted driver. She turned into the lane fast, braked hard, and rolled down the window. "Why are you here?" she asked. "I told you I had plans tonight."

"I'm worried about you, Lizzy. Why didn't you tell me that somebody had broken into your house and left muddy tracks on your kitchen floor?"

"How did you know that?"

"I know a lot of people. They gossip. You had a state trooper out to investigate and you didn't say anything about it?"

"There wasn't anything to tell. It was a prank. The officer said so."

"Well, whoever the joker is, he's back." He pointed to her house. "He left a present on your back step."

76

Liz didn't wait to hear more. She stepped on the accelerator, drove up the lane, and pulled up by the gate. Lying in front of the door was a large funeral wreath of dead flowers. She got out and ran to the steps. The gilt letters on the faded purple ribbon were peeling, but there was no doubt as to the original wording. *Beloved Mother.*

Cursing, Liz grabbed the arrangement to hurl it off the porch. Then she froze and clamped a hand over her mouth. Hidden under the flowers were two dead mallard ducklings, with their necks twisted at an impossible angle. Bile rose in her throat as she threw the wreath onto the grass. Racing down the steps, she kicked and stomped the ruined blooms and stems into the grass.

Jack stopped his bike just behind her car, shut it off, and came toward her. "No need to kill the wreath. I think it's already dead."

"Is this you?" she cried, whirling on him. "Did you do this?" She pointed at the limp, brown and yellow ducklings.

He stared at her, an expression of disgust on his face.

"Nothing awful happened to me until you showed up in my life," she said. "Nothing—"

"You found a dead girl in your office. Think I did that too?"

She looked down at the crushed roses and swallowed hard, trying to hold back the tears. "How do I know?" she whispered. "How do I know anything?"

He moved to take her in his arms, and she laid her head against his chest. Jack smelled of aftershave and tobacco, and she refused to let herself think just how good he felt.

He held her for a long moment, and then let her go. "This isn't like you. You were always a lot tougher. And you really ought to lock your door when you go out."

"What?" She looked toward the house and noticed that the screen door was closed, but the interior, eighteenth-century Dutch door stood wide open. "I did lock it," she said, hurrying up the steps and into the house.

"Don't touch anything," he called after her.

Liz glanced around the kitchen with its white-plastered walls and smoke-stained, hand-hewn beams. The redbrick floor was as clean as she'd left it. A blue china pitcher of daffodils stood in the center of the table beside the Hunter Morgan novel she'd been reading. Over the doorway that led to the hall, her great-grandfather's ten-gauge shotgun hung undisturbed. Nothing seemed out of place.

Jack followed her in. "You could wait outside while I look—"

"I locked my damn door."

"Go outside, Lizzy."

Where was her cat? "I don't see Muffin," she said. "Kitty, kitty, kitty!"

"I'll look for the cat. You stay here."

Ignoring Jack's order, Liz went into the parlor. Again, everything seemed to be as she'd left it. The twenty-dollar bill that Michael had advised her to leave on the mantel was still there. "Kitty, kitty!" she repeated.

Jack's footsteps sounded on the stairs. A minute later, he called down. "Cat's fine. Up here, sleeping on a bed. I'll look in the other rooms."

She went into the small room in the front of the

78

house that she used as an office. Her computer, printer, and fax were there, and the blue glass butter dish full of quarters hadn't been touched. She pulled open her filing cabinet. Her can of pepper spray was there, still in its shrink-wrap, unopened.

Liz's heart rate slowed to a near normal rhythm. Was there a possibility that she'd left the back door open? She'd been in a rush to get to the funeral on time and . . .

No, she hadn't forgotten. Locking up the house was as ingrained in her as fastening her seat belt when she got into a car. She hadn't left the back door open, and she hadn't left funeral flowers on her own porch.

Was it possible that Jack . . .

"Nothing."

His voice came from right behind her. Startled, she turned to face him. "There's . . . there's no one here."

"You want to call the cops?"

"No, I don't. I'm fine. There's no need for you to—"

"I don't want to leave you here alone."

"Why did you come, Jack? After I told you—"

"Shit, you think it's me, don't you? You must think I'm Superman. I murder Tracy, drown Wayne to throw the blame on him, break into your house twice, and bring you flowers. I'm a busy boy."

She wanted to say she didn't think he was guilty, but the words wouldn't come out. The possibility was there. "I—"

"Right. Forget it. Just forget it." He took three steps toward the doorway, and then turned back. "Get yourself a gun and learn how to use it, Lizzy. If you're going to play games with guys like me, you need all the help you can get."

* * *

"He's right about that," Michael said, hours later over supper. "Until they find Wayne's body, there's a possibility that Wayne is behind this. And if he's not, your boyfriend's a good second choice."

She took a sip of wine. Yellow Tail, Michael had called it. It was Australian, earthy, with a hint of berry and very good. Wine with dinner didn't break any hard and fast rules, not as long as she wasn't drinking alone. She shrugged. "Jack isn't my boyfriend."

"You two had something going years ago, didn't you?"

"I was a stupid kid then," she said. "I didn't know any better." She shrugged. "I had a crush on him, but when I wouldn't put out, he consoled himself with my big sister." How could that still hurt after so long? But it did. She averted her eyes to keep Michael from seeing how much it hurt.

"You were a good kid. Decent."

She shook her head. "It wasn't morals that kept me from having sex. I was afraid of getting pregnant, of being stuck here with no education, an illegitimate baby to support, and no future."

"He would have done that to you?"

"Maybe." She shrugged. "Probably."

"I'm your friend, Elizabeth. I don't have the right to tell you whom to see, but Rafferty is scum. I can't imagine you with somebody like that."

"Jack's not scum. At least, he never used to be."

"People change."

She nodded. "You're not the first one to tell me that." She swirled the red wine in the crystal Lenox glass.

"I care about you. I don't want to see you hurt. This thing with the muskrat trap and the flowers—it could be a college prank, some asshole kid that you gave a failing grade, or it could be somebody you should be afraid of."

"I don't scare easy."

He nodded. "I know you don't, but there's a difference between being easily spooked and overly confident."

Heidi got up and came over to lay her head on Michael's knee, and he stroked her back and scratched behind her ears. The dog closed her intelligent eyes to slits and uttered a deep rumble of contentment.

"I bought that handgun I told you about," Michael continued. "I'd like to teach you how to use it. And I want to loan you Heidi, just until this is over."

"Heidi?" Michael adored both of his dogs, but the female was his darling. "I couldn't," Liz said. "She'll never stay—"

"Heidi's well trained." He refilled her empty wineglass. "She'll obey you. And she'll be no trouble."

"Michael . . ."

He took a deep breath. "Please, Elizabeth. Take Heidi as a favor to me. I'll sleep better if I know she's guarding you."

"I hate to admit it," she answered. "But so would I. I'll borrow her, but I'm not sure about the gun. You know how I feel about firearms."

"Guns aren't evil. It's the people who misuse them."

"So you keep saying."

"Tracy wasn't killed with a gun."

"No." Liz's heart sank. "She wasn't, was she?" She stood up and began clearing dishes off the table. "Thanks for asking me over tonight," she said, changing the subject. "Your crab cakes are the best."

"You gave me the recipe."

She chuckled. "Dad got it from his grandmother. But they never come out right for me. Either I burn them or . . ." She broke off as her cell phone jingled "Take Me Out to the Ballgame."

She dug it from her purse on the third ring and was delighted to hear her daughter's voice. "Katie, hi!"

"Ask her how she likes Ireland in the spring," Michael said.

"What's up, sweetheart?" Liz asked.

"Daddy called."

"On his own dime? There's a switch."

"That isn't funny."

"I wasn't trying to be amusing. It's just odd that we should both hear from your father at the same time. He called me—"

"I know, Moms. He told me you said you weren't paying my tuition for next semester—that I had to come home. You didn't say that, did you?"

"What was our agreement? I told you that paying Aunt Crystal for her share of Clarke's Purchase, plus all the repairs on the property, took our savings and ran up the credit card. Your father was supposed—"

"Money. Is that all you ever think about? You can't make me come home. It's not fair. I've got to spend at least another year—"

"This isn't the time to discuss this. I'll have to call you later, from home."

"I want to talk about it now," Katie insisted.

"I don't."

"Fine. Have it your way. You always do."

"Don't whine."

"You tell me I might have to drop everything and come home, and I'm not supposed to complain? Besides, it's been a bloody day."

"Lovely talk. This is the education I'm paying for?"

Katie's voice lost its defiant tone. "Somebody sent me flowers."

"What's wrong with that?" Liz asked.

"Now, don't get all freaky on me, Moms. It was probably that jerk Larry that I broke up with last fall."

"Explanation, please," Liz said.

"The florist delivered an arrangement, addressed to me. Somebody's idea of a sick joke."

A cold chill washed over Liz. "What kind of flowers?"

"It's a hoot, really. Nothing to get in a spin about. White funeral lilies tied in a black ribbon that said *Beloved Daughter*."

Chapter Five

Liz gasped and stared at Michael as fear gripped her. "Katie? Are you alone? Is anyone there with you?"

"Moms. That's really not any of . . ." The exasperated sigh on the other end of the line was all too familiar. "If you must know, Niall is here. But it's not what you think. He just—"

"Good. Ask him to stay the night! I don't want you alone." She sank into a chair, shocked at her own level of panic for her daughter's safety. "Niall—"

"Moms, have you been drinking?"

"What is it?" Michael asked. "What's wrong?"

"Just a second," Liz said to Katie. "Don't hang up." She pressed the phone against her chest and told him about Katie's flower delivery. "What do I say to her?"

Michael reached for the phone. Reluctantly she passed it over and sat numbly as he asked questions and then told Katie about the similar floral arrangement on the back step at Clarke's Purchase. Her daughter's reaction didn't need to be relayed—Liz could hear her swear. Michael grinned, offered a practical lecture on personal safety, and handed the cell phone back.

"Some sick bastard must be having fun at our expense," Katie said.

"Where did you pick up that language?"

"From you."

"True. But I want you to listen to Michael and—"

"No need to freak. I'm in Dublin. What idiot is going to pop for a plane ticket to play Halloween when he can access the internet for free?"

"You're right," Liz agreed, beginning to breathe normally again. "I'm trying to think who would have your address there. Your father, certainly, and the latest Mrs. Montgomery. We're barely on speaking terms, but she's never struck me as—"

"It's not Danielle. She likes me. Remember the pink silk sweater I got for my birthday? Dad certainly didn't send it," Katie reminded. "I wouldn't put it past Larry or that creep who's been stalking you—Cameron Whitaker."

"He's not stalking me. He's a nuisance and a major loser. But I've never given him your address."

"He's a grad student," Katie said. "How hard would it be for him to get into your office files?"

"I keep the filing cabinet locked."

"Right, and I could pick that lock with a hair clip. It's probably his idea of a joke. Mystery solved. Got to go. Stop worrying. I can take care of myself."

"Katie, wait—"

"Love ya. Bye." There was a distant click and then dead silence.

Still gripping the phone, Liz turned to Michael. "What do—"

"She's an ocean away." He refilled her wineglass. "And you are definitely staying here tonight."

"No, I can't. I—"

He held up a hand, callused palm out. "No argument, Elizabeth. I insist. Tomorrow I'll call someone about alarm systems. If you can't pay for it, I'll—"

"Absolutely not," she said. "I was thinking of that myself. I can manage. But I don't want to take advantage of your . . ." She grimaced. "Katie's sleeping with her Irish boyfriend. He's probably a terrorist—some kind of munitions expert, and his enemies are trying to get to him through my daughter. And I have just advised her to have him spend the night with her."

Michael grinned. "Maybe you should give up teaching and write thrillers. You have a great imagination. She's a college student. If she wasn't sleeping with her boyfriend, I'd worry. Drink your wine. I'll light a fire, and we'll sit in front of it and mull over this mess."

She couldn't help smiling. "Certain you don't want to get me drunk to take advantage of me?"

"It's crossed my mind. You're staying here tonight. Doctor's orders. You can be the brave, independent woman tomorrow. Tonight, I'm going to take care of you.'

"Thanks, Michael. You're a good friend."

"That's me, friend in need." He raised one brow quizzically. "You know I'd like to be more than that."

"Tempting, very tempting."

By the time she'd finished clearing away and loading the dishwasher, Michael had a blaze going in the hearth. When she joined him, he indicated her half-empty wineglass. "More?"

"No, this is wonderful." She curled up on the leather couch. "I've had enough alcohol for one night." She yawned. "Excuse me. Mmm. If I'd known we were having a sleep-over, I'd have brought my SpongeBob pj's."

"I think I can find you something to wear." Muscles corded his forearms as Michael swung himself from his wheelchair into a high-backed and over-stuffed chair. He pulled an ottoman close and lifted first one leg and then the other onto the footstool before retrieving his imported beer from the carrier on the back of his chair. "If you want popcorn, you'll have to make it yourself."

She chuckled. "No, I couldn't eat another bite." She leaned down and patted Heidi's head. Both dogs were sprawled on the rug, seemingly content to be near Michael and the fire.

Michael began to tell her about a warbler he'd seen the day before in the trees along his driveway. As always, they never failed to find enough to talk about. For the better part of two hours, they avoided mentioning Tracy's murder or the intruder at her house.

Finally, she said, "You know what really got me about those muddy tracks across my kitchen floor? They bring back memories of when I was a kid. Things I'd rather forget."

Michael's compassionate gaze met hers. "Sometimes talking about bad stuff is better than trying to bury it."

She sighed. "I suppose." She swallowed in an attempt to ease the lump in her throat. "I know I've told you before about that crazy hermit. The one who lived out in the marsh."

"Buck Juney."

She nodded. "Yes." Unease prickled the skin on her arms and she grimaced. Buck was long dead, and she was no longer a child. But, try as she might to shake him, he remained a shadowy specter lurking in the dark places of her mind, poised to pounce if she lowered her guard. If she let herself, she could still smell the sweaty flesh and rotting hides that radiated from his shuffling form.

"I've never lived anywhere that there wasn't one crazy in the neighborhood."

"Buck was worse than that. People said all kinds of things about him," she said softly. "That he was a war hero who came home shell-shocked and murdered his wife and child in their beds. That he cooked and ate their bodies, and avoided being hanged for it only by claiming insanity and spending years in a mental institution." She grimaced. "Sonny Shahan swore that Buck had fits, ate his meat raw, and howled at the moon like a werewolf."

"And what did your father say?"

"That Buck's wife deserted him the same way Mom left us, and maybe that gave him the right to be a little addlepated." She examined a chipped nail. "Daddy thought that Buck was harmless. If we left Buck alone, he'd do the same by us."

"Is your mother alive, Elizabeth?"

"Honestly, I don't know. My sister heard from her a few years back, after Daddy was declared legally dead. She wanted to know if there was anything in the will for her. When Crystal told her there wasn't,

Mom hung up. She didn't leave a number, but Crystal said the call came from an Alabama area code."

"You've never seen your mother since she left your father?"

"I can't even remember her face. And Daddy tore up all of her pictures. I was little, but Crystal said Mommy-Dearest took off two days before Christmas. Went to Wilmington with a girlfriend and walked away with every cent Daddy had in his wallet and an advance on his next week's pay from Jack's father. After that, it was just the three of us."

"Never curious about her? About why she ran away?"

Liz finished her wine. "Nope. Daddy said Crystal favored her in looks and temperament. When I asked about her, he claimed Mom was pretty but not much of a mother and even less of a wife. Crystal claimed that they argued a lot, mostly about money and living out here on Clarke's Purchase. She hated the solitude."

"And it never bothered you, growing up? From what you've told me, you and Crystal were alone on the farm a lot while your father was out fishing."

"Bothered me? No. Crystal hated Clarke's Purchase. Most days when we weren't in school, she'd hitchhike to Dover or shut herself in her bedroom and watch soaps. But I loved the old place. Other than burying myself in a book, I was happiest fishing or crabbing, or building forts in the marsh grass. I still love it, Michael. And I won't be frightened away from my home by some nut."

Firelight cast shadows on his rugged face. "I don't blame you. There's a peace here that I haven't found anyplace else. There's room to stretch out, to be yourself. Even if that self is a little eccentric."

She smiled at him. "I'd hardly call you eccentric. You're the most normal person I know."

He glanced at his custom wheelchair. "In spite of my mode of transportation?"

"Absolutely."

Michael lifted his beer bottle in salute. "I'll take that as a compliment."

"And on that note, I think I'd better get to bed. Unless I've had more to drink than I thought, that clock says 11:15. I've got to work tomorrow. And I've got to get up early if I'm going to go home and change before school."

"Sure, go ahead. I'm ready to turn in too. If the weather is decent tomorrow, I'd like to drive out to Bombay Hook just after the sun comes out and see if I can get my duck count up. I saw a Gadwall listed on the rare-bird alert, and I haven't seen one this year."

He set his beer down, his second of the evening, barely touched. "Take Heidi with you tomorrow. Let her into the house first, and leave her in while you're at school. I can guarantee that you won't have any prowlers inside."

She rose and kissed his cheek. "What would I do without you?"

Despite taking two nighttime tablets, sleep didn't come much easier for Liz in Michael's comfortable guest room than it had at home. Half of her felt silly for hiding out here instead of going home, and the other half was relieved that she didn't have to face an empty house tonight. Not empty, she reminded herself; she'd have Heidi. The dog would be company, and as Michael said, she wouldn't have to worry about an intruder with the German shepherd on duty.

She glanced at the antique clock on the nightstand. It was just after midnight here, but three hours earlier on the West Coast. A little past nine. Crystal would be awake. Talking about their mother with Michael had brought back memories of more than Buck Juney.

On a whim, she dug through her purse and came up with her palm pilot. Before she lost her nerve, she located Crystal's number in Santa Barbara. Her sister picked up on the second ring. "Hi, Crystal. It's Liz."

"Liz? Is everything all right? Nothing's happened to Katie, has it?" There was a blare of TV in the background. "Wait until I turn down the box."

"Is this a bad time?"

"No. Five hundred stations and I end up watching reruns of gay guys picking out furniture for straight men's apartments. You're sure nothing's wrong? You haven't developed some weird disease and need a kidney or something?"

"Nope. No fatal diseases this week. How's work?" Liz was a receptionist for a plastic surgeon through the week and worked as a cocktail waitress on Friday and Saturday nights. Or at least, she had. "Still at the same apartment?"

"Why would I move?" Crystal had gotten the condo as part of the settlement from her second husband, a gambler and would-be club manager. From what her sister had told her, the place was small and beginning to show its age, but it had a pool and was in a good location.

"Hold on while I get an ashtray." More clatter, a crash of glass, cursing, and Crystal's throaty voice returned—still oozing with a Delaware accent and the results of decades of smoking. "I've got a new neighbor. Cute, but bald as an egg. He wants to take me to Reno for a weekend. Not exactly Mr. Right, but not bad. At least he's a gentleman."

"Are you going to go?"

"Maybe, depends on how bored I am. Okay, sis, you didn't call to hear about my love life—or lack of it. What's up? Have you come to your senses and realized how crazy you were to move back to the swamp? I'm not giving back a cent of—"

"No, I like the farm. Always did."

"Fix up the house, sell, and buy a condo in Ocean City. I would if I was a big college professor with a fat bank account."

"Me? A fat . . . You have no idea, Crystal. If the price of oil doesn't drop, I may be toting drink trays on the weekends."

"Sure. Right. I'll believe that when I hear you've struck oil on the family plantation. You're not getting married again, are you?"

"No, at least not in the immediate future."

"Preggers?"

"No, not with child. I just thought I'd call and see how things were going with you. We are sisters."

"Yeah, Daddy claimed we were." Liz heard the clink of ice in a glass. " 'Fess up, baby girl. I know you better than that. You didn't call because you had an uncontrollable desire to hear my voice."

"Maybe I did," she admitted. "I was talking with a friend about Mom. You haven't heard from her, have you?"

"That old bitch? Not likely. I've got an unlisted number, and unless she's come into millions and wants to leave it all to me, there's nothing I have to say to her. She didn't want us and she didn't want Daddy. She made that clear."

"She might be dead by now."

"So? Why get sentimental about poor white trash? She never did anything for you but let you burn yourself on the wood stove when you started walking. Oh, yeah. I almost forgot. Once, she let you wander off and tumble off the dock. The Lab pulled you out. Blackie. Remember him?"

"Yes, I remember Blackie."

"Bad-tempered old dog, but he saved your neck. You looked like a dead fish when you stopped puking. Yeah, dear old Mom. You think Daddy had a drinking problem? I can't remember ever seeing her sober. Good riddance, I say. Why would you want to get in touch with her?"

"I didn't say I would. I was just thinking about her, about old times when we were kids."

"Not me. I try not to think about them. I washed that bay mud off my feet a long time ago. I'm strictly a California girl, Liz."

"So things are good for you?"

"Could be better. I'd like to lose ten pounds and win big at the slots. Not thinking of coming West for a vacation, are you?"

"No, too much to do here. If I did take a vacation, it would be to go to Ireland. Katie's in college there."

"Ireland? See! What did I tell you? Miss Rich

Bitch. You're loaded, Liz. You don't know how the other half lives. Maybe I should have gone to college. Or I could have been a flight attendant. Or a cosmetologist. Opened my own shop and charged forty dollars for a wash and cut."

"It's not too late, Crystal. Lots of women go to school—"

"Not me. At least, not college. I've got a friend in Las Vegas. She says dealers make good tips. I've been thinking about renting this place out and moving there to see how I like it. Or Hawaii. I've always wanted to live on the beach in Waikiki."

"Be certain you give me your new address, if you do move. I e-mailed you after Christmas, but—"

"I don't have time for that. Waste of time. I didn't use that internet service enough to make it worth my while. I can use the one in the office if I want. You can always get me there."

"We should keep in touch. There's only the three of us." Crystal had never had children, never wanted any.

"Right. You've got a birthday coming up. I'll give you a ring then."

"Okay," Liz said, knowing Crystal wouldn't bother. Years had only widened the breach between them. There were no common ties to strengthen. "It's getting late here."

"If you get to Ireland, send me a postcard. Or better yet, a bottle of Irish whiskey."

"Will do. Bye, Crystal. Love ya."

"Back at you, sis. Ciao."

Liz turned off her phone and then the light. Trust a conversation with Crystal to make her wonder whether she had done the right thing to move back to Clarke's Purchase. An owl hooted outside, making her feel lonelier than ever. She missed Katie's laughter and even her loud music echoing through the farmhouse.

"I'm glad you're far away," she murmured into the pillow. "Safe." The pills were beginning to work, and she felt the warm haziness of sleep easing her unrest.

She tried to picture Katie's smile and the freckles on her nose, but her thoughts kept drifting back to the mother she'd never really known. And the biggie hissed at the back of her mind—the gremlin that had ridden around on her back since she was old enough to put thought into words. *If my own mother couldn't love me, who will?*

The Game Master shut his car door and stepped out onto the overgrown dirt road on state game lands. The dark blue, ten-year-old sedan was a recent acquisition. He'd picked it up at the Philadelphia airport in long-term parking and replaced the New York tag with a Maryland one. The Chevy would suit his needs for a few weeks, and then, if no one noticed it, he'd trade up for another model. He liked American cars with their large trunks, much more convenient for transporting his cargo. When he was working, he never drove anything flashy, and he was a cautious driver. It didn't pay to attract attention or give any reason for the cops to stop him.

It was close to two o'clock and dark as pitch, but he didn't need light to guide him. He knew where he was going and he had his night-vision goggles. He'd driven the road that ran past the professor's lane twice. Though it was impossible to tell if anyone was parked in the yard, he knew that no state troopers were patrolling the area. Still, he took no chances, crossing woods, fields, and marsh to approach the brick dwelling without the possibility of being seen.

No cars were behind the house or pulled up beside the nineteenth-century barn or in the sheds. He entered the house, as he had before, through the outside cellar entrance. The heavy board-and-batten door was locked, but opening it was child's play, easier and faster than letting himself into the professor's office had been.

Inside, he moved slowly and silently down the brick steps and across the main room. An open passageway, leading to several smaller rooms, ran the length of the structure. A wooden staircase rose from one of these narrow chambers. Using a tiny flashlight, the Game Master climbed to the first-floor hall and made short work of that lock as well.

The house sounded empty, but he took no chances, examining each room before he set to the task of removing electrical switch plates and floorboards to plant electronic devices in strategic positions. The last of these, miniature cameras, he installed in the professor's bedroom and the largest bath. The tasks were time-consuming, but setting up the game board was a necessary part of the game.

Lesser men might be content with the satisfaction of the kill, the scent of blood, and the cries of their victims. Those aspects were enjoyable, even immensely fulfilling, but it was the sport of the chase that thrilled him the most. Stalking his lovelies, watching as ever-increasing fear consumed their lives, kept the game new and challenging. That . . . and—something he prided himself on—the fact that he escalated the danger to himself with each challenge.

He longed to look deep into the professor's eyes at the moment of her death, had imagined killing her in so many delicious ways, but he could wait. Patience made his appetite keener and his ultimate prize greater. He promised himself that when the time came, he would deny himself nothing. He would taste and feast on her blood and flesh. He would consume her bit by bit, and he would keep the spark of life in her sweet body for a long, long time.

These little toys would serve twofold—frighten her, and let him fully enjoy each move of the game. He would know what she was thinking—planning—perhaps even before she did. And he would savor each bite of her terror until the moment of his triumph.

He glanced at his watch, then turned to glance at the old-fashioned iron bed. It was covered with a floral spread, not expensive, probably from some mail-order house. He wondered when she'd last changed her sheets and if they would retain her scent.

He went back to the bed, lifted the coverlet and bent to sniff a pillowcase. Percale. Not new, but acceptable. But she didn't hang her sheets on the line to dry. No, these had been dried in a dryer, probably with one of those little white sheets of fabric softener. Women today were so slothful, unwilling to take the time to properly care for a home.

He fluffed the pillow and smoothed the bedspread over it. "Sleep well," he said softly. "Enjoy your bed while you can. Your next bed will be somewhat colder." He smiled at his own joke. "And damper," he added with a chuckle. "Much, much damper."

"Are you reading my mail?" Liz flung her briefcase on a chair and advanced on Cameron. Administration had assigned her a space in this glorified storage room while her office was being painted and new carpet laid, but the worst part was that she had to share the area with Cameron Whitaker. "Have you lost your mind? What gives you the right to—"

"A simple thank-you would do," he said. "You don't have to bite my head off." He looked around at the stacked chairs lining one wall. "I could have let you set up your own computer."

"Please get out of my chair." She glanced at the screen, scanning the screen names and the ever-present advertisements for enhanced sexual organs and weight loss.

"Your filing cabinet's over there." He gestured toward a corner of the room. "They dented it up moving it in here."

"Have you been snooping in that as well?" She glared at him. "Did you send flowers to Katie?"

"Katie who?"

"You know damned well what Katie. My daughter. In Dublin. Was it your idea of a sick joke?"

"Look, Liz. I know you're upset about what happened to Tracy, but there's no need to make absurd accusations. We're colleagues—friends."

"Friends? Hardly. Now, get out of my chair and away from my computer before I file a formal complaint against you for violating my privacy. And I'd prefer that you address me as Dr. Clarke."

"Pulling rank? Considering that we are more than acquaintances, I think—"

"That's it, Cameron. That's all we are."

"Funny, I'd say that you showed more interest than that. You went out with me."

"Shared dinner in a public restaurant," she said. "Nothing more. I met you there, if you recall, and I paid for my own meal."

"I offered." He scrolled down and tapped a key. "Look at that. Weird, isn't it?"

Liz stared at the screen. The image of an oyster knife revolved from left to right. Under it, written in red, were the words *Your move, Professor.*

"Oh, God," she murmured. "Look at—"

"Want me to—"

The screen went to blue.

"Oops."

"Did you delete that?" she demanded.

"What?"

"Didn't you see it—right in front of you?"

"See what?" Cameron asked smugly.

"Damn it." Liz's heart thudded against her ribs. "You deleted it. Bring it back. What was the screen name?"

"It was spam. You wanted spam?"

"Am I interrupting something here?" Amelia stuck her head in the open doorway. "What's up? Are you two—"

"There was an e-mail," Liz said. "And a picture. Of a knife."

Cameron stood up. "I didn't see any knife."

"There was a knife," Liz repeated. "An oyster knife."

"I think she's imagining things," Cameron said.

"You had to see it," Liz insisted. "There was a message, in red. You saw that, didn't you? It read, 'Your move, Professor.'" She glanced at Amelia. "He deleted it. But it's got to be in the hard drive, doesn't it? I'm going to call security."

Cameron backed away from the computer. "There was some junk, the usual stuff. It might have been red. I think you're losing it, Liz."

She sat down and ran the mouse over recently deleted mail. "Wait, it's got to be here," she said. "I'll prove it to you."

Amelia approached the chair and put her hand on Liz's shoulder. "I think your class is waiting for you, Cameron," she said.

"Oh, yes, Roman Pottery Along Hadrian's Wall."

"I can't find it," Liz said. "Where could it have gone?"

"I told you, I didn't see—"

"I think you'd better get to your students before Liz makes you the second victim in this wing," Amelia said.

"I'd get her to a therapist if I were you," Cameron said as he headed for the doorway. "She should be on different medication."

Liz swore between clenched teeth. "I'm telling you, I saw it. I'm not losing my mind."

"Probably just another of Cameron's attempts at humor," her friend said. "You know what a computer whiz the prick is. If there was some twisted message, he probably sent it to you."

"Maybe," Liz said. "I think he sent flowers to Katie. Funeral flowers."

"To Katie?" Amelia glanced at her watch. "I've got

two hours before my next class. Why don't you cancel your morning lecture and come home with me for some real coffee and you can tell me all about it."

"I shouldn't. My kids—"

"Your kids will be delighted. Come on, Liz. What is the administration going to do? Discipline you? You shouldn't even be back to work this soon after what's happened." Amelia's beautiful, chocolate features creased with genuine concern. "What do you say? Coffee, Irish cream, and a shoulder to cry on. What more could you ask for?"

Chapter Six

"I've got the house to myself for a few days," Amelia said as she poured coffee into bright orange pottery mugs adorned with stylized African wildlife. "Thomas left for Virginia Beach this morning." She ran slender fingers through her close-cropped salt-and-pepper hair. "Bad timing, but we had some repairs done to the deck, and he wants to be certain the contractor completes the work before he writes the check. The same contractor who built the place for us—the man Thomas brags is so reasonable, the man we've never had a minute's trouble with. But . . . you know how anal-retentive Thomas is. He has to check up on everything."

Liz smiled in sympathy and then glanced out the window at Amelia's elegant back yard with its marble bench and fountain, and beyond that at the greenhouse where Amelia's husband grew prize-winning orchids. "You said you'd lost some shingles in that March storm."

Amelia took a chair across from her at the small

breakfast table. "One of the joys of owning property a block from the ocean."

The coffee was rich and dark, too hot to drink, but Liz lifted the gazelle cup to inhale the aroma. "Mmm, trust Thomas to buy the best." Amelia's husband did all of the shopping and most of the cooking. Liz knew that Thomas was particular about his coffee, buying only organically grown beans and grinding them himself. "Will your nieces be coming for the summer again?"

"Not Natasha, but Regina will. Natasha got an internship in Washington. Regina's coming, and she's bringing her roommate, Yejide. Lovely girl. You've got to come down while she's with us. She's Nigerian, but she grew up in Cape Town. Pre-med." Amelia chuckled. "It should be an interesting ten weeks. According to Regina's e-mails, Yejide's had quite a time adjusting to American life. Yejide's parents had numerous household servants, and the girl had no idea how to make her bed or wash her clothes. Regina said Yejide drowned the dorm laundry in suds and ruined two loads of her good clothing with bleach."

"Should keep you and Thomas from getting bored."

Amelia toyed with a gold hoop earring. "His idea. On the plus side, Yejide doesn't date and attends church twice a week." She stirred cream and artificial sweetener into her coffee. "However, Regina claims that Yejide's half of the room looks like the aftermath of a hurricane. I'm giving Yejide the crow's nest, the attic room with all the windows on the third floor, a view of the ocean, and her own whirlpool bath. Thomas doesn't need to see the mess until September, and by then the Merry Maids will have worked wonders."

"Sounds like a plan. So long as she doesn't do laundry."

Amelia's liquid brown eyes grew thoughtful. "It's you I'm worried about. I can only imagine how you must feel. No one should have to go through what you did. Why don't you stay here for a week—for as long as you want? There's no need for you to be out there all alone, not when you're being stalked by some nutcase."

"Thanks, but . . ." Liz cradled her mug with both hands, met her friend's gaze, and exhaled. "Amelia, I think it's Cameron."

Amelia sat back in her chair and folded her arms over her chest. "I know he's an annoying prick, but funeral flowers and threatening e-mails? If he's guilty, he could go to jail. He'd certainly lose his slot at Somerville and probably any hope of working for anyone else in the academic world."

"I've thought of all that, but I can't come to any other conclusion." She placed the cup deliberately on the striped tablecloth and gazed at it.

"You don't believe he murdered Tracy Fleming, do you?"

Liz looked up from her musing and smiled. "Hardly. He may be taking advantage of the situation, but I don't believe it's in Cameron's nature to be violent. And to give the devil his due, I've never seen Cameron speak to any of the girls outside class. I think he reserves his lechery for older women."

"Well, if he didn't kill her, who did?"

"Jack says it was her boyfriend Wayne . . . who may well be dead himself, now."

"Jack. The just-released-from-prison Jack? The drug runner ex-item?"

For a minute, Liz was sorry she'd revealed so much of her past to Sydney and Amelia that night at dinner. "It was Jack on the motorcycle that we saw coming out of the parking lot that morning."

"Any chance he could be the murderer?"

"No-o-o." Liz felt her cheeks grow warm. "At least, I don't want to think he could be. Jack's a little rough around the edges, but . . ."

"Still hung up on him, aren't you? Why is it women never get over their first lay?"

Liz nibbled her lower lip. "He wasn't, actually. He wanted it. I wanted it. But I didn't completely trust him, and I was scared that giving in would mean an end to my dreams."

"So you didn't trust him then, but suddenly he's worthy of your trust now?" Amelia asked.

"Jack can be a real bastard, but I can't believe he'd murder Tracy—or any woman, for that matter."

"But he's capable of killing a man?"

Liz sighed. "You don't know watermen. It's hard to explain. They're a breed apart. They make their own laws and live by a code that's almost archaic. It's a macho thing, tied up with honor and loyalty. If you haven't grown up with them, it's difficult to understand."

"You're avoiding my question."

"Yes, I suppose that under the right circumstances, Jack could kill someone," Liz said. "But, given extraordinary conditions, any of us could." She paused and asked, "If it was life or death, don't you think . . ."

"No, Liz, I don't. I can't imagine any circumstance

that would force me to take a life. And I don't think you could either."

"You couldn't kill someone to save Thomas?"

Amelia shook her head. "You're losing your perspective, Liz. You should talk to someone."

"The police? I've—"

"No. Professional help, a counselor. You've had a terrible shock. You may not be thinking logically." Amelia arched a perfectly tweezed eyebrow. "This isn't something you just get over, Liz. Finding a murdered girl in your office . . ."

"You think I'm losing it?"

Amelia tasted her coffee, then added another spoonful of dark honey and stirred. "It's only been a week. Seven days. You need to seek help."

"All right, I'll think about it. But I'll be honest. I don't have much respect for shrinks. The doctor I saw when Russell and I were in the process of divorce was useless. She kept suggesting that I be more sympathetic to Russell's gambling addiction. Easy for her to say. He put us thirty thousand dollars in debt and took a second mortgage on the house. And he cheated on me. Repeatedly. Once, Katie came home from school and found her father and his receptionist in our . . ." She shook her head. "It doesn't matter. Russell is history." She finished her coffee and stood up. "We should get back to school." She leaned over and hugged her friend. "I don't know what I'd do without you and Sydney."

"You know we're here for you. If you need anything, or if you just want to talk, don't hesitate to call me, day or night."

Liz sighed and nodded. "Okay."

"And you're in no shape to teach. Take the rest of the week off."

"It's too close to the end of the term."

"Then take a few days."

"Maybe you're right."

"No maybe about it. I'm right. No one in administration will give you any hassle."

"I'll think about it."

"No, promise me that you'll do it. Three days, at least."

"Yes, Mother. I'll take a few days off."

"Three," Amelia insisted. "You can load the kids up with work for the weekend."

"They'll love me for it."

Amelia dumped her purse on the table, opened a compact, and freshened her coral lipstick. "It's not a popularity contest. And they adore you."

"Not all of them. Someone's threatening me."

"You said it was Cameron."

"I said I thought it was Cameron."

"Mmm-hmm." Amelia squeezed her lips together. "Either him or a disgruntled student. Are you failing anyone?"

"Unfortunately."

"Any students who look capable of building a bomb?"

"Thanks a lot." Liz grimaced. "Now I should worry about being blown up every time I start my car?"

"Why not? You're a fan of the *Sopranos*. Isn't that how Tony gets rid of his enemies?"

"Michael and Jack both think that Tracy was killed by her ex-boyfriend. And now it looks as though he might have committed suicide. I doubt I have a murderer stalking me."

"Isn't that what I've been telling you? All this is probably some moron's idea of fun. They'll soon tire of the game and find someone else to pester."

"But they broke into my house! How would you feel if—"

Amelia rose. "I promised you scones and I never even offered them—"

"No, thanks. Honestly. The coffee and the shoulder to cry on were what I needed. Your scones are fabulous, but I'm not hungry."

"All right, but I'm not letting you off. Call Dean Pollett's secretary and tell them you won't be in for the rest of the week."

"Two days," Liz offered.

"Three."

Liz chuckled. "You drive a hard bargain."

"I know. Thomas says that all the time." She poured herself another half cup of coffee. "More?" Liz shook her head. Amelia crossed to a wall phone, punched in the number of the dean's office, and handed the receiver to Liz.

When she'd finished with the call and assured the secretary that she would return on Friday, Liz passed the phone back to Amelia, who hung it up.

"Now, wasn't that easy?" Amelia asked.

"I suppose, but I feel like a shirker."

"Don't. Go shopping. Buy shoes. I'll give you the number of that counselor, and I want you to make an appointment as soon as possible."

"I'll think about it," Liz said.

"Good, and think about visiting us at the beach house. Any time, for as long as you'd like."

"That, I'll gladly accept. I'm looking forward to it." She stood and picked up her briefcase. "I've already bought a new bathing suit in Ocean City. That shop I was telling you about—where they make the suits to fit you? It's a blue and green leafy print, two-piece."

"Great. Buy another one. You'll need it. I'm a beach fanatic. I toast on one side, then oil, and bake on the other." Amelia chuckled. "As if my tan needs it." Her eyes narrowed. "And I'm serious about you coming to stay here in this house for a few days. I want you to consider it."

Liz shook her head. "I can't. People have been trying to drive my family off Clarke's Purchase for hundreds of years. I ran away when I was seventeen. I won't do it again, not if it kills me."

"That's comforting, considering what just happened."

"Michael's loaned me one of his guard dogs. And he's just down the road. He says I have nothing to worry about, no matter who killed Tracy. If the murderer had wanted to cut my throat, he could have found me there any morning. I can deal with slimy Cameron, but—"

Liz broke off in mid sentence as her cell phone rang. She checked to see who was calling before answering. "Russell? How did you . . . ? Never mind. *What* is it?"

"I need to talk to you, honey. Can I come by the house?"

"No, you cannot come by my house. And I don't want you calling my cell. Katie shouldn't have given you this number." She glanced down at her watch. "What do you want? If it's money, you can—"

"This is urgent. Please, Liz. If I can't come to the farm, meet me in Dover. Dinner? Tonight?"

"Impossible."

"Coffee, then. That restaurant at the mall. We'll make it early. Five o'clock. Please, I wouldn't ask, but—"

"Russell, I work for a living."

"Please, for old time's sake."

"Fifteen minutes. Not a second more."

"Great, you're a lifesaver. Tonight. Five sharp. I'll be there."

"Idiot," Liz said when Russell hung up. "I'm an idiot." Why did she still let him manipulate her? It was always some dire emergency, which turned out to be a plea to borrow money. "Comic relief, I suppose," she muttered, "but which one of us is the clown?"

Hours later, amid a steady stream of mall patrons, Liz glanced at her watch. Russell was late. What did she expect? Russell was Russell.

Had it ever been good between them? After Jack broke her heart, she hadn't dated anyone for over two years. She'd convinced herself that education was what mattered. Not men, and not the life she'd put behind her. She'd sworn she'd never be "one of those Clarke girls from out in the sticks" again. She'd vowed to become a woman of taste, sophistication, and independence.

Inevitably, in trying to choose a man as different from Jack as bay water from champagne, she'd allowed herself to believe she could be happy with Russell Montgomery.

Educated, attractive, upper-class, and worldly . . . and a lying sack of shit.

"Liz!" He leaned forward to kiss her mouth. "You look great."

She turned her head so that his lips brushed her cheek. "You're late." He was impeccably dressed, as always. Brown hair styled in a medium cut, a steel-gray, single-breasted Prada suit, and Bruno Magli shoes. Russell's striped tie matched his pinstriped maroon shirt perfectly.

"Sorry about making you wait." He flashed his gold Rolex. "Traffic on I-95 was a bitch; backed up all the way from the train station to—"

"Fifteen minutes," she reminded him. "Not a minute more."

He took her arm as they entered the restaurant. Liz decided that her ex's taste in cologne hadn't changed. Too much and too expensive.

"Certain you're not hungry? My treat." He motioned to the hostess. "A booth, please."

Russell had put on a few pounds around the middle since she'd seen him last. And his hair was definitely thinning, but it showed not a hint of gray. If he was dyeing it, it was a professional job. Russell's locks had a hint of curl, and Katie had inherited the same rich brunette color, her father's dimple, and his beautiful blue eyes. Fortunately, Russell had passed on to his daughter little else.

It took exactly six minutes for Russell to dispense his quota of charm and move on to his temporary cash-flow problem. From there he swept enthusiastically to his opportunity to purchase the property his business had been leasing. "A once-in-a-lifetime

111

deal," he assured her. Desperation showed in his eyes. "The heirs want—"

"Russell, are you gambling again? Not one cent. I don't have any money to lend you. I wouldn't give you any if I did."

"I don't need a penny from you. All I want is your signature. You co-sign the loan and I—"

"Have you lost your mind? Sell your watch. I wouldn't co-sign a note for you if—"

"God, Liz. Danielle said you'd be like this. I'm not asking for—"

"No. Nada. Not a cent." She opened her wallet and counted out three dollars and laid it on the table. "I've gone this route too many times, Russell. I'm finished."

"Don't walk out on me," he said, pinning her hand with his larger one. "I need—"

She jerked free and glared at him. A bead of sweat glistened on his upper lip. "Go to hell, Russell."

"Liz!"

She dodged a chubby brunette waitress carrying a full tray of drinks and food and walked swiftly to the restaurant entrance that opened onto the parking lot. Russell followed her, but not fast enough. She reached her vehicle, unlocked the door, and got in. He approached just as she was putting the car into reverse, and she missed backing over his shiny new shoes by inches.

"Liz, wait!" he shouted.

She raised a middle finger in salute and drove out of the mall and onto northbound 13.

Twenty minutes later, Liz slowed and pulled into a parking spot beside the dock where the Raffertys moored their boats. Even with the air-conditioning on, she could smell the salt water, the not unpleasant odor of diesel fuel, and the oily scent of newly caught fish. She put the car in park and sat there sipping a warm Diet Pepsi and listening to the Stones as she tried to summon enough nerve to go in search of Jack.

Across the lot, a sport fisherman tightened the straps that held his nineteen-foot Grady White securely to the boat trailer. His buddy emptied beer cans and paper into a black container bearing a smiley face and a notice stating "NO BOTTLES OR CANS" and climbed into the cab of the big Dodge truck. As Liz watched, the driver got into the Dodge and pulled slowly away, leaving her alone in the lot.

The parking area, with its public ramp, was surprisingly free of trash. A yellowing life preserver and a coil of rope hung from a post at the water's edge. At the base of the pole, a calico cat trailing two bedraggled kittens tore hungrily at a trout skeleton. The song ended, and Liz turned off the ignition and put down her window part way. She could hear the purr of an outboard in the distance and the slap of waves against the pilings. An odd sensation of peace seeped through her. She'd been away so long, but she could still feel at home here. She closed her eyes and let the familiar sounds and smells soothe her troubled soul.

"Hey, girl!"

Startled by the hard rap on the front passenger window, Liz nearly spilled her soft drink.

"Elizabeth Clarke? It's me, Nora!" The woman laughed and knocked again on the glass. "Well? Are you going to sit there? Or are you coming out to give me a hug?"

Liz got out, and Nora hurried around the vehicle and threw her arms around her. "God, you look good, girl!"

"You too," Liz said. "You haven't changed a bit." Jack's mother was stuffed into a too-tight pair of blue jeans and a men's plaid cotton shirt that hung over her ample belly. High-top black sneakers with a hole in one toe completed her ensemble.

"Like hell I haven't. Forty pounds and a head of gray hair. But you could pass for twenty-five."

"Now who's throwing the bull?" Liz asked, smiling back at her. "You've been around those sons of yours too long. You're beginning to sound just like them."

"Thirty-five, anyway." She hugged Liz again. "Come up to the house. Jack's out with a charter, but supper's nearly—"

"I can't," Liz protested. "I didn't intend to intrude on your—"

"When did you know me not to make enough food to feed an army?" Nora's disheveled ponytail bounced with indignation and her glasses shifted forward on her nose. "Lima beans and dumplings," she said, pushing back the frames. "And you can't pass on fresh trout."

"Fried?"

Nora laughed heartily. "Is there any other way? My doctor says my cholesterol worries him, but I told him that there's no sense in both of us getting ulcers. Come eat with us. I insist. Jack's dad's making biscuits."

"I don't know," Liz teased. "Arlie? Sounds risky."

"Old Arlie's softenin' up a little in his golden years. Suddenly decided my pies and biscuits weren't like

114

his mother used to make, so he started messin' in the kitchen." She winked. "His biscuits are better than mine, but don't you dare tell him. He'll get so big-headed that he'll not fit through the door."

"You haven't changed," Liz repeated. "You never do." She smiled affectionately at Jack's mother and then grew serious. "I'm so sorry about what happened to Tracy. I wanted to talk to you at the funeral, but—"

"I wasn't at the funeral. I don't do funerals. I thought I could do more for Tracy by cooking for her wake. It was a terrible thing that happened to her, and terrible that you had to come on it."

"You knew?"

Nora's pleasant face grew strained. "For all its growing up, this is still a small place. Not much happens in Kent County that I don't know. And Jack—"

"He told you."

Nora nodded. "Jack feels he's partly to blame. He took her to school that morning."

"No more than I do. She was meeting me. That's why she came so early. My car wouldn't start, but if I'd been on time, Tracy might be alive."

"I doubt it. What's supposed to happen usually does. Like George gettin' caught. I suspected he was up to no good. His charters brought in too much money, and he always had more cash than he should have. Arlie didn't suspect, but I was worried about him for a long time. I tried to talk sense into him, but you know George."

"It must be terrible for you and Mr. Rafferty."

"Not as bad as it could be. Ten to fifteen years they gave him, but Georgie will be out in eight or nine, tops. He's still got time to turn his life around. If Arlie doesn't kill him when the state turns him loose. It about tore his daddy to pieces. He can't abide drugs. Seen too many young lives destroyed by them."

"I really shouldn't stay," Liz said. "I'm not hungry, and—"

"The biggest mistake Jack ever made was to drop you for that worthless sister of yours," Nora said. "You're the one I wanted for my Jack. He wouldn't have turned out nearly as wild if he'd had you to keep him straight." She locked an arm through Liz's. "No argument, now. Come and eat supper with us. It's not as though you haven't done it a hundred times before."

"Thank you," Liz said. "Maybe I could eat a piece of trout. Nobody fries fish like you do."

"It's all in the flour coating and keeping the oil hot enough. You can't overcook fish, or it's tasteless and tough. And you've got to have at least one of Arlie's biscuits. And I know you like lima beans and dumplings. I bought four bushels at Spence's last August and froze them. They're about gone, so if you miss these, you're out of luck." Nora squeezed her arm. "You grew up fine. I'm proud of you. You always said you were goin' to college, but Jack says we have to call you Dr. Clarke now."

"Not you," Liz assured her. "For you and my old friends, Liz will do just fine."

"You may as well drive up to the house," Nora said. "Kids have been vandalizing trucks and boat trailers. Arlie caught two of them throwing paint on one of his boats last week. Lucky for them, they could run faster than he could. I just went around to the one's mother and told her that my husband was crazy and carried a forty-five on his hip. I warned her that if she didn't want her son dead, she'd keep him off this dock."

"Would Arlie have shot them?"

Nora laughed. "Hell, no. But he would have busted some asses and probably landed in county jail. Kids can do what they please nowadays. Not like it used to be. But Arlie hasn't been locked up in ten years, and I'd like to keep it that way." She walked around the car, waited for Liz to unlock the passenger door, and then got in. "You know the way."

Liz chuckled. "I should. I spent enough time at your house."

"You're a good girl, Lizzy, and we're all proud of you. I wish it could have worked out between you and Jack. I worry about him a lot."

For an instant, Liz thought of what it would have been like if she'd given her virginity to Jack that summer when she was seventeen. Would they have broken up, or would her love for him have trapped her here in this small fishing town? Would her ambition have been buried under the strain of too many babies and too little money?

". . . Idiot girl he married," Nora continued, breaking through Liz's reverie. "Jack's got the Rafferty temper, wild as Injuns, all of them. Arlie's mother was half Nanticoke, and the Raffertys have as much Lenape Injun in them as Irish. Used to be, fishing, running charters gave a man a solid living if he was willing to work hard, but no more. Fish are about gone; water's polluted with mercury and God knows what other filth. I worry about my Jack, I surely do."

"He'll be all right," Liz assured her with more conviction than she felt. "He said he'd had some college and that he—"

"Hmmph," Nora scoffed. "Didn't brag on what kind of trash he's associating with, did he? If he doesn't keep his nose clean, he could end up worse than Georgie. He could end up dead."

Liz pulled into a wide driveway behind a blue compact Toyota and a Ford pickup with black-and-white plates. The two-story rambling Victorian house didn't look any different from when she'd last laid eyes on it. Half the front had been painted a creamy white, but the paint cans and brushes sat on the bare dirt area that passed for a front lawn. What grass there was clung to the edges of large clay pots bearing wilting pansies and herbs. A crumbling brick walk led to wooden steps, worn smooth by time and weather, and a wide porch that encircled the front and two sides of the house.

A disassembled boat motor held the place of honor near the front door, along with several rocking chairs and a porch swing. The front door was fashioned of colored glass panels and boasted a tarnished brass doorknob and a mail slot that had never been used for mail delivery. Original shutters, painted black, sagged at each side of the large, twelve-paned windows.

Liz couldn't help smiling. She could have been fourteen again as she followed Nora into the wide front hall with its braided oval rug and brass stands that held, not umbrellas, but fishing poles. The house smelled of lima beans and dumplings and hot biscuits, fresh from the oven. The furniture looked as worn and comfortable as the exterior, not so much untidy as lived in.

"Arlie, look what I found down near the dock!" Nora called.

Her husband, grayer and more stooped than Liz remembered, came through the archway that led to the dining room, a can of Budweiser in one hand. "God-amighty! Look what the wind blew in," Arlie said. "Look at you. Donald Clarke's girl, all grown up. You're a sight for sore eyes." He grinned, showing the Rafferty clan's perfect teeth, still intact and only slightly yellowed by age. "We're just sittin' down to supper. I'll set a plate for you."

"I already asked her, Arlie," Nora said, shooing the two of them through the formal dining room and into the kitchen. "We don't eat in there much," Nora explained, "not unless it's Thanksgiving. Just the three of us here now, and Jack usually stirs up something for hisself on the *Dolphin III*." She pushed an orange cat off a cushioned chair. "Sit, sit," she ordered.

"You took long enough," Arlie said to his wife. "Did you find it?"

"I swear, men are born without a findin' gene," Nora said as she filled a tall glass with ice cubes and followed with cold tea and a slice of lemon. "Arlie lost the phone number of Saturday's charter, and I had to go lookin' for it down at the dock. He'd lose his ass if it wasn't glued to his pizzle. Good thing I was down there. You would have sneaked off without comin' for a proper visit, wouldn't you?"

"I meant to come by and—" Liz started.

Arlie took his seat and passed a plate of biscuits to her. "When? You've been back at the old place for a couple of years, haven't you? Don't think we didn't hear about it. Joe what's-his-name who shingled

119

your roof, he goes out with me regular when trout are running. He said you and your daughter had fixed up the old place."

"Working on it," she answered. "It all takes time."

"And money," Nora put in. She slid a helping of lima beans and dumplings onto Liz's plate.

"Your daddy would be proud," Arlie said.

"I hope so."

"A pity they never found his body," Nora said. "He deserved a proper burial on Clarke's Purchase like the rest of his people."

"I know," Liz said. "I used to grieve about it, but . . ." She sighed. "It can't be helped. You know the Delaware Bay. He's not the first to be lost overboard without a trace."

"Arlie, want to offer grace?" Nora asked.

Liz bowed her head for the familiar words and then let herself enjoy the company of old friends and the food of her childhood. Nora was full of talk about people and boats that Liz had known, bad storms, tourists, and a run of good-sized trout that were biting on squid.

After supper, there was coffee and homemade apple pie. When Liz drove home, sometime after nine, she felt stronger than she had since she'd discovered Tracy's murder.

Some things never change, she thought. She'd spent years running from her old life, and in the process, she'd almost forgotten the good times.

When Liz arrived home, Michael's female German shepherd was waiting for her in the circle of light by the back door, head cocked, ears alert. Liz gave a little sigh of relief when she saw the guard dog. Whoever was playing these stupid games would be in for a huge surprise if he tried to sneak around with Heidi on guard.

"Hello, there." When the dog didn't respond, Liz remembered the silent whistle in her purse. She dug it out and blew on it to signal Heidi that she was off duty. The reaction was immediate. This time, when she called Heidi's name, the animal trotted toward her, tongue lolling, eyes wide and friendly. "Good girl, good Heidi." Liz took a dog biscuit from the bag on her car seat and offered it to her. Heidi nibbled it daintily and wagged her tail. "Yes, you're a good girl," Liz assured her.

She crossed to the porch. It was as clean as she'd left it—no grisly flowers, and no dead animals. Humming to herself, Liz unlocked the back door, pushed it open, and called Heidi in.

The phone on the kitchen wall was ringing. Liz ran to get it. "Hello!"

A tinny, almost mechanical voice crackled, "Ready or not, here I come."

Chapter Seven

"Who is this? What sick game are you—" The line went dead, and Liz slammed the phone down. She stared at it, trying to shake the unease that pricked the skin on her upper arms. She took two deep breaths and went to the back door, jerked it shut, and turned the deadbolt.

Heidi whined and looked up apprehensively.

"It's all right," Liz said. "Just a jerk-off." But was he? Since she'd discovered Tracy's body and the disturbing events had started happening here at the house, she'd tried to think rationally. She'd been angry, even unnerved, but she hadn't been afraid for her personal safety. Not really.

"Suppose I've been deceiving myself?" she murmured. "Suppose some psycho is after me and I'm too dumb to realize it?"

The dog tilted her head, a curious expression in her tawny eyes.

Liz wondered if she should call Michael and tell

him about the call, but decided that she didn't want to worry him. What she needed was reassurance, and Michael was a typically paranoid cop who saw perverts behind every tree. He'd only make things worse.

Jack . . . Jack was laid-back. He'd laugh and tell her that most phone harassers were harmless.

She pulled open a cabinet drawer and flipped through the phone book. Not the yellow pages, too expensive. He'd probably list . . . Yes, there it was. Rafferty, Jack.

"Be there," she murmured as the phone rang, twice, three times. "Answer it, damn you. Pick up the—Jack." She let out a sigh of relief when she heard his voice. "It's Liz."

"I know who it is. Mom told me that I just missed you. I had a charter, and we pulled in to the dock right after you left. Hold on a minute. I just got out of the shower. I'm dripping all over the floor. Let me get a towel."

"I'm talking to a naked man?" Pleasurable memories of their passionate interlude in her back yard washed over her.

His deep chuckle drove back the shadows. "Okay, Lizzy, I'm now decently covered. What's up?"

"I just got a crank call."

"What did they say? Did—"

"Could you come over? Just for a little while. I'd rather . . ." She swallowed her pride. "I need some company. I don't think I'm in danger. I've got a friend's German shepherd here, but—"

"How about supper?"

"Your mother stuffed me with trout and lima

beans with slippery dumplings." She leaned against the table, suddenly feeling much better.

"No, not you. Me. I haven't had anything and I'm starved. How about if I pick you up? We can go out to Rick's Crab Shack. I'll eat, and you can have a beer with me or eat again. Rick still makes a hell of a soft-crab sandwich. I'm buying. What do you say?"

She hesitated. She remembered Rick's as having great food, but attracting a rough crowd on weekends. This was Monday, and she had told the school she wouldn't be in until Friday, so . . . "There's no need to take me out. I could fix you something to eat here."

"Are you trying to proposition me? Lure me into your house with food and then take advantage of me?"

She laughed. "Is that what it sounds like? Do women make a habit of making excuses to get you to come over?" In her mind, she could almost see Jack, towel wrapped around his lean hips, hair dripping. She wondered if he'd shaved. She was certain she'd caught the scent of Obsession on him at the funeral.

"I'm not in the mood for a grilled cheese sandwich and tomato soup. Live recklessly. Come with an old friend and have a drink. You can tell me all about this phone call that has you spooked."

"All right," she answered.

"Good. Give me twenty minutes."

He was there in eighteen. And shortly after, she had her arms wrapped tightly around Jack's waist as they sped down Clarke's Purchase Road in the cool darkness on his Harley.

"You okay?" Jack shouted as he approached a stop sign and applied the hand brakes.

"Yes."

"Having fun?"

"Yes." She realized that she was. She was wound as tight as a spring and needed a release after the past several days. And it had been too long since she'd done something on a whim. Sometimes she felt closer to sixty than forty. She'd always had to be more mature than her age, had to be the responsible one. Her twenties and thirties had slipped by all too fast, and if she didn't allow herself a little fun, she'd be too old to enjoy it. Being close to Jack felt good, and she had a suspicion that before the night was over, she'd be even closer.

Other than the prices, Rick's Crab Shack, built on pilings sunk into the bank of a tidal salt creek and mudflats, hadn't changed in the years since Liz had last been there. Rick's scarred wooden tables were still covered with newspaper, the beer was still served in oversized, chilled mugs and pitchers, and the jumbo hard-shell crabs were so spicy they made your nose run.

Crude chairs made from barrels and springy plank floorboards added to the ambience, as did the lobster and crab pots hanging from the ceiling. Most of the light came from the 1970's Budweiser sign hanging over the bar and a few naked sixty-watt bulbs wired inside the lobster traps.

The country music, courtesy of WDSD, wailed from a lime-green radio bolted to a side wall with a hand-printed warning underneath that read, *"Rick don't care if you swear. Rick don't care if you smoke. But touch this dial and he'll rearrange your smile."* Someone had crossed out the word "smoke," but Liz noticed that at least half the customers ignored the Delaware law prohibiting smoking in public places. Rick's did not cater to a particularly sophisticated crowd.

The small restaurant was noisy, but several additions to the main room jutted out over the water, and Jack steered Liz toward a secluded table where they could talk. As usual, he ordered as if it were his last meal: crunchy salads, thick fries, a platter of raw oysters and clams, two of Rick's infamous soft-crab sandwiches, homemade coleslaw, and a brimming pitcher of cold beer.

"Who's joining us?" Liz teased as a sixty-year-old waitress in tight jeans and a Ravens sweatshirt delivered their order.

"Bet you can't get food like this in California," he said.

"I'll have you know that California is known for its fine food. They have wonderful seafood."

He slathered tartar sauce on a sandwich and took a bite. "Better eat that while it's hot."

She bit into a crab sandwich and savored the taste. "Delicious," she said. "I haven't had soft crab in twenty years. But Pacific crab is good too."

"I hear you." He grinned and took a sip of his beer.

Talking with Jack had always come easily, and tonight was no exception. For more than an hour they laughed and chatted about old times. They finished the pitcher and most of the food before his expression grew serious.

"Now let's talk about whoever's trying to scare you. Do you have any idea who it could be?"

"There's a grad student who's been pestering me to go out with him. Cameron Whitaker."

"A grad student, hmm?" Jack raised a dark eyebrow. "Isn't he a little young for you?"

"Not this one. Actually, I did go to dinner with him. Once." She grimaced. "He's a total jerk. Rude to the waitress."

"So you think Cameron is stalking you?"

"I don't know if I'd call it stalking."

"Breaking into your house? Leaving dead animals and dead flowers on your porch? Threatening phone calls? That's stalking in my book."

"I have Caller ID. I had it turned on earlier in the week, but the kitchen phone is so old it doesn't show the numbers."

"So you have a second phone in the house."

"Sure. In my bedroom. That . . ." She broke off. "I'm an idiot. That should give the number of the crank call, shouldn't it? Regardless of which phone I answered. I didn't think—"

"We'll check it when I take you home."

"Certain that's not a trick to get into my bedroom?"

"Maybe." He caught her hand and squeezed it. "Want me to have a talk with your grad student? I could probably—"

"No, I don't need your strong-arm tactics to deal with Cameron. He's about as dangerous as a beached catfish. I could whip his butt with one hand tied behind my back."

"I've missed you, Lizzy. And now that I've found

you again, I don't intend to let anything happen to you. If you need me, all you've got to do is shout."

She looked away, unsure if she wanted to hear this. Things were happening too fast, and as much as she enjoyed his company, she wasn't willing to trust him just yet.

"Hey, Jack!" a red-bearded man in a faded watch cap called from the bar. "Heard you got into a mess of trout today." He lifted his beer in salute. "You Raffertys always did have more luck than good looks!"

Jack replied with a cheerful insult that brought laughter from Red-beard's buddies.

Liz found herself shocked at how comfortable she felt here in the midst of these rednecks. Was she slipping back into the past she'd worked so long to escape? A few more hours and she'd pick up the accent she'd taken speech lessons to get rid of.

Her childhood had often been harsh; she'd endured things that she never wanted Katie to imagine. Yet she had to admit that there had been good times too. When he was sober, she couldn't have asked for a more loving father than Donald Clarke. There was an innate sense of solidarity among the families of the watermen, with hospitality offered freely, no matter how strapped for cash the host might be.

Jack pulled her from her reverie by stroking her cheek. "Hey, are you listening to me?" His fingertips were rough, but his touch excited her and filled her with heady anticipation.

Jack was hot and more than a little dangerous. A bad boy, and one she'd never gotten over. And, hands down, a better lay than any other man she'd ever been with.

"Come on," he said, taking her hand. "It's too crowded in here." He left two twenties on the table and pushed open a door that said *O EXIT*, leading to the narrow dock that ran around Rick's Crab Shack.

"I don't think we're supposed to use this door," she protested halfheartedly, suddenly wanting to be alone in the dark with Jack.

"It's an emergency. I can't keep my hands off you any longer."

The weathered deck and unpainted cedar railing were lit by a dim string of Christmas lights. Jack led her only a few steps past the window before shoving her up against the cedar shakes and kissing her. "Lizzy, Lizzy," he said as they came up for air. "Do you know what you do to me?"

His mouth covered hers, and it seemed the most natural thing in the world to open for his kiss, to thrill to the taste of his hot, velvety tongue and the feel of his hands moving over her. She shut her eyes and tilted her head back so that he could kiss her neck and nuzzle the damp warmth at the vee of her sweater. She slid her fingers up his chest to caress his shoulders and tangle in his hair, and all the while, he kept kissing her until she was giddy with need for him.

On the far side of the thin restaurant wall, a Southern voice on the radio sang about broken hearts and lonely nights, but all Liz could think of was getting closer to Jack. She could feel the heat of his arousal through his worn jeans. She made no protest when he unzipped her pants and tugged them down over her hips.

"No panties," he whispered in her ear.

"Complaining?" Her breath was coming in short, quick gulps.

"No, ma'am."

"Have you got a—"

"Yep."

She heard the faint rip of a foil packet and smelled the unmistakable odor of a new condom. "Always prepared?"

"Hell, yes."

She was wet and ready for him. She trembled as he lifted her to slide inside, stifling her cries of pleasure with a searing kiss. Her reward came fast and intense. Rocked by waves of sensual pleasure, she clung to Jack as he reached his climax.

He groaned. "Better than drugs."

"You do drugs?"

"A little weed. And that was a long time ago. I gave it up when I found something better."

"Not crack?"

He chuckled and nibbled her throat below her ear. "Sex."

For long minutes they remained as one, while aftershocks of sensation washed over her. Then Jack lowered her feet to the deck and produced a clean handkerchief from his pocket. Laughing and whispering furtively, they managed to perform basic hygiene and get their clothing in order.

Liz ran her fingers through her hair in an effort to make herself presentable. "I'm not going back through the restaurant," she warned. "They'll all know what we were doing out here."

He chuckled. "They might guess, Professor, but they won't know. My lips are sealed."

Unease spilled down her spine. "What did you call me?"

"Professor." He grinned. "Or would you prefer Dr. Clarke? It's what you are, isn't it?"

"Yes . . . It's just . . ." She looked away at the black water. The tide rushed out, exposing the muddy banks and filling the air with the scent of decaying vegetation. Suddenly she felt chilled. "We'd better get back. I'd like to check on that number on my upstairs phone."

Professor. Jack hadn't called her that before. And the message on her computer monitor—the one with the image of the oyster knife—had called her "professor." It was a coincidence, nothing more, but it spoiled the mood of the evening for her, and she wanted to be alone where she could reason this out.

If Jack was the one trying to frighten her, she was in a lot more trouble than she'd realized . . .

Still holding her hand, he led the way around the deck to the front of the restaurant and the unlighted gravel lot where they'd left the motorcycle. About a dozen cars and trucks were parked there, but Liz saw no one walking to or from the Crab Shack. Jack's bike was about halfway down the first row, front tire a foot from the chain-link fence that kept inebriated patrons from driving off into the marsh. Behind the Harley, a pickup idled, lights off. In the moonlight, Liz could make out two men in the front seat. A third figure leaned against the driver's door, the tip of a cigarette glowing red in the darkness.

Jack stopped and stared at the truck. "Go back inside," he said.

Puzzled, she glanced up at him. "Why?"

"Don't argue, just go!"

Abruptly the truck lights came on, temporarily blinding her. The pickup engine revved, and the vehicle shot toward them. Jack grabbed her arm and pulled her aside as the truck screeched past and braked to a halt, blocking her escape route to the restaurant. The doors flew open and the men piled out. One carried a baseball bat.

"Fine e-evening, J-Jack." The smoker threw his cigarette on the gravel and ground it out with the toe of his boot.

"Wasn't bad until you showed up." Jack stepped in front of her. "What do you want, Sonny?"

Liz recognized the name and the stutter, although she hadn't heard it since she was a child. Sonny Shahan. His close-cropped head was nearly bald and shiny in the moonlight, and he had a beer belly on him, but his aggressive stance and attitude hadn't changed a bit. Once a bully, always a bully.

"We want to t-talk to you."

"Yeah," the man with the bat said, his voice slurred with drink.

"Got nothing to say to you, Randy. You either, Daryll."

"What d-did you d-do to Wayne?" Sonny asked.

"Nothing. Liked to. Looked everywhere for him, but I couldn't find him."

"You're a damned liar," the third man said. He was close enough that Liz could smell whiskey on his breath. "Wayne's our buddy, and if you killed him, you got us to—"

"Walk away, Lizzy," Jack said. "She's no part of this. Let her go inside."

A mosquito buzzed around Liz's head. The breeze

carried a rank smell off the marsh, as though some-thing big had died out there. Her knees felt sud-denly weak. She took a step backward.

"And h-have her c-call the c-cops?" Sonny took another stride closer. "You m-must think we're s-stupid." A knife gleamed in his hand.

"You boys have had too much to drink and you've been watching too much television. I told you, I didn't lay a hand on Wayne. I'm not looking for trouble. What passed between us is just that. In the past."

Randy laughed. "Talking a different story now, ain't you?"

"Not so tough without your gun, are you, Jack?" Daryll taunted.

"Leave us alone," Liz said. "I'll scream for help."

Daryll raised the bat. "Try it, bitch, and I'll knock your teeth down your throat."

Jack lunged at Daryll. With a curse, the redneck swung the bat, a blow that would have taken Jack's head off if it had connected. Jack spun on one foot and delivered a karate kick to Daryll's groin and fol-lowed it up with a quick chop to the back of the neck. Daryll fell, curled, gagging and whimpering, into a fetal position.

Before Liz could utter a sound, both Sonny and Randy charged Jack. She heard the dull smack of a fist smacking flesh, and Randy collapsed on top of his now sobbing and vomiting brother. Sonny and Jack circled each other.

"He's got a knife!" Liz cried. She snatched up a rock and hurled it like a baseball at Sonny. The rock struck him hard in the shoulder, and he let out a yelp. Sonny turned his head to glance in her direction, and Jack brought the side of his hand down against the bully's wrist. Bone snapped. The knife dropped from Sonny's fingers, and he clutched his injured hand to his chest.

Jack stepped back just as the first shotgun blast struck the right headlight of the pickup. Glass shattered. Ears ringing, Liz whirled to see Rick standing at the edge of the road, a twelve-gauge in his hands.

"Didn't I tell you to stay the hell away from my restaurant, Shahan? Now get your drunk ass out of here before I call the state troopers to lock you up!"

"You s-shot m-my truck! I'll s-sue you, you b-bastard!"

Jack grabbed Liz and pulled her out of the line of fire.

"Sue away," Rick answered, "but if the cops come, you'll get your third DUI, and I'll press charges for assault and attempted robbery!"

"R-Robbery? Wh-What did I s-steal?"

"I'll think of something," Rick said, breaking open the shotgun and shoving in another shell.

"You s-son of a—"

The twelve-gauge roared again, destroying the truck's left headlight and blowing a hole in one tire. "Get your trashy ass out of here," Rick warned. "I got plenty more shells."

Speechless, Liz watched as the three bullies piled into the cab, Randy started the engine, and the truck wobbled onto the main road with the left front tire rim grating on the blacktop.

"H-How the h-hell we s-supposed to see to d-drive?" Sonny shouted out the window.

"Beats me," Rick replied. "Come back here again, and I'll take out the rear tires." He looked at Jack. "You all right? Need the E.M.T.'s?"

"We're good," Jack answered. "Thanks for the help."

Liz's hands were trembling so badly that she couldn't fasten the straps on her helmet.

"Let me do that," Jack said.

"You're hurt."

He rubbed his jaw. "Nothing a little ice won't fix. I'm sorry about this, Lizzy. I never meant—"

"You never do," she said softly. "But it wasn't your fault. You did your best to talk your way out of it."

"I never meant to put you in danger."

"Maybe it was a mistake for me to come back to Delaware. Things like this never happened in California."

"No?"

She realized how foolish that sounded. "Well, it never happened to me. Not in my world, Jack. No fistfights. No crazy vigilante bartenders with shot-guns."

"Just college girls getting their throats cut?"

"That's not fair," she protested.

"No, it isn't," he said. "But shit happens. And when it does, you've either got to be strong enough and smart enough to save yourself, or you end up like Tracy. Which are you, Lizzy?"

It was a little after two a.m. when they arrived back at Clarke's Purchase. Despite her insistence that no intruders could be in the house because of the guard dog, Jack stood firm on personally inspecting every

135

room, checking every door and window, before leaving. He'd made sure that the interior door that led to the basement, and the closed stairway to the attic, were locked securely.

Caller ID on the upstairs bedroom phone had registered two calls, the one she'd received just after nine from her stalker, listed as a blocked number, plus a second that Liz recognized as Amelia's.

"I'll stay the night if you want," Jack offered.

"No, I'll be fine," she answered. Their impulsive sex at the restaurant and the incident in the parking lot had shaken her, making her wonder if this whole thing with Jack was a huge mistake. "You said you have a charter tomorrow. You'd better go back to the boat and get as much sleep as you can before dawn."

"I can cancel the charter. Or Dad can take it. Mom can handle Dad's regular head-boat run."

"No. I don't need a babysitter. I can take care of myself."

"I said I was sorry. I didn't know we'd run into Sonny or the Hurd brothers. Or that the idiots would be drunk enough to—"

"Just go, Jack. Please. I'm tired."

"I'll call you."

"Let's take it slow, shall we? A lot has happened, and—"

"Right." His face hardened. "You call me when you've got a mind to go slumming."

"Jack, don't—"

"Good night, Lizzy. It's been"—he shrugged—"almost like old times."

"Not quite. It was *me* with you tonight, not Crystal."

"Low," he said. "Low and dirty."

Apprehensively she watched the lights of his motorcycle grow smaller and smaller as he pulled away down the lane. Calling the dog to come upstairs with her, Liz showered and then climbed into bed, exhausted and certain that she would fall asleep in minutes.

The Game Master shuddered with pleasure as he brought up image after image of his past adventures on his laptop. *The sophomore*'s photos were particularly enjoyable. The colors on his new digital camera were fantastic. Looking at the spreading pool of blood on the professor's office rug, he could almost taste the sweet, salty tang on his tongue.

Idly he fingered a small leather pouch.

This, his newest challenge, promised to be the most rewarding. *The professor* was tough and resilient, a worthy opponent. The Crow Indians believed that a man could be judged by the quality of his enemies. He agreed with that. *The professor* was the finest quarry he'd ever stalked, and he was convinced that she was also the most dangerous.

He undid the knot on the drawstring and removed a plastic bag. Opening it, he sniffed the shriveled finger. How fragile it was. It might have been a child's digit, if it weren't for the bright cherry nail polish. Sadly, the polish was chipped. *The sophomore* hadn't been as careful about her appearance as she should have. He wondered if the remaining flesh would attract crabs. Maybe he'd try an experiment when he was finished with *the professor*. There wasn't enough of *the sophomore* to go around, and he wasn't willing to give up his only souvenir.

Still, it was time to turn up the heat on his current interest. Once she was irrevocably his, he could take his time disposing of her. He inhaled slowly as he thought of the hours . . . days, perhaps even weeks that she would be his to enjoy. But then, as he gazed at *the sophomore*'s pale and lifeless body, his joy faded, to be gradually replaced by a deep and gnawing hunger.

He knew the familiar feeling. Hadn't he lived with it for years? Soon he would be unable to sleep, to take pleasure in his trophies, or in food or drink. All too soon, the need to possess her would become the most important thing in his world. It was a need that must be satisfied before it consumed him utterly and destroyed him as surely as he destroyed his victims.

Liz's night was far from restful. The wind rose and rattled the windows, and a thunderstorm blew in from the west. Sheets of rain slanted against the bull's-eye glass panes. The electricity flickered off and on, causing Liz's bedside clock to lose power and revert to a flashing 12:00 p.m. several times. Outside, tree branches swayed and brushed against the second story, and above her the attic floors creaked and thumped. Liz's dreams were troubled by a girl's voice—a voice that sounded much like Tracy's—and the faint ring of an imaginary telephone. Twice, Liz started awake to Heidi's shrill barking from downstairs. Both times, she got up, took her flashlight, and went down to investigate. And each time, the dog had stopped barking by the time she got there. Liz slept fitfully and woke red-eyed and tired to face a gray and foggy dawn.

She rose and went to the window, staring out over

the bleak marsh. Her barn, dock, and outbuildings were swathed in mist. She could see only portions of her back yard, the grass sodden and green. The lonely cry of a single Canada goose seeped through the glass, and Liz raised the window.

Despite the fog, the familiar lapping of the waves against the dock and the rustling sighs of the tall phragmites were reassuring. Not a single car horn honked, no rush of traffic or wail of sirens marred the peace of the morning.

But there was something . . . something she couldn't quite place, a *scrape, scrape, scrape* sound of wood against wood. Curious, Liz pulled on a pair of jean cutoffs, a bra, and a blue T-shirt bearing the image of the great pyramids at Giza that she'd bought at the Met last fall. Barefoot, she hurried down the kitchen stairs to find Heidi pacing by the back door.

Liz undid the lock and opened the Dutch door for the dog, then followed her outside. The noise was louder in the back yard. She crossed the wet lawn to the dock and stopped short. Rocking against the Sampson post on the far side was a rotting, flat-bottomed rowboat.

Liz's breath caught in her throat as she stared at the waterlogged craft. Decaying fish heads, a single worm-infested oar, and a rusty fishing pole littered the bottom. And piled haphazardly in the bow of the nightmare boat was a heap of rusty traps, some holding the decaying corpses of muskrats.

Liz clamped her hand over her mouth, but the unspoken name screamed in her head. *Buck. Buck Juney.* She groaned and backed away.

On the wet dock, muddy footprints led from the place where the boat was tied to within two yards of where she stood . . . led and stopped as completely as if the owner had vanished into thin air.

Chapter Eight

Liz shook her head. Fear made her giddy.

Rational. She had to be rational. She was an educated woman; she'd earned a doctorate. She wasn't a ditz. She didn't believe in ghosts, and she wouldn't allow a dead crazy man to terrify her. This had to be some bizarre coincidence.

Glancing around, Liz drew in a ragged breath. Nothing seemed out of place. Her car was near the back gate where she'd parked it last night. Heidi lay stretched on the damp grass not far away. A mockingbird trilled an elaborate song from a top branch on the Macintosh apple tree.

Heidi wasn't barking.

Dogs possessed keen hearing and a sense of smell hundreds of times greater than humans. Surely, if a stranger were nearby, the German shepherd would have scented him. And this wasn't just any mutt; she was a trained guard dog. As long as Heidi thought that the premises were safe from trespassers, Liz had no reason to be alarmed.

Liz swallowed, trying to ease the tightness in her throat. She needed a strong cup of coffee, maybe two. Tracy's death had affected her far more deeply than she'd realized. Perhaps Amelia was right. Maybe she did need to consult a counselor.

"I'm not eleven years old anymore." Hadn't she told Jack that she could take care of herself? It was useless. No amount of reasoning could prevent the buried memories from seeping back to haunt her.

How many times during long-ago summers had she been terrified by Buck Juney? He'd been real, and her fears had been real, not the imagination of a hysterical child. Buck had stalked her, like a hunter stalks a deer.

And no one, not even her father, had believed her.

Time and time again, Buck Juney's boat had materialized as silently as a wraith out of the marsh reeds. He'd followed her through the woods as well. Even now, her heartbeat quickened as she remembered the ominous snap of twigs behind her as she fled down the familiar trails and caught glimpses of him through the trees. Once, Buck had startled her by rising from a green brier thicket, almost within arm's length. And another time, he'd stepped out of the fog almost within reach as she'd walked to the barn with a bucket of water for her pony.

"Hello, girly," he would grate slyly before bursting into hollow laughter. His rusty voice had been so much like the one that she'd heard on the phone yesterday that thinking about the prank call made her stomach clench.

No, rational thought couldn't erase Liz's memory of Buck or of the mangy pack of slat-ribbed hounds slinking in his wake. She shuddered, remembering the nights that she'd sat bolt upright in her bed, her sheets tangled and soaked with sweat while eerie howling echoed through the open windows of the farmhouse. She'd wondered then, as she wondered now: Had she heard the baying of flesh-and-blood dogs, or was it the crazy old man?

But it couldn't be Buck Juney's rowboat scraping against her dock. That was impossible. Liz steadied herself on a post at the water's edge and tried to slow her breathing before she hyperventilated. She needed caffeine, and she needed to talk to someone she trusted. Calling Heidi to follow, she went back inside, made herself presentable, and drove to Michael's. Usually, Tuesday and Wednesday were his days off. She hoped today wasn't an exception and that he'd be at home.

Liz found him planting flowers at the base of the marble angel in the brick-walled graveyard. Michael's spacious ranch house stood on the site of an eighteenth-century farmhouse. None of the original buildings survived, but the plantation cemetery remained in a grove of cedars a few hundred yards from his back door.

Michael had told Liz that when he'd purchased the acreage, he'd hired workers to repair the crumbling bricks, clear the area of green briers and saplings, and straighten the sagging tombstones.

"I never expected to bury Barbara here," Michael had explained the first time he'd taken her to see the restoration. "But Barbara loved the peacefulness of the old cemetery." He'd been close to tears that day,

as he seemed to be this morning. It was obvious to
Liz that Barbara had been the love of his life and that
he still mourned his dead wife deeply.

"I'm sorry to disturb you," Liz said as she pushed
open the elaborate wrought-iron gate. Otto, Michael's
male German shepherd, wagged his tail and frisked
around her in what she supposed was a plea for attention or a biscuit. She petted him, amazed as always at
how gentle and loving both of the guard dogs could
be when they weren't working.

Michael glanced up and smiled. "You know better
than that. I'm glad for the company."

After Barbara's death, Michael had ordered ma-
sons to replace the old oyster-shell walkway with
one that he could easily traverse with his wheelchair.
A raised bed with a retaining wall provided an area
that he could plant with seasonal flowers.

"I knocked, but when you didn't answer the door,
I thought you might be out here."

"Otto's a good listener, but not much of a conver-
sationalist." Michael carefully pressed the topsoil
around a fragile seedling. "The tulips are about
gone. I'll replace the bulbs in the fall. I'm putting in
impatiens and strawflowers for summer."

"Survivalist and romantic," Liz teased. "You really are a Renaissance man." She sank onto a bench
and watched as he finished watering the seedlings.

"It's been five years," he said. "But it seems like
yesterday."

Liz wondered if anyone would ever love her that
much . . . if anyone but Katie would care if she died.
"I wish I could have known her. Barbara must have
been special."

"She was to me." Michael dusted the dirt off his

hands and looked at her. "You lose power last night?"

She nodded. "Off and on."

"I thought so. My clocks and the microwave needed resetting this morning. I heard thunder, but I slept through the rain." He slid his tools back into a canvas bag and hung the watering can on a hook on the back of his chair. "How's Heidi working out for you?"

"She's good, but . . ."

Michael's mouth firmed. "More problems? Come up to the house. I'll put on a fresh pot."

"Lifesaver." Over a cup of French roast, she told him about the phone call and what she'd found at her dock this morning, carefully omitting any mention of Jack or the fight at Rick's. "I have to admit, seeing that rowboat scared me."

"Did you report the threatening phone call to the police? It could have something to do with Tracy's murder."

Liz grimaced. "You're not supposed to say that. You're supposed to tell me that it's some kid I'm failing in Women and Property Rights in Seventeenth-Century America: Middle Colonies. I was counting on you."

"Cops are paid to deal with these things. You aren't helping yourself if you don't make a complaint. You don't have one isolated incident. There's a pattern."

"A pattern. You're damned right, there's a pattern, but who's going to believe me? You should have been there when that trooper came to answer my last complaint. He treated me as though I was a hysterical idiot."

"You should have called me. Retired or not, rank

still has some pull. You'd never have gotten such a response when I was on the road. These troopers today . . ." He shrugged. "The trouble is, they've lowered the standards."

She leaned forward. "Chauvinist."

"Nothing to do with women or minorities. It's character, intelligence, and strength. Show me a recruit who can keep cool in an emergency, do the job, and back up his partner, and I couldn't care less about race, ethnic background, or gender."

"I can hardly blame the police. It's the laws. It's almost impossible to prove harassment, even when the victim knows her harasser. Some of the women I counseled at my last school went through hell. And when they did get the bastard who abused them into court, the judges would let them off with a slap on the wrist."

"Let me reach out, Elizabeth. I still have friends on the force."

"My father never trusted the police. If he had trouble, he took care of it himself."

Michael grinned. "You don't know how many times I've heard that. But times change, and a woman can be prey to some ugly characters. I promise you that there will be an investigation. From now on, don't answer the phone. Let voice mail pick it up. Then, if your caller makes threats, the detectives have somewhere to start. And if it continues, we . . . *they* can put a trace on your line." He refilled her cup. "Have you given any thought to my other suggestion?"

"That I learn to use a firearm?"

"Yes."

"It goes against everything I believe."

"It may mean the difference between life and death."

"I know."

"Or moving away from Clarke's Purchase."

"I can't do that," she said softly. "You're right. It's time I acquired a gun."

"You'll let me instruct you?"

"If you want."

"I taught recruits for three years. I wouldn't trust anybody else." Michael moved to a rolltop desk, unlocked it, and produced a small revolver. "I told you I had just the thing for you."

She eyed the weapon anxiously. "When do we start?"

"What's wrong with this morning?"

Despite the ear protection Michael had insisted she wear, Liz's ears rang with the echo of gunshots as she drove into her own yard late that afternoon. She parked the car and walked down to the dock, half expecting the rowboat to be gone. It wasn't, but Michael had offered to tow it away and anchor it somewhere in the marsh, once the police had taken a look.

She didn't have as much faith in the authorities as he did. She massaged her wrist and stared down at the boat. It could be Buck's. Stranger things had happened. She supposed that the craft could have lain on a bank or been mired in mud . . . For a quarter of a century? She was kidding herself, letting her imagination run away with her. Either it was a coincidence or Cameron was cleverer than she imagined.

Reluctantly she entered the house, checked all the windows and doors, and went up to listen to her voice mail. There were three messages: one from

Katie, one from Sydney, and a third from Al, the manager at Atlantic Book Warehouse, telling her that the book she'd ordered was in.

Liz was on her way back down to throw a load of towels in the washer when the phone rang again. She waited to let voice mail pick up, and then grabbed the receiver when the caller identified himself as a representative of the Delaware State Police.

"Yes, this is Dr. Clarke." Michael must have pulled some strings, she thought. But instead of questioning her about the boat, the man was seeking donations for a summer camp the force ran for disadvantaged children. Liz rejected the sales pitch and hung up. So much for the strong arm of the law.

She tried to think of what she normally would be doing on a weekend. Usually, the days flew past, without her finishing half the chores she'd laid out for herself. Now the hours stretched ahead of her, and she didn't have the slightest inclination to tackle any of the tasks on her waiting list. As much as she loved teaching, she couldn't force herself to go over her coming week's lesson plans or to make last-minute changes in her finals.

She settled on mowing the lawn, a no-brainer. All she had to do was stay on the John Deere and steer in circles. She had approximately two acres to cut around the house and barn. The rest of the farmland she either let lie fallow or rented by the acre to farmers. She did like to mow a strip on either side of the long lane to keep the weeds and saplings from swallowing her driveway. The problem was that she didn't have to think, and her mind kept wandering back to Tracy's death and—when she could evade that nightmare—to Jack.

She had to be out of her mind. Certifiable. Had she really let him make love to her in her back yard in broad daylight? And on the deck outside the Crab Shack? Let him, hell—it had been an equal-opportunity seduction. Jack had been hot. Better than good. She'd come more times than . . . She smiled in spite of herself. Jack could certainly give her ex-husband a few lessons.

She'd never adopted celibacy by choice. She'd been a virgin when she married Russell, and despite his cheating, she'd never broken her marriage vow. Her other two relationships had been satisfying, warm and comfortable, but nothing like what she'd experienced in the last week. Nothing like Jack.

She wanted a repeat performance. Like an alcoholic in pursuit of a drink, she longed to feel the way she had in his arms. And that was what terrified her.

Once burned . . .

But, oh, how the fire beckoned.

"Face it, Lizzy, your choice in men sucks," she shouted above the hum of the lawn tractor.

Not that she'd had any examples to follow. Her parents' relationship had hardly been noteworthy. What had the two of them ever seen in each other? Her mother had been nineteen when she'd married her dad. And from all accounts, Donald Clarke had been a piece of work in his younger days.

"All his life," she murmured. She glanced toward the dock, half expecting to see her father's boat snubbed to the Sampson post. Or to hear him cursing as he fought with the chronically ailing water pump. Ball cap on backward, face and hands stained with grease, her father had pitted his considerable mechanical skills against aging motors and twisted props.

149

What in the name of all that was holy had prompted her to come back here? She and Katie had been doing fine in California. No one she knew had come to a violent death there. Russell and his notions about Katie studying in Dublin had been three thousand miles away, and so had Jack Rafferty.

She'd call Jack tonight.

At ten o'clock that evening, Liz gave up on Jack. Either he was night fishing or he had other fish to fry. Probably the latter. She wished she'd called Sydney or Amelia and asked if they wanted to see a movie. A romantic comedy would be good, something to make her laugh, but anything would beat sitting here alone with only Heidi and her cat to keep her company.

At ten-thirty, she cut an inch off her hair and colored what remained. It was hard to find an auburn that wasn't brassy, but she hated the occasional gray strand that sprouted around her face, making her look like an aging schoolteacher. "It's what you are," she told her reflection in the bathroom mirror. "You're never going to be thirty again, girl."

Not that thirty had been great. She'd always kept herself reasonably fit, more out of necessity than concern for her looks. She'd been blessed with good teeth, a normal nose, and nice hair. At least, people told her it was attractive. When she was young, her sister had teased her about the color, calling her carrot-top, but the red had darkened from a shocking strawberry blonde to a presentable auburn.

She snipped another lock. Pam, her hairdresser, would pitch a fit. "Who's been hacking at this?" she'd ask and follow with a derogatory remark.

Maybe she was paranoid. She always cut her hair when she was stressed. Pam had warned her never to use color immediately after a trim because the ends would self-destruct—turn fuchsia or something—but they didn't. Liz could see little difference in the shade as she towel dried. She didn't like to use her dryer unless time was critical. Her hair had a little natural curl, and blasting her head with hot air tended to make it frizzy. She trimmed a few stray hairs on top and decided that it was time to make an appointment with Pam.

Liz was cleaning up the sink when Heidi began to bark. Wrapping a towel around her wet head, Liz hurried down the stairs. The dog scratched at the back door and whined.

Liz's heart rose in her throat as she switched on the porch light. No one was visible, but there was something furry lying on the floor just beyond the mat. She was tempted to open the door, but she didn't. Whatever it was could stay there until morning. No way in hell was she opening this door tonight.

Leaving the light on, she went to the other kitchen windows and looked out. Nothing. Heidi paced and whined. Liz reached for the phone. She'd give Jack another ring. He might be—

The telephone rang, and she jerked her hand back. Liz swore and picked up the receiver.

"Professor Clarke."

Liz's mouth went dry. It sounded like Tracy's voice. She stepped away, still clutching the receiver in her hand.

"Please . . ." the caller said. "Don't hurt me. Don't—" There was a terrified shriek, and the phone went dead.

Liz dropped the phone and raced up the steps, two at a time. She caught a quick glimpse of a message on her bedroom phone. *Insufficient data.* She snatched up the receiver. "Who are you, damn it?" she shouted.

The only response was a persistent beep, reminding her that she'd left the kitchen phone off the hook, followed by the mechanical recording: "If you'd like to make a call, please hang up and dial again."

A scrape on the sill caught Liz's attention, and she whirled around to see Heidi standing in her bedroom doorway, head cocked, eyes wide and curious. Muffin hissed and flew up to the top of the maple dresser.

"Enough already," Liz said. Heart thumping, she sank on the bed and tried calling Jack's boat again with the same results.

The night seemed long with creaks, groans, and rustling coming from various corners of the house. Once, Liz drifted off to sleep only to awake certain that she had heard someone whispering. She tossed and turned, and then turned on the light and read a book until after two. She was about to try sleep again when the phone rang. This time, she had sense enough to wait for the caller ID to identify the caller.

It was Jack.

She answered, trying to sound as though she'd been asleep. "It's you," she said.

"You rang."

"Hot date?"

"What's up, Lizzy?"

She swore. "You don't make this any easier, do you?"

"You're the one who wanted space."

"What am I supposed to think? For two decades I don't see you, don't hear a word, and then you just happen to call on the night I find a dead girl in my office?"

"Did you call to fight, or do you want something?"

"I'm scared, Jack," she admitted.

"Something wrong? More problems at the house?"

She slid back and propped her head on the pillow. "More problems than I know how to handle. And you're right in the middle of them."

"How's that?"

"We had sex, twice."

"You could say that."

She could almost see his slow grin. "Do I have anything to worry about?"

"We used protection."

"I want more than that. I want some reassurance." She paused and started again. This was harder than she imagined. "I think it's time we had 'the talk.' Intimacy carries risks these days."

"Why didn't you bring that up when we went for crabs?"

She sighed. "Embarrassed, maybe. I'm not exactly experienced at this."

"That's my Lizzy, pure as the driven snow."

"If you feel that way, why are we having this conversation?"

"All right. Let's clear up your worries on that count. One, I used a condom both times. Two, I've been lucky. No H.I.V., no STDs. I was tested nine months ago in prison, and I haven't been with any woman but you since I got out."

Relief made her giddy. "You swear?"

"Oh, it gets better. You don't even have to worry about me getting you pregnant."

"I'm on the pill."

"No, you've got to hear this. Here's irony for you. You turned me down that summer you were seventeen because you were afraid of getting pregnant."

"Daddy would have killed you."

"It was more than that. You didn't think I cared enough about you to do the right thing if we got caught."

"I didn't want a baby, Jack. I was seventeen."

"And you had big plans for getting away from your father's farm."

"I won't apologize for that."

"No, you shouldn't."

"I loved you as much as any seventeen-year-old can, and you broke my heart."

"I know."

"Would you have wanted to be a father then?"

"No worry on that score," he answered. Some of the sarcasm drained out of his voice. "I shoot blanks, Lizzy. My inability to father a child is one of the reasons my marriage failed. Some guy from the air base gave my ex what she wanted. I offered to accept the baby as my own, but she said it was too late. She divorced me and married him. The last time I saw her brother Steve, he told me that they'd had two more kids, and were living in Oregon."

"I'm sorry," she said.

"I'm not. Noble offers aside, neither of us was mature enough to be married. It wouldn't have lasted six months. I won't pretend I've been an angel since, but I can tell you that you don't need to worry about getting pregnant or STDs."

She hesitated. "I haven't been tested, but I haven't had sex in four years. Until . . . until you."

"So much for the sexual revolution."

"Exactly." She chuckled.

"Want me to come over?"

"No, it's all right. I just wanted to hear a friendly voice."

"That's me. A friendly voice in the night."

"Jack . . . I'm overwhelmed. I'm not ready to . . ."

"No strings. Wasn't that your idea?"

"Could we talk about something else?"

"Don't jerk me around here, Lizzy. Either we're friends or we're not."

"I believe the kids have another term for it. Boinking buddies."

"That's what you think?"

"You told me that you and Tracy were friends. Did you have the same kind of relationship with her?"

"I told you what was between Tracy and me. If you don't believe me, then there's nothing I can say to convince you."

"Can you blame me? You just got out of jail. Is it any wonder I don't accept everything you say hook, line, and sinker?"

"What kind of talk is that for a professor? Still got a little of that bay water in your veins, don't you?"

"Did you do it?"

"Cut her throat?"

"Were you part of George's drug running?"

"That's a no-win conversation." He made a sound of impatience. "If I claim innocence, you'll assume I'm lying."

"I want to hear you say it. I understand about the Hurd brothers. If you tried to kill them, you probably had good reason. But drugs . . . If you—"

"We're done talking about that. If I'm guilty, it's of not stopping George before it got out of hand."

"Now who's playing games?" she said. "Were you innocent of the drug charges?"

"Dad asked me the same thing. I can tell you what I told him. What's innocent?"

"Why can't you just give me a straight answer?"

"Why can't you trust me? You've always known me."

"But I don't know you now."

"Can I come over anyway?"

"No."

"I can be there in—"

"Good night, Jack."

At six a.m., Liz discovered the water-soaked body of a red fox on her porch, one paw cruelly sawed or bitten off. The sight made her gag. She would have thrown up if she'd had anything in her stomach.

She was tempted to call the police, but knew that if she did, she'd appear a kook. She'd already made a complaint about the crank call and the boat. Michael had insisted she do so yesterday from his house. The desk sergeant had seemed amused, had said that it was a busy day, but he'd promised to send an officer to investigate, if she insisted. To her knowledge, no one had come. She'd tried Detective Tarkington's number and left a message on his voice mail, but he hadn't returned her call.

Now she had a dead fox to add to the puzzle. Was she overreacting? There were foxes in the fields and woods around Clarke's Purchase. Any stray dog could have dragged the carcass there. But she knew in her heart that it hadn't been a dog. Not a dog, and not the ghost of a dead man. Somebody was still playing sick games with her. She didn't know who or why, but she'd find out. And she'd raise the stakes.

More resolute than angry, Liz went to the barn, got a shovel, and buried the animal at the edge of the field. Before the day was out, she'd return to Michael's and put in more target practice. She didn't want to harm anyone, but she was tired of being a victim, and she was tired of being afraid in her own home.

After showering and washing her hair, she phoned Amelia, apologized for calling so early, and asked her if she wanted to meet for breakfast.

"Actually, I wanted to talk to you."

Liz noticed that Amelia's voice sounded strained. "Did you want me to give Sydney a ring and see if she's free to join us?"

"No. Just us," her friend replied. "I don't know about you, but I had a rotten night's sleep."

"Missing Thomas?"

"Yes. After a fashion."

The tightness in Amelia's tone remained. Something was wrong. "Are you all right?"

"No, I'm not. My alarm system went off in the middle of the night. The company called me and then alerted the police. I had two officers here about two o'clock. My trashcan was turned over, and the door to the screened porch was open. The police thought maybe a stray cat or a raccoon—"

"A raccoon?" Liz said. "I could understand it if

you kept cat food out there, but you don't. Why would a raccoon wander onto your porch?"

"You know how paranoid Thomas is about doors and windows being locked. I think I might have had a prowler. He triggered the motion detector, and the alarm scared him off."

"And you want me to spend the night there? In town, where it's safe?" Liz chuckled, trying to hold back a sense of growing concern.

"I know. It gives me the creeps. We've never had any trouble here. The Rehnards, over on the next street, had a coin collection stolen last year, but it was while they were on vacation."

"Maybe the wind blew the door open."

"I've never left the porch door unlocked. If it was wind, it was gone by the time the patrol car got here. I was outside in my robe answering questions, and not a breeze was stirring." Amelia paused. "There's something else, Liz, something I didn't mention. I received a very nasty e-mail Friday. I printed it off and saved it."

"Worse than the ads for larger sexual organs?"

"A lot worse."

"What did it say?"

"It read, 'You're next.' And then a racial epithet, one no one has ever directed at me."

"That's terrible. Do you know who sent it?"

"No, I don't."

"Did you show it to the police? Why didn't you tell me?"

"Because it came from the college. With your screen name."

"Me?" The stiffness in Amelia's tone became immediately understandable. "You don't think I—"

"Of course I don't. Give me some credit. But I'm scared. I keep thinking about Tracy."

"Me too."

"And this isn't 1960. I won't be threatened, and I won't stand for being racially harassed."

"No, I wouldn't expect you to."

"It makes me so damned angry. I know these things still go on every day, but not at Somerville, and not to me."

"Is it still on your computer? Did you save it?"

"Just the copy. I was so furious that I didn't think."

"You should have told me."

"I was embarrassed. Afraid that you'd be offended."

"Me?"

"It's complicated, Liz. Not being black—"

"You think I wouldn't understand?"

"Okay, so I'm an idiot. Can you be at the Pancake Kitchen in half an hour?"

"My hair's still wet. Make it forty-five minutes."

"Can do. And Liz . . ."

"Yes?"

"Be careful."

Chapter Nine

Thirty minutes later, Liz braked at the end of her drive to drop her electric and telephone bills into her mailbox. She used her shoe to squash a spider that had taken up residence, inserted the two stamped envelopes, and raised the flag. As she returned to her car, she noticed a vehicle parked on the side of the road some distance away.

Out of curiosity, Liz turned right and drove along the blacktop until she reached the hedgerow that marked the edge of state game lands. The car, an early 90's dark blue Honda, looked familiar. She slowed and inspected it carefully, noting the Somerville faculty parking sticker prominently displayed on the rear window.

Liz stopped and got out, leaving her car in the middle of the road. As she approached the Honda, a bevy of quail exploded into the air twenty yards away on the right side of the line of intergrown cedar trees and wild roses.

Underbrush crashed and snapped, and a man

cursed. A few seconds later, Cameron Whitaker appeared through a gap in the bushes with a pair of binoculars hanging around his neck.

Anger flared in Liz's chest. "What are you doing here?"

"Bird watching, if it's any of your business," he said. "This is public land, and I have every right to be here."

"You're wrong. This hedgerow is the dividing line between my farm and state lands, and you're on the wrong side. You're trespassing."

"Touchy, are we?" Cameron retorted. His face was scratched, and a trickle of blood ran down one cheek.

"I don't believe you! I think you've been spying on me."

"Prove it." He slipped as he tried to jump the ditch beside the road and sank one white athletic shoe ankle-deep in muck. "Doing something you're ashamed of again?"

"Get off my property, Cameron. And stay off, or I'll have you arrested for trespassing."

"Like hell you will. What's the matter? Afraid someone will see what you're doing in broad daylight with that drug runner?"

Liz's palm itched. It was all she could do to keep from smacking the smug expression off his face. "Have you been calling my house and making threats?"

"Bullshit!"

"I won't be harassed. If you are the one, I'll have you arrested. I'll prosecute, and I'll see that you're dismissed from Somerville."

"Just try it! You think I won't tell a few things on

you?" Red-faced, swollen with mosquito bites, Cameron shoved past her and yanked open his car door. "Maybe your students would like to hear what turns you on. A few pictures of you and lover boy on the picnic table would really make you popular. I could post them on the student website."

"You bastard! I'm swearing out a warrant against you."

"Watch who you're insulting, whore!" Cameron raised his middle finger as he slid behind the wheel of the Honda. He turned the key and stamped on the gas. The vehicle shot past her, barely missing the right front bumper of her car.

Liz was still furious as the waitress poured her a second cup of coffee. She and Amelia sat in a corner booth of their favorite Dover breakfast restaurant. "Cameron was spying on me," Liz said. "He admitted it, but you know he'll try to lie his way out of it. He threatened me, too."

Amelia shook her head. "He's got to be mentally unbalanced."

"I'm wondering if he's unbalanced enough to have killed Tracy."

"Being slime doesn't make him a murderer."

"No, it doesn't, but it doesn't make him innocent either," Liz said. "And if he's sneaking around my house, he might be the one who set off your burglar alarm."

"And sent the filth mail."

"You know how Cameron loves computers. He threatened to put porno pictures of me on the web."

Amelia's eyes widened. "What are you going to do?"

162

"Press charges and hope he's bluffing. It's one thing to get close enough to spy on me with binoculars, and another to get pictures clear enough for anyone to recognize my face."

"You didn't dance in a strip joint to put your way through college or something, did you?"

Liz chuckled. "No, but I did apparently put on quite a show for Cameron in my back yard. He had to be trespassing, spying on me with binoculars, or he couldn't have gotten the view he did." She rubbed the side of her neck. "Jack and I . . . we . . ."

"Did the nasty?"

"You've been at my house, Amelia. There's no one for miles. I thought . . ." She sighed. "Well, obviously, I didn't think, but I didn't expect a peeping Tom, or in this instance, a peeping Cameron."

"I think it's obvious that Whitaker is the one who's been stalking you." Amelia spread grape jelly on her bagel. "Once he's arrested, I'm certain your trouble will come to an end."

"I don't know," Liz mused. "Why would Cameron have started all this immediately after Tracy's murder? He came into my office just after I did. Either he was as shocked as I was, or he's the best actor I've ever seen. I can't believe he killed her."

"You need to follow up on this. Today."

Liz nodded. "I know." She pushed a strip of bacon around on her plate with her fork. She hadn't taken a bite of her scrambled eggs. The hunger she'd felt when she'd phoned Amelia and invited her to breakfast was gone. "Russell wanted me to co-sign a loan for him. I told you. He never calls unless he wants something."

"Did you refuse?"

"Amelia, I wouldn't give him a quarter for the parking meter. He gambles on everything, and he always loses. Once, he bet on a harness race, a sure thing. The horse came in dead last, and Russell lost his entire Christmas bonus."

"Ouch."

"Yes, and I didn't have a single credit card that he hadn't maxed out. I had to borrow money from an aunt for Katie's Christmas."

"I didn't know you had any family, other than your sister and Katie."

Liz shrugged. "I don't. Aunt Sally passed away more than ten years ago. She was my great-aunt, my grandfather's sister. She was a Baptist missionary in China for over thirty years."

Changing the subject, Liz asked, "Why did you want to talk to me alone, without Sydney?"

"You know I love her, but sometimes she can be so"—Amelia shrugged—"so politically correct. I wanted to talk to you about the e-mails I've been receiving."

"Without blowing them out of proportion?"

"Exactly. I don't need protesters carrying signs in front of the college, and I don't want reporters trampling my lawn to get interviews with the latest victim. Thomas would be mortified."

"I'm disgusted that anyone would harass you like they did."

"Seeing the n-word isn't going to kill me, so long as it's just an empty threat. I'm frightened, Liz, really frightened, not just for you, but for me. I'm going to Norfolk next weekend, and I'm going there to stay for the summer as soon as I can."

"I don't blame you."

"Come with me."

Liz shook her head. "I'd like to, but I can't. I've got to see this through." She chuckled. "Actually, it's a relief to know that I'm not the only one jumping at shadows. I was beginning to wonder if I was paranoid."

"No," Amelia said, "you're not. If anyone is, it's me." She glanced around and then leaned closer. "You probably will think I've lost it, but I dreamed of white lilies this week." Her brown eyes widened expectantly.

"I don't understand."

Amelia sighed. "Okay, maybe I'm superstitious at heart. But the women in my family have this . . . this thing. When we dream about lilies, usually somebody dies." She grimaced. "Tell anybody and I'll make a voodoo doll in your image and drive pins through its heart."

Liz laughed and clasped her friend's hand. "It's okay. I understand. I still throw spilled salt over my shoulder. We're allowed to be educated and human, too."

Amelia laughed with her. "It's crazy, I know it's crazy, but it happened to my mother all the time. And my grandmother. I dreamed about white lilies twice before, once when I was ten and again in college. Both times, someone close to me died within weeks."

"It's Tracy's death. We are both so spooked that—"

"Now you know why I didn't want Sydney here," Amelia managed between giggles.

"I didn't . . ." Liz giggled. "Heaven help us." She

squeezed Amelia's hand again. "Go to the beach and forget all about this. By the time September comes, it will just be a bad memory."

"I hope so." Amelia glanced at her watch. "Have to run. I've got a conference in forty-five minutes. I wish I could go with you to the police, but—"

"Go to school. I'm capable of handling Cameron by myself." The waitress returned with the coffeepot, and Liz shook her head. "Just the check, please." She smiled at Amelia. "It's my turn. You paid last time."

Amelia hugged her.

"No more bad dreams," Liz said.

"Or at least I'll try to dream about daisies," Amelia quipped over her shoulder as she hurried off.

Liz pushed back her untouched breakfast and opened her laptop to check her mail, something she hadn't bothered to do yesterday after she'd downloaded it.

There were four messages from school, one from Michael, three from Cap'n Jack, two from Katie, and one from a screen name that she didn't recognize but had *Katie Montgomery* in the subject line, and the usual spam. Liz opened the e-mails from her daughter first.

Moms. Go, me! 96 in Dead Irish Poets. I deserve a reward. Daddy says you're being bitchy again. Can't you forgive and forget? He needs financial aid. Me too. Send money for books and essentials. I signed up for a dream summer course. Now I have to stay. Love, Katie.

Liz clicked the next message, which was dated the same day.

Don't forget to send money. Bren, Mary & I got tickets to a folk concert on the Burn for next weekend. Taking the bus. Staying with Bren at her grandfather's cottage on cliffs overlooking Atlantic. Will take camera. Leaving tomorrow. Back Sunday. Will call then. Please be nice to Daddy. It won't kill you to co-sign his whatever. Hugs. Katie the Peacemaker

Liz frowned. Katie was not known for her letters home. On the phone, she could talk for hours, but snail mail was rare and e-mails minimal. And the repeated requests on Russell's behalf meant that Russell was playing dirty pool, trying to use Katie to get his loan.

"Damn you," Liz muttered.

"Excuse me?" The waitress stood, mouth gaping, beside the table.

"Sorry," Liz said. "Not you. Ex-husband." She threw too large a tip on the table, closed her laptop, and walked to the cashier's station to pay her check.

When she reached the car, Liz opened the laptop again and read the rest of her mail. Michael wanted to know if she was free for target practice at one o'clock or tomorrow morning. She wrote back, accepting for this afternoon. The messages from work weren't urgent. She skipped over Jack's e-mails and opened the last one.

Russell, now apparently calling himself "Reliable 3981," had nothing to say about Katie. Instead, he repeated his request for her to co-sign the loan and promised to repay her for two years' back child support *if and when* his *no-lose* deal panned out. Liz deleted the message and opened one of Jack's.

The first was a cartoon of a fisherman stranded on

a deserted island, making sweet talk to a seagull. The second was six lines of very bad poetry telling her how much he missed her, and the last was an invitation to join him for a late supper on his boat. She smiled, punched in his number on her cell phone, and countered with an invitation for spaghetti dinner at the farm.

"Eight sharp," she said.

"No can do. Can we make it nine?" Jack asked.

"Nine it is. Don't be late. I hate reheated bread."

"Scout's honor. I'll be there at nine."

Sure, Liz thought as Jack broke the connection, *but you were never a Boy Scout.*

"You've got to hold the gun perfectly still," Michael said.

Liz fired off two more shots that hit the target but missed the bull's-eye by more than a foot. "What did you say?" she asked, easing off her ear protectors.

"I said, you've got to hold your hand steady. You did better yesterday."

"Yesterday I wasn't this mad. Those idiots at the court told me I don't have enough evidence to convict Cameron of trespassing. Without a witness, I can't prove he was on my land. Otherwise, it's my word against his and a waste of everyone's time. I tried to tell the clerk about the funeral flowers, the rowboat, and the dead fox, but he said that if I didn't see Cameron do those things, I couldn't charge him with them. If I insisted, I could sign a warrant against him for trespassing, but he didn't know when it would be scheduled on the docket, and the judge would throw it out when it did get there."

"So you're going to let Whitaker get away with it?"

"No, I'm going to talk to Tarkington, the detective in charge of Tracy's investigation. I think he should be aware of what's been happening."

"I agree. Nathan's a good man. I remember him from when he first came on the force. Nathan's smart and pays attention to details. He never rushes a case."

"I called him but got his voice mail. I asked him to call me back. I said it was urgent."

"If he doesn't get back to you by Friday, try again."

Liz nibbled at her lower lip. "Amelia DeLaurier's burglar alarm went off the other night. It's possible that Cameron could be trying to frighten her as well."

"Do you want me to handle him?"

"No. He's a jerk, and now that I know he's the one doing all this stuff, I can handle him." She pursed her lips, pulled the headset back in place and fired the remaining shots in the weapon.

Her results were less than admirable.

"Be patient," Michael said, taking the weapon and checking to make certain that it was empty. "Do you feel confident enough to take the gun home with you? I can arrange a license for you to carry it."

"No." Liz wiped her hands on her jeans. "Not yet. I hate handguns. I hate the stink of gunpowder, and the sound. I suppose I'm just a nonviolent person."

Michael motioned for her to step back out of the way, then reloaded the revolver and sank every shot into the black center of the target. Otto lay beside Michael's chair, but the dog never blinked an eye. "Nothing wrong with the gun," Michael said. "Keep practicing."

Michael's outdoor firing range was as safe as any the professionals used. The straw-backed targets stood in front of an earthen bank six feet high and ten feet across. The handicapped-accessible concrete pad and walkway made it easy for Michael to practice his sport.

"I didn't thank you for getting rid of that rowboat for me," she said.

"No problem. I just towed the thing downriver and anchored it in my marsh. As leaky as it is, the rowboat will sink in a few days, and make a good habitat for crabs."

"You didn't leave the traps in there, did you?"

He chuckled. "No, I didn't. They went to the landfill. You didn't want them, did you?"

She knelt beside Otto and fished a dog biscuit from her pocket. "You know better than that." The German shepherd daintily accepted the treat.

"If it was up to you, he'd be as fat as I am," Michael teased.

"You? I don't think you have an ounce of fat on your body." Michael's legs were as hard and tanned as his muscular arms. Liz knew he spent hours working out every day, and in good weather he often rowed or biked for miles. Michael owned a three-wheeled racer, especially adapted for his handicap.

Maybe she should forget Jack, Liz thought as she and Michael headed back toward the house and a pitcher of iced tea. If she said the word, she knew that Michael would ask her to marry her. And why not? They were best friends, with so much in common.

Liz couldn't ignore that they were sexually attracted to each other. She'd never asked him the details about his paralysis, but they'd gotten into some heavy petting once, and she'd learned that he was entirely capable of an erection. Their sex life might be different from most couples', but she had no doubt that it would be rewarding.

As if reading her mind, Michael stopped and glanced up at her. "I'm thinking of driving up the coast to Maine and Canada this summer. Birding there is spectacular. Would you like to come along?"

"Maybe," she answered. "When?"

"July. I'm planning on at least three weeks. What do you say? With Katie staying in Ireland, you've got the summer on your own."

"Let me think about it, Michael," she said.

"Not too long. I want to make reservations."

"I'm not certain I can afford that long a vacation. I—"

"No," he said, taking her hand. "I'm inviting you. I'll pay for everything. All you have to do is ride shotgun for the cripple."

She leaned and hugged him. "Don't say that. You know I hate it when you talk like that." She blinked back tears. "I'll think about it, I promise."

"I'll hold you to that," he said as he held open the kitchen door for her.

"I love you," she said. "I really do."

"'Ah, but how does she love him?' the man asks," he replied with a chuckle. "Brotherly, or something more . . ."

Definitely not brotherly, Liz thought, but what it was, she had to figure out. "I take the Fifth," she protested.

"You can run, but you can't hide. I want an answer by June first. Got it?"

"Affirmative, Captain," she answered with a smile. "I hear you loud and clear."

Liz threw basil and chopped garlic into the sauce, stirred, and turned the gas flame as low as it would go. She always made spaghetti sauce from scratch. When tomatoes were in season, she used fresh ones, but this was May and those available in the grocery store were as expensive as gold and tasted like the packing boxes they were shipped in.

She cooked sauce in a heavy copper pot that had been passed down from her great-grandmother Clarke and only God knew how many more greats. The pot was far bigger than Liz needed, but it was a fixture in the old kitchen, resting when not in use in a place of honor on top of a built-in, countertop-high wooden cupboard. Above the kettle were open shelves, as nicked and scarred by the passing years as the other woodwork in the kitchen. Once painted yellow, the bull pine had achieved a dark patina that Liz thought perfectly matched the faded redbrick floor.

Neither the kitchen nor the copper pot found favor with Amelia, but the spacious old room with exposed beams and deep fireplace suited Liz fine. When she'd married Russell, they shared a new apartment on the third floor just outside of Wilmington. The kitchen had been all electric, tiny, and equipped with the latest appliances. The dishwasher was the only thing she missed here at the farm. Washing dishes had never been a favorite chore, and in every apartment or condo she'd occupied after the divorce, the first thing she asked was whether there was a dishwasher. Here, dishes were washed and usually air dried in the fifty-inch, double granite sink under the casement windows that overlooked the water.

Liz hummed as she dropped sliced mushrooms and a pinch of cinnamon into the spaghetti sauce. Stainless-steel state-of-the-art dishwasher or not, she wouldn't trade her kitchen for Amelia's modern one. And she wouldn't swap Clarke's Purchase for any house she'd ever seen. With all its sloping floors and creaking stairs, this was home. She wasn't about to let trash like Cameron Whitaker or Wayne Boyd run her off her farm.

For the first time, she thought about what it would be like to have another child. Katie hadn't been able to grow up here, and she was almost on her own anyway. Chances were, she'd never come home to live in the old house. And if Katie didn't, who would?

But Jack had told her that he was sterile.

Liz took a clean spoon, dipped it in the sauce, and blew it cool. A little more pepper, she thought. She'd have at least four quarts when it was done. Thank God for freezers. She'd freeze what was left and think about having some of her students over for spaghetti before finals. They could relax, stuff themselves, and go over a few points she wanted them to remember.

A baby? Was she totally out of her mind?

Jack couldn't father a child, but maybe Michael could . . .

What was she thinking? Had the shock of Tracy's murder affected her sanity? But Sydney's adopted twins weren't two yet, and Sydney was only three years younger than she was. It wasn't as though she were a senior citizen. Clarke women reached puberty late and kept their ability to have children until nearly fifty. She had at least four, maybe six or seven years of fertility left, but she'd never expected to hear that biological clock ticking again.

"I've been inhaling oregano," Liz muttered to Heidi. "I skipped lunch and I must be light-headed. It's temporary insanity. A plate of spaghetti, and the thought will never darken my head again." She stirred the sauce with a long-handled wooden spoon and began to sing a shameless ditty her father had taught her when she was little.

Shadows of twilight stretched across the back yard, but the sweet scent of wisteria and the brassy scolding of a Carolina wren drifted through the open window. Liz leaned on the granite sink and let the last remnants of tension drain out of her neck and shoulders. She stood there for several minutes, feeling at peace for the first time since Tracy's death.

. . . Until her reverie was broken by the phone.

She considered running upstairs to check Caller ID or just letting voice mail pick up, but she thought it might be Jack. He'd said not to expect him until nine, but she took the chance and answered.

"Liz!"

Russell. She almost hung up without speaking to him, but her temper got the best of her. "Do I have to change my number to get you to stop calling?" she asked.

"Liz, please. Listen to me. I really need—"

"I don't care what you *really* need. I am not going to help you. What do I have to say to make you understand? No, Russell. There is nothing you could say that would influence my decision. For Katie's sake, can't we be civilized about this?"

Russell's voice was thick. He'd been drinking and was about to burst into tears. His nose always ran when he cried, and thoughts of it were more than Liz wanted to consider. "Please, Liz. You don't understand. This is—"

"This is good-bye, Russell. And if you call me again, I'll start leaving sheep heads in your mailbox or calling your creditors and telling them to blacklist your name." She hung the phone up, spent two minutes obsessing about what a pest her ex was, and began to set the table.

"We will not allow Russell Montgomery to ruin our evening, will we?" she said to Muffin, the cat, who sat on a step halfway up the back stairs glaring at the German shepherd. "Russell and Cameron and Wayne Boyd will all have a special corner in hell, and we will not give them the dignity of any more consideration."

When the napkins were folded, candles arranged in their pewter holders, and the salad prepared, Liz put a bottle of wine in the refrigerator to cool and arranged the fresh flowers she'd bought at Sam's Club in a blue granite-ware pitcher.

She'd showered when she'd come home from Michael's, but she needed to put on some makeup and find something special to wear. She was looking forward to dinner, but even more to what was inevitable afterward. This time, she and Jack would make love in her bed, on clean sheets, with no worry about privacy or time constraints.

A night of good food, laughter, cool wine, and hot sex was exactly what the doctor ordered. Everything else could wait until tomorrow.

Chapter Ten

Tiffany turned the key again. This time, the motor didn't make that *ee-ee-ee* sound—meaning the battery was as dead as a used condom. "Damn! Damn!" She slammed the wheel of her 1987 land barge with her fist. "Damn piece of shit!" She winced as the nail on her right index finger snapped off at the quick.

"Hell!" Was it bleeding? The nail hung by a fragment and hurt like the dickens. She bit the remainder of the attached nail between her teeth, chewed it off, and spat it out. "Great, just great." These were her nails too, none of those fake jobs. The missing nail would take months to grow out, and she'd just done them this morning. Three coats of Plum Pearl Lustre!

Tiffany grabbed her purse, her cigarettes, and the two-liter bottle of Code Red she'd just picked up at Dora's Stop 'n' Shop, climbed out of the aging hardtop, and slammed the door. The catch didn't hold, and the door swung open a few inches—as usual.

"Shit!" She wasn't in the mood. Leaving the door ajar, she began to walk south.

Route 9 was a desolate blacktop that snaked through marsh, woods, and overgrown farm fields along the shore of the Delaware. Nothing but salt water and mudflats on her left—Tiffany wasn't certain where the river became bay—and empty wetlands on her right.

Two crotch rockets shrieked past, going eighty if they were moving at all. She hated the cheap foreign motorcycles. Give her an honest Harley any day. Her favorite cousin, J.J., had gotten creamed on one of the slick imports the first month he'd owned it. He'd hit a tree going ninety, and his brother told her that there wasn't enough left of J.J. and the red bike to fill a bushel basket.

Tiffany had to scramble into knee-high grass to keep from being run down as the motorcycles passed. Bastards! They didn't care who they killed so long as they had their thrill ride. One dead squirrel on the road, and they'd be shit on toast. Damn if they'd take her with them.

It would be dark soon, and Aunt Carol's doublewide was a good five miles away, maybe six. Her aunt had to be at work at the Harrington Slots by nine. Tiffany had been late to watch the kids twice this week, and if she was late again, Aunt Carol would fire her. Without this job, the electric in the trailer would go the way of the telephone: Shut off for nonpayment.

She cursed Kenny with every step. He'd sworn the old Caddie was a steal despite the pukey two-tone paint job. Claimed that the odometer reading of 86,432 miles was for real, not rolled over! Swore that the battery was cherry! "Piece of shit," she muttered again. "He can put the Caddy where the sun don't shine!"

The damn soda was getting heavy, and it was hard to carry without a bag, but Tiffany hated to abandon it along the road. She hadn't opened it yet, and the Code Red had been on special. Plus she'd been lucky enough to find a fifty-cent coupon in the parking lot, and when could you get two liters for eighty-nine cents at Dora's Stop 'n' Shop? Hell's bells, Dora hiked everything practically double. The last time Tiffany ran out of tampons, she had to pay $2.79 for a little sample pack that would have been a buck at the Big Wall.

Tiffany wished she'd thought to lock the Code Red in the trunk. She could drink some, but it was warm. Nothing worse than warm soda unless it was flat soda. And if she drank it, suppose she had to pee? What was she supposed to do, hide in the poison ivy? Hell, on this godforsaken road, she wouldn't even have tires on the Caddie when she got back—and she was worried about two liters of Mountain Dew?

The waistband on her jean shorts was tight, and the straps on her new wedge sandals rubbed her heels with every step. The shoes were white imitation leather and already grass-stained. She'd had to hide tips from Kenny for three weeks to buy the shoes. Had to lie and tell him her mom had bought them for herself and found out they were too small. A damn shame when a girl couldn't buy sandals with her own money without taking crap from her old man. Like she wasn't working two nothin' jobs, and him still looking for something right.

Her sister had warned her that Kenny was trailer trash who managed to get his lazy ass fired from two perfectly good jobs in the past six months. Maybe Amber was right. Maybe she should start sockin' a little bit away every week until she could buy her own wheels. Then she could crash with Amber or Aunt Carol until she saved money for the deposit on a place of her own.

If she had a cell phone, she could have called Aunt Carol or even Pops. Her granddad would come rescue her—if he wasn't sleeping off a six-pack. What she needed was one of those voice phones, the kind you didn't need to punch in numbers but could just say "Home" or "Carol's," not the cheap-ass one Kenny had bought her for Christmas and then smashed against the wall when he found out you had to pay every month to use it.

As she crossed a concrete bridge over a muddy creek, another car rounded the bend toward her, and Tiffany moved over against the wall. The car slowed and came to a stop. The driver leaned across and rolled down the front passenger window.

"Need a lift?"

Tiffany considered brushing him off, but he looked normal, not some perv. Haircut, shaved. Cute, too. "My car died on me," she said cautiously. "You got a cell? Maybe you could call my aunt to come get me. It's not a pay call."

"Sorry. No phone." He turned off the ignition. She saw that he had an open can of Bud in one hand. "How far is your car? Maybe I could do something with it."

"Yeah, push it off into the swamp."

He chuckled. "That bad, huh?"

"You don't want to know." A mosquito drilled into her left thigh, and she slapped it. It was still light enough to see the smear of blood on her bare leg.

"Ouch," he said. "Gonna be a bad year for them. I told my wife to spray the kids good when they go out to play."

"Got a wife, huh?" Tiffany wondered why every working guy in the state was already taken. Maybe the good guys were invisible unless you had special eyeglasses, like 3-D ones, and if you didn't own them, all you could see were jerks. If anybody needed a pair, she did.

"Mosquitoes are nothing to fool with," he said. "They keep talking about shit you can get from mosquito bites. Lyme and sleeping sickness."

"I think that's ticks," Tiffany leaned on the open window and glanced around the interior. The car was clean. No trash, no smell of pot. Nothing on the front seat but a cooler with five unopened beers. She was suddenly thirsty.

"I could call somebody for you when I get home," the guy offered. Then he appeared to notice her looking at the beer. "Thirsty?"

"I wouldn't say no to a cold one," she admitted, lifting one foot to ease the pressure on her heel. She knew she must have a blister. She reached down and touched it. Yeah, a blister. She could feel the gooey bubble.

"Help yourself. I'm Jim Carny. My wife and I just bought a house outside of Delaware City. Maybe you've seen it? It's a seventies bi-level with a little wooden bridge on the lawn."

He smiled, and she noticed that he had good teeth. Really white, as if he had just used those strips. He didn't look like a guy who'd paste paper strips on his teeth at night. Maybe he was just born with nice, straight teeth. Lucky bastard. She had a mouth full of cavities and no money to get them filled. Not that she was anxious to climb into a dentist's chair. She hated dentists with a passion.

"The bridge doesn't go anywhere yet," he said.

"Bridge?"

"On our front lawn," he reminded her. "Terry's got this cutout of a boy with a fishing pole in front of the bridge. But her heart's set on one of those fish ponds, the kind where you dig a hole and lay plastic over it to fill it with real water."

"Terry's your wife?"

"Yeah. She's a checker in the new Super G in Bear."

Another mosquito circled. Tiffany swatted it away from her face. "I really need to get to my aunt's," she said. "I'm supposed to watch her two foster kids tonight while she's at work. One's twelve, and Aunt Carol should be able to leave them alone. But the kids aren't wound too tight, and the state's funny. They'll take them away if she doesn't do everything just right. It's only about four miles back that way. Could you . . ."

"No problem. Hop in. I'd have offered, but I didn't want to come on like some . . . Hell, I could be a serial killer, for all you know."

"Right." Tiffany laughed. "And so could I. Remember that woman in Florida who was shooting and robbing guys along the interstate? They made a movie about her."

Jim's expression sobered. "Whoa." He held up an

open hand. "I'm just on my way home from work. I'm not looking for anything—"

"No, no, it's okay," Tiffany said, unlatching the door and moving the cooler to the floor so she could get in. "No guns, no knives. But I warn you, I do have a warm bottle of Mountain Dew, and I'm not afraid to use it."

He laughed and she laughed with him, breaking the tension. "Roll up that window, if you don't mind," he said. "No sense letting all the mosquitoes in."

"I'm Tiffany Henderson," she said, doing as he asked. Once the window was up, she popped the top on the Bud. She took a sip. The beer was cold and wet, and it went down easy. "I really appreciate this."

"So you baby-sit for your aunt regularly?"

"Yeah."

"Like kids, do you?"

"Not particularly. These two she's got now are real hellions. You know how foster kids are."

"Trouble, I guess. They probably get moved around a lot."

"No wonder. If they were mine, I'd probably run out on them too. The oldest one's real weird. Likes to play with matches. That's the main reason my aunt can't leave them alone."

"Good of her to take them in, though."

"Yeah, I guess. The state check comes regular. Pays her rent." Tiffany's foot struck something, and she glanced down.

"That in your way? Sorry." Jim reached down and lifted what looked like a black briefcase off the floor and tossed it on the backseat. He started the car and drove across the bridge. "It's a laptop. A computer," he explained.

"That little thing?"

"My wife's. She does all this e-mail stuff with her friends. I think it's a waste of time, but then, I don't even know how to turn the damn thing on. Usually she uses this car, but it needed gas, so she took my truck this morning."

"I don't know nothing about computers," Tiffany said. "I was thinkin' about gettin' my GED, study typing and stuff. Get a job in a bank, or maybe some doctor's office. Sit on my ass all day." She relaxed a little and fastened the seat belt. The little compact still had a new-car smell. She could see herself behind the wheel of one of these. Probably got good gas mileage. Anything would be better than the land barge. When it was running, she couldn't get more than ten miles to the gallon on it. "Where do you work?"

Jim turned into a farm lane and backed onto the road. "The county. Soil service." He put the vehicle in drive and recrossed the bridge.

"Oh. Are they hiring? My boyfriend's looking for a job."

"They might be. The county always needs summer help. The pay isn't bad, but no benefits for temporary workers."

"That's okay. Kenny hasn't had a job with health coverage yet." Tiffany kept well over on the seat next to the door. Jim kept his hands on the wheel and drove at a reasonable speed, not too fast and not too slow. "Honestly, I appreciate this," she said. "You saved my life."

GET UP TO
5 FREE BOOKS!

Sign up for one of our book clubs today, and we'll send you
FREE* BOOKS
just for trying it out...**with no obligation to buy, ever!**

HISTORICAL ROMANCE BOOK CLUB

Travel from the Scottish Highlands to the American West, the decadent ballrooms of Regency England to Viking ships. Your shipments will include authors such as CONNIE MASON, CASSIE EDWARDS, LYNSAY SANDS, LEIGH GREENWOOD, and many, many more.

LOVE SPELL BOOK CLUB

Bring a little magic into your life with the romances of Love Spell—fun contemporaries, paranormals, time-travels, futuristics, and more. Your shipments will include authors such as KATIE MACALISTER, SUSAN GRANT, NINA BANGS, SANDRA HILL, and more.

As a book club member you also receive the following special benefits:

- **30% OFF** all orders through our website & telecenter!
  (Plus, you still get 1 book FREE for every 5 books you buy!)
- **Exclusive access to** special discounts!
- **Convenient** home delivery **and 10 days to return any books you don't want to keep.**

There is **no minimum number of books to buy**, and you may cancel membership at any time. See back to sign up!

*Please include $2.00 for shipping and handling.

YES! ☐

Sign me up for the **Historical Romance Book Club** and send my THREE FREE BOOKS! If I choose to stay in the club, I will pay only $13.50* each month, a savings of $6.47!

YES! ☐

Sign me up for the **Love Spell Book Club** and send my TWO FREE BOOKS! If I choose to stay in the club, I will pay only $8.50* each month, a savings of $5.48!

NAME: _____

ADDRESS: _____

_____

TELEPHONE: _____

E-MAIL: _____

☐ **I WANT TO PAY BY CREDIT CARD.**

☐ *VISA*   ☐ *MasterCard*   ☐ *DISCOVER*

ACCOUNT #: _____

EXPIRATION DATE: _____

SIGNATURE: _____

Send this card along with $2.00 shipping & handling for each club you wish to join, to:

**Romance Book Clubs
20 Academy Street
Norwalk, CT 06850-4032**

Or fax (must include credit card information!) to: 610.995.9274. You can also sign up online at www.dorchesterpub.com.

*Plus $2.00 for shipping. Offer open to residents of the U.S. and Canada only. Canadian residents please call 1.800.481.9191 for pricing information.

If under 18, a parent or guardian must sign. Terms, prices and conditions subject to change. Subscription subject to acceptance. Dorchester Publishing reserves the right to reject any order or cancel any subscription.

JOIN NOW!

"No trouble. Just don't tell my wife. She's pregnant with our third child, and she gets a little jealous if she thinks I'm looking at a pretty girl."

Tiffany smiled and took another sip as a warm glow spread through her chest. She'd been with Kenny for two years, ever since she'd quit high school in her senior year. He hadn't called her pretty since the first few weeks they'd lived together. She sat up a little straighter and crossed her legs. So long as Jim wasn't coming on to her, she didn't mind showing off her best asset.

"Uh-oh." Jim took his foot off the gas and turned the wheel hard right. The car rolled off the hardtop and down a steep incline.

"What the hell?" Tiffany demanded, grabbing the dash to keep from slamming against it. Her head jerked back as fear made her voice shrill. "What are you—"

"It's all right!" Jim said. "Shit. The gas. I forgot the gas."

The car came to a stop on a packed-dirt area beside a boat landing. A sick feeling filled Tiffany's belly. "Oh, no!" she said. "I'm not that stupid." Scared, she seized the door handle and shoved it down.

Nothing happened. The door didn't budge.

"Let me out of here, you bastard!"

"Easy, easy. We're out of gas, that's all."

"Bastard! Bastard!" she repeated. She grabbed the Mountain Dew off the floor and heaved it at him.

"Are you nuts?" Jim opened his door. "Get out of my car, you crazy bitch."

Tiffany struggled with the passenger-side door handle. This wasn't happening. Not to her. This had to be a nightmare. She was so scared she thought she was going to pee on herself.

"The handle sticks," he said. "Slide out my side."

She began to roll down the window and scream. "Help! Help me!"

Jim ran around the car and opened the door. "Here," he said. "Get out!"

She leaped out of the vehicle and crashed into something solid. Her cry broke off as she tasted blood in her mouth. He'd hit her. The bastard had hit her. She began to sob. "All I wanted was a friggin' ride to my aunt's. You didn't—"

He struck her again, smashing her head back against the car. She gasped, felt something hard in her mouth, choked and spat. A tooth. He'd knocked out her tooth. Tears were running down her face. Her knees crumpled, and she slid down the car onto the ground.

"Please," she begged, more frightened than she'd ever been in her life. "Don't hit me again. I'll do whatever you want."

"Yes," he said. "You will."

Something in his voice turned Tiffany's fear to terror. She tried to crawl away, but he followed and kicked her hard in the ribs. "Please," she wailed. He kicked her again, and she sank facedown in the dirt. She felt cool air on the bottom of her left foot. Where had she lost her sandal?

"Who are you?" he crooned, looming over her.

She clamped her eyes shut. It was a bad dream. This couldn't be happening. She'd wake up and smell stale cat litter and Kenny's rotten coffee. "Tiffany," she managed between swelling lips. "I'm Tiffany."

"No, you're not," he said. "You're a tramp. Say it!"

She screamed as he drove his shoe into her side and bone grated on bone.

"Say it."

She groaned. "Twamp."

"Again."

"Jesus," she prayed. "Sweet Jesus, help me."

"You're not listening," Jim said.

"Jesus." She moaned.

Pain shot through her as her tormenter rolled her onto her back. She tried to look at him, but one eye was swollen shut, running hot blood down her cheek. She coughed and choked as blood clogged her mouth and made it hard to breathe.

Gloved fingers closed around her throat.

Tiffany closed her eye and stopped struggling. He was too strong, and it hurt too much. She'd rest a minute, and then she'd fight. She'd scream. She'd throw sand in his eyes and run back to the road and flag down a car.

"Shush," he said. "Go to sleep, little tramp."

Tiffany couldn't breathe. Her lungs convulsed. She had to have air. She opened her mouth to scream, but nothing came out. Her heels drummed the ground.

The gloved hands tightened.

And then she felt nothing.

A minute passed, and then a second. It occurred to him that his car lights were still on. Not good. Not good at all.

The Game Master released his grip on her neck and took hold of her head. A sharp crack told him there was no way that little Tiffany could scream again. He returned to the car, turned off the lights, and opened the trunk.

He removed a blue plastic tarp, spread it on the ground, and rolled her onto it. One shoe was missing. He retrieved the sandal from under the car and tucked it under her chin. She was light, but then she was only a little tramp. He doubted she weighed more than ninety-five pounds.

He placed her in the trunk, removed a clam rake and a flashlight, and proceeded to rake the area around the car. The Game Master was glad he'd brought the flashlight. In the strong beam of light, he caught the gleam of a bloody tooth. He picked it up, carried it to the muddy bank, and threw it out into the river.

The Game Master knew that he'd been bad again, that he'd broken one of his own rules. She hadn't been in the plan. He hadn't even known she existed until a few minutes ago. But the sheer audacity of the killing was exhilarating. He was beyond laws, really. And he deserved some small measure of enjoyment. He'd been so meticulous with the professor. A man needed release, didn't he? And dealing with the results was good exercise; it would keep him sharp.

A few beer cans, a broken gin bottle, and a McDonald's bag lay in a gully. Disgusting. People were pigs. All this beauty, and they didn't have the slightest compunction about fouling it with their waste.

The Game Master took a trash bag from the trunk and gathered the cans, paper, and broken glass and returned the bag to the car. He'd deposit it in the first roadside container he came to. He knew that his efforts would have little effect, compared to the tide of ignorant litterers, but if all the good citizens did their part, they could make a difference.

He inspected again the ground where he'd killed the tramp. Was that a spot of blood? It wouldn't do to leave evidence. He sighed, and reluctantly removed a can of used motor oil from the trunk. Motor oil could cover a multitude of sins.

Eight-thirty came and went. The next time Liz glanced at the clock, it was five to nine. She closed the window over the sink and pulled the curtains. She was reaching for the phone when it rang.

"Lizzy, sorry. I'm going to be a little later than I said. Hold supper. I'm starved. For food and you."

"I've been heating the water for the noodles since eight-thirty," she said. Her romantic evening was fast evaporating. "Where are you?"

"I'll make it up to you. Cross my heart. Have a glass of wine."

"What's the holdup?"

"Bike's not running right. I've been working on it. But I'll borrow Mom's car and be there in half an hour."

"What's wrong with your truck?"

"Is this Sixty Questions? It's in the shop. Brakes and tune-up."

"Jack, I—"

"I'll be there. If Mom's low on gas, I'll have to run into Dover and fill it."

"Promise?"

"I swear."

"I'm eating at nine-thirty, with or without you."

"I hear and obey, Professor."

* * *

Jack arrived at ten to ten, a bouquet of flowers in one hand and a bottle of wine in the other. "Mom couldn't find her keys," he said when Liz opened the door. "I'm sorry. You finally let me come over, and I mess up your evening."

Heidi stiffened, rolled her lips up to show her teeth, and made a threatening sound that stopped just short of a snarl.

"It's all right," Liz said. "Good girl, good dog." She patted the dog on the head.

"Nice pup," Jack said, handing Liz the flowers. "Any ninjas hidden in the woodwork?"

"I can shut her in another room if you want," Liz offered. "She'll be fine so long as you don't make any sudden moves."

"Locking her up might be a good idea. I'd hate to get bitten in the ass if I couldn't resist putting a move on you."

"Funny," Liz said. "Okay, I can shut her in the front parlor."

"No argument from me. She looks like she'd enjoy taking chomps out of me."

"She's sweet and well behaved, which is more than I can say for you," Liz said as she took hold of Heidi's collar and led her down the hall. "I hope you don't mind reheated noodles. I put them on at nine-thirty."

"Ouch," he said.

When Liz came back, Jack leaned to kiss her and she turned her head so that his lips brushed her cheek. "I said I was sorry."

Liz sighed. "Okay. It's just that I planned . . ."

He looked at the table settings. "So we eat a little

later. I should have called you when I first found the problem with the bike, but I thought I could fix it in five minutes."

She smelled a hint of beer on his breath. "Where have I heard that before?"

Jack groaned and clutched his heart. "Got me! I was late for our first date, wasn't I?"

"You were late for half of our dates," she reminded him as she put the flowers in water. "You never come when you say you will. I hate that about you, Jack. I always did."

"Mom says I run on Indian time."

"It's time you caught up with the rest of the world. It's rude." She set Jack's flowers on the counter where the copper pot usually reigned supreme. "Thank you for the flowers. They're beautiful."

"But I see you've already bought your own flowers."

She shrugged. "A woman cannot have enough flowers. Or shoes."

"No shoes in my jean pockets."

"I can buy my own shoes, thank you."

"So speaks the twentieth-century woman."

"Twenty-first," she corrected.

"Right. I've been away," he reminded her. "In the Big House."

"Russell called," she said, refusing to be charmed and abruptly changing the subject.

"Russell as in the worthy father of your child?"

Liz poured boiling water into the noodle pot, drained them a second time, and dumped them into a yellow crockery bowl that she'd wiped with olive oil and sprinkled with garlic and chopped chives. "I don't have any more spaghetti noodles, so we'll have to heat these in the microwave if they aren't hot enough."

"I'm used to cooking for myself in a galley. If the sauce is hot, your noodles will be fine. I'm easy to please, Lizzy." He carried two plates to the stove and held them while she forked noodles onto the faded stoneware. "Smells great."

"Russell keeps trying to get me to co-sign a loan for him. He claims it's a business opportunity, but I'm afraid he's in debt to someone over his gambling."

Jack glanced away.

"What? What is it?"

He hesitated. "Believe me, you don't want to get involved in Russell's financial problems."

"You've never been reluctant to say what was on your mind before."

"All right, but what I tell you goes no further."

She scooped sauce from the kettle and held it over a plate of noodles. "Tell me."

"Your ex has been sitting in on a big-time poker game in the city. He owes five figures or more to a contractor who has connections with some unsavory characters in the drug trade."

"How do you know that?" she demanded. "How do you know anything about Russell?"

"Small state, big business." Jack put the plates of food on the table. "I have a lot of friends, and I'm curious about anything concerning you."

She stood in the middle of the room as an uneasy feeling rippled down her spine. "You scare me."

"Me?" He lit the candles. "Salad in the fridge?"

"How do you know these things? You're supposed to be a commercial fisherman who's just gotten out of jail. Every other fisherman I know is broke, but you've got cash in your pocket and you reappear in my life the night a student of mine is murdered. Shouldn't I be a little cautious?"

Jack put the bowl of salad on the table and took her in his arms. "You're right again, babe. You should be cautious." He tilted her chin up and kissed her tenderly. "But you have to trust somebody in life, don't you?"

Sweet sensations curled in the pit of her belly. It felt so good to have Jack hold her, to be kissed like this. He looked down into her eyes.

"You're special to me, Lizzy. You always have been. And you have to know that I'd never do anything to hurt you." His mouth covered hers, and he ran a powerful hand down the curve of her spine, pulling her against him.

She thrilled to his touch, kissing him with equal fervor, tangling her fingers in his thick hair and molding her body to his. "Damn you, Jack," she murmured as heat flared between them.

They never made it to the bed this time, either. Much later, as they shared a hot shower, Jack massaged shampoo into her scalp and soaped every part of her body. They finished the second bottle of wine on the thick bathroom rug. Then, wrapped in clean towels, they made their way down the steps to reheat and devour dinner amid laughter and more love play.

It was after two when they finally sought Liz's bed. "Against the wall," he said, "so you can't escape. I've got a confession to make, and I need you to listen."

Her eyes widened as she knelt on the bed. "What is it? If you tell me you're a drug kingpin—"

"Let that rest," he said as he slid in beside her. "I don't deal drugs and I don't use them. But I did do something I'm not proud of tonight."

She waited, throat tight, the sting of tears gathering behind her eyes.

"I lied to you," he said. "About why I was late. No, wait. Just listen." He exhaled softly, and his eyes grew serious. "There's nothing wrong with my bike. I was doing something, and the time got away from me."

"What?"

"I can't tell you. It's personal. You'll just have to trust me."

"What's so important that you have to lie?"

"It's private, Lizzy. Take it or leave it. I was wrong, and I won't lie to you again. That I promise."

She dropped back onto a pillow and stared at the ceiling. "Am I allowed to ask any questions?"

"No, not about this. Someday maybe I'll tell you. But it's nothing I'm ashamed of—other than deceiving you."

Her thoughts raced with possibilities.

"Do you want me to leave?"

"No." She spoke too quickly. But she didn't want to be alone tonight. As long as Jack was here with his broad shoulders and ready grin, she could hold back the shadows, forget Cameron's spying, Tracy's horrible death, the muddy tracks on her kitchen floor. "Stay," she said. "Stay the night with me."

He pulled her into his arms, and she nestled against his warm chest. "No drugs," he whispered as he stroked her damp hair. "I swear. No drugs."

* * *

Liz awoke to the scent of fresh-brewed coffee and pancakes. She rubbed her eyes and pushed herself up in the tumbled bed sheets. Then she remembered last night and couldn't stop herself from smiling.

"Rise and shine," Jack called from the stairs. "The sun's up, and fish are biting. Hit the deck, mate!"

By daylight, Liz's worries were easy to dismiss. During breakfast she allowed Jack to talk her into a fishing trip on the bay. She didn't have to be back at school until Friday, and she was reluctant to let the nightmare of the past two weeks return.

"I hard-boiled some eggs and raided the fridge for grapes and cheese. I've got half a loaf of sourdough bread in my galley. With luck, we'll catch a few fish to fry. Pack your swimsuit."

"I have no intention of going in the water today."

"Chicken," he teased. "You didn't used to be so fussy. Remember the time we went skinny dipping off the Port Mahon Lighthouse in March?"

"Do I remember? I got pneumonia and was sick for a month."

"It's May—you're not going to get pneumonia."

"You swim if you want," she flung back. "If I take my suit, it will be to catch a few rays on the deck. Put a knife in your teeth and dive in to hunt sharks, for all I care. I'm not going in the water."

"Harsh." He offered a forkful of pancake and syrup. "Eat, wench, you're falling away to skin and bones."

"That will be the day."

"Yes, Tarzan like woman with meat on bones," he said with caveman gestures. "Round bottom, man can get hands on."

She couldn't help laughing at his antics. "Tarzan you're not," she proclaimed. "But braid your hair and stick lit candles in it and you could pass for Blackbeard."

"Umm," Jack agreed. "Pirate. Pirate like round woman, too."

"Keep it up," she threatened, still giggling. "If you think I'm going out on the bay with a madman, you'd better think again."

"Woman afraid? Afraid Cap'n Jack catch more fish than her?"

"That'll be the day," Liz retorted. "Ten bucks says I catch the biggest fish."

"Edible," he qualified. "Sharks excluded."

"You're on."

Jack took the boat south in search of tautogs, a prized blackfish that favored rock piles, wrecks, and reefs. The boat was sleek and spacious, and the cabin looked like something out of a marine catalog. Liz couldn't help being impressed.

"Pretty nice," she commented. He'd given her a tour of the boat, which included a small living area with built-in bookcases full of best-sellers and classics, a galley, a head complete with minute shower, and a compact stateroom.

"You still like to read," she said, scanning his titles and noticing that among the Grishams, Pattersons, and Clancys, Jack had a worn copy of Gore Vidal's *Creation*, *Envy* by Sandra Brown, the latest Hunter Morgan mystery, and Dan Brown's *The Da Vinci Code*. "Impressive."

"Yes'm, and I can make my letters too."

"Seriously, Jack, this is really nice."

"Everything a pirate could ask for."

"And you live on board?"

"Pretty much," he replied. "I still store a lot of stuff at Mom's, but I never did need much room. It suits me."

The tide was going out, and they were able to anchor close to a lighthouse where Liz pulled in her first tog within five minutes of dropping her line. The fish was well over the legal limit and fought for all it was worth.

Conceding the contest and saying they only needed one fish, Jack pulled anchor and motored north to a secluded spot well out of the channel. The two shared icy beers and great sex on the deck in the early heat of afternoon.

When Liz came out of the tiny shower clad in her new bathing suit, Jack had already cleaned and filleted the fish. "I'll just fry two of these up," he said, "to go with lunch. There's more beer in the fridge, or soda or bottled water if you prefer."

"I'll have water. One beer is my limit. At least out here."

"Too bad some of our paying clients don't feel the same way. Pop says we could take half of them to Rick's Crab Shack and let them drink themselves silly and they wouldn't care if they ever got their lines in the water. Most don't want the fish if they do catch them." He rolled a fillet in flour and sprinkled it with pepper and lemon salt. "Dig me a spatula out of that drawer, will you, babe?"

Liz pulled open the cabinet drawer and picked through the cooking utensils and tableware. "I wish my kitchen was—" She stopped in mid sentence as a block of ice formed in her throat. She stared at the object in her hand and took a step backward.

She was holding an oyster knife, the blade razor-sharp and shiny, a knife so new that it still bore a price sticker from Dover Hardware.

Chapter Eleven

"What's wrong with you?" Jack asked. "See a ghost?"

Liz dropped the knife back into the drawer and, suddenly cool, rubbed her upper arms briskly. "No, no ghosts." She felt a rush of blood suffuse her throat and cheeks.

"That's not the oyster knife that killed Tracy," he said. "The cops found that one under her."

"I know," Liz said, feeling ridiculous. "I've got at least three of the damned things in my house."

His eyes narrowed. "But not new ones?" He swore softly as he pulled the frying pan off the burner. "You've lost it, Lizzy. Now you think I'm the murderer?"

"No, I don't think that," she snapped back. "I picked it up and . . ." A faint frisson of doubt lingered in her mind. "You're right. It was a moment of temporary insanity."

"Wayne killed Tracy. When the cops catch up with him—if he's not already dead—he'll admit it."

She sank onto the bench on the other side of the small, built-in table. "But if Wayne killed Tracy, he'd have no reason to make my life miserable."

"You told me that you were certain you knew who your stalker was."

"I do, and I don't." She covered her face with her hands. "It's complicated, Jack. There's stuff . . . It's just too eerie. You remember old Buck Juney?"

Jack nodded. "Crazy as a love-struck opossum."

"I keep thinking about him. He used to follow me, you know. All one summer, he kept leaping out of hiding places and scaring me half to death."

"He's got to be long gone. No one's mentioned him for . . . Shoot, Lizzy, he was gone before you and I started hanging around together. Pop said he probably drowned in that leaky rowboat. He'd take it out on the bay in all kinds of weather."

"It must be finding Tracy that makes me like this," Liz said. "I'm not usually a basket case."

"Nope," Jack agreed. "At least, you weren't." He crossed to the drawer and fished out the spatula. "If the fillets are black on the bottom, it's your fault, not mine." Returning to the stove, he turned the fish and pushed the pan back over the heat.

"I guess I could help by setting the table," Liz offered. She found paper plates and forks and knives. "Napkins?" She opened a narrow cabinet door, noticed a laptop on the floor, and reached for it. "Wow. I'm impressed. Is this a Dell?"

"Yes." Jack motioned for her to leave the laptop alone. "It's mine, and I'm paranoid about anybody touching it." His tone was sharp and carried a thread of unease.

"Sorry." She closed the door. "I didn't mean to pry."

"Napkins are over the fridge." He shrugged, attempting to cover the guilty expression in his eyes. "I guess you're not the only one who's wound too tight, babe. Pop messed with my last laptop, spilled a beer on it, and frigged it up big time. It took me days to get tax records out of it. This one's more expensive and—"

"I had no intention of—"

He put his arms around her. She stiffened, but he didn't let go. "I'll admit it," he said. "I'm a screw-up and a jerk. Forgive me?"

"This isn't going to work," she said.

"What isn't going to work?" He kissed her eyebrow and the tip of her nose. "Tell me that this hasn't been fun."

"It has."

"And tell me that you aren't going to let one stupid remark ruin last night and today's fishing trip." He looked into her eyes. "I'm trying, babe." His lips thinned. "You can play with my laptop. Hell, you can dance on it if you want."

"No, thanks." She took a deep breath. "We're not the people we were. Things change."

"Not inside. You may have a title and an important position at the college, but you're still Lizzy Clarke of Clarke's Purchase." He released her and flashed the Rafferty grin. "And you still can eat your weight in fried fish."

"Which reminds me," she said, trying to ease the tension between them; "you owe me ten bucks."

"Tarzan not know what Jane talk about. Ten bucks

too many deer to trade for one small fish that jump into boat. Maybe five bucks, one doe."

"Jane hungry," she lied. "Feed woman, then talk about ten bucks Tarzan owe her."

As Jack cut the engines to enter the mouth of the harbor, Liz saw a fourteen-foot bass boat motoring out. "Look," she said. "That's Cameron Whitaker." The grad student was alone in the boat and obviously struggling to keep the aluminum craft with the powerful motor on a straight course.

Jack rested a hand on the throttle. "Wonder how much wake he can take."

"Behave yourself."

"No, seriously," he replied, straight-faced. "I could run him down. I've got a million dollars in liability, and no one could prove it wasn't an accident."

"That isn't funny," she said, but it was funny in a sick way. For an instant, she considered what a perfect ending it would be for Cameron Whitaker, a man who'd bragged that he'd never fished in his life and considered the sport one step above cockfights and dwarf tossing.

Cameron recognized her and waved. Liz didn't see a pole, net, or tackle box in the bottom of the boat. Cameron was wearing a camera case around his neck, and on the seat beside him was what could only be binoculars.

"Slimy little bastard," Jack said. "Come on, babe. Let me do the world a favor."

Liz squelched a desire to give Cameron the finger and turned away. Jack was definitely a bad influence. Next she'd be mooning passersby and chewing wads of Red Man tobacco.

"Wonder what kind of sightseeing he's up to," Jack said.

"I can guess. If he knows what's good for him, he'd better stay away from my farm. I'll turn Heidi loose on him."

"Oh—I can't run over the asshole, but you can make dog chow out of him."

"Better yet, I'll take pictures of him sneaking around my house and send him up on a stalking charge."

"That would be nice. Pretty boy wouldn't last a week in Smyrna."

She touched Jack's arm. "You . . . I mean, no one . . ." She trailed off, unable to ask if anything terrible had happened to him in prison.

"Me?" Jack smirked. "The trick, little lady, is to be the baddest, craziest sonofabitch in the unit. Besides, I was in for attempted murder. Most of the other inmates were scared of me. With good reason."

"I'm sorry," she said. "I was prying again, wasn't I?"

"It's not an experience I care to repeat. Or one I care to talk about." He pointed. "There's Mom. On the dock."

Nora was waving.

"Wonder what's up," Liz said. Her first thought was that something was wrong. She hoped it wasn't Jack's dad. Arlie had a bad heart.

Jack nosed the bow of the *Dolphin III* gently into the slip. He put the engines in neutral and motioned for Liz to take the wheel, then climbed out on the bow and tossed his mother a line. Nora snubbed it expertly to a mooring post. Liz turned the wheel gently, and the vessel glided against the row of tires that acted as bumper guards and came to a halt.

"Pop okay?" Jack called to his mother. Obviously, he'd been thinking along the same paths as Liz.

"He's fine," Nora replied. "They found Wayne Boyd."

Jack threw her a second rope, and she fastened that as well. "Shut it down," Jack called to Liz.

She came off the bridge, and Jack stepped onto the dock and helped her ashore. "What did you say about Wayne?" she asked Nora.

"A tourist with a metal finder was hunting for coins on Big Stone Beach. He found Wayne, or what was left of him, washed up on the sand."

"Drowned?" Jack asked.

Nora grimaced. "Who could tell after that long in the water? Rumor has it that the crabs had been at him."

"That's more than I wanted to know," Liz said.

"I imagine that will wrap up the murder investigation," Nora said. "Most folks suspected that Wayne killed Tracy all along. Killing hisself left their baby an orphan, but the little one's better off without a father like that."

Liz felt a rush of relief. She supposed she should be ashamed of herself, but if Wayne was guilty and he'd committed suicide, the students at her school wouldn't have to look over their shoulders every day.

"Want to come for supper?" Nora asked Liz. "I'm cooking up some clam chowder, corn bread, asparagus and dumplings, and strawberry pie."

"It sounds wonderful," Liz said. She didn't add that supper wasn't high on her list of priorities with thoughts of Wayne's demise fresh in her mind. "But I've got to prepare finals for my students. I should have worked on them today, but Jack twisted my arm."

"If I remember, the last time he twisted your arm, you cold-conked him with a lunchbox," Nora replied with a grin.

Nora had twisted her hair up into a bun today, but stray locks had come loose and were curled around her face and neck. She wore patched jeans cut off at the knees, a red checked shirt, and not a dab of makeup. Liz hoped she'd look as full of life at sixty-three as Jack's mom.

"I was ten years old," Jack protested. "Do you have to keep bringing that up?"

"Shows you were an uncivilized troublemaker as a child," Liz said.

"What about you?" Jack said. "Knocking a play-mate senseless is proper behavior for a young lady? All I was doing was showing you a wrestling move that—"

"That George used on you," Nora said. "He called this morning. He wants you to send him some ciga-rettes."

"Smoking's a nasty habit," Jack said. "He should quit."

"And you should go visit him," his mother said. "No matter what he's done, he's your brother."

"It's you he wants to see, Mom. And Pop."

"That place gives me the creeps," Nora replied. "When they slam those cell doors, I want to run for the wall."

"I'm not too crazy about those steel bars, myself,"

Jack agreed. "If I never see them again, I'll be just as happy."

Nora motioned to her blue compact, still parked in the lot where Jack had left it. "Do you still need my car?"

"Yeah," Jack said. "I'm going to drive Liz home. I think she's had enough sun for one day."

"Did you bring me any fish?" Nora asked.

"There's more than half of a tog left, but Liz caught it."

"Take it and welcome," Liz said. "I'll probably just have a salad for supper."

"I'll accept your fish in trade," Nora answered with a quick smile. "Jack, you just come by the house and get a pint of chowder and a slice of pie for Liz to eat tonight. Fair's fair."

"What about me?" Jack teased.

"Liz is giving me fresh tog. If you want supper, you can come around early enough to finish painting the front porch. I'm not running a boarding-house for grown sons, you know."

Jack groaned. "You see how she treats me? Makes me wonder if I'm really her child. When I was little, she used to say that I was a stray orphan who came to dinner and just stayed."

"Oh, you're a Rafferty, all right," his mother retorted. "Tongues as sweet as honey, all three of you." She glanced at Liz. "You wouldn't think it, to look at Arlie now, but he cut a wide swath when he was young and frisky. He could talk his way out of anything and make up lies so smooth the Pope would swallow them hook, line, and sinker. I always said, 'Arlie, if you put those tales on paper, you'd never have to fish again. You could write a book and we'd all be rich as Solomon.'"

Jack was unusually quiet as he drove Liz home after they had cleaned up the boat and gassed the *Dolphin III* in preparation for the next trip. Nora's '99 Toyota was compact, but neat, and Liz supposed that it must get better mileage than her own four-door sedan.

"I've been thinking about getting another car," she said to Jack. "An SUV or a pickup, something that will pull a boat."

"Planning on giving up teaching and fishing full time?"

She laughed. "Not likely. But Katie and I need a boat. There's always been one at Clarke's Purchase. The dock looks lonely without a boat tied there." She tried not to think of the derelict vessel she'd found there a few days ago.

"I'll ask Mom," Jack said, keeping his eyes on the road. "She knows every boat in the county, who's selling, and who's had their boat in the shop for engine work. Unless you're looking to buy new."

"No, definitely a used one. I'd rather not go to a dealer."

"I hear you," he agreed. "You know, George's sixteen-footer is sitting in the shed. He doesn't have more than a hundred hours on the Mercury engine. It's got a good deep hull, what you need for this bay."

"Do you think he'd consider selling?"

"Maybe. He don't need it where he's at, and by the time he gets out, there may be no fish left to catch."

When silence rose between them, Liz tried to recover the comradeship they'd shared in the morning. "Thanks for taking me out. I love your boat."

"Just don't care much for the captain."

She turned to look at him. "That's not true. It's just that things have gotten more serious than I expected."

"Sorry about it?"

"No, not sorry. I care for you, Jack. You know I do, but—"

"It's all in the *but*, isn't it? Is this the part where you tell me how you want us to be friends?"

She smacked his arm in frustration, not hard enough to hurt, but to get his attention. "Sometimes you overwhelm me," she admitted. "I don't know whether I've got solid ground under me or water. You scare me."

"That's the second time you've said that."

"I mean it."

He hesitated, and then said, "There are things in my life that I'm not willing to share, Liz."

"Not with me, or not with anyone?"

"I've got my reasons." He slowed to make the turn into her long drive.

"Can't we just take it slow between us?" she said.

"If you want."

"I'll sleep better tonight, knowing that Wayne's body was found."

"I can come back later, if you want," he offered.

"No, not tonight."

"Saturday evening? We could drive down to the beach. Eat somewhere nice."

"Call me Saturday morning."

"Got a date with your neighbor?"

"What do you know about Michael?"

"It's a small state, Lizzy. Hard to keep secrets."

"My seeing Michael isn't a secret," she said, a little too defensively. "We're friends. Among other things, he's teaching me to shoot."

"You?"

She nodded. "What's wrong with that?"

He shrugged. "Wonders never cease." He pulled up beside her car and got out to open the door for her. "I'm coming inside to check the place out, if you'll get hold of the beast."

"It will be all right," she assured him. "Heidi wouldn't let anyone in the house."

"You going to let me in, or am I going to sit out here all night?"

"Suit yourself, but it's not necessary." She didn't want him to come into the house. She wanted to be alone, to think, but Jack was Jack. Once he made up his mind, there was no stopping him.

She turned Heidi outside while Jack made a quick inspection upstairs and down. "All clear," he said when he returned to the kitchen. "But you should be leaving that dog outside at night. If she's a guard dog, that's where she'll do you the most good."

"I know, but I hate to put her out. I'll be fine. Now go home and paint your mother's porch."

"Tarzan hear woman," he said. "Tarzan go, but he be back when moon is full. Two days." He held up four fingers.

"Call me," she repeated. "I'm making no promises."

"I am. I'll be here Saturday night."

She called the dog back into the house and locked

the kitchen door as Jack pulled out of the yard. She wasn't certain if she'd go with him on Saturday night or not. Liz refused to think about that now. She had material to prepare for tomorrow's classes.

Why? Why had he done it? And how had he, a master of the art of murder, exhibited such weakness? He'd never been a man ruled by base emotions; he was far too intelligent.

But he had never lied to himself, and it was impossible to deny that he had acted on impulse last night.

The Game Master swore softly as he removed the tarp-wrapped corpse from the car trunk. With only moonlight to guide him, he strode purposefully through the woods into the reeds and deposited the stiffened remains in the bottom of the boat. Last night, when the tramp sat on the car seat beside him, luring him with her pale flesh, disposing of her had seemed an adventure. A quick kill.

He could still feel the hot pulse of blood in her throat, hear her cries . . . remember the excitement of her futile struggles. But the killing was nothing more than a cheap thrill, without risk, lacking the slightest degree of finesse. Any common thug could have done the same.

Like shooting fish in a barrel.

Maybe if he'd strangled her with his bare hands instead of muffling his sense of touch with gloves . . . perhaps then he wouldn't have such abject disgust for what should have been a memorable experience.

Now, disposing of her was a chore, with none of the rewards usually associated with his sport. Instead of spending a leisurely night watching The

Professor shower or undress for bed, he was here, fending off mosquitoes and poling through salt marsh. He had to forgo the amusement of listening as sounds echoed through the old house, and the dog whined and bristled at each creak and footstep.

This pursuit of *the professor* had gone on longer than he'd planned. He'd known she would be a rare subject, but even he had not guessed how challenging the game would become. He wanted her . . . longed to taste her blood . . . to feel the grate of her bone against his teeth. What trophies she and the daughter would provide.

This was a milestone, a level of sport that few would ever know. When he was old and past his prime, he could revel in the memories of this hunt, sucking every drop of joy from these days of high adventure.

But he was human, not a god or an immortal.

A thinking man, even a genius, learned from his mistakes. He had acted rashly in taking the tramp, out of season, as it were. And he must pay the price, forgoing his fun for the night to "mop things up."

The Game Master reached the cedar pilings and snugged the bow of his boat against the corner of the thick plank platform. It was low tide; in high tide, water covered the surface, washing away the residue. The boards were slippery, but he was used to keeping his balance when he butchered.

His actions became routine. First he stripped himself naked, removing every stitch, even his boots and socks. He deposited his clothing in a plastic garbage bag to keep them dry and clean, before lifting the carcass onto the five-by-six raised area. Next he unwrapped two filleting knives and a whet stone. If he struck bone, his knives lost their edge, and it was important to keep them sharp.

Dividing the remains into small enough sections to fit into crab traps was surprisingly simple. He was strong, experienced, and eager to dispose of the evidence. His strokes were quick and sure, dividing flesh and bone into neat sections. Even the buzzing mosquitoes didn't bother him particularly. They rarely bit him. Perhaps his blood was too rich for the insects' liking. Once he'd returned the baited traps to the boat, he used a bucket and sponge to wash down the platform, cleaned his knives, and put them back in the oilcloth case.

The Game Master dressed quickly. All that was left to do was to place the traps in the best spots. Actually, he could have caught a bushel of prime crabs here, but it seemed unsporting. No, his tried-and-true methods were best. He glanced up at the moon. If he hurried, there was still time to get his traps out, return home, and get a few hours' sleep before dawn.

He removed a small nubbin of flesh and bone from between his lips, rolled it in plastic, and dropped it into his jeans pocket. The crabs wouldn't miss one pinky toe with a tiny, polished nail, not with the feast he had for them tonight. And wouldn't it add to his collection nicely?

Friday morning dawned bright without a cloud in the sky. Two of her classes met this morning, the first a freshman-level American History, and the second, her Heroines of the American Revolution, reserved for history majors.

To her relief, nothing unpleasant waited on her

porch, in her back yard, or at her dock. She fed and walked Heidi, turned the dog loose in the house, and left for Somerville with a lighter heart than she'd had in weeks. She parked in her usual space in the lot, passed Cameron in the hall without speaking to him, and arrived fifteen minutes early for her first class.

Ava Johnson, a grad student who usually worked with one of the senior history professors, came in to assist. Since Liz had planned a slide show and presentation, the period was over in what seemed record time. H.A.R. was a favorite of Liz's. Most of the students were interested in the material and well prepared. She wished them all well on their finals and was about to join Sydney for lunch when a tall, olive-skinned girl who worked in the office approached her in the hall.

"Professor Clarke? I have a message for you. Mrs. Ryder didn't call because she was afraid of interrupting your lecture."

"Thank you, LaShondra." Liz opened the note. There was a number, a man's name, and the word *insurance*. *Insurance* was underlined twice.

"Mrs. Ryder said that it sounded important and that Mr. Klinger would be at his desk all afternoon," LaShondra said. "Just give his receptionist your name. She's expecting your call."

Liz returned to the empty auditorium and took her cell out of her briefcase. In less than a minute, Philip Klinger was apologizing for disturbing her at the college.

"Ordinarily, I would have called you at home, Ms. Clarke. I've sent out a letter, but I wanted your verbal okay on this policy."

"What policy?" Liz asked. "And it's Dr. Clarke."

"Yes, of course. Dr. Clarke. Something came across my desk that . . ." He went on to explain that the policy was written by one of his junior employees, an eager young man who'd recently received his license to sell life insurance. Apparently, that agent, whose name Mr. Klinger omitted, had recently sold a substantial life policy to a Mr. Russell Montgomery.

"I don't understand what this has to do with me," Liz said. "Russell and I have been divorced for years."

"Yes, but—"

"There's a current Mrs. Montgomery, Danielle. She's probably who you want to speak to."

"No, Dr. Clarke, it's definitely you."

"What is the value of this policy?"

"One million dollars, with a double indemnity for accidental death."

"Three million if the insured is killed by a stray asteroid or a rampaging elephant?"

"Yes."

"I still don't see what this has to do with me," Liz said. "The policy is on Russell, isn't it?"

"No, actually, it isn't, Dr. Clarke."

"Then who? Our daughter, Katie?"

"On you."

"Me? A million dollars? Without my consent? Is that legal?"

"I'm looking at a signature on the policy. Am I to assume that you didn't sign this?"

"Who is the beneficiary?"

"Russell Montgomery."

"Son of a bitch!" Anger flared within her.

"Excuse me?"

"Cancel it," Liz said. "Immediately."

"It would be better if you could examine the signature, make certain that you didn't—"

"I think I'd know if I'd given my irresponsible ex-husband consent to take out a million-dollar insurance policy on my life."

"You definitely believe that this is a mistake?" Klinger asked.

"A mistake? Not likely." Was Russell hoping to profit from her death? Liz sank onto a bench by the door. How far would he go to get his hands on that kind of money? "My ex-husband is a gambler," she said as calmly as she could. "I have reason to think he may be in debt to some unsavory characters."

"Oh, I see." Philip Klinger cleared his throat. "Naturally, we'll cancel this immediately."

"See that you do," she said. "And I'd like a copy of the cancellation letter." She gave him her home address and was concluding the conversation when Sydney opened the door to the corridor.

"Liz? Oh, sorry, I didn't know you were on the phone," Sydney said.

"No, I'm finished." Liz thanked Philip Klinger for contacting her and closed her cell. "I would have come looking for you," she said to Sydney. "I can't meet you for lunch."

"Why not?"

"I have a date with my ex," Liz replied. "And it's not going to be pretty."

Chapter Twelve

Russell's receptionist reluctantly ended her personal phone conversation and wiggled the fingers on her left hand in the air in an attempt to dry her nail polish. "Let me check to see if he's in the office, Dr. Clarke," she said in a patronizing tone.

Liz had dealt with Lorraine before and wasn't impressed with her office skills. Russell claimed she was an excellent employee, and from past experience with her ex-husband's secretaries and receptionists, Liz supposed that the young woman must have other attributes that only a man could appreciate.

Lorraine's flowing mane of hair was dyed a garish plum, but her perky 38D breasts, tiny waist, and long legs were stunning, nearly as impressive as the silver tongue stud that garbled her South Philadelphia accent. "On second thought, I think you just missed him. Mr. Montgomery had an important lunch meeting," which—due to the wad of chewing gum or the stud—came out as *"Un sekka tat, eye tinka youse yust mist'm. Litha Montgummy hatta porta heet'n."*

"Oh, Russell's in. I saw his car parked in the side lot." Years of being the first Mrs. Montgomery had taught Liz a few of Russell's tricks. No doubt, the silver Mercedes convertible was leased in the current Mrs. Montgomery's name. But if Liz knew Russell, he was at least two months' payments behind, thus the necessity of keeping the car's location less than obvious.

The receptionist rose and attempted to block Liz's path. The young woman was quick, but her four-inch open-toed sandals slowed her just enough for Liz to brush by.

"Mr. Montgomery might be on the phone."

Liz flung open her ex-husband's door. "Hi, Russell."

The small, windowless room smelled of Chinese take-out and mountain pine air freshener. Liz glanced around, taking in the peeling paint on the walls and the cheap, rented furniture showing signs of wear. Two cardboard containers marked *Jade Palace* stood on the desk amid a folded newspaper, crumpled napkins, a racing schedule, and piles of manila folders.

"I tried to stop her," Lorraine said. "She—"

"It's all right." Russell rose so quickly that he knocked over a nearly empty cup of latte. "Liz, it's good to see you again." He stabbed plastic chopsticks into an open carton of rice and mopped the coffee spill with a napkin.

"Better me than the police," she answered. "What the hell do you think you're doing?" When his face paled and he began to stammer, she raised her hand. "No, you be quiet and listen to me."

Lorraine fled the office.

Russell pushed the door shut behind her. His complexion had gone from ashen to puce. "Sit down, Liz." It was more of an order than a request. "There's no need to make a scene."

"Oh, there's need. You're lucky you're not being arrested for fraud. Of all the sneaky, underhanded tricks! I expect deceit out of you, but how dare you take out a million-dollar policy on my life without my consent?"

"Ah . . . you're overreacting. It's not what it appears," Russell said, obviously stalling while he concocted an excuse. His gaze darted around the room, almost as if he were expecting a SWAT team to burst through the skylight.

Something was very wrong. She'd expected lies, but not hostility. Or was it desperation?

"You're a bastard," she said. "A deceitful, conniving lowlife. But I never thought . . . Were you planning on killing me for the insurance?" She folded her arms over her chest as impossible thoughts clouded her reason. "You wouldn't have the guts to try it yourself," she said. "Did you hire someone to do your dirty work?"

"I wanted to protect Katie."

"From what?"

"A girl was murdered in your office. It could have been you. And then where would Katie be?"

"You expect me to believe that? Stop lying to me. I want the truth, Russell."

"Don't go to the police."

"Why shouldn't I?"

Moisture glistened in Russell's eyes. "I came to you for help. I begged you, but you wouldn't listen. I'm in trouble, Liz; big trouble."

"Maybe you should be the one going to the police.

You're in debt because of your gambling, aren't you? Admit it."

"You have no idea what the last few weeks have been like for me. I've been threatened."

"Does Danielle know?"

"Don't drag her into this." His voice thickened. "I didn't know what to do."

"So you decided to kill me to get the money?"

"I wasn't thinking straight. I panicked. But I never could have gone through with it. You're the mother of my oldest child. I'm not a violent person. Whatever you think—"

"Did you have anything to do with Tracy Fleming's death?"

He shook his head. Tears coursed down his cheeks. "What do you think I am?"

"I think you're a pitiful excuse for a man. Stay away from me. And from Katie."

"Liz. For God's sake . . ."

"Leave Him out of this."

"What am I supposed to do?"

"Find a rock and crawl under it. Or go to the authorities and ask for protection. You have to do something. Danielle isn't to blame. And she has young children."

"If you'd just sign for the loan, I can—"

"Go to hell, Russell." She opened the door and glared back at him. "If you come near me or Katie, if you try to involve us in your schemes, you'll wish that all you had to worry about were loan sharks."

Liz's phone was ringing when she unlocked the farmhouse door and entered the kitchen. She snatched up the receiver.

"Moms? Moms, this is me." Katie's voice was high, bordering on hysterical.

"Katie? What's wrong?"

"Dad's in terrible trouble. You've got to help him. He says his life's in danger."

"I know. I just left him. Did he call you?"

"Yes, about half an hour ago. I'm scared, Moms. Can I come home?"

"No. You stay where you are."

"You've got to help him. He said he begged you, but you wouldn't—"

"You know how he is, Katie. You know that he's addicted to gambling. I can't fix that."

"I can get a flight home tonight."

"Don't even think about it. I'm serious. Stay there and finish out the term."

"But Daddy—"

"I can't help him, Katie. This time he has to solve his own problems."

"You're still blaming him. It's a sickness. He can't help it. All he needs is a little help to—"

"I can't. We can't. Your father got himself into this mess, and he—"

"You think more about money than Dad's life? How can you be so spiteful? Just because he's happy with Danielle and the—"

"Is that what he told you?"

"He never wanted the divorce. It was you who wanted out. You who wanted a career instead of—"

"We aren't having this conversation," Liz said. "He's your father, and you love him. That's all he is to me, Katie—your father. He's cost me too much over the years. I won't put up another penny to—"

"I'll never forgive you if something happens to him."

"Katie, don't—"

"You're right, we're not having this conversation. I can't talk to you when you get like this. Good-bye, Mother."

Liz heard the loud click of the receiver being slammed down and then silence. She stared at the phone, wondering if she should call back, and then decided against it. Katie's temper was too much like her own. It would take a day or two before her daughter would be willing to listen to reason.

Heidi nosed against Liz's ankle. "What's wrong, girl?" Liz asked. She dropped to her knees and embraced the dog. "What else could go wrong?"

The German shepherd wiggled free and regarded Liz with a hopeful expression. Liz nodded, stood, and went to the cookie jar on top of the refrigerator where she kept a supply of dog biscuits. "Is this what you want?" she asked. "Treat?"

Heidi's dark eyes lit with anticipation.

"Sit," Liz told her. When the dog obeyed, Liz offered the snack. Heidi took it gently from her fingers. "Good girl," Liz said. "Good dog." She patted the animal's head. "You miss Michael and Otto, don't you?" Maybe she should return the dog. With Wayne dead and Russell's double-dealings exposed, there wasn't really any reason to keep Heidi any longer.

She wondered if Russell had been trying to frighten her. He knew about Buck Juney; at least, he knew that the hermit had disturbed her dreams for years. And Russell certainly was familiar with the house. Could he still have a key to the front door? She'd changed all the other locks but that one. But, if it was Russell, what reason would he have for wanting to frighten her?

Of course, Russell wasn't the only person who knew about Buck Juney. Jack knew, and she'd told Michael. She nibbled at her lower lip. Until today, she'd been certain that Cameron was stalking her—that he'd been the one who'd left the boat at her dock and tracked mud through her kitchen. But what if he wasn't? What if it was Jack? Had great sex made her blind to his faults? She'd known him once, or thought she had. But how much did she really know about Jack now? And what was she going to do about Russell? Should she bring charges against him?

She picked up the phone and tried Katie's apartment. No answer. Either she had gone out or she didn't want to talk to her again. Katie's response hurt, but they would come to an understanding in a few days. Katie was still young enough to believe that her mother was usually wrong. And Russell, the absent father with the silver tongue, remained the misunderstood victim.

For now, Liz's biggest worry was Russell. Maybe she should report his attempt to take out the policy on her life to the police. She didn't really want to see Russell go to jail, but neither did she want to see some bookie break his legs. Should she call the detective investigating Tracy's murder?

"My dealings with the long arm of the law have not exactly been successful," Liz said to Heidi.

She needed advice from someone she could trust. But who? Amelia would insist that she prosecute

Russell to the fullest, or think Liz was the worst kind of fool if she didn't. As much as she respected Amelia and Sydney, neither of them would be in a position to offer an unbiased opinion. She couldn't ask Jack either. He hated Russell; she could guess what he'd say. She needed to talk to Michael, and the sooner, the better.

She had reached for the phone again when she remembered that Michael had told her he wouldn't be at school on Friday because of some routine medical tests he was having at Christiana Hospital. He'd said they'd be keeping him overnight, and releasing him at noon on Saturday.

She'd offered to go over and look in on Otto, but Michael had said the dog would be fine. Michael usually left the dogs outside when he went on short trips. Liz knew he had an automatic water bowl and feeder for the animals in his garage. Otto could come and go as he pleased though a dog door.

"My luck," she said to Heidi after an unsuccessful call to Amelia, who said she was going to drive down to spend the weekend in Norfolk with Thomas. "On to Sydney."

Her friend was home, but expecting company. "I'll call you tomorrow," Sydney said. "If I forget, you call me. You're welcome to join us for dinner if you like. We're going to drive out in Maryland to Suicide Bridge, that restaurant on the water. Terrific seafood."

"No, thanks," Liz answered. "I'll give you a ring tomorrow. Have a good time." She hung up and looked back at the dog. "Well, what do you say?" she asked. "Jack or Detective Tarkington?"

Heidi wagged her tail and looked hopefully at the cookie jar.

"No more treats until after supper," Liz said. "Michael won't forgive me if I send you home ten pounds heavier." Reluctantly she punched in Jack's number.

"The *Dolphin III* is out catching fish," Jack's recorded answer proclaimed. "Leave your number and a message, and the captain will get back to you tomorrow. Unless the fish are biting." At the beep, Liz hesitated and then hung up without saying anything. What could she say in twenty words or less?

She sighed, realizing how much she'd hoped that Jack would pick up, listen, and have sensible advice. She dug in her purse for Nathan Tarkington's number.

"Leave a message at the beep."

"I hate voice mail," Liz said to the dog. "It's . . . it's barbaric." She considered explaining her fears about Russell's safety to a desk sergeant, but then decided against it. It was time Russell started behaving responsibly and cleaning up his own mistakes. She couldn't spend the rest of her life taking care of him. She'd tell Detective Tarkington everything on Monday and let him take it from there. Besides, maybe Russell had already taken her advice and asked for protection.

Taking only a quick break for a grilled cheese sandwich, a salad, and a bowl of ice cream, Liz spent the rest of the evening preparing her exams. Heidi paced the hallway and front staircase, occasionally barking, but whenever Liz went to see what was upsetting the dog, she couldn't find anything wrong.

Liz flicked through the channels to see if there was anything worth watching on television. Too restless to settle for reruns or comedies with canned laugher,

Liz did a load of laundry, let Heidi outside, and gave the command that would turn her from companion to watchdog. A light rain was falling, but Michael had assured her that the German shepherd was oblivious to the weather. She'd been thinking about what Jack had said, that Heidi would be a better watchdog if she wasn't in the house, and decided that he was probably right. By the time Liz was ready for bed and a few chapters into the best-seller she was reading, it was eleven-thirty.

"Maybe I should take Michael up on his offer," Liz murmured to Muffin. "Board you in a kennel and enjoy a vacation." Muffin didn't answer, merely staring back with slitted eyes and an irritated twitch of her tail.

Liz fluffed her pillow. If she went with Michael, it wouldn't be just a few weeks away, it would be more . . . It would mean breaking with Jack once and for all.

And what then?

"You can't have your cake and eat it too," her father always said. But what kind of sense did that make? Liz wondered. If you had cake, you usually ate it. Funny, she'd never questioned that old chestnut before.

Michael or Jack? Or keep both as friends and go on alone as she had been for so many years? Somehow, independence didn't seem as appealing as it always had before.

She switched off the light.

The Game Master found dealing with the guard dog difficult. He hated waste, and this animal was both beautiful and highly trained. But the German shepherd presented an obstacle, and obstacles had to be disposed of as efficiently as possible.

The poison was quick, deadly, and nearly painless. He injected it into a slice of raw liver and left it in a spot the animal, with her excellent sense of smell, was certain to discover. The results were predictable.

The Game Master glanced at his watch. 3:34. He waited. Fifteen minutes passed before he was certain that the dog was dead. He carried the still-warm body to the back porch and posed the carcass in a lifelike position near the kitchen door, where the professor would be certain to discover it in the morning.

He entered the house using a key that he'd duplicated from a spare set in the professor's top bureau drawer. Surprisingly, he'd been able to remove the original from the key chain and return it, once it had served its purpose, without her ever knowing it was missing. Even the ones who believed themselves so smart proved to be foolish compared to his intelligence. Having the key made it easier to enter her home, but even if she'd changed the locks after he'd stolen the key, he would have gotten in anyway. And, he suspected, it would have been more fun.

Once inside, the Game Master made his way to the larger of the two attics to collect his videos and check his audio equipment. It was wonderful how science made observing his victims easier and easier. He couldn't wait to get home and view the footage of the professor in the shower and the bedroom. He'd installed two cameras in her bedroom, so that he could view her antics from every angle. A woman let loose her wildest fantasies between the sheets.

Heat flashed under the Game Master's skin, and his breathing quickened. Videos made the best mementos. He could enjoy them over and over, long after his game pieces were history. He glanced at his watch again, pressing the tiny button to light the display. He'd been in the house forty-two minutes. Where did the time go? Dawn came early to the shores of Delaware Bay in late spring. He would have to move quickly.

He descended the stairs and made his way through the hall passageway to the professor's bedroom. Disappointingly, her door stood ajar. Foolish, foolish woman, he thought. Where is your sense of self-preservation? Haven't you heard that smoke kills before fire? If an accidental fire started anywhere in the house—and old houses were known as firetraps—your smoke alarms might not sound until it was too late. Worse than silly, she was stupid. And he had little patience with stupidity.

Pushing open the door, he entered the room. His night-vision goggles made it child's play to navigate around the furniture to the foot of her bed. She lay sprawled on her stomach amid the tumbled sheets, clad only in a worn green T-shirt and red boxer-type shorts. One slender bare foot protruded tantalizingly from beneath a furry object that he couldn't identify at first glance. The professor's nails were painted, but he couldn't be sure of the shade. Were they pink or red? Surely not blue or black. He hated dark polish on women's nails. It was too butch.

His gloved hand hovered over the professor's bare foot. He had the strongest urge to stroke it, to hold it in his hand, but he resisted. He was not a man of impulse. No sexual act could satisfy as greatly as seeing a woman at her most vulnerable, no longer tough or abrupt, speaking to a man as though she were his equal. He performed coitus skillfully enough to please the females he'd had in the past. It was physically rewarding to him, and apparently, he was as good at giving pleasure as receiving it. No one had ever complained.

He'd known the pain and satisfaction of union with his own sex, too. That and self-induced pleasure had been necessary during the years of enforced confinement, but neither of those alternatives were his first choice.

The Game Master liked women. He liked their scent and the texture of their skin. He loved their voices, especially the sighs and squeals they made during intimacy or at the point of death. Yes, he was all man, superior to the majority of his gender, but human. He knew that he was attractive to women; he had been gifted with good genes, regular features, and a powerful physique that he maintained by his vigorous lifestyle. And, contrary to the nature of other males, he continued to evolve.

The furry object moved, and he realized that it was a cat. The animal focused on him, recoiled, and hissed. He hissed back, and the creature flew off the bed and vanished through the open doorway.

A pity. He could have added the cat's body to that of the German shepherd . . . placed it between the dog's paws. What a delightful package the two would make. But the cat was gone, and he would have to forgo that bit of fun. There was always later, and cats were much easier to contend with than larger animals. Cats were so . . . so breakable.

He'd experimented with cats as a young boy, often devising clever ways to rid the earth of them. They had outgrown their time and usefulness in the world. No one needed them to catch rats and mice anymore. Poison was much more effective, and it didn't have to be fed daily, brushed, and taken to the vet for expensive shots.

He really preferred dogs. Dogs knew their place. And no matter what you did to a dog, they never held a grudge.

He checked his watch again. Twenty minutes? Had he really stood here for twenty minutes staring at the professor's naked foot? Exasperated with himself, he turned away, pulled open a dresser drawer, and inspected the contents. Socks and what appeared to be panty hose and silky short stockings. He tried the drawer directly below that one.

The wood protested.

The Game Master caught his breath. Was the professor deaf, that she didn't hear the squeak? She stirred, rolling over onto her back, so that her shorts rode up and revealed even more white thigh. If she opened her eyes, he would be forced to end the game here, to overpower her and carry her to the boat.

He waited.

She murmured something and burrowed under a pillow. Her breathing grew more regular.

He glanced at the east window. Soon the sun would break over the horizon and the bay would sparkle with a million diamonds. He had stayed too long. He was in danger of losing all for the sake of small pleasures.

He loved walking the edge. Tonight was proving to be all that he had hoped. Keen arousal made his body taut. Recklessly he slid the drawer open and plunged his hand inside.

The feel of slippery fabric brought moisture to his eyes. His throat tightened, and his heart leaped in his chest. His fingers trembled as he brought the panties to his nose and inhaled deeply, relishing the smell of detergent, fabric softener, and woman.

When he was certain that he'd not missed a single undergarment, he returned the panties to their drawer.

In three minutes, the Game Master was out of the house and crossing the back yard to the dock. He untied his boat, pushed off the mooring post, and let the current carry him away. He'd wait to start the engine until he was out of sight of the bedroom window. There was no sense in taking unnecessary chances.

He wished that he'd thought to place a camera on the back porch. The professor thought she was so safe now that Wayne Boyd was dead. But the best would be when she opened her back door and found his surprise waiting for her.

It would be an expression to die for.

Chapter Thirteen

"Wake up, Professor. It's time to wake up."

Liz opened her eyes. Sunlight streamed across the painted wood floorboards of her bedroom. Cool morning air wafted in the open window. Beyond, in the big yellow poplar, she could hear a mockingbird singing.

She yawned and listened. Nothing unusual. She could have sworn she'd heard someone call her name, but she must have been dreaming. Beside her on the bed, Muffin slept, head tucked into her fur, tail wrapped around her.

Liz rose and looked out a window. There were no vehicles in the yard other than her own. The surrounding yard and marsh teemed with birds, rabbits, and other small creatures. If someone was out there, the animals would be more wary. A great blue heron flew up gracefully from the river's edge and sailed over the house. At the tree line where meadow and woods met, a quail called cheerily, "Bob white! Bob white!"

Odd, Liz thought. She'd been so certain that she'd heard a voice. Still yawning, she left the bedroom and walked down the hall to the back kitchen stairs. The uncarpeted steps were cool against the soles of her bare feet, and the kitchen lay in shadow. She paused at the bottom step and listened again, but— other than the steady hum of the refrigerator motor—the house was quiet.

Automatically, still only half awake, Liz went through the motions of making a pot of coffee and opened two windows to let in the fresh breeze off the river. She ducked into a downstairs bathroom off the kitchen, brushed her teeth, splashed water on her face, and ran a brush through her hair before securing it in a short ponytail.

For a long minute, she stared into the age-spotted mirror over the 1950's sink. "Pretty damn good for forty and not a stitch of makeup," she proclaimed. Well, not exactly forty, she mused; nearer forty-three. But, hey, she wasn't being graded on candor here. She wondered if the sparkle in her eyes was the result of her sexual adventures with Jack. She grinned, feeling slightly giddy and not the least embarrassed. After all, wasn't she a free woman? Entitled to life, liberty, and the pursuit of the perfect orgasm?

The blessed odor of coffee filled the kitchen. Liz filled a tall cup adorned with a painting of Bob Marley and a palm tree, sniffed the half-and-half to be certain it wasn't sour, and added just enough. She inhaled the flavor of the coffee, wanting to take a sip but afraid to burn her tongue as she'd done all too often lately. She slipped into one of the comfortable old chairs at the round table. Today, she'd regain her life. Starting this morning, she'd take control and take stock of what was happening to her.

She'd begin by driving down to Port Mahon to see if the migrating shorebirds had arrived. Delaware Bay was one of the premier birding spots in the world, and she and her dad had always made the effort to witness the annual flocks as they stopped to feed on the horseshoe-crab eggs. Donald Clarke hadn't owned a pair of binoculars. He couldn't tell a black-necked stilt from an avocet, but he'd taken pleasure in the mid-May event and he'd defended with both fists the rights of horseshoe crabs to come ashore unmolested. "It's all the same," he'd say to his daughters, whenever they watched the prehistoric crabs crawling up the sand to lay their eggs. "Horseshoe crabs got a purpose just like every bird, fish, and mussel. Grind the crabs for fertilizer and you might as well do the same to the crabbers and the fishermen. Kills the bay as much as oil spills and chemicals."

At ten, when Atlantic Books opened, she'd stop and pick up the book she'd ordered before Tracy's death. And this afternoon she'd take Heidi back to Michael's and tell him to return the pistol to the gun shop. Giving in to fear and practicing to kill someone went against everything she believed. Now that she had an explanation for everything, she could go back to living her life.

After Heidi was home, she'd stop and buy a new kitchen telephone, one equipped with Caller ID, and then she'd go to Troop 3 and demand to speak to someone about the pattern of harassment she'd faced since the murder. She'd not leave until the police took her suspicions seriously.

As for Jack . . .

Liz sipped her coffee, sighing with delight as the warm liquid slid down her throat. She'd worry about Jack once she'd cleared her desk of her current agenda.

Thinking about Heidi reminded Liz that the German shepherd needed to be fed. She washed out the dog bowl and filled it with the special chow Michael had sent over. He didn't buy dog food in the supermarket; Heidi and Otto ate only high-protein meal supplemented with chicken, fish, and beef.

Liz unlocked the back door and opened it. "Heidi!" she called. "Here, girl . . ." Her voice trailed off as she saw the dog on the porch. "Heidi?"

The bowl of dog chow slipped through Liz's fingers.

She screamed.

By the time the state trooper—a tall, muscular young woman—arrived, Liz had dressed, thrown up her first cup of coffee, and drunk a second to fortify herself. She'd called Michael before she called 911 but had gotten no answer.

The officer, who identified herself as Trooper O'Neal, took down Liz's statement in a matter-of-fact manner. "And you say the animal was running loose last night."

"Yes," Liz agreed, "but she's . . . she was a guard dog. She wouldn't leave the vicinity of the house. Someone has been stalking me. I've made several other complaints."

"It's illegal for dogs to run loose." Trooper O'Neal examined Heidi's collar.

"That's true," Liz said, trying to answer calmly.

"But only if the property is less than twenty acres. This is a farm. I own much more than twenty acres."

"I see that her license and rabies are up to date. This is your dog, Dr. Clarke?"

"No, it's my neighbor's, Michael Hubbard," Liz explained. "He's a retired captain, Delaware State Police." She knelt beside the dog's body and stroked her head. "I don't know how I'm going to tell him. He adored her."

"Then Captain Hubbard's dog was off his property?"

"No, that's not it at all. He lent me Heidi."

"Captain Hubbard should be making the complaint if the animal is his. You say that you found it on your porch?"

"Look, Officer, why don't you call your desk sergeant? I'm sure there will be a record of a break-in here less than two weeks ago. Someone is stalking me. And . . . and please contact Detective Tarkington. I'm the one who discovered the murdered college girl at Somerville College. I've been trying to reach Detective Tarkington myself. I'm afraid there might be a connection between the attack on Tracy Fleming and what's happened here."

Trooper O'Neal wrote a few more words on her report, returned to her car, and made a call, presumably to the troop.

Liz waited, arms folded. The kitchen phone began to ring, but she ignored it. Whoever it was could wait.

"Yes," Trooper O'Neal said. "Clarke. Dr. Elizabeth Clarke." She gave the address. After a minute, the officer nodded. "Yes. This time it's a dead dog, possibly poisoned. No, that's not definite." The conversation continued, but Liz couldn't make out the rest of it.

"Well? Did they find my last complaint?" Liz asked when Trooper O'Neal approached the porch a second time.

"Yes. I received confirmation that you are a witness in a recent murder at Somerville College, and that Detective Tarkington is in charge of that investigation."

"That's correct," Liz said. "I didn't witness the crime, but I was the first one to discover the dead girl. In my office."

"In your office," Trooper O'Neal repeated. "And do I understand that you feel that several unexplained incidents have occurred here at your home since the day of the crime?"

"Yes," Liz replied, exasperated. "Someone, perhaps even my ex-husband, has been trying to frighten me—or worse."

Trooper O'Neal frowned. "Your ex-husband?" She examined her report. "And his name is?"

"Russell. Russell Montgomery. I've just found out that he tried to take out a large life-insurance policy on me."

Trooper O'Neal snapped her ballpoint back on the clipboard. "I would suggest that you take the animal to your vet, or have Captain Hubbard do that. Then, if it's certain the dog was poisoned, we can continue the complaint. You really should discuss all this . . ." She shrugged. "Your suspicions that someone is stalking you, this insurance matter. You should tell that to Detective Tarkington."

The phone rang again.

Trooper O'Neal replaced her hat. "If you find out that the dog was poisoned, you can contact the troop again. Or Captain Hubbard can. It might be better if he did, since you say the animal is really his. But I don't know that we will have much luck in finding out who poisoned the dog. It's a rotten business. I have an Airedale myself. But my yard is fenced. As I said, it's an infraction of the law to let dogs run loose in the county."

The phone continued to ring.

"Thank you for your trouble," Liz said. "Be sure I will take this up with Detective Tarkington, provided I can ever reach him."

"I'm sorry," Trooper O'Neal said. "There really isn't anything more I can do at this time." Her voice grew warmer. "Have you thought of having someone come to stay with you? Finding a dead body must be a terrible shock. It was for me, my first time. You might think about seeking professional—"

"Thank you," Liz said. "I've already considered that option. Sorry to take up your time."

"No problem, that's what we're here for."

Liz ran inside to answer the telephone. To her surprise, the voice on the other end of the line was that of Dean Pollett. She glanced at the kitchen clock, wondering why he would be calling this early on a weekend.

"Is there some problem?" Liz asked.

"Yes, I'm afraid there is. Could you come in to my office? There's a serious matter we need to discuss."

"If this is about my days off this past week—"

"No. I'd rather speak to you in person. As I said, this is serious."

Liz leaned against the wall and exhaled softly. What now? What else could go wrong? "Has anyone been hurt?" she asked.

"No, not exactly, but—"

"I'll be glad to take this up with you on Monday morning, but to tell the truth, I'm having a hell of a day so far. If you can't give me some idea of what the problem is, it will have to wait."

Dean Pollett cleared his throat. "Very well, if you insist. I'm attempting to save you further embarrassment, but since your weekend plans are obviously—"

"Dean, someone just poisoned my best friend's dog while it was in my care. Michael Hubbard's German shepherd. I have to take the animal to a vet for an autopsy, and I have to tell Michael. You'd be doing me a big favor if you'd just get to the point. What have I done wrong?"

"A graduate student has come to me about your behavior, Dr. Clarke."

"A grad student? Not Cameron Whitaker?"

"Yes, as a matter of fact, it is Mr. Whitaker. He claims that you have been calling his home, following him in your car, and making inappropriate suggestions to him. In short, Cameron Whitaker is threatening to charge you with sexual harassment and to name Somerville College a party to the harassment."

"Concentrate, Elizabeth," Michael chided as they examined the target. Of her dozen shots, not one had come near the bull's-eye. Instead, they were all over the perimeter of the cardboard cutout of a guntoting, masked intruder. "You have the basics, but your aim is erratic. You're all over the target. You'll never put an assailant down with shooting like this."

She sighed and glanced away, unable to meet Michael's accusing gaze. "Maybe I don't want to," she said quietly. "I don't like guns. I find the idea of taking a human life repugnant."

"You're an intelligent woman with good reflexes and excellent vision. I can't understand why you aren't getting any better."

It was nearly five o'clock, and acute grief at the loss of his canine companion still etched lines into Michael's handsome face. When she'd told him about Heidi's death, he'd turned away from her, barely able to contain his emotion. And when he looked back, she could see tears in his eyes.

White-hot anger had quickly replaced sorrow. Michael had taken the Smith & Wesson from the drawer and insisted that she practice her shooting. "I want you to take the gun home with you," he'd said. "And I want you to keep it with you. Do you understand? Take it to bed with you. Take it in the shower. Don't be without it for a minute."

"I don't have a license to carry a concealed weapon," she'd protested.

"Who gives a damn? We're talking about your life, Elizabeth. This isn't a game. I'm trying to keep you alive."

"I can't take it to school. Weapons are forbidden on school property."

"Right," he'd flung back. "That stupid bastard Ernie Baker carries a revolver. I do. So does Barry."

She'd stood firm. "I won't carry a firearm at Somerville."

"All right, but if I pull some favors and get you a license, will you promise me to keep it with you and lock it in the car when you get to school?"

She'd nodded. "I suppose I can do that."

Earlier, before Michael arrived home from the hospital, Liz had taken Heidi to the vet's office. Dr. Miller had said that she wanted to get an okay from Michael as he was the dog's legal owner. So long as Michael agreed to the autopsy, Dr. Miller could have a definite cause of death by Wednesday at the latest, perhaps as early as Monday afternoon.

"I should have kept her inside," Liz said for the third time as she and Michael returned to the firing position on the range. "If I'd let Heidi sleep in the house with me, she'd be alive."

"It's not your fault," Michael had said. "I told you to leave her outdoors to patrol the house. Whoever killed her did it to frighten you. He wanted you to know that you aren't safe, that he can do what he pleases."

"There's more," she said as she reloaded six bullets into the revolver. "Dean Pollett called this morning." She told him then about Cameron's threat to bring charges against her for sexual harassment. "The dean doesn't want to take sides. He just wants the problem to go away. If I can't prove that Cameron's lying, I could lose my job."

"Whitaker's bluffing, covering his a—" Michael caught himself and substituted, "his *butt* by threatening to sue you. You should have let me deal with him when he first started making a nuisance of himself."

That's what Jack said, Liz thought as she raised the handgun, steadied her arm with her left hand, and sighted down the barrel. "But what if it isn't

Cameron? I just can't believe he could be vicious enough to poison Heidi. What if it's Russell or someone else who's doing this to me?" *What if it's Jack?*

"They'd have to have a motive. Squeeze the trigger gently. All in one motion. Raise, aim, fire."

The recoil from the revolver was minimal. A hole appeared in the right of the target, a good three inches away from the bad guy's left elbow.

Michael swore under his breath.

Liz lowered the weapon, keeping the barrel pointed at the concrete pad. The Smith & Wesson had no safety, so she removed her finger from the trigger.

"Why do I think your heart isn't in this?" Michael asked.

"It isn't."

"What can I say to make you understand?" He took the gun from her hand, raised it, and fired off five shots in succession. When he lowered the gun, a dark hole showed in the target's forehead. Every bullet had struck within a two-inch circle.

"You're a master marksman," she said.

Michael shook his head. "It isn't just marksmanship. Self-defense eludes most civilians because they hesitate when they should shoot. They don't have survival instincts. While the average Joe is deciding whether or not to pull the trigger, the assailant takes them out."

"What if they shoot some innocent—"

"An innocent bystander isn't charging into your bedroom with a weapon in his hand. Anyone who crosses your threshold is looking to hurt you, Elizabeth. And all this that's happened, it isn't going to stop. It escalates."

"Stop," she said. "You're frightening me."

"Good. You should be scared. Whoever is after you won't be satisfied with your job or your money. This has gone too far. He wants your life. He won't stop until you're dead."

Michael had wanted her to spend the night at his house, but Liz knew she couldn't. If she was too afraid to go home now, she'd never be able to. She'd run, just as she had at seventeen. And she'd spend the rest of her life jumping at shadows.

After leaving his house she drove to her favorite bookstore in Dover. Al, dark-haired, slim, and smiling, was at the front register. She'd known him since they were in elementary school, although she was several years older. He was smart, an avid reader, and she always enjoyed chatting with him.

"What did you think of Marshall's first one?" he asked as he retrieved her book from a shelf along the wall and rang it up.

"Excellent. I hope this is as good. I don't know when I'll get to it, though. Things have been . . ."

He nodded sympathetically. "I read about it in the paper. Terrible."

She handed him her credit card.

"For what it's worth, I thought *No Remorse* was great, maybe better than the first," Al said. "You know, there are rumors the author lives in the area, that John Marshall's just a pseudonym."

"Is that right? I suppose anything's possible." She accepted the bag, thanked him, and returned to her car.

After a quick stop at Radio Shack for a new phone, Liz drove back to the farm. She took the revolver from under the seat, gathered up the books and the bag containing the telephone with Caller ID, and hurried inside. Once safely in the kitchen, she locked the door behind her.

Removing the older model phone and installing the new one took ten minutes, some cursing, and a broken fingernail. But once she heard the comforting dial tone, the first thing Liz did was call Russell's home.

Danielle answered on the second ring. "Russell?"

"No, it's Liz." She heard a small sound of disappointment. "He's not there, is he?" Liz said.

"No. I don't know where he is. He said he was going to Atlanta on business, but he didn't take any extra suits. I called the Doubletree on Peach Street where he was supposed to have a reservation, and they said he wasn't a guest. The clerk couldn't find any record of a reservation either." Danielle sounded as though she'd been crying. Liz could hear one of the twins shrieking in the background.

"Do you know if he went to the airport?"

"I dropped him off there at seven-thirty this morning. Russell had been out all night, and he came home in a cab. I don't know what happened to his car, and he wouldn't answer any of my questions. I suspected that he might have been with that secretary of his, Lorraine."

"Yes, I've met Lorraine."

"She's a piece of work."

"I agree with you," Liz said.

"Russell's Mercedes is leased, but I don't think he's been making the payments." Her voice broke and she began to weep. "The bastard," she said. "It's all coming apart, Liz. My father had to lend me the money for our mortgage payments twice since Christmas."

"Russell's gambling again." Liz knew he was, but she wanted to hear Danielle confirm it.

"There's more. I told you I suspected that he and Lorraine were having an office romance, but now I'm not sure. Lorraine came to the house just before lunch. She was raving. She took her paycheck to the bank, and the teller refused to honor it. They said the business account had been closed."

"Did you check your personal accounts?"

"Empty as the twins' college fund. I think he's run out on us, Liz. I wouldn't count on any back child support if I were you."

"Russell tried to get me to co-sign a loan for him." Liz slid down the wall and sat cross-legged on the kitchen floor. "When I wouldn't, he admitted that he was in debt big time. He was afraid for his life."

"He'd better be. If I find him, there won't be enough left—"

"Russell tried to take out a policy on my life, Danielle. A big one, but the insurance office notified me. Maybe you'd better check around to see if . . ."

Danielle swore. "Thanks. I'll do that."

"Will you be all right?"

"No. Yes. Probably better than I've been for the past year. I'll have to sell the house, of course. Move home until I can find a job." She began to cry again, and Liz couldn't help feeling sorry for her. "I feel like . . . like such a fool," Danielle said. "You tried to warn me, but I thought you . . ."

"Why should you believe me? Do whatever you have to do, but if you do hear from him, will you let me know?"

"Yes, of course, if you want."

"I'm so sorry, Danielle. I really am."

"Is this what he did to Laura?"

"Pretty much. Only the second Mrs. Montgomery only lasted two years. Two little girls, but Russell claimed that one wasn't really his." Liz cut the conversation short and hung up the phone.

"The bastard," she said. If he hadn't caught a plane until this morning, he could have been at her house last night. But why would he? What would he gain by poisoning Heidi, or hurting her when she'd already canceled the insurance policy?

She went through the house, checking all the window and door locks, and found nothing out of place. Had it been Russell all along? And if it had, did that mean it was over? She decided to call Michael and tell him what she'd learned from Danielle.

"So you think he's in Atlanta?" Michael said. "I could find out if he took a flight out today."

"You could do that?"

He chuckled. "Give me a few hours. I'll reach out."

"You've got a lot of friends in high places."

"A cop who doesn't won't solve many cases. Let me see what I can find out for you, Elizabeth."

A few minutes later, Jack called to see if she'd decided to have dinner with him. She begged off, claiming cramps and a headache. She didn't tell him about Heidi, and once he'd hung up, she wondered why. Was she beginning to suspect Jack? Or was she so crazy she'd begin to think Amelia was stalking her next?

At eight-twenty, Michael called back. "Bull's-eye," he said. "Your Mr. Russell Montgomery arrived in Atlanta at two o'clock and took a flight on to Miami ninety minutes later."

"Miami?" she said incredulously. "You're kidding."

"No, and it gets better. He landed safely in Miami and caught another flight to the Dominican Republic. I lost his trail there, but I found out that he'd purchased the tickets Friday and paid for them with two different credit cards, an American Express and a Visa. Both cards were in the name of Danielle Montgomery."

"The rat ran."

"I doubt he'll be a problem for you or Katie, at least not in the next few years. He's been writing bad checks. There are at least two warrants out for him in Maryland." He paused. "And I checked with another buddy. The Mercedes wasn't repossessed."

"So what do you think happened to it?"

"Either he abandoned it or sold it. And since he was planning on making a getaway, I'd imagine he sold it."

"How could Russell sell a car without a title?"

"Elizabeth, you're such an innocent." Michael chuckled. "He could easily forge a title, or he could sell it to a buyer who wasn't particular. And, there are chop shops that regularly buy vehicles and disassemble them for parts. They pay pennies on the dollar, but the seller generally claims the vehicle stolen and collects insurance."

"I suppose I should be relieved," Liz said. "But I feel bad for Katie. She loves her father. This is one time it's hell to be right."

The phone by the bed woke Liz at quarter to three in the morning. She switched on the bedside light and checked the Caller ID before answering. The message read *unknown caller*, but she picked up. "Hello?"

"Liz?"

Her foggy brain recognized her sister's voice. "Crystal? What's wrong? It's the middle of the night here."

"I know what time it is. You are not going to believe this."

Liz sat up, adrenaline pulsing through her body. She heard something more than sarcasm in Crystal's tone. "Are you all right?"

"I'm fine. Didn't know you gave a damn. Hey, maybe we're both mellowing a little." Crystal sounded sober. "It's her," she said.

"Her? Her who?"

"Jeez, Liz, I know you're not stupid. Patsy, our sainted mother. I've been away. Well, I moved, not to Nevada, but to Arizona. It's a long story, but that guy I told you about?"

"Guy?"

"You know, the one without hair, the one who had the hots for me?"

"Yes, I remember. What about him?"

"We went to Las Vegas for this long weekend and he hit the slots pretty big, fifty thou big, if you can imagine. Anyway, we both did some celebrating, and before I knew it, he asked me to marry him."

"You're getting married?" Liz asked. Had her sister called her at three o'clock to tell her she was engaged? "But what's that got to do with Mom?"

"Not *getting* married, *got* married. Ring, minister, and certificate. I am now Mrs. Henry Webster, can you believe it? Turns out that Henry's fixed better than I thought. His family has this chain of funeral homes in Phoenix. Don't laugh. Okay, laugh, but they're established businesses. His uncle and his father were in it together, and the father's real old, but the uncle died. So, we moved into the uncle's house—you should see it—four bedrooms, a pool, and a three-car garage. Henry's a good guy, Liz. You'd like him. He treats me like a queen. He might not be the handsomest, but he makes me laugh. And there's nothing wrong under the hood, if you get my meaning."

"That's wonderful news, Crystal. I'm so happy for you. But what does this have to do with our mother?"

"Oh, yeah. It was because of me marrying Henry and moving, sudden like, that my phone got turned off. Henry had the mail forwarded, but I got this letter from a nursing home in Texas, some little nothing town outside Dallas. They said Patsy Clarke was a patient there, and they were trying to locate her family."

"You didn't get the letter tonight?"

"No, I got it two days ago. Henry read it, and he thought I should call the nursing home. I mean, if she's dying or something, he felt as though I should know. I would have ignored it. To hell with her, I say. She didn't want us, so why should we bother with her now? But—"

"Is she? Dying?" Liz shivered. How could it hurt? Her mother was a stranger. She hadn't laid eyes on her in decades.

"Yep. Henry called this morning, and talked to a Dr. Maria Gonzales. She said that Mom was too sick and too sedated to talk. She's got about everything wrong with her that you can have wrong and still be alive, and she's in a lot of pain. I'd guess cancer, but Dr. Gonzales didn't say exactly. She did say that they don't expect Mom to last out the week, and they'd like a relative to tell them whether or not to . . . you know . . ."

"Resuscitate?" Liz supplied.

"Right. I said I'd have to check with my sister. I wanted to call you, but I misplaced your number in the move. Then, just a little while ago, I got a call from a Paul Sutherland in Texas. He says he's a Baptist minister and has gotten to know Patsy since she's been at Riverview Rest. Sounds like a graveyard, doesn't it?" Crystal made a sound of amusement. "Riverview Rest? Give me a break. Anyway, the old gal's on her way out and wants to see us."

"So how did you get my number tonight?"

"Henry called the operator and said it was a life-and-death emergency. He used a business phone, so the operator gave him your unlisted number."

"Henry and everyone else, I suppose. Are you going?"

"To Texas? Hell, no. Henry told the doctor that we'd take care of the funeral and interment. Henry wants to have her cremated and the ashes mailed here. There's room for her in this wall they have for those little urns in the Webster Memorial Park. Henry's family owns that too. I don't see the need for a service or anything, but Henry said we can put her name and birth and death dates on this little bronze plaque. You don't have to worry that she's going out with the trash or anything."

"Do you have the number?"

"Of the nursing home? Sure. She's on the second floor of Riverview Rest, East Wing. I bet there's no river either, probably just a muddy ditch. She doesn't have a cent, so I don't imagine that it's the

Ritz." Crystal read off the number. "You don't want to talk to her, do you?"

"No," Liz answered. "I want to go there and see her."

"Are you crazy?"

"Maybe."

"It's a waste of time and money. Don't you have to teach school or something?"

Liz swallowed. "I've spent a lot of time hating her, Crystal. Maybe it's time I forgave her."

"She's not worth it. Patsy wouldn't cross the street for you if there wasn't something in it for her."

"It's not for her," Liz said thickly. "It's for me."

"She won't appreciate it."

"I don't expect her to. But I'm glad you called me, and I'm glad you've found someone who makes you happy."

"Me too," Crystal said. "Don't be a stranger. Maybe you could come out and see us this summer. Spend a few days hashing over old times."

"I'd like that."

"I'm serious. We've got plenty of room. It's just us and the spaniels knocking around in this house. Henry's got these two King Charles spaniels. Spoiled rotten, but really cute. You'll love them."

"Thanks, sis."

"You're really going to see the old bitch before she croaks?"

"Yes, I am."

"Don't expect me. We're doing enough for her, what with Henry offering to foot the bill."

"I'll share it with you," Liz said.

"No need. Henry says he gets a special cut rate on

the cremation. Something about professional courtesy. This one's on me."

"I'll call you when I get there."

"Okay, you do that," Crystal said. "But if she's dead when you get there, and you wasted your money on a plane ticket, don't blame me."

Chapter Fourteen

Barefooted, naked except for a twist of dull green cloth around his loins, the Game Master paced the confines of his secret place. Being here, underground, almost in his mother's womb, usually brought him some measure of peace. Not tonight. Tonight, tonight, his cravings ate at him, gnawing at his vitals, urging him to strike now—to finish the game—while the professor remained within his reach.

The Game Master admired her, even felt some measure of pity for her. He'd played cat-and-mouse with the professor for months, had planned this game for nearly two years, yet he could not deny that destroying her unique personality would be a sacrifice. But now, with the shriek of steel doors slamming shut in his head and salt-sweat oozing from his pores, he could delay no longer. The agony would not end until he tasted her hot blood. This was survival of the fittest, and one of them must die that the other could live.

He'd read that some so-called serial killers wanted to be caught, but that had never been true of him. He was far too intelligent, and he loved life. He had never fit the mold of ordinary humans, and he wasn't a carbon copy of those sick bastards who killed out of lust or for financial gain. He was what he was, and there were no others of his kind. Had the world been a more enlightened place, he would be admired rather than mocked.

The Game Master knew that he was a creature born in the wrong time. There had been times in human history when women understood their subservient roles and willingly served men as they were meant to do by the Creator. Power was never meant to be held by the weaker sex.

He'd understood—almost from the moment of birth—the injustices that stemmed from society's departure from sanity. A man had only to turn on the television or open a newspaper or magazine to find evidence of the decline of civilization. He supposed it had begun simply enough: allowing women to speak freely in the presence of their masters, permitting them to vote and hold public office, allowing them to control money, even to discipline male children. The sheer mass of compounded errors sickened him, yet even his own suffering at the hands of these female monstrosities did not slice away at the core of his will like it did with so many men.

No, the Game Master did not seek his own destruction. Such drivel was absurd. He walked faster, keeping pace with the thoughts that raced through his mind. Ten paces west, then twelve south. Stop, turn, now east.

"Why would I want that?" he shouted. "Why

would I want to be arrested—to come under a depraved legal system where a mindless female might sit in judgment of me? Where a woman could theoretically condemn me for acting as my primal nature demands?"

Ten paces exactly. Stop; pivot north. He threaded his fingers together, clasping both hands behind his back, blinking to clear his eyes of the sweat trickling down his forehead.

Voices echoed and reechoed in his ears. Weeping, begging, shouting. He ignored them.

The same intellect that ruled his every action recognized the need to pit his wit against ever greater challenges and to escalate each level of play. "If it were not so, might I tire of the great game?"

He gritted his teeth against the grinding pain in his head.

Had his skin been a different color, he might have found happiness in the more primitive societies in Africa or Asia, cultures that recognized the superiority of men and the right of the strong to prevail over the weak.

But he had been born here in this insignificant spot, and he was what he was. Stop, turn, walk. The Game Master could not allow himself to grieve over what had happened in his past, his cruel confinement behind barred windows and steel doors, the indignities he had been subjected to by lesser mortals. He was the Game Master. Control was his. His power increased with each sunrise, and soon he would not count his trophies by dozens but by hundreds.

"Why? Why have I allowed her to live this long?"

It remained an enigma. She was no longer in the full bloom of youth, certainly not as beautiful as others in his collection. But, in fairness, he had to admit that she possessed other qualities that he admired. She was wary and bold, and despite her attempts to hide her true feelings, he knew that she lusted after his magnificent body and the carnal pleasure he could give her.

"Does your daughter possess those same qualities? Or is she weak like her father?"

A smile tugged at the corners of his mouth. He stopped, closed his eyes, and sank to his knees as he imagined watching the daughter stepping naked and dripping from the shower, her young breasts proud and jutting, her legs long and sleek and shapely.

"She's young," he said. "But has she inherited the professor's courage?" Would she have the nerve to return to the farmhouse after her mother's disappearance, or would he be forced to hunt her elsewhere?

The two were a package now in his mind; first the professor, and then the daughter. Their photos, which he planned to take at the exact moment of death, would fit perfectly here on the south wall between *the cop* and *the hooker*. He regretted that he didn't have pictures of all his *girls* in his gallery.

The Game Master brushed a spiderweb away from the hand-knotted net that hung on the cedar-shingled wall. The spider, a small gray one, ran up his wrist. He caught it and squashed it between his fingers.

Various mementos, secured on rusty fishhooks,

adorned the net. Sometimes even he was forced to make do with a souvenir. If he was lucky and had the time, as with *the sophomore*, he might get both photos and a slender finger complete with polished nail, a dainty earlobe and earring, or some other choice item. Pinky toes were his favorite, but he refused to handle any that showed careless hygiene. He was a man of refined taste.

How he hoped the professor's daughter wouldn't disappoint him as the little tramp had done. Too easy . . . no more difficult than snuffing the life from a kitten. A few screams, futile thrashing, and she was dead. A pity.

It was his own fault. Had he known how inadequate the tramp was, he would have driven past without stopping. Let the bitch walk; he could have found finer game.

The same compelling urge that troubled him tonight had driven him to seek out the stranger. He could have taken the professor instead, had planned to close the trap.

The Game Master closed his eyes and balled his fists as energy built within him. A moan escaped his throat. He could feel the killing rage turn him from a man to something more, a creature apart. His face contorted and he arched his back in an attempt to harness the churning power. His muscles locked. He opened his mouth, threw back his head and howled.

Blackness took him.

Later, much later, he became aware of himself again. He lay on the dirt floor, his legs and diaper fouled with his own vomit, urine, and feces. His head pounded, his mouth tasted of rotting meat.

He wept.

How long? How long must he suffer the agony of torture that he knew would recede into shadow when he tasted her blood? He would have peace. He would walk among men and be almost one of them for weeks . . . months . . . until the need to seek his next victim flared within him.

The thought that he should spare the professor, much as a sportsman releases a trophy catch, flashed through his mind. He could do that. The Game Master rose shakily to his feet, stumbled, and caught himself on the section of tree stump that served as his chopping block.

His hand brushed the bloodstained hatchet, jerking him back to reality. He could no more forfeit the game than he could chop off his own hand. No, mutilating himself would be easier. He chuckled, wrenched the hatchet from the scarred stump.

Closing his eyes again, he savored the tangy richness of the old blood. Strength flowed through him, renewing his spirit and soul. He had soiled himself, but no one would discipline him. No woman would beat him with leather belts or wire hangers. No whore would kick or starve him, and none would shame him with jeers and curses. The weak, sniveling cub had become a lion. All feared the lion, and well they should.

. . . The professor most of all. She had caused him mental anguish, and he would repay the favor many times over.

Three phone calls, five cups of coffee, and ten hours later, Liz drove out of the Dallas airport in her Budget rental car. She'd purchased an egg muffin, two bottles of water, and a road map on the main concourse. She hadn't bothered to pack more than a few necessities because she fully expected to be back at school on Monday afternoon at the latest. She'd e-mailed Michael, Jack, Amelia, and Dean Pollett about her travel plans, saying only that it was a family emergency. She didn't mention her mother.

Curiously, although she was on her way to a deathbed visit with the woman who'd abandoned her when she was a young child, Liz didn't feel depressed. She felt almost lighthearted, as though a great weight had lifted off her shoulders.

On the plane, Liz had tried to recall her mother's voice, but she couldn't. She remembered bitter arguments between her parents; scoldings; Mom switching her daughters' legs until they bled; finding her mother lying on the bathroom floor, drunk, in her own vomit on Christmas morning. Were there any good memories? Liz hadn't recalled any before she'd fallen asleep. She didn't wake until the flight attendant tapped her shoulder to inform her that they would be landing in a few minutes.

And now, fighting traffic and watching for the right exit on unfamiliar expressways, Liz found herself humming a tune, almost as if she were on her way to a vacation resort. She supposed she should feel guilty or at least sad, but she didn't. She'd spent too many years wondering why her mother had left, and hoping that she'd show up on her doorstep full of apologies and heartfelt regret.

Liz couldn't suppress a smile as she remembered one Christmas in California when things were tight and she'd been forced to sell the engagement ring Russell had given her to pay the tuition for Katie's spring term at preschool. They had no furniture except a picnic table and benches, and a fold-out sofa bed. Most of Katie's toys and books had been purchased secondhand, and after she'd bought a tiny Douglas fir, there hadn't been any money left for decorations. She and Katie had strung popcorn, cranberries, and spray-painted pine cones on the tree instead of bulbs, and they'd topped it with a tinfoil star.

That year, for some reason, Katie had been full of questions about grandparents. She knew that her Grandfather Clarke and Grandmother Montgomery were both dead. Russell's mother had died the year after Liz and Russell were married. His father was living in Boca Raton with a girlfriend half his age, and had never shown the slightest interest in Katie. That left one grandmother, Patsy Clarke, unaccounted for. Every night before she'd gone to sleep, Katie had demanded to know all about Grandmother Clarke, where she was, and when she was coming back.

When Liz had told Katie that Patsy was probably in heaven with Grandpop, Katie had insisted she wasn't. She began to include her grandmother in her prayers, and she confided that she'd asked Santa to bring Grandmother Clarke home for Christmas.

And somehow, Katie's certainty that her grandmother would show up for Christmas dinner became Liz's secret hope. She imagined what Patsy would look like and what she'd say. Caught in the magic of holiday make-believe and her daughter's prayers, Liz had half expected her mother to appear. Of course, she hadn't, but Liz had mourned her loss all over again.

Now the lost lamb was found, but it was too late.

Liz no longer wanted or expected anything from her mother. She'd come for selfish reasons, certain that by letting go of the bitterness and heartache, she could find a peace that had always eluded her.

Liz reached Riverside Rest a little after six, and guessed by the smells and clink of dishes and trays that it must be time for the evening meal. She went to the reception desk, introduced herself, and told the attendant she was Patsy Clarke's daughter.

"Upstairs." The middle-aged R.N. looked tired, as though she were finishing a twelve-hour day shift, rather than being two hours into the evening one. "That elevator's not working. You'll have to take the steps. Go to the second floor, turn right, go through the double doors. You'll see the nursing station. Dr. Gonzales is on the floor. You'll want to speak with her."

Liz followed the woman's directions. The nursing home was old and out-of-date, but appeared clean. Several orderlies pushed wheelchair-bound patients through the halls while others carried trays into rooms.

At the top of the steps, an elderly gentleman in robe, pajamas, and slippers waddled past shouting for a Miss Jeanne. Liz smiled at him, but the filmy eyes he turned in her direction were vacant, and he didn't seem to see her.

"What's for dinner?" a painfully thin black woman in a bad wig demanded. She wore a pink jogging outfit and orthopedic shoes, and edged forward hunched over a walker.

"Salisbury steak and rice with green beans, Mrs. Roberts." A gangling Hispanic youth with a wide smile removed a covered tray from a serving cart. "Orange Jell-O for dessert."

"Salisbury steak? Ain't nothing but cheap hamburg. I'm sick of orange Jell-O. Why can't we ever have lime? I like lime."

Liz pushed through the double doors. In spite of herself, her heart began to race. She wanted to turn away, go back down the steps, and go home. Why had she thought that coming here would help anything?

"Liz?"

She turned to see Crystal coming through a doorway marked *Family Lounge*. "Hey," Liz answered. "What are you doing here? I thought you weren't coming."

"I know. I know." Crystal shrugged. "Dumb as you, I guess."

Crystal was thirty pounds heavier, and her hair was light brown rather than the unnatural white-blond that it had been the last time they'd seen each other. A pleasant-looking bald man in a black suit and striped tie followed her out of the room.

"Liz." Crystal hugged her. "You look great. This is my husband, Henry. Henry—my baby sister, Liz."

"How do you do?" Henry said formally. His voice held the hushed cadence of a funeral director, but his smile was genuine and his handshake firm. "Crystal has told me so much about you. I'm sorry that we have to meet under these circumstances."

Sensing his unspoken message, Liz glanced at Crystal.

She nodded. "Patsy's gone—slipped off right after we got here. Didn't know me. At least I hope she didn't. All she said was that I'd stolen her false teeth and she was going to have me arrested." Crystal snickered. "She still had quite a mouth on her. Guess that's where I get it."

Liz inhaled deeply. Dead. Her mother was dead. She waited, expecting to feel sadness, regret, but there wasn't anything. "I came as soon as I could," she said. "The first two flights to Dallas were full, and I—"

"No matter," Crystal said. "The old girl's better off." She shook her head. "She'd had a hard life, I expect. The nurse said that if she hadn't died from heart trouble, the lung cancer would have gotten her within the month."

"Mrs. Clarke's gone to a far better place," Henry intoned. "She's home with the Lord, and she's left all pain and earthly cares behind."

"Yeah," Crystal said. "Do you want to see her? We waited. Henry signed all the papers, but the doctor's still here if you want to talk to her."

"How long has Mom been here?"

Crystal looked at Henry. "Ten months?"

"Yes, that's what the nurse said. She was transferred here from a hospital in Dallas, and before that there was at least one more nursing home. No assets."

"Are there any . . . relatives? Friends?" Liz asked, wondering how her mother had slipped away without anyone to mourn her. "Anybody?"

"No, I'm afraid not," Henry answered. "I asked if anyone should be notified. The nurse said that Mrs. Clarke never had a visitor, a phone call, or a letter since she's been here at Riverview."

"I think I'd like to see her, to say good-bye," Liz said. She was dry-eyed. Whatever feelings she'd once possessed for the dead woman, none were left.

"Not me. I'm done," Crystal said. "Henry, you go in with her."

"Yes, dear." He squeezed Crystal's hand affectionately. Henry was shorter than her sister and perhaps ten years older, but neither of them seemed to notice or mind. Henry was clearly smitten by his new bride. And Crystal obviously doted on him.

"No, thank you," Liz said. "If you'll just show me where M . . . where she is, I'd rather do this alone."

"Certainly," Henry agreed, not in the least offended. "Perfectly natural." He led her back through the family lounge and pointed to a closed door. "In there. Just push aside the curtain. She looks quite peaceful, much better than when she was alive."

Liz stepped through the doorway and shut the door behind her. The room was still except for the hum of an air conditioner. Her mother lay on clean sheets in a narrow bed. If Crystal and Henry hadn't told her who the dead woman was, Liz would never have recognized her. Patsy Louise Clarke was in her early sixties, but looked twenty years older.

Paper-thin, age-spotted skin stretched over sharp bones. Her hair was sparse and gray; her nails bitten or cut to the quick. She couldn't have weighed more than eighty pounds, and she had once been a tall, attractive, full-breasted woman. Now all that was left of her was an empty shell.

Liz took one of the bony white hands in hers. "Good-bye, Mom," she whispered. "I forgive you."

A fly buzzed against the glass. The window air

conditioner churned noisily as the compressor came on. The dead woman lay motionless, bloodless lips drawn back over artificially white false teeth.

"I wish . . ." Liz began, then released her grip on the lifeless hand. A phrase of her dad's came to mind. "Keep the wind at your back, Mom."

She waited for perhaps another five minutes, saying nothing more, simply standing there, before nodding and backing out of the room.

"I told you it was a waste of time and money for you to come," Crystal said.

"No, it wasn't," Liz replied. "I got to see you, didn't I? And I got to meet Henry." She smiled at him. "I can't thank you enough for—"

"Not another word," Henry said, beaming. "This is what I do. I console the living and give the dead a decent send-off."

"You have to let me share in the expense," Liz offered. "There must be something I can—"

"I told you," Crystal said. "Henry has taken care of everything."

"Were you planning on staying or driving back to Dallas tonight?" Henry asked.

"I have to get back. I have finals tomorrow. At the college."

"Yes, yes, of course. Crystal told me you were a professor. Wonderful. And you're young for such a position. I can see that beauty runs in the family."

Crystal blushed and giggled.

The couple walked back to the rental car with Liz. "You have reservations on a flight back?" her sister asked.

"Yes, it leaves at 2:45 a.m., straight through to Baltimore."

"Then you've plenty of time to have dinner with us," Henry said. "No, no, my treat. I won't hear of you leaving us without eating. They don't feed you on the airlines anymore. Stale pretzels and tepid soda pop."

"Yes," Crystal insisted. "Join us for dinner. We haven't had a chance to talk."

"All right," Liz said. "I'd like that."

"You must come to Arizona and visit us in happier times," Henry said. "If you can't afford the plane fare, I'll take care of it. We really want you to come. I can't wait to meet that new niece of mine. Katie? Crystal says she's a charmer."

"Smart, too, just like her mother," Crystal said. "We can see who got all the brains in the family."

"Now, I won't have you putting yourself down," Henry said. "I love you just the way you are."

Crystal smiled. "What did I tell you, sis? He's just a big, cuddly teddy bear."

"And who's my Mama Bear?" Henry cooed, hugging her.

Crystal giggled. "Don't worry any more about Patsy, sis."

"Absolutely not," Henry agreed. "We'll have a proper interment for her. Pastor Bob is a Baptist. He does most of my services—unless you'd prefer another denomination."

"No," Liz assured him. "Baptist will be fine, but I don't know if she ever attended church, or even if she believed in God."

"Doesn't matter," Henry said. "God believes in her. We'll take care of it. Now, follow us. I understand there's a wonderful Mexican restaurant about a mile from here. Do you like Mexican?"

"Love it," Liz replied.

"Good," Crystal said. "So do we." She kissed Liz's cheek. "It's good to see you, baby doll. Don't make it so long between phone calls next time."

"I won't," Liz said, and meant it.

Liz arrived back at the farm at quarter of nine Monday morning, showered, dressed, and hurried to school. She'd slept on the plane, but it hadn't been enough, and she needed two cups of coffee and a donut to feel nearly human. The day of finals was hectic, but a good kind of hectic. The energy and excitement of the students was contagious, and she found herself rediscovering how much she loved teaching.

Somehow, it was mid-afternoon before she realized that she hadn't bothered to check her office e-mail or voice mail. There was a call from Jack saying he would be out of town until the following weekend, and two messages from Michael, asking if there was anything he could do. She wondered what could take Jack away at the busiest time of the year for fishermen, and why he hadn't said where he was going.

She didn't see Cameron all day, but she did pass Nancy Steiner in the hall, and the professor made a point of snubbing her. There was a note in her in box from Dean Pollett asking her to make an appointment to see him. Liz ignored it. She had no intention of discussing the matter of Cameron's stalking until she could locate and hire an attorney.

The week passed without incident, other than a call from Crystal telling her that the funeral had gone off without a hitch. They'd spent a few minutes chatting, and Crystal had repeated her invitation for Liz to come out to visit. Liz made excuses but promised she'd try to come for Thanksgiving. Although she was sure that she and Crystal would never be best friends, it was good to know that her sister had a real life and cared about her.

School was equally uneventful. Dean Pollett, apparently caught up in the rush of the last week of the session, failed to contact her a second time. Liz had lunch with Michael on Tuesday, and with Sydney and Amelia on Wednesday and Thursday. By Thursday afternoon, Cameron's absence had become an object of speculation.

"Where could he be?" Sydney said as she dumped an armload of papers into the trash. "Nancy's face is screwed up like a shriveled prune, and it'd cost your life to say 'good morning' to her."

"Cameron's desk is bare," Liz said. "I'd check the drawers, but that would be stooping to his level."

"I haven't heard a word," Amelia said. "My sources are as much a blank as we are."

"You'd think that Dean Pollett would say something to me if he's been dismissed," Liz said. "Wouldn't you?"

"I doubt it," Sydney said. "It might mean apologizing to you. I'd hold off on finding an attorney, if I were you. Why spend the money if the little rat has already gotten his just deserts?" She picked up her briefcase. "Sorry, you two. I'd love to stay, but Bob and I are driving to Connecticut first thing in the morning, and I'm not packed. Bob's nephew is graduating from a prep school. Surprised me. I never thought he'd make it. It goes to show that if the tuition is high enough, anyone can succeed."

"Me too," Amelia said. "Have to run. I have an appointment with the unhappy parent of a freshman who didn't succeed, and then I'm meeting Thomas. We're going to Christiana Mall to pick up something for his Aunt Charlotte's birthday, and then on to an early dinner with her and her two sons and their wives. Thomas is driving back to Norfolk in the morning, and I'm following tomorrow evening. I've got one more class tomorrow afternoon."

"You're shutting the house and staying for the summer?" Sydney asked.

"I am. You know how nervous I've been the past week. I am ready for vacation. Sun, sand, and catching up on my reading."

"Amen to that," Liz agreed.

"Anything I can help you ladies with?" Ernie Baker asked.

Liz turned to see the security guard standing just inside Sydney's office. She wondered how long he'd been there and how much of their conversation he'd overheard.

"No, thank you," Sydney said. "I'm just about to lock up. You have a good summer, Ernie."

"Glad to carry anything to the car for you," he said, not budging.

"We've got it covered," Liz said.

Ernie flushed. "Just call if you need help."

"Good-bye, Ernie," Amelia said. And, after the door closed behind him, she grimaced and whispered, "He really does give me the creeps."

Sydney laughed. "He admires your boobs." She glanced down at her own fashionably flat chest and narrow hips. "Me? I'm not even in the running."

Liz smiled. "The gospel according to Ms. Size Two. I'd give anything to have your figure."

"But would you give up Ernie?" Sydney teased. "You know, it wasn't my books he wanted to carry. It was a chance to leer at two size 36C's in the same room."

"If he wanted to see flesh, he'd be smarter to stay in the halls," Amelia said. "I thought one of the girls in my last class had walked out of her dorm in her thong panties, but they were just short shorts. Very short."

"Mmm-hmm," Sydney said. "And you didn't wear them like that yourself in college?"

"Not me," Liz replied. "I was the girl in the back row in her Sesame Street pj's and yellow fuzzy slippers."

"Or me," Amelia said. "That was my serious period—wire-rim glasses, black skirts, white blouses starched and pressed, sensible shoes. The intellectual black girl with strong opinions and a chip on her shoulder."

"As opposed to?" Sydney chuckled. "The marshmallow we know and love today?"

Amelia laughed with them. "You've been talking to Thomas. He swears I should have studied law. I believe he's insinuating that I'm opinionated."

"Amen to that," Liz agreed. She glanced at her watch. "Got to go. I've got an appointment to see a breeder about a puppy."

"You're getting a dog?" Amelia asked.

"Yes, I am," Liz admitted. "A Newfoundland, if you can believe it. Having Michael's German shepherd around was good, until . . ." She left the rest of the sentence unfinished, but both of her friends knew what had happened to Heidi. "Anyway . . ." She sighed. "I'm getting the biggest dog I can fit in my car. I've been reading up on Newfs, and they're supposed to be sweet-natured."

"What will they do, lick a burglar to death?" Sydney asked.

"Maybe," Liz said. "But just the same, after everything, I think I'll sleep better with a very large friend beside my bed."

"What about in it?" Amelia asked. "I know a certain retired policeman who'd be quite happy to fill that empty spot in your bed."

"Are we talking about Michael?" Sydney chimed in.

"I take the Fifth," Liz answered.

"I hear you, girl," Amelia said. "But I, for one, won't be surprised if I hear there are wedding bells in your future, and sooner rather than later."

"It is a distinct possibility," Liz said, "but a woman reserves the right to change her mind."

"Just don't wait too long," Sydney advised. "And don't let Jack Rafferty complicate your decision. He's definitely not in your league. When it comes to a choice between Captain Hubbard and Rafferty, there's no choice at all."

"Maybe not," Liz said.

"No maybes about it," Amelia agreed. "He's nothing but trouble, and you owe it to yourself to stay as far from him as possible. He may be good in bed, but it's what he does the other twenty-three and a half hours in the day that matters."

Chapter Fifteen

Amelia felt the tension in her neck and shoulders drain away as she followed Route 13 south through the small Virginia towns that hugged the main four-lane highway. Traffic was moderate, occasionally clogged by tractors or logging trucks crossing the intersections, but the flat rural countryside and good road made for easy, if somewhat monotonous, driving.

Not wanting to get a ticket, Amelia kept her speed to an even eight miles above the limit. The convertible top was down, the air warm and balmy. The stress of the murder at Somerville, the nasty e-mails, and the scare at the house faded. Amelia's thoughts fixed on the coming evening with Thomas, the bottle of California merlot tucked into her large canvas bag, and sleeping late tomorrow morning to the music of waves on the beach.

The girls wouldn't be arriving for another week, and she'd have those precious hours of sun and sand to unwind. Actually, Thomas had said that the forecast called for rain. She didn't mind; there was nothing quite as decadent as lounging in silk pajamas with a good book and a bowl of fresh strawberries on a stormy day.

She'd begged Liz to come down this weekend, but now with the rush of preparations behind her, she was secretly glad that she and Thomas would have the privacy to really relax, perhaps even engage in a little unscheduled and uninhibited sex.

Thomas was a wonderful husband, he really was, and she'd never been unhappy in her choice of men. But now and then she enjoyed a bit more vigorous intimacy. There was nowhere that Thomas was more likely to let down his hair than at the beach. If she donned her new red Victoria's Secret lingerie and poured her anal retentive husband a few stiff martinis, anything could happen.

Twilight was fading into purple dusk as Amelia slowed to pay the toll for the Chesapeake Bay Bridge-Tunnel, a whopping ten dollars, one way. She glanced at her watch, barely able to make out the numerals. If there were no delays, she'd be at the house an hour before she'd told Thomas to expect her. He would have already eaten, but she knew he'd have a large shrimp cocktail and a small Caesar salad waiting in the refrigerator for her. She'd skipped lunch; too much to do. She'd had to pack, arrange for the mail to be forwarded, prepay the yard people, and close up the house. Why was it that men always managed to evade the domestic chores?

The water was relatively calm tonight, no more than a three-foot chop. Amelia had seen the waves so high here that they splashed over the roadway. Driving the bridge-tunnel was an ordeal for

Thomas, but she didn't mind. The drive could be tedious if you got behind a camper or a poky tourist, but she seemed to have hit it at exactly the right time today.

She'd not gone far when she noticed in her rearview mirror a large dark truck with a massive steel bumper and headlight guards. She was driving her normal eight miles above the posted limit, but the truck quickly ate up the distance between them. She increased speed, leaving a safety window between them. The driver took the hint and slowed until he was traveling at the same speed as she.

Amelia removed the soft-rock CD and replaced it with one of her favorite Beatles albums. She passed through the tunnel at the deepest part of the channel and found herself singing along to the classic with Ringo, John, George, and Paul. They seemed to be the only ones on this stretch of the bridge, perhaps the only people in the world.

The black truck loomed out of the darkness, suddenly only a few car lengths from her back bumper. Amelia held her speed steady, refusing to be bullied. The driver behind her accelerated, coming close enough to nudge her car.

Amelia's heart thudded against her ribs. What was the fool trying to do? She pressed down on the gas pedal, and her red sports car leaped ahead. Amelia fumbled for her cell phone in her open purse. Road rage was a menace on the highways, but a quick call to 911 might clip his wings. To her dismay, the purse slid off the seat onto the floor. At this speed, she couldn't reach it without taking her eyes off the road, and the guard rails were flashing by much too fast.

The truck engine roared behind her. Amelia's hands began to sweat. Her muscles tensed. She leaned forward, gaze fixed on the solid yellow line. She knew the convertible wasn't at full speed; the little sports car could certainly outrun him. But flying down I-95 in broad daylight was one thing, and driving like this at night on a narrow bridge was another scenario altogether.

A cluster of white feathers ahead on the road surface made Amelia touch the brake. The bodies of greedy seagulls occasionally littered the bridge, and they could make the surface slippery. If she slowed, the fool would be forced to pass her in a no-passing zone or slow down as well. At fifty-five, perhaps even fifty, she could reach her purse, retrieve the cell, and have police waiting for him at the south end of the bridge.

The truck pulled left, and Amelia released her pent-up breath with a sigh. She eased off on the gas as the driver brought the truck up alongside her convertible. She glanced over, unable to make out anyone in the high cab through the tinted windows.

Incredibly, the truck drifted closer, crossing the solid line, crowding her against the rail. Amelia's mouth went dry. Her fingers tightened on the wheel. Out of instinct, she sped up again. The truck kept pace, going faster and faster. She pushed down on the pedal, and the nose of her car inched ahead of the big vehicle. Her right front bumper came perilously close to the rail, and it scared her so badly that she applied less pressure to the gas pedal.

"Pass me! Pass me!" she cried.

When his right bumper was level with Amelia's door, the driver veered right, smashing into her.

Amelia screamed as metal shrieked against concrete. The wheel wrenched out of her hands and glass shattered. "Jesus!" she cried as pain knifed through her left arm and shoulder. The massive truck kept coming, plowing into her, sending the sports car ricocheting off a post and bouncing end over end to somersault over the guard railing into the bay.

The last sensations that Amelia felt were the icy embrace of water and blessed, blessed silence.

Smiling, the Game Master slowed, straightened the wheel, and continued on. In time, some do-gooder would notice the bits of glass and metal on the road and notify the proper authorities, but by then he would be well off the bridge and lost amid the throngs and traffic jams of Friday-night Norfolk motorists. He knew just the spot to dispose of the truck, a wooded swamp in North Carolina only two miles from a truck stop. The Game Master had already filed off the serial numbers, but he'd change the plates at least once more before he burned the truck. Details were important, and he was nothing if not efficient in his planning.

He regretted leaving the roadway in such a shambles. Littering went against his grain, and the next vehicle might well shred a tire. But tonight was an exception to a lifetime of picking up after other people. Let someone else share the burden of housekeeping this time. Doubtless, they'd have to close the lanes to clean up the shards of glass and metal.

A pity, he thought. It might be hours, days even, before the wreckage of the red convertible was pulled out of the water. And the professor's friend might not even be in the car any longer. Had she been wise enough to wear her seat belt? So many women didn't bother. They believed that they were invincible, immune to death.

What would the professor say when the phone call came? A tragic accident. A friend's life cut short all too soon.

Poor, poor little professor. Bit by bit, he was stealing her life. Soon she would have nothing left to live for . . . He chuckled. This had been fun. He'd have to try it again some day, just pick a car at random and send it flying over the side of the bridge. It took skill, planning, and luck. Additional traffic wouldn't necessarily prevent him from success; other cars could add to the thrill. He grimaced, regretting the overabundance of cell phones. Science moved too quickly. Life was better when one didn't have to worry about every Tom, Dick, and Harry playing hero by interfering in his pleasures.

What would the professor do when she heard the news? He hoped she would be within range of one of his cameras when she took the call. It was one of those Hallmark moments that were too good to miss.

Liz was awakened just before eight on Sunday morning by the crack of a windowpane breaking. She leaped out of bed, dug the revolver out of her nightstand drawer, and ran to peer cautiously out another window.

Jack was standing on the lawn with a sheepish expression on his face. "I'm sorry," he said as she pushed up the window. "I didn't mean to . . . I'll fix it."

"You're damn right you'll fix it," she called down to him. "You're lucky I didn't shoot you!"

Heart thumping, Liz emptied the shells from the Smith & Wesson and returned both handgun and bullets to the drawer before hurrying downstairs to open the kitchen door. "You've got to be a madman," she said.

Jack grinned and held up a bag labeled *Red, White, and Blue Bagels.* "Tarzan bring peace offering from Big Apple."

"Red, white, and blue bagels?"

"Not to mention Wawa coffee and the Sunday *News Journal.*" He leaned down and kissed her. She turned her head at the last instant so his lips brushed her cheek and eyebrow.

"I had a newspaper in my box at the end of my lane."

"Tarzan know. Where Jane think he get this one?"

She laughed. "Enough with the theatrics. It's too early. And why did it seem like a good idea to throw rocks at my window?"

He shrugged. "If the bike didn't wake you, what was I supposed to do?"

"Knock?"

"I did knock. Back door and front. You were snoozing pretty good there, Lizzy." He pulled a chair out from under the table and sat down. "High tide's at one. I thought maybe you'd like to sneak out for a little trout fishing."

She took cream cheese, jelly, butter, and a carton of half-and-half from the refrigerator. "I love bagels, but I've never had blue ones."

Jack rose and fetched two cups and spoons. "If you don't mind. I hate paper cups." He poured coffee from a tall container into the mugs. "I got plain, onion, and all-grain, but they're the normal color for bagels. I got them from a little bodega off Broadway. I think the red, white, and blue is a new American's attempt to show patriotism. If I had to guess, I think the owner was Tibetan or a Laplander. Anyway, he makes good bagels."

"A Laplander? What would make you think that?" she asked, knowing she was being set up for more of Jack's nonsense. Broken window or not, she was glad to see him this morning. More than glad, she was delighted.

"I don't know, maybe the live reindeer at the register or—" Liz threw a bagel at him. He caught it, and they both laughed.

Within a few moments, the awkwardness that had marred their last day together vanished and Liz found herself telling him about her emergency flight to Texas and her mother's death. He listened, as he always had, not saying anything until she was finished.

"So, while I can't say that there was any deathbed reunion between me and Patsy, it was good to patch things up with Crystal."

Jack licked cream cheese off his fingertips. "It sounds as though she's found something good."

"Henry's nice. Dull, sweet, and nice. I'd given up hope of her ever dating anybody normal, let alone marrying again."

"It just goes to prove that even the good ones can be captured with the right bait."

"Crystal?" Liz asked.

"Nope." Jack chuckled. "The fifty thousand Henry won in Vegas. Money strips a man of his wits faster than anything else."

"I suppose that means that you're better off poor?"

He grinned. "Didn't say that, either. Money you work for is one thing, windfall's something else. They say most big lottery winners end up broke and unhappy."

"So you don't buy lottery tickets?"

"Nope. I don't like the odds. I prefer to bet my hard-earned dollars on a sure thing." He laid his hand over hers, closing his fingers around hers and turning her hand to kiss the underside of her wrist.

"Jack," she murmured.

He pulled her out of her chair and into his lap. His kiss sent a tingle of excitement to the tips of her toes. "Mmmm," he said. "You taste like onion."

"I thought we were going fishing."

"The fish can wait." He kissed her again.

This time they made it to her bed.

The afternoon on Jack's boat was carefree. They caught a half-dozen trout, and drank a bottle of red wine from a local winery. Once the fish stopped biting, Jack took the boat in closer to shore and anchored.

"Ready for a swim?" he asked Liz.

"No. The water's not warm enough yet."

"I knew it. All that education made you soft." He stripped off his jeans and shirt and dove in.

Liz contented herself with stretching out on a blanket on the bow. "Do you have any hamburger or liver?" she asked. "If I throw out a little chum, maybe we could lure a few sharks—"

"No sharks," he said in mock horror. After a few

minutes, he climbed the ladder at the stern, wrapped a towel around his hips, and joined her on the bow deck.

"I expect you to repair my window when we get home," she reminded him. "There are panes from a matching one in the barn loft. My carpenter wanted to haul it to the dump, but I've got too much of my dad in me. If you remember, he couldn't throw anything out."

"Will do," Jack promised, stretching out beside her. "I like having you here, Lizzy." He nuzzled her neck, and when she laughed, he kissed her lips. "I could never forget you."

"Like a bad case of poison ivy?" she teased.

"Exactly."

She closed her eyes and listened to the sounds of the waves lapping against the boat hull and the cries of seagulls overhead. "I like being here," she said.

"With me?"

"With you."

"Even if you did try to kill me this morning?"

"I did not try to kill you. You told me that I should have a gun, so I have one. What can you expect when I wake up to some wild man breaking my windows?"

"Guilty. It didn't work like that in that movie."

"What movie?" A fish jumped about ten yards from the boat.

"I don't remember the title. *Sleeping in Seattle*?"

She chuckled. "There were no rocks flying through windows in *Sleepless in Seattle*."

"It was one of those movies. The hero pitches the rocks. The heroine leans out in her lacy black nightie."

"Right. I hope you saw what I sleep in."

"The same as that girl in *She's Got Mail*."

"No. Jack, you are hopeless when it comes to movies."

"No, I'm sure I'm right. Mom's got the DVD. We can borrow it and watch it at your house. Is your TV in your bedroom?"

"No. You were in my bedroom," Liz answered. "Did you see a television or a DVD player there?"

"We'll have to remedy that. Or we could watch it here on the *Dolphin*. I like to watch movies in bed. Sometimes I even watch X-rated ones."

"By yourself, I'm sure." She handed him a tube of sunblock and rolled onto her stomach so that he could rub it on her back.

"Who else would I watch them with?"

"I can't imagine." She groaned as he rubbed the cream into her skin. "That feels heavenly. I haven't had anybody do that for me since Katie went to Ireland. You'd like her, Jack. Strangely enough, I think she'd like you too."

"Strangely?" He made a sound of amusement.

"You have to admit, you're one of a kind. More of a nineteenth-century man than a twenty-first. But I suppose a lot of watermen are."

"Your dad included?"

"Daddy especially. He was such a great father— when he wasn't drinking. And even when he was, he never lifted a hand to Crystal or me."

"Wish I could say that about Pop. Although I have to admit that George and I deserved a taste of the belt now and then. And Mom was the real disciplinarian. If you didn't jump when she said jump— look out."

She smiled, remembering some of the mischief

the Rafferty boys had gotten into. "Do you mean the time you two chained the bumper of a police car to a post at the end of the dock? Or when you dumped the half ton of aging fish in the mayor's cellar?"

Jack grinned. "I'm innocent. George made me do it."

"I'm sure. I don't think either of you ever grew up, not really." She applied sunblock to her knees and calves. Curiosity made her ask, "What were you doing in New York, anyway? I wouldn't think the fishing business would take you to the city. You always said you hated cities."

"I did, but they have their uses."

"You still haven't told me why you went. Is it a secret?"

"Yes."

She sat up. "Sorry, I didn't mean to pry. It's a terrible habit of mine. I—"

"It's all right, Lizzy. I can trust you." He hesitated a few seconds. "I had some business to conduct, but I also went to see George."

She glanced at him. "Your brother? I thought he was in Smyrna prison."

Jack took her hand, turned it over, and rubbed her palm with his thumb. "George won't be coming home. He's gone into the witness protection program. I haven't even told Mom and Pop yet."

"He what?" Liz's eyes widened in surprise. "Isn't that only for—"

"Gangsters? I suppose, but it's mostly for people who are willing to testify about what they've seen other people do. Sometimes knowing too much can get you killed."

"Is this about drugs?"

"It's about money."

Unease made her suddenly chilled. She stood and picked up her towel. "I think I've had enough sun." Jack steadied her as she made her way back to the main deck. "I won't say anything, of course," she said. "But does this mean he can't come home? Not ever? Your parents—"

"George didn't want them to know until it was a done deal. Something bad happened up in Smyrna. Luckily, George had a buddy to help him out. But he couldn't count on that a second time. Next time, he might end up dead."

"Where are they sending him? No, don't tell me. That was a stupid question." She pulled a shirt on over her bathing suit. "I don't want to know."

"Good, because I don't know either." His eyes narrowed. "It's for the best. If he did get out early, he'd be right back in the business again. This way, he has a chance."

"Tough for your parents."

He nodded. "In a way, but not so hard as burying him, or knowing that he's rotting inside that concrete cage. The sound of those steel doors shutting— it gets to you. If they'd given me twenty years . . ." He took a deep breath and went up the steps to the bridge. "I'm not cut out for life in a box."

"But George won't be in prison now, will he? He'll be protected, set up in a new life someplace else?"

"So he told me. They want him to testify against some nasty people. That's why he's in a safe house in New York City for a while. He told the feds he wouldn't agree to it if we couldn't spend some time together first."

"I'm sorry, Jack. I always liked George. But he was

crazy, even as a kid." She folded her arms. "Not in a bad way, but he scared me. So did you."

"You had reason to be scared. Maybe you still do." He started the engine. "I'd best get you home. I'll tell Mom and Pop tonight. It's not something I'm looking forward to, but the sooner, the better."

"Thanks for sharing it with me. I won't let you down."

"In a few months, it will be common knowledge. Word gets around in prison. Hopefully, by then George will be a few thousand miles away with a new name and a new identity." He gestured to her. "Come on up here."

She joined him, and he stepped back to let her take the wheel. "It handles like a dream," she said after they'd gone about half a mile.

"George wants you to have his boat. He told me to run it up and tie it at your dock. I thought I'd better tell you, instead of letting you come out and find it— after the last boat you found there."

"That's great. But I can't accept it as a gift. Let me pay for it, and give the money to your mother."

"Can't do that."

"Why not?"

"George loves that boat. He'd never sell it. If he wants you to have it, that's good enough for me. And for Mom."

"You Raffertys are a stubborn bunch."

"Yep, so I've been told."

"Michael's driving up to New England this summer. He's asked me to go with him."

Jack's arms tightened around her. "I don't know much about your neighbor, but what I've seen, I don't like."

"He's more than a neighbor. He's a good friend."

"How good of a friend?"

"We haven't . . . well," she stammered. "Not like it is between us. He's a nice guy, and he's had terrible luck."

"Are you going with him?" His voice hardened. "Don't go, Lizzy."

"Are you telling me or asking me?"

"Take it either way."

"I haven't decided yet." She let him take back the wheel. "I've known Michael over two years. And you—"

"All your life."

"This time. This time, I've known you . . . what? Three weeks? I'm not ready to make any commitments, Jack."

"Have I asked for any?"

"No, you haven't. And that means I'm still free to take a vacation with a friend. He's handicapped. You've seen him. It's not the same."

"I've seen him," Jack said. "But handicapped or not, it's more than friendship. If you go with him . . ."

"Are you giving me ultimatums?"

"Maybe. Take it for what it's worth."

She returned to the main deck, found her twill shorts, and put them on. "You can't tell me what to do," she said.

"I just did. Don't go with him. And if you do, don't expect to find me on your porch waiting for you when you get back."

The call came at eight that evening. Jack had long gone and Liz was lingering over photos of the New-foundland breeder's most recent litter of puppies.

She checked to see who was calling, recognized the Virginia exchange, and picked up on the third ring.

"Elizabeth?"

"Yes. Thomas? Is that you? How's the—"

"There's been an accident," Amelia's husband said. His voice was clipped, each word cut off precisely.

Liz blinked. Her hand holding the receiver felt detached, as though it belonged to someone else. This couldn't be happening. It had to be a nightmare. "Is . . . Amelia hurt?"

Thomas began to cry.

Chapter Sixteen

Stunned, the Game Master stared at the front page of the *Delaware State News*. The two-inch-high headlines read: "CRAB TRAPS YIELD GRUESOME DISCOVERY." A color photograph featured two local boys holding fishing poles and standing next to a stack of commercial crab pots. Taking up half of the page, the article related how the teenagers had snagged a crab trap while fishing in the backwaters of a creek leading off the Delaware Bay. Police confirmed that the wire cage contained human remains. There were additional quotes from a retired medical inspector and a separate piece on forensics and the scientific advances that could identify bodies and convict murderers years after a crime had been committed.

"No! No!" The paper fell from the Game Master's numb fingers to drift to the floor in scattered sections. Rage consumed him. It wasn't possible that he could be robbed of his prize by mindless teenagers. The bones were his. His alone. He dropped to his knees and rocked back and forth, fists clenched, mouth gaping wide in a silent scream. He would find them. Make them pay. Peel the skin from their flesh while they were still alive.

A low groan of anguish escaped his throat. If there were remains, the boys must have discovered his little tramp. There could be nothing left of the others but fragments of bare bone. She'd been a mistake from the moment he allowed her into his car. He'd known it then, but he hadn't followed his instincts and thrown her out along the road.

One small deviation from his game plan . . . This was bad karma, brought on by breaking his own rules.

The Game Master scrambled for the paper, spread it on the table, and read line by line. *Discovery. Investigation. Autopsy.* The words knifed through his gut with the force of steel needles driven into his flesh by a nail gun. *Information officer . . . Unable to determine the sex . . . Shocked . . .*

Were they imbeciles? How could they hold a woman's bones in their hands and not know they were female? Even the rotting bones and hair of a woman's corpse smelled of female.

The Game Master was shattered. Near tears. What kind of God would permit such injustice under heaven? And if one crab pot had been found, would they dredge up others? Would they rob him of everything he had worked for? What could he do to prevent an even greater loss? Should he retrieve what remained in his scattered traps? Or would attempting to salvage his prizes put him at risk?

He felt as though he would vomit.

He had to calm himself, to think clearly. The game

was what was important, not the loss of offal as insignificant as the remains of the little tramp. Nothing must prevent the professor's harvest. She was his, and he had waited too long to finish it.

The throbbing behind his eyes had returned with even greater intensity. He lowered his head and clasped it between his hands as lights pinwheeled and a myriad of accusing voices chanted, "Stupid piss pants, stupid, stupid."

"I'm not," he protested.

"Bad, stupid boy!" they howled. "You pissed the bed!"

"No! I'm not stupid. I'm not a boy." He groaned, and his voice thundered out of his chest. "I'm the Game Master! And I always win!"

Cameron Whitaker folded his newspaper and dropped it into the oversized trash container at the back of the Better Burger parking lot along with his empty soda container, chicken tenders wrapper, and fries bag. He'd noticed a pay phone at the side of the restaurant, but he didn't want to park next to it.

His fingers were sticky with chicken sauce, but washing them would mean returning to the restroom inside. A friendly Hispanic clerk had been scrubbing the stall floors with a mop, and if he went back, the man might remember him and initiate another conversation. Cameron wished he hadn't finished all his Diet Coke. He could have used the liquid to remove the residue. Now the soiled napkin would have to suffice.

He wondered if he should have worn gloves. But if anyone did see him using the phone, they'd wonder why someone would be wearing gloves in late May.

He thought about using what was left of the napkin, but decided instead on his handkerchief.

Strolling casually to the telephone, he dropped two quarters into the slot. Covering his index finger with a corner of the cotton handkerchief, he punched in 911. On the fourth ring, a snotty-voiced woman demanded to know if he had an emergency.

"*Sí,*" he answered, covering his mouth with the wadded-up material.

"What is the nature of your emergency?"

"Es poleese matter," he said, trying to mimic the sing-song accent of the custodian. "Por favor. Must speek to estada poleese."

"I'll connect you."

"Sergeant Andruskie. Delaware State Police. Troop Three."

"Jack Rafferty," Cameron said, failing in his attempt to sound Hispanic.

"Yes, Mr. Rafferty," the sergeant said. "How can I help you?"

"No. Yo no . . . No ees me."

"Excuse me, sir, could you speak louder?"

"Bones. Newspaper. Een craba trap. Hombre you vema . . . look. Jack Rafferty."

"Could you give me your name and address, sir?"

"*No hablo inglés.*"

"Sir? Are you referring to the discovery of the human bones in today's paper?"

"*Sí.* Capitano catch *pescado.* How you say? Fisherman. Hombre es Jack Rafferty. Ask heem about bones."

"Sir? We—"

Smiling, Cameron hung up and walked away. That should fix the bitch. Given half a chance, the authorities would lock that redneck lover of hers back in Smyrna prison and throw the key away. Cameron crossed the street, lingered in the shadows for a few minutes while he watched to see if any police cars approached. When nothing out of the ordinary occurred, he returned to his car and drove back to his apartment by a roundabout route.

He wished he could be at the docks to see the surprise on Rafferty's face when they came to arrest him. Maybe Professor Elizabeth Clarke would be with him. That would look good in the papers, too. But . . . Cameron grimaced. If he were present when the police came to question Rafferty, it might be obvious who had made the phone call, and that wouldn't do. It wouldn't do at all.

Liz answered her door to find Jack's mother standing there. Her eyes were red and swollen, as though she'd been crying. "They took Jack," Nora said.

"Who took him?" Liz asked, stepping back and motioning Nora inside. Her first thought was that Sonny Shahan and the Hurd brothers had come after Jack in retaliation for the fight at Rick's. "Have you called the police?"

"The police took him away." Trembling, Nora folded her arms over her chest. "I was afraid this would happen. The troopers said they were taking him to Troop Three for questioning, but that's what they said last time, and he ended up in prison." Nora's distraught face was pale and blotched, and she wasn't wearing any makeup. For the first time, Liz thought that Nora looked older than her age.

"What can I do?" Liz's voice came out ragged as she put an arm around the older woman's shoulders.

A dozen questions surfaced in her mind. "Why did they take Jack?"

"I'm not sure. I heard them say something about crab pots. Oh, God, Lizzy. You don't think this has anything to do with the story in this morning's paper?"

"What story? I didn't get my paper this morning. I called the delivery driver, but he insisted that he'd put it in my box as usual." Liz waved to the table. "Sit down. I'll put on a pot of coffee."

Nora sank into a chair. "You've been crying too, haven't you? Is it something that Jack—"

"No, nothing to do with him. My friend Amelia— my best friend. She was killed Friday night in an accident on the Bay Bridge-Tunnel. I've been on the phone with another friend, Sydney. I was trying to comfort her, and . . . My mother died over the weekend and now Amelia. I can't believe it."

"You poor baby." Nora rose and embraced her. "You didn't need my trouble on top of all this." She patted Liz's shoulder. "They say everything comes in threes. Some people say it's superstition, but there's truth to it. I've seen it too many times."

Liz pushed her gently away and blinked back tears. "No, it's all right. It's just that it doesn't seem real. Amelia wanted me to come down to the beach house and spend time with them. I can't believe she's really gone."

"First poor Tracy, then Patsy, and now your friend Amelia. It's enough to make you shed a few tears. No need to be ashamed of being human."

"There are mugs in that cupboard," Liz said, pointing. She busied herself with filling the coffee maker. "Amelia's being cremated. Her husband wants her ashes scattered at sea."

"Lots of folks doing that," Nora observed as she took her seat again. "Always seemed unnatural to me."

"The service will be in Norfolk." Liz switched on the coffee maker and returned to Nora. "I'm going, of course." She took a deep breath. "What's this about an article in the paper?" And how would it concern Jack? Fear constricted her throat. "Was it about drugs?"

"No," Nora said. "Worse. Two boys out fishing or robbing other people's crab traps found a commercial crab pot in your river. There were bones inside, human bones. Either some sick bastard is robbing graveyards or there's been a murder."

"In my river?" Liz shuddered. "Gross."

Nora nodded. "There was long blond hair in the pot and . . . other parts. They say it might be a woman's body."

"And the police suspect Jack?" Liz's stomach clenched. It was all coming apart. Everything. Her dreams . . . her life . . . What if Jack was the man that Michael suspected? What if she'd been sleeping with a monster who thought nothing of murder or of dealing in illegal drugs? Immediately she rejected the idea. It wasn't possible. The Jack she knew, the man she was coming to care for more than she wanted to admit, couldn't be a killer. Could he?

"Jack wants me to contact this man at his home. It's an out-of-state number. He wants me to ask him to hire a criminal lawyer, a good one. Jack said that money is not a concern."

"What?" Liz stared at the name scribbled on a receipt from a local fish wholesaler. Gregory McMann. There was a number below, and she recognized the area code as Manhattan. "He wants you to call and ask this man to find him a lawyer?"

"Yes. I told him that I could get the same attorney who represented him last time, but he said, "No. Call McMann. He'll know what to do.""

"Did you?"

"No, I didn't." Nora's eyes clouded with doubt. "I'm in way over my depth here, Lizzy. You know how I feel about talking to strangers. And lawyers?" She shrugged her shoulders. "My tongue gets tangled. I'll make a fool of myself, say the wrong thing, let Jack down. Will you do it?"

"What is Jack involved in?" Liz felt nauseous, as she had long ago when she was seasick in a nasty storm on the bay.

"Please. He'll be mad at me for worrying you instead of doing what he asked myself."

"I'll do it for you, but . . . I don't know what to think. I can't imagine why . . . And you say he told you that money was no object?"

Nora nodded. "That's what he meant."

"How? Jack doesn't have that kind of money. A criminal defense attorney could charge him twenty thousand, forty—more if this goes to a drawn-out trial."

"Just do what he wants. I've lost one son. I can't lose another."

"He told you about George?"

"Last night." Tears ran down Nora's cheeks. "Georgie should have let us know—let me see him one more time. Let Arlie see him. It's not fair. It's just not fair."

"At least this way, you know he's safe." Liz got up, found a box of tissues, and handed it to her.

Nora looked up. "What's safe if a woman in Kent County can end up as crab bait? Georgie's always been wild . . . and it looks as if Jack might be just as bad."

"Jack wouldn't commit murder."

"No," Nora agreed. "He wouldn't kill someone without a good reason." She blew her nose. "I'm sorry to put this on you. I could have—"

"I'll do it." Liz took the piece of paper and went to the phone. On the sixth ring, Liz heard a click.

"This is . . ." A deep, male voice with an upper-class British accent repeated the number Liz had just punched in. "Please leave your name, a message, and a number where you can be reached."

"Hello, Mr. McMann. I'm a friend of Jack Rafferty's. I'm sorry to bother you, but this is urgent. Please call me immediately, no matter the hour." She repeated her home number and cell number and hung up. "Either he isn't there or he's letting an answering machine pick up," Liz said. "If he doesn't call back, I'll try again later."

"Thank you," Nora said. "I knew you wouldn't let us down. Your daddy was rough as a cob, but he never deserted a friend. You're his daughter all right, a Clarke through and through." She got to her feet. "I'd better get home and see if Jack's called. Arlie's in a real spin."

"I'm sure Jack's not involved in anything criminal," Liz said, but she wasn't sure at all. She was nearly as frightened as Jack's mother. She walked out to the car with Nora, and the two hugged before the older woman slid behind the wheel. "I'll let you know if I hear from Mr. McMann," Liz assured her.

"You do that," Nora said. "I don't care if it's three in the morning. You call me. Hear?"

"I will," Liz promised.

The phone was ringing when she walked back into the kitchen. She checked the caller ID, but the screen read: *Unknown*. Liz answered.

"Moms? It's me. Have you heard anything from Dad?" Katie sounded young.

"Hi, honey. How are you?"

"I'm okay. It's Dad I'm worried about. Has he called you?"

Liz stretched the receiver cord and sat back down at the kitchen table. "No, he hasn't."

"I'm coming home."

Fear made Liz's voice sharp. "No. You are absolutely not coming home." She made a mental note to cancel Katie's credit card immediately. "You haven't bought a ticket, have you?"

"No. Why can't I come home? What if something bad happens to him? What if—"

"You wanted to stay. I've paid the tuition for your summer session. You can't change your mind now."

"That's not fair. It's because of Dad, isn't it? You hate him and—"

"I don't hate him, honey." Liz took a sip of the cooling coffee. "I'll come to see you in August. Maybe we'll take that trip to Paris you've been wanting."

"What about Dad? You're treating me like a child. You don't tell me anything, and you expect me to—"

"If I didn't tell you, it's because I didn't want you to be hurt."

"Has something terrible happened to Dad? Is he in the hospital?" It sounded to Liz as though her daughter might burst into tears.

"No, nothing like that. He's run out on Danielle and the kids."

"You don't know that. Something might have—"

"Katie, I'm telling you the absolute truth. Your father took a lot of money and left the country. Michael traced him to Miami and then to the Dominican Republic. I doubt if he's coming back." There was absolute silence on the other end of the line. "Katie? Are you there?"

"I suppose that makes you happy, doesn't it?"

Liz's palm itched to slap the teenage superiority out of her. "No," she replied as calmly as possible. "No, it doesn't make me happy. Your father's been gambling again. He maxed out all of Danielle's credit cards before he got on a plane. I'm sorry, honey. I really am. But I couldn't—"

"Couldn't or wouldn't? I suppose there's really no use in carrying this conversation any further, is there? It must delight you to be right and have everyone else wrong."

"You're right, Katie. There isn't any reason for us to continue this conversation. It's not my fault that your father is a shit or that you have to hear it from me. Call me when you've had time to think this over and decide who the villain really is—because it's not me." Liz hung up the phone and kicked the cat's water dish halfway across the kitchen floor.

"Has everyone gone stark raving mad?" she shouted. How in hell could her daughter blame her because Russell had done to Danielle what he'd done to them and to wife number two? She didn't hate Russell. She was just sick to death of cleaning up after him.

Liz poured herself another cup of coffee, drank it black, and called Katie back.

"Moms, I'm sorry," her daughter said. It was obvious that she had been crying. "It's not your fault that Dad . . . that he let us all down again."

"He started out right," Liz said gently. "But addiction and bad choices have messed up his life so bad that I don't know if he'll ever get it straight again."

"I know," Katie replied. "I know that he never keeps his promises, and I know you always do. I just kept thinking that this time . . . I love you, Moms."

"And I love you more."

"I love you much."

Liz smiled. It was an old game that they'd played since Katie was tiny. "Love you mostest."

"Is mostest correct English for a full professor?" Katie's voice wavered between tears and laughter.

"Did you get the letter I sent you?" Liz asked her. "About Aunt Crystal and my mother?"

"Yeah. I did." Katie paused. "I guess Grandmom's not coming to Christmas dinner, is she?"

"No, she's not. But we'll go out to Arizona together and say a prayer at her memorial."

"I'd like that. Sort of hello and good-bye all at once."

"Katie?" Liz's eyes welled up with moisture. "There's something else."

"What?"

With a sigh, Liz told her about Amelia's accident. Katie listened and then offered to come home.

"For you, Moms. You need me."

"I need you where you're at, finishing the summer term. If you want to stay another year, we'll decide about that together when I come over. Fair enough?"

"Deal. I really miss you," Katie said.

"And I miss you." They exchanged good-byes and Liz hung up a second time, relieved that in the middle of everything else, Katie was safe and an ocean away from Clarke's Purchase.

Liz put the dirty cups in the sink, rinsed out the glass carafe of the coffee maker, and put a fresh filter in for the morning. She swept the floor, retrieved the cat dish and washed it. When the kitchen was reasonably neat, she again tried the number that Nora had left. This time, Gregory McMann answered.

"Yes, I got your earlier message. May I ask who you are?"

"Elizabeth Clarke. I'm a friend of Jack's."

"And he gave you my private number?"

"Yes," she said. "I'm sorry to bother you, but this is an emergency. Jack's in trouble." She explained Jack's request that Mr. McMann contact an attorney specializing in criminal law. Surprisingly, McMann didn't hang up on her and didn't ask if she'd lost her mind.

"You say these were Delaware State Police who took him in for questioning? I assume that this is Kent County?"

Liz assured him that it was. Then she passed on the information that Jack wanted the best representation, regardless of cost.

"That goes without saying," McMann answered. "Tell Jack that I'll have someone there tonight."

"Tonight?" It was already seven-thirty. How could

he find an attorney of that caliber at this hour? "Could I ask what your relationship is with Jack?" she asked.

"I'm sorry, but that's privileged information, Ms. Clarke. I can tell you that I also consider Jack a friend. Tell him not to worry. I'll handle this."

As soon as she had completed that conversation, Liz called Nora to tell her that McMann had promised to find a criminal attorney for Jack. Nora was thanking her once more when Liz heard the sound of a vehicle coming up her lane.

"I've got to go," Liz said. "Someone's here. And don't worry; I'm sure this is all a mistake." She placed the receiver on the hook and went to the back door in time to see Michael's van pulling to a stop beside the gate.

As she approached, Michael powered down the front passenger window. "Hi," she said. "What's up?"

"Get in," he said.

She opened the van door and stepped inside. Michael was holding a bouquet of long-stem yellow roses.

"For you," he said, handing them to her. "I'm worried about you, Elizabeth. So I brought you some company." From the back of the van, she heard Otto's excited whimper.

"Oh, Michael, thank you for the flowers. They're beautiful. But I can't accept Otto. Not after what happened to Heidi."

"That wasn't your fault. If you keep him in the house with you, he'll be safe." He raised a hand. "Wait, let me say this before I lose my nerve. I know my timing couldn't be worse. It's been terrible for you," he said. "Your student's death, your home being broken into, your mother's passing, and now the loss of your friend. You've had more than enough to break you, Elizabeth, but you haven't cracked. You're strong. But sometimes life can be too much, even for the strong. I want you to take the trip with me. And if it's all I think it will be, I want you to consider becoming my wife."

Liz leaned back against the door. "You're right, Michael. I feel like I'm ready to come apart. It has been too much. And I'm too crazy right now to think straight."

He took a deep breath. "I'm not done. All I ask is that you hear me out. You're a beautiful woman. You're smart and you love life. I'm not asking you to go into an unnatural marriage. I promise you that I'll be able to satisfy you sexually. I'll be a father to Katie, and I'll protect you both from anything the world throws at you."

"Michael, I . . . I'm honored, but . . ." The thought that she loved him but wasn't in love with him rose in her mind, but before she could utter it, he went on.

"I'm not asking you to give me an answer anytime soon. I just want you to know how I feel about you. Think about it, Elizabeth. Aren't friendship and respect a stronger foundation for marriage than infatuation?"

"Yes, they could be," she admitted.

"I never expected to marry again after I lost Barbara. I didn't think anyone could take her place until I met you."

"If . . . if I did decide to say yes, and I'm not saying I will," Liz said, "I could never take Barbara's place. I wouldn't want to."

He cleared his throat and reached for her hand. "I love you and I want to take care of you."

Liz tensed. "I have to be completely honest. I've been dating Jack Rafferty."

"I know. You deserve better than that. He'll never make you as happy as I can."

"Jack and I have been intimate, Michael."

"Has he asked you to be his wife?"

"No, he hasn't. And I couldn't make that commitment to him if he did. Not now. To be truthful, my life is in such turmoil, I can't decide what I want for dinner, let alone what I want to do with the rest of my life. I need time, Michael."

"I can respect that. I wanted you to know where I stand."

"How did you know about me and Jack?"

Michael shrugged. "It's Delaware. Everybody knows everything, don't they? I don't care. I want you to be my wife. I want us to be a family—you, me, and Katie. Promise me you'll think about it?"

"I will." Liz felt stunned. She'd known that Michael's interest in her was more than friendship, but she hadn't expected this. "You're a good man, Michael."

"For a cripple."

"Don't say that. You have to understand that I've been independent for a long time. I made a terrible mistake with my first marriage, and I'm not certain I can trust my own judgment. If I do marry again, I want it to be for keeps."

"Me too." He raised his hand to her cheek, caught her chin between his fingers, and leaned to kiss her on the mouth. She closed her eyes and kissed him back.

Maybe I should say yes tonight, she thought. Marriage to Michael would be solid; he'd provide the father figure that Katie had never really known.

But could she? Could she turn her back on the passion she and Jack shared? Was what she felt for Jack love, or had she been lured by the excitement of playing with fire?

"You keep Otto with you," Michael said. "You heard about what those boys found in the river? There's a crazy out there, and I won't take chances with your life."

"I don't think I need—"

"Please, Elizabeth. For me. I lost one woman I cared for. I couldn't bear to lose a second."

"All right. I'll take him, but only for a little while. And I can't tell you how long I'll need to think about this."

"You'll never want for anything if you marry me. You have my word on that." He kissed her again.

Michael's lips were warm and firm, but they weren't Jack's lips. "Would you like to come in?"

"No, you go on in and get a good night's sleep. I'd like to drive you down to Norfolk for Professor De-Laurier's funeral next week."

"Thank you. And thank you for the beautiful flowers." She got out of the van, opened the side door, and called to the big German shepherd. "I'll be good to him," she said. "I won't let anything happen to him."

"It's you I'm worried about," Michael said. "I'll sleep better knowing that Otto's looking after you."

Chapter Seventeen

It was ten-thirty when the telephone woke her. Liz hadn't been asleep more than a few minutes, and she was groggy as she raised the receiver.

"Lizzy. It's me. I'm sprung."

"Jack?"

Otto got up from the rug by the bedroom door and fixed her with a keen gaze, obviously picking up on the apprehension in her voice.

"Did I wake you?"

She pulled the phone onto her bed and wiggled to a sitting position. The German shepherd's ears pricked up, and muscles coiled beneath his sleek hide. Liz covered the bottom of the receiver with her hand and spoke to the dog. "Easy, boy." She removed her hand and said into the phone, "The police let you go?"

"I'm coming over."

"No, not tonight. I'm tired, Jack. And I think you owe me an explanation."

"Do you think I'm a homicidal maniac? That I

murdered someone and chopped them up for bait?"

"No, I don't. But you haven't been completely honest with me. I've got too many unanswered questions."

"Trust me. I've got reasons for—"

"No, I'm tired of your dancing around the truth. Is McMann F.B.I. or some sort of government agent? Is he a business associate of yours? What's your connection with him, and why would you call him to find you an attorney?"

"I'd rather not go into it now."

"That's your right. Mine is to cool things between us for a while."

"What?"

"This has all happened too fast. I think I'm losing control. I can't deal with us now. Hell, I don't know what I can deal with. I'm thinking of going to Ireland for a month after Amelia's funeral. Maybe there I can put things in perspective."

"Look, Lizzy, I know—"

"Do you, Jack? Do you have any idea? As if my life hasn't been crazy enough these past weeks, tonight Michael Hubbard asked me to marry him."

"Are you serious?" he demanded. "What about us? Does he know—"

"I told him we'd been dating."

"Is that what you call it? Dating?" Jack swore softly. "Lizzy, I won't let you do this."

"I don't know what I'm doing. And you being arrested tonight doesn't help. What am I supposed to think?"

"I wasn't arrested. They took me in for questioning. How many times did your father spend a night in jail?"

"That's a cheap shot. You're the one who wanted a high-powered criminal attorney."

"Mom shouldn't have pulled you into this. I asked *her* to call McMann, not you."

"Good night, Jack. Call me when you're ready to stop playing games."

It was after one a.m. when the Game Master, face darkened with body paint and garbed in a black wetsuit, paddled his kayak silently out of the marsh to the dock at Clarke's Purchase. There was no moon; the clouds hung thick and heavy with rain, and the mournful cries of night birds mingled with the rustling of reeds and the croaking of frogs.

The house lay quiet, illuminated only by an overhead porch light and the flood lamp in the back yard. The Game Master slipped into the water and pushed his kayak under the dock. The cool water closed around his lower body as he snugged the craft to a tarred post with unsteady hands.

He was not himself.

Since he'd stopped for the tramp, everything had gone wrong—her too-easy disposal, the discovery of her bones, his loss of control. Even tonight, his blood pulsed with the echo of the taunting voices that plagued his existence and would not let him sleep.

Was this the professor's hour? He didn't know. He wouldn't know until he laid eyes on her. If she slept, he might grant her mercy for another week . . . another day. But if the dog woke her, if she caught him in her bedroom, both she and the animal would have to die.

Resolute, he waded along the shadowed side of the dock to the shoreline and crouched behind the last piling. He inhaled the night air, relishing the scents of marsh and woodland . . . intoxicated by the sweet, rotting tang of a bloated fish that the outgoing tide had stranded on the sand.

The feeble circle of light didn't deter him. He would circle around to the end of the house, enter from the cellar door. Locks and bolts couldn't keep him out. He moved stealthily, his eyes and ears missing nothing.

The Game Master flexed his powerful fingers, hoping that he'd not have to choke the life from his professor tonight. If he captured her alive, there might be time for a lingering good-bye before he had to move on to sweet Katie.

He hated to be rushed, but the professor no longer trusted him. He must strike soon, before she evaded him completely. And the voices plagued him, pushing, pushing, urging him to act before he could cautiously plan the final moves of his game.

He wondered if the professor would scream. He'd switch on the tape recorder taped to his chest before he climbed to the second floor. If he had to act prematurely, he would have the consolation of her final cries to relive over and over. His gut churned in anticipation.

He could taste her.

He rose and took no more than two steps through the shallow water when he heard a branch snap. Instantly he retreated to his hiding place and listened intently. What had disturbed the night? A dog? A deer? The sound had come from the front of the dwelling. What wild animal would venture so close to the house? And for what reason?

The Game Master held his breath and waited. A

tree frog chirped; the wind rustled the phragmites, and from the deep woods came the muted cry of a screech owl. The Game Master waited. Blood pulsed in his head. His lungs burned as seconds stretched into minutes.

And then he heard it—the unmistakable crunch of a footstep. He resumed breathing. A man. Not a woman, but a man. He didn't know how he knew, but he knew. There was no question. His instincts were as finely tuned as those of a marsh hawk. The Game Master smiled. Power flowed to his limbs. Flames ignited from his glowing core.

The hunt was on.

Time stopped as he circled the sprawling brick house, loping between old trees, beach plums, and boxwood with the grace of a dancer. No twig snapped under his feet. No leaves crunched. He felt as one with the darkness, a fierce predator guided by will, self-preservation, and superhuman intellect.

The man never heard him coming.

One final leap and the Game Master's left hand closed over the intruder's mouth. At the same instant, the point of the knife in his right hand severed the victim's spinal cord. One quick thrust and the man collapsed. The Game Master didn't loosen his grip until his quarry had given several convulsive jerks and lay limp and still.

Blood loss was minimal.

The Game Master pulled a length of black plastic from the pouch at his belt and wrapped it quickly around the dead man's neck and head. Then he lowered himself to a crouching position and waited to see if the professor or the dog had heard the slight scuffle.

When no lights came on and the house remained silent and sleeping, the Game Master slung the warm body over his shoulder and returned to the two-man kayak. Fitting the corpse into the backseat and balancing its weight so that it wouldn't tip was tricky, but he managed as he managed most difficult situations.

As he pushed the kayak away from the dock and climbed in, he cast a longing look at the house. The professor would have to wait a little longer. It was more important to dispose of the intruder's remains, and he knew the perfect spot, a bottomless sinkhole in the marsh.

A pity to rid himself of the body so quickly, especially since this was only the fifth male he'd ever eliminated. The Game Master wondered if he should keep some sexual token as a novelty. As a courtesy to the superior sex, he'd never saved trophies from men. Well, hardly ever. He had carried *the crabber's* tongue on a key chain for years. Ridding himself of the professor's father had been almost as easy as silencing the little tramp. The murdering fool had been drunk and unable to defend himself, even when he knew why he had to die and who was carrying out the sentence.

The Game Master turned to glance back at his passenger. "Enjoying the ride, are you?"

The intruder's head wobbled as the kayak moved into the channel and the force of the outgoing tide.

"No use complaining now." The Game Master chuckled at his own little joke. "You should have stayed away from the professor."

* * *

The following morning, Liz called Nathan Tarkington's office to see if she needed to remain in contact for the next few weeks, and to share her concerns about the lack of response she'd had from the State Police in general. When she reached the detective's voice mail, she left a brief request for him to call her.

Tarkington picked up just as she was about to disconnect. "Yes, Dr. Clarke. I'm sorry I haven't gotten to touch base with you. Things are hectic here."

"Maybe I'm getting neurotic, but I felt as though you were avoiding me."

"No, no. The investigation is under way, and I'm not at liberty to disclose information. I assure you, I'll call you when and if you're needed."

The detective was saying all the right things, but Liz had the feeling that she was getting the brushoff. "Did you get a report from a trooper who responded to a complaint at my home? Someone poisoned Michael Hubbard's guard dog, a valuable German shepherd. Do you know Michael? He's my neighbor, and he lent me the animal to—"

"Yes, I know Captain Hubbard well. I'm sorry, but I'm late for a meeting. I promise that your concerns will be given the attention they deserve."

"Did the officer mention the insurance policy that my ex-husband took out on—"

"Yes, Dr. Clarke, I have that information. You must understand that—"

"This isn't coincidence. I'm being stalked."

"I'll get back to you on this. We appreciate your cooperation. Thank you, and have a good day."

"Thanks for nothing," Liz muttered to the German shepherd after Tarkington hung up. "Daddy was right. The police are not our friends."

What she needed was to get out of the house and do something—anything physical—to work off her annoyance at the detective and the tension gathering in her shoulders and the back of her neck. After spraying herself and Otto liberally with insect repellent, Liz put the dog on a leash and slid the .22 revolver into an old holster of her father's so that she could comfortably carry the gun on her walk. She felt a little foolish, but she had promised Michael that she'd keep the weapon handy when she was alone. You couldn't get much more alone than the old logging trail that ran into State Game Lands.

She walked and ran for the better part of two hours, returning in an easier frame of mind than she'd been in for days. She'd decided to contact Nancy Steiner and ask her point-blank about Cameron's abrupt departure, and she'd made the decision to refuse Michael's offer of marriage. No matter how it altered their friendship, she couldn't settle for security. She'd been independent too long to marry for emotional security and companionship.

What to do about Jack still plagued her, but a trip to Ireland was beginning to look better and better. Jack hadn't been honest with her, and without honesty between them, good sex wasn't enough. There was too much danger of sliding into his world and the possibility that his life mirrored that of his brother George.

She cared for Jack, but she'd proved that she could make tough decisions where he was concerned. She'd done it once, and she could do it again.

As she and the German shepherd entered the kitchen, a blinking red light on the kitchen phone alerted her to a missed call. Caller ID listed it as the Delaware State Police, and she listened to the message. Detective Tarkington was polite, but succinct. He apologized for not answering her primary question when they'd spoken. She was free to go on summer vacation so long as she left a contact number.

She had scarcely better luck with Nancy Steiner. Liz reached the professor by telephone at Somerville, but found her less than friendly.

"Considering the charges that Mr. Whitaker has made against you, I'd suppose that you'd be more than willing to drop the entire matter," Professor Steiner said.

"I was not stalking him," Liz replied. "Quite the contrary. It was Cameron who—"

"I'm really not interested in your excuses. Whatever your slant on the problem—"

"Slant?" Liz said. "I have reason to believe that Cameron threatened me both by e-mail and repeated calls to my home phone. He trespassed on my property, and admitted taking photographs of a highly personal nature."

"Dr. Clarke, I see no reason for this conversation to continue further. This is not California, and whatever conduct might have been acceptable in your last position is not sanctioned here. Mr. Whitaker is no longer an employee or a student at Somerville, and his reputation and future career have suffered irreparable damage. Haven't you done enough to him without pursuing—"

"Has he left Dover?"

"I would suggest you contact Dean Pollett, although I highly doubt he will share confidential information with you either."

"Did Cameron do something to you? A simple yes or no will suffice," Liz said. "Why would he accuse me of wrongdoing and suddenly leave Somerville?"

There was silence on the other end of the line.

"Nancy . . . all I'm asking is—"

"I should think I've made myself quite clear."

"He did, didn't he?"

"Good-bye, Professor Clarke. Do not attempt to discuss this matter with me again." A loud click ended the connection.

Liz swore under her breath and punched in Dean Pollett's number. His secretary answered and informed her that the dean would be out of his office for the next week.

"Can you tell me if Cameron Whitaker's accusations against me have been dropped?"

"That's for Dean Pollett to—"

"Phyllis. Nothing happens in the school that you aren't on top of. Please. At least, tell me—"

"Dr. Clarke, you really shouldn't be discussing this with me. Dean Pollett will be back on—"

"Yes or no, Phyllis?"

"I can't say."

"Just tell me if I should hire an attorney. It's an expense I can't afford at this time, but—"

Phyllis cleared her throat. "I believe . . ." she began hesitantly. "I believe you could hold off on that action . . . for the time being."

"Thanks, you're a life saver. I'll sleep easier tonight."

"Would you like me to make an appointment with the dean for you?"

"No. I'm thinking about taking a trip to Ireland, to see my daughter. Tell Dean Pollett that I'll speak with him when I get back." She thanked the secretary again and hung up.

"One more monster slain," Liz said to the dog. She washed out the water bowl and refilled it. "There you go, Otto, nothing's too good for you."

She felt like calling Amelia and telling her the good news, and then remembered that there would be no more heartfelt chats with her best friend. She could share Cameron's downfall with Michael, but she wasn't up to talking to him yet. If she did, she'd feel compelled to tell him that she couldn't marry him . . . that if she'd led him to believe otherwise, she was sorry . . . that all she felt for him was friendship.

Instead, Liz tried to reach Sydney. When voice mail picked up, Liz left a message for her friend to call. Then she grabbed a quick peanut butter and jelly sandwich and threw herself into the task of cutting the grass.

Liz finished the back yard as the first drops of rain began to fall. Driven inside, she swept and mopped her kitchen floor and settled down with her computer to check out fares to Ireland. When she couldn't find anything reasonable, she put in a call to Dot at the travel agency in Dover that she'd used several times before.

Everyone Liz knew seemed to find great rates on the internet, but she was old-fashioned enough to prefer the services of an experienced travel agent for overseas flights. Due to a computer glitch, a friend in California had once purchased two tickets to Italy for the same day. Getting a refund from her credit card company had proved a nightmare, and Liz wasn't willing to make a similar mistake.

Dot called back in twenty minutes with several possibilities. "I can get you a much better deal if you're willing to wait at least ten days," the agent said cheerily. "You'll save four hundred dollars if you stay at least three weeks."

Liz groaned. "Ten days? Can't you schedule now?"

"No. It's a special promotion. Iceland Air. It includes a twenty-four-hour layover at a good hotel in Reykjavik. We aren't supposed to tell anyone about it, but it's common knowledge. I know you'd love to see your daughter sooner, but I'd wait if I were you."

"Okay, so what now? Do I call you in ten days?" Liz asked. "I'd like to think about it. I might want to leave sooner."

"If you do, let me know. Otherwise, I'll call you on the first day of the special. And meanwhile, if anything better comes up, I'll let you know. There's always the possibility of a special to Heathrow or Glasgow. Then you'd have to book transportation to Dublin, but that's minimal."

"No, I'm not that fond of air travel. I'll fly straight through."

"I'll talk to you soon, then," Dot said. "Bye."

"Yes, that's what I said." Liz laughed. "I'm coming to Ireland." It had taken her the better part of the evening to reach Katie, but now that she had, she felt a hundred times better. "I can't wait to see you," she said. "I've got so much to tell you."

"I've missed you too, Moms. Really. And I'm sorry about what I said—about Dad. I know he can be a real jerk sometimes, but . . ." Katie sighed. "He's really gone and done it this time, hasn't he?"

"I'm afraid so."

"Does this mean I'll never see the twins? I know you and Danielle never hit it off, but they are my half—"

"I'd never try to keep you from seeing them. So long as it's okay with Danielle, and I'm certain she'd be glad to have you visit with them."

"You don't mind, really?"

"No, I don't mind. It might be nice if you'd send Danielle a photo of yourself. See if you can find a plastic frame, something the little Tasmanian devils can't eat or tear apart."

Katie laughed. "Be nice, Moms. They're only babies."

"Actually, honey, I think Danielle could use a little emotional support. Call her if you like. But just do it when the rates are low."

"I hear you. Do you think you could pick me up two pairs of jeans, the ones I like, in a size eight? And Kraft macaroni and cheese? As many boxes as you can stuff in your suitcase. Ireland's fantastic, of course, but sometimes, I could die for Grotto pizza or Thrashers' fries with vinegar. Even the Coke tastes different over here. I think it's sweeter."

"No Cokes. I draw the line at trying to smuggle cans of soda through customs."

"What made you decide to come here instead of driving to New England with Michael? You said you were thinking about it."

"It's too long to explain over the phone. I'll tell you everything when I get there. Let's just say that I couldn't stand the thought of not seeing you."

"Hmm," Katie teased. "I think the plot thickens. Give with the dirt."

"Nope, you'll have to wait. I was wondering if you'd like to do some sightseeing, maybe rent a car and see some castles?"

"Sounds great. I'll ask around, see if I can get a line on some neat places to stay. I know it's kind of cornball, but I'd really love to go to one of those medieval dinners where everyone's in costume."

"I know you have classes, but I might even take a mini tour, the ones where you bike through quaint villages. There are some standing stones in the north."

"Moms, there are stones everywhere! And sheep. Tons of sheep. They're gorgeous from a distance, but they can really stop traffic. I know there's some other stuff I need from home. I'll e-mail you a list."

"I don't doubt it. Just keep in mind that I can only bring two suitcases, and I need room for my own stuff."

They talked for another ten minutes, and then Katie had to run to meet a friend at the library. Liz hung up the phone with a grin on her face. For a little while, she'd reached out and touched the Katie she loved more than anything in the world. She knew it was natural that they'd hit a few bumps in their relationship. Katie was growing up, and she was as adamant about her independence as Liz herself had been at that age.

Liz realized she was hungry. It was too late for a real dinner, so she settled for a frozen low-cal pizza, a salad, and an apple. She thought about calling Michael and telling him her decision, but decided that the phone was a coward's way out. No matter how hard it was, she had to do it face to face. She had just poured herself a glass of iced tea when the phone rang.

Caller ID showed a local number and the name A. Rafferty. Was Jack calling her from his parents' home? She didn't want to talk to him any more than she'd wanted to speak to Michael, but she picked up anyway.

"Lizzy?"

She was surprised to hear Nora's voice rather than Jack's. "Hi, Nora."

"I wanted you to know that I'm bringing Georgie's boat over tomorrow morning. No, before you start arguing with me, this is what my son wanted. It has nothing to do with you and Jack."

"I can't accept it," she said. "I'd love to buy the boat, but—"

"Hush that talk, girl. Of course you can take it. Georgie loved it, and it's the last thing I can do for him. You'll take it, or I'll know the reason why."

"Nothing is settled between me and Jack. I'm scared, Nora. Too much has happened, too fast. I'm going to Ireland to visit Katie, and—"

"You're scared? You're not the only one. But you're not to worry your heart over takin' Georgie's boat. There's more reasons than you being the nicest young woman I know or you and Jack liking each other . . . It's got nothin' to do with Jack."

Liz stretched the cord so she could reach her tea and took a sip. "What does it have to do with?"

"Your daddy and Georgie. You were too little to re-member, but my Arlie used to drink as bad as Donald. Only, your daddy was a happy drunk, and whiskey made Arlie mean. He was hard on his boys, too hard. And I'm ashamed to say that I wasn't much better. I used to take a belt to them, but Arlie was worse. The two boys were stubborn and ornery. Always sneakin' off from chores, or talkin' back. Georgie was the oldest, and he caught the most hell. Your daddy used to stick up for him. Said a boy without spunk wasn't worth salt. Once, he and Arlie come to blows over it, and Donald took Georgie home to Clarke's Purchase and kept him for two months."

"I didn't know that."

"It's true," Nora said. "You can ask Jack. He remembers the bad times. I think it was thinkin' he was losin' Georgie for good that made Arlie see the light. Or it was just time we grew up and started actin' like a mother and father ought to. We started going to church. I quit drinkin', and Arlie gave up the hard stuff. It made a new man out of him. Oh, he takes a beer now and then, but it don't set him off like the moonshine used to. You know your daddy made whiskey, didn't you?"

"No-o-o." Liz sank onto the kitchen stool, the glass of iced tea clutched in her hand. "I didn't know that."

"Oh, yeah. He made good whiskey. Had him a still on a high spot deep in the marsh. That old Buck Juney worked for him on and off for years. It's the reason he let Buck build a shack on your land. I always thought your daddy made up some of those crazy tales about Buck to keep people away from the still."

Gooseflesh rose on Liz's upper arms. "He worked for Daddy? Are you sure?"

Nora chuckled. "Who can be sure about anything, now that they're both dead? But Georgie's the one who told me, and he thought the sun rose and set on Donald Clarke." Her voice grew serious. "Take the damn boat, Lizzy. It's either that or start a family feud between the Clarkes and the Raffertys. And you know watermen. Once a thing like that gets teeth, it will last for at least three generations."

"I'd like to pay something."

"Nope. Consider it a gift from your daddy. I'm bringing it first thing in the morning. I should be there by nine at the latest. I'd appreciate it if you'd give me a ride home. If it's not convenient, I can have Arlie—"

"Nonsense, Nora. Of course I'll drive you home."

"Good. Arlie and Jack are going to have their hands full tomorrow anyway. You heard the weather reports, haven't you?"

"No. I haven't had the TV on in days."

"That hurricane that made such a mess down in the islands, it's headin' straight up the East Coast. Hurricane warnings are already being posted for the Carolina coast. It's one reason I didn't want to wait to bring Georgie's boat. That old shed is rickety, and it's liable to fall in on the boat and do real damage. You make sure you've got batteries and kerosene in case the power goes out. We haven't had a bad blow in a while, and we're about due."

"I'll check to be certain I'm prepared. I saw something about the hurricane in the paper yesterday, but it was supposed to be losing strength and turning east."

"Well, Cassandra changed her mind. Winds are 120 and gaining speed. We're safe here for another forty-eight hours, but after that . . ."

"I'll check the weather station on the internet."

"Okay, honey. I'll see you in the morning then. And Lizzy . . ."

"Yes?"

"When you go to bed tonight, say a prayer for my Jack. He needs all the help he can get."

Later, after Liz had finished her meal and gotten to the computer, she found the weather forecast as dire as Jack's mother had warned. If the storm continued on track, it would pass directly over the DelMarVa. And when she went to her e-mail, she found three messages that had all come in after seven p.m.. The first, from Michael, said that he'd located a six-month-old German shepherd pup on eBay, out of the same bloodline as Heidi, and he was driving to Pittsburgh to see her. The second was from Jack. It read simply, *Let's talk this out. Jack.* Finally a brief note from Amelia's husband, Thomas, explained that he'd decided to postpone the memorial service for another week due to the threatening hurricane and travel difficulties for relatives driving up from the Deep South.

Thomas's spare message brought back the loss of her friend, and Liz broke down and wept for the second time that day. She tried to imagine what school would be like in the fall without Amelia, and she couldn't. How could the life of such a brilliant teacher end on a simple drive to her beach house? It was so unfair.

As she crawled into bed, eyes red and swollen, Liz mentally went over her emergency supplies and decided to run into Dover after she took Nora home in the morning. The hurricane might veer out to sea or it might hit the Carolinas and weaken, but it paid to be prepared, especially in such an isolated area. Hurricanes didn't particularly worry Liz. She'd been far more apprehensive about the continual earthquakes in California. The brick walls of this old house had stood for three hundred years and probably would be standing long after she was dead.

Clarke's Purchase had seen its share of heavy weather. Liz could remember once, when she was small, water rising within a few feet of the back porch and her father tying his rowboat to the gate. Luckily, the old house was built on a rise and the ground around it was sandy. There had been plenty of electric failures, but no water damage, unless you counted the rain that poured through the attic roof when high wind tore off a few shingles. Still, Liz was glad that Katie was safely away in Ireland.

"Everything bad comes in threes," Nora had said. Three people around Liz had died. If the old superstitions were true, her run of tragedy was over. Wasn't it?

Morning dawned gray, and the air felt still and heavy without the hint of a breeze. A quick check of the morning news told Liz that Cassandra was still moving north-northwest, bearing down on the Carolinas. Evacuations were under way all along the coast, and Norfolk was under a storm watch that extended all the way to Cape Cod.

Liz hurried though her shower and breakfast, then took Otto out for his morning run. She had found several heavy mooring ropes in the barn and carried them to the water's edge before she heard the first rumbling of a boat motor. She walked to the end of the dock and watched as Nora rounded the bend in the river.

"Mornin', Lizzy!" Nora waved as she covered the distance between them and brought the craft expertly to the dock. "Runs like a clock," she called as she cut the engine and let the bow nudge the piling.

The two women quickly secured the runabout to the posts. It had been decades since Liz had helped her father ready their fishing boat for bad weather, but it all came back to her. The wind would likely push the tides much higher than usual, so she and Nora had to leave enough line so that rising water wouldn't sink the boat, and at the same time, the line had to keep the craft snug enough against the dock to prevent damage.

"Would you like to come in for coffee?" Liz asked when they were finished.

"Love to, but I can't," Nora replied. "I need to get back and give Arlie moral support. Plus I promised to drive old Mrs. Horsey to the foot doctor. Those daughters of hers both work and can't seem to find time to take her. And she don't drive anymore. Not since she got caught going the wrong way on Route One. It's her eyes. Her mind works fine, but she can't see worth a damn."

"No problem. Thank you for bringing the boat. I love it. It's just what I wanted. I wish you'd let me pay you what it's worth."

"No more of that talk," Nora said. "We've hashed that out. Georgie wants you to have the boat, and I brought it to you. Enough said. Enjoy it—that's the best thanks you can give my son."

Liz got her purse from the house, put the dog inside, and she and Nora got in the car. She stopped at the end of the lane to put a bill in the mailbox and noticed what looked like a police car parked on the road a few hundred yards away. "That's odd," she said. Anxious to see what was wrong, she turned right and drove to the end of her property line.

"Wonder what he's doing out here," Nora said.

Liz pulled up behind the state trooper. A young officer stood beside a second vehicle that had been parked on a grown-over lane and was nearly hidden from the road by the trees. The policeman seemed to be writing a ticket. "Wait here," Liz said to Nora. She got out, barely able to conceal her rising anger.

The policeman glanced up and frowned. "Is this your car, ma'am?"

"No, but I know who owns it." The Somerville parking sticker on the window removed all doubt. "I live there." She pointed to her property. "The owner has made harassing phone calls to my home, trespassed repeatedly, poisoned a valuable dog, and threatened me. His name is Cameron Whitaker, and I want him arrested on charges of stalking."

Chapter Eighteen

It was late afternoon when Liz returned from Dover. After she'd driven Nora home, she'd stopped at Wal-Mart to pick up extra batteries, raisins, granola bars, another flashlight, and bags of ice to fill her cooler. She'd wanted to purchase a battery-operated lantern to replace her propane one, but those were sold out. While she was there, she stocked up on fresh fruit, three new paperback novels, and a selection of goodies to snack on if she got bored. Storms always aroused her sweet tooth, and since she'd lost six pounds since Tracy's death, she could afford to indulge herself. As she pushed her grocery cart out into the crowded parking lot, the sky was darkening and cold needles of rain were falling.

Filing the warrants against Cameron took nearly two hours, and more than once, she wished that Michael were there for moral support. She had the impression that the officer taking her complaint thought *she* was the kook. By the time she arrived back at Clarke's Purchase, Liz almost hoped that

Cameron would show up at her door. If he did, she wouldn't need Otto's protection; she was angry and frustrated enough to take him or any peeping Tom on single-handed.

Instead of turning into her drive, Liz kept going, passing the spot where Cameron's vehicle still sat, a soggy yellow tag hanging out of the driver's door. Odd, she thought. If he left it here much longer, the state would have it towed, and that would cost him. She imagined that Cameron might have seen the policeman, cut through the woods, and hitched a ride home. But why hadn't he returned for his car?

As she pulled up to the back gate, Liz reached under the front seat and retrieved the revolver Michael had given her. She felt like a criminal, and she supposed that, technically, she was guilty of carrying a concealed deadly weapon. If she were caught and charged, that might be cause enough for her to lose her job at Somerville. A few weeks ago, after Katie, her professorship was the most important thing in her life. Now, her teaching position didn't seem as vital. After losing both a student and a friend, she wondered if she could ever pick up her life where she'd left off.

Too much had happened. Everything had suddenly become more complicated, and if she didn't get away to sort things out, she wasn't certain she'd retain her sanity. She'd never considered herself overly emotional, yet ever since she'd learned of Amelia's accident, she'd found herself bursting into tears without warning. She'd come close to it in the check-out line in Wal-Mart today when a tall, slender black woman walked by. For a split second, she'd thought the stranger was Amelia and nearly called out to her. Her friend's death had hit her much harder than her mother's, and she wasn't sure she'd ever get over it.

The house, the dock, and the yard were quiet, as she'd left them. Everything seemed secure, but to be certain, Liz carried the handgun with her as she dashed to unlock the back door and let Otto out. The German shepherd trailed her back and forth through the pouring rain as she carried her purchases inside. On the final trip, she heard the phone ringing.

It was Michael, asking if she'd been following the progress of the hurricane. When she assured him that she had, he said he'd be stopping in Valley Forge to visit an old buddy, another ex-cop, who'd been in a physical therapy rehab with him, and that he'd definitely be home sometime after midnight.

"Why don't you bring Otto and come to my place in the morning?" Michael suggested. "I'll make breakfast and we can keep each other company during the storm."

Liz sighed. "No, thanks, I'll stay here. Go down with the ship, as it were. You're sweet to worry, but I'm okay. Did you buy the pup?"

"No, too high-strung. It takes a steady temperament to make a good guard dog. I'll keep looking." He paused and then asked, "Have you thought about the big question?"

"Yes, I have, but I'd rather wait to talk to you in person." She kept her tone light. She'd didn't mention finding Cameron's car either. There wasn't anything Michael could do about it from Pennsylvania, and it would only cause him more worry. "You drive carefully," she warned. "From what the weatherman says, the earliest that the hurricane could hit here would be late tomorrow morning, and there's still a possibility it may turn east over the ocean."

After she hung up, Liz found a raincoat and boots of her father's in the closet under the stairs and went out to move her car to the barn. For the next three hours, she kept busy, filling water containers, securing the heavy wooden shutters that protected the windows on the ground floor, and moving her lawn furniture, grill, and trash cans to a low shed.

"I'll do all this, and the hurricane will miss us completely," Liz commented to the dog. When she looked at the NOAA weather site on the internet, Cassandra seemed to be stalled over the Carolinas and had been downgraded from a category 3 to a 2. Even at 80 mph, the storm had done considerable damage, knocking down trees and flooding streams and rivers, but traveling over land had decreased the power of the hurricane, and so far, there were no reported deaths.

While Liz was studying the Doppler maps, she received an instant message from Sydney asking if she'd heard that Amelia's memorial service was postponed. Liz answered that she had, and they chatted for a few minutes before Sydney's husband alerted her that the twins were awake and wanted her attention. Sydney sent her love and hastily signed off. There was a second message from Jack, but Liz didn't open it. She was no more ready to parry with him than she was with Michael.

Rain continued through the night, and by morning gusts were whipping around corners of the house and raising whitecaps on the river. Liz attempted to call Michael to see if he'd gotten home all right, but there was no answer. When her phone rang a few minutes later, she grabbed it without checking Caller ID. She'd thought it would be Michael calling back. Instead, she heard Jack's voice.

"You're ignoring my e-mails," he said. "You're being childish. We need to talk. I want to come over."

For an instant, she was tempted. If he came, they'd end up arguing and then making love. It was a given, and she wasn't ready for that. Not until she'd decided that Jack could be trusted. "No," she said firmly. "I meant what I said before. You haven't been honest with me."

"Give me a chance. I'll tell you everything."

"Later, when I get back from Ireland. When I've had time to sort things out. Good-bye, Jack."

"Lizzy, don't hang—"

Only she hadn't. She been about to press down the button and cut him off, but the line had gone dead first. She tapped it. Nothing. "Damn," she muttered.

She'd wanted to call Michael's house and see if he'd gotten in safely, but her phone was definitely out. She knew that it was probably the rain. It had been pouring all night, and sometimes it seemed that she lost the telephone lines every time there was a hard rain. Not that she wasn't used to losing phones and electricity here on the farm. Several times when she was a child, and once since she'd returned to Delaware, a Nor'easter had dumped so much rain on Kent County that rising water had flooded out the bridges on either end of Clarke's Purchase Road.

Liz's cell was in her purse, and she used it to try Michael. She got a busy signal, and had no better luck with his cell phone number. She wondered if she should drive over and see if everything was all right, but if Michael was there, it would mean going in. It would mean telling him that she'd decided not to marry him.

She put her cell phone on the charger on the counter and busied herself making a pot of vegetable beef soup and a loaf of bread. Punching down bread dough was always good for releasing tension.

Jack would be furious, certain that she had hung up on him in a display of childish temper, but she didn't care. It might be good to upset him for a change. She chopped onions and carrots, browned meat, and threw spices into the pot. The soup grew beyond anything she'd ever eat in a week, but it would freeze, and she could always take some to Michael. She was certain that it was impossible to make soup for one person; hers always fed at least ten.

Liz watched the television coverage of the coastal storm damage as the delicious scent of baking bread and soup filled the downstairs. According to the latest reports, Cassandra was weakening and heading northeasterly into the Atlantic, rather than sweeping directly up the Chesapeake Bay. The drenching rains continued, but the winds that whipped the tree branches and tore at the shutters were not hurricane force.

Twice, Liz tried the phone again, but the lines remained dead. The dish signal flickered and then went black; her picture was replaced with a message that said she had lost the signal. When the news program didn't return, she curled up in her favorite chair, put in a DVD, and watched Harry Potter try to outwit his nasty relatives so that he could escape to school. The lights went out, then on and off again before going out for good sometime after eleven, and Liz gave up. Laden with a glass of ice water, the revolver, the new flashlight, and an extra pack of batteries, she climbed the creaking stairs to make ready for bed.

When Liz entered the room with the flashlight on, she found her cat already curled on a pillow, nose tucked under her tail. She turned off the flashlight and put it on the nightstand beside the handgun. In five minutes, her teeth were shiny clean, and she was sliding between the sheets in the dark to the symphony of wind and rain.

The thick walls of brick fired three hundred years ago in a kiln in the west field muffled the storm, but attic timbers groaned and squeaked, and glass panes rattled. The German shepherd paced the bedroom and hall, whining anxiously. In contrast, Muffin showed little concern for the hurricane. Liz could hear the cat's soft, peaceful breathing only inches from her face and wished that she could sleep as soundly.

Liz didn't fear the darkness; she'd spent too many summer thunderstorms in the farmhouse without power to be concerned by the lack of electricity, and she was too old to believe in ghosts. Reason told her that this was one night when she didn't have to worry about Cameron prowling around the house. No one, peeping Tom or pervert, would be abroad on a night like this. But still, she couldn't shake a feeling of uneasiness. She lay awake for hours, tossing and turning, always bordering on sleep but never quite drifting off. The wind weakened and changed direction, and the deluge of rain dwindled to a light patter on the windows.

When she got up to use the bathroom, thunder was rumbling menacingly overhead. Liz wasn't surprised. Yesterday's paper had mentioned the possibility of hurricane winds and sudden shifts in temperature causing violent thunderstorms in the South. A bolt of lightning momentarily illuminated the room brightly enough that she could read 2:15 on the bedside clock, which had a battery backup. Seconds later came another roll of thunder.

She didn't bother with a robe or slippers, but padded barefoot to the toilet. She wouldn't have taken the flashlight either if she hadn't been worried about stepping on the dog in the dark. But as she directed the beam around the bedroom and up and down the wide hall, Liz realized that she hadn't needed the light. The German shepherd wasn't anywhere to be seen. She assumed that he'd gone back downstairs to his favorite spot in the kitchen.

When she returned from the bathroom, Muffin was still curled on the same pillow on the bed. "Still here, are you?" Liz murmured sleepily. The cowardly cat hated thunderstorms. If the booming grew louder, Muffin would dive under the bed and wouldn't come out for hours.

Liz had just switched off the flashlight when she heard Otto growl and then bark furiously from downstairs. She froze, heart thumping against her ribs, held her breath, and listened. Just as quickly as the German shepherd's warning bark had come, it was cut off. Liz reached for the flashlight again, and her fingers closed on the gun.

Her cell phone—where was her phone?

She reached down on the bottom shelf of the nightstand where she kept her purse, but it wasn't there. Had she left her purse and the cell in the kitchen?

Grabbing the flashlight in her left hand and keeping the revolver in her right, she got out of bed and went to the bedroom door. She stopped and listened. The faint screech of metal came from the hall below. Cold panic seized her as she recognized the familiar sound. The door leading to the cellar was original, the heavy iron hinges rusty with age.

Gooseflesh rose on Liz's bare skin. She wanted to call for Otto, but she was afraid. If there was someone in the house, the intruder wouldn't know she was awake. Instinct bade her to slam the bedroom door and throw the wide brass bolt. But she couldn't be sure. The possibility that she'd conjured the squeaking cellar door out of her own terror made her creep down the hall to the top of the front staircase, the one that led not to the kitchen wing but down to the wainscoted, formal entrance hall. The cellar door opened onto that passageway, but that door was always locked. She'd checked it herself when she'd returned from Dover.

Lightning flashed through the window at the far end of the hallway. A few heartbeats later, thunder crashed, reverberating through the house. Liz gasped as Muffin, eyes wide, back arched and hair and tail bristling, darted through the bedroom doorway. Hissing, the cat raced past and leaped down the staircase in two great bounds. Seconds later, the cat's wail rose to an enraged shriek. Otto yipped in pain, snarled, and went silent again.

Liz heard the bottom step creak under a heavy weight. Time seemed to stand still as fear paralyzed her and images of Buck Juney rose in her mind. Then a clap of thunder shook the house. Deafened, she twisted around and fled back to her bedroom. Closing the door as quietly as she could, she shot home the bolt with stiff, trembling fingers. Her stomach churned. Her mouth tasted of copper. She could almost smell the rotting stench of Buck's clothes and hair—feel the heat of his fetid breath in her face.

Was she losing her mind? Buck Juney was dead. He couldn't be here in the house. Her stalker was someone else. Not a specter but a living, breathing monster . . . someone who meant to kill her. Had he already killed Otto as he had Heidi? Was it Cameron? And if not Cameron, who?

Not knowing was terror beyond any she had known. She wanted to fling open the door and shine the flashlight beam in the intruder's face. But if she confronted him, it would give away her last advantage. And if she held the flashlight, she couldn't use both hands to raise and aim the revolver. If he had a gun . . .

No. She had to wait. If she couldn't see him in the darkness, he couldn't see her. If he tried to force his way through the locked door, she would have to shoot. A black chasm yawned at her feet. Could she do it? Could she take someone's life and live with herself? Reason told her that this couldn't be happening. Not to her. Not twice in the same house.

Logic shattered as the doorknob turned.

Liz dashed to a window, pushed up the sash, and knocked out the screen. The waistband of her pajama shorts was too loose to hold the gun, so she threw the weapon out onto the lawn. She climbed onto the windowsill as a heavy weight slammed against the door.

"Game over," a harsh male voice shouted through the door. "You're dead."

Liz turned onto her stomach and lowered herself out the open window until she was hanging on by her hands. The door splintered. She let go and dropped, smashing into a boxwood and sliding onto the wet grass amid a tangle of leaves and sharp twigs.

The storm was directly overhead. Rain fell in torrents. Lightning shattered a dead tree in the orchard, illuminating the house and yard and half blinding Liz. She scrambled to her feet, oblivious to the scratches on her face and body.

"Ready . . . not! . . . come!" bellowed the shadowy figure at the upstairs window.

She couldn't hear all the words, but her mind filled in blanks. Where was the damned gun? She looked around frantically. "Please, please," she prayed. Her fingers closed on the steel barrel of the weapon and she snatched it up, thankful that it hadn't gone off and killed her when she threw it out of the window.

She only had seconds. Run! But where? She dashed around the house toward the barn. Another jagged bolt of lightning and crash of thunder rocked the earth; but her fear of the monster was greater than that of the storm. Rain battered her face and exposed skin, and the muddy ground sucked at her bare feet, but she knew every step of the way.

The car was locked. She knew it was locked, but

she tried the door handle just the same. Gasping for breath, she dropped to her knees on the barn floor and dug for the spare key she kept taped to the driver's tire well.

It wasn't there. "Yes, it is!" she cried, leaning her head against the car. "It's got to be!" A shred of sticky electrician's tape dangled, but no key.

Run. Not in the barn. Not where he could trap her. The marsh. If she reached the safety of the tall reeds—

"Lizzy!" Jack stood in the open double doors.

She grasped the pistol in two hands and aimed it at him. "No! Get away!" she screamed.

"Wait! I—"

Lightning made the barn as light as day. Liz shut her eyes against the glare, and in the split second she was blind, Jack lunged at her and grabbed her wrist.

"Drop the gun!" he shouted. His voice was nearly lost in the blast of thunder.

She struggled to hold on to the weapon, but she was no match for his strength. He twisted her arm, forcing the revolver down. "No!" she screamed. "No!"

"Lizzy, I—"

His words were drowned in Otto's snarl. The German shepherd burst out of the rain and struck Jack with enough force to send him staggering to one knee. Liz slammed her fist into Jack's face and broke from his grasp. Jack swung the gun barrel back over his shoulder against the dog's head, and Liz heard Otto yip and then bark furiously as she fled away from the barn toward the water's edge. A gunshot cracked and then another.

Liz looked back to see Jack pounding after her. Otto's yelp had become a howl of agony, but the dog was on the attack. A third bullet slammed into a post, not four feet from her head, sending splinters flying like missiles. One embedded itself in her upper arm, another in her side, but she ignored the pain and ran faster.

A narrow opening appeared in the tall reeds. Liz ducked into it. Her feet sank into mud. The water rose over her ankles, but she kept moving, slipping, falling, pulling herself back up to her feet. Behind her, she heard Jack shout her name.

The gun went off again. Instinctively Liz ducked. The reeds opened to a small hummock of ground. She didn't need daylight to know there were two gnarled cedars here, dwarfed and twisted. The water rose over her knees, making each step more difficult.

To the left, through a tangle of grass, phragmites, and mud bank, lay the river. If she could reach that, she could swim to—

A beam of light found her. "Game over, Professor."

Liz turned and threw up a hand to shield her eyes from the powerful mag light. The monster loomed out of the shadows, his big hands smacking together in an eerie parody of applause. But the voice wasn't right . . . it couldn't be . . .

"Jack?"

"You lose."

Realization flooded though her. She didn't need the flicker of lightning to recognize the man in the hood and black clothing. "Michael?" But if Michael was here, where was Jack?

He laughed.

"Michael? It can't . . . You can't . . ." He was standing—had run after her through the marsh. How could he? His legs . . .

He took a step toward her. Liz threw herself against the wall of reeds, clawing against the tall grass, forcing her body through the morass toward the river.

"Enough. My play."

A blow to her head made her ears ring. She fell forward, rolling onto her back and kicking at him. Something hard slammed against her ankle, and stars pinwheeled behind her eyelids. She cried out and struggled as he leaned down to grab her injured leg.

"I said, 'enough'!"

"You son of a bitch! What did you do to Jack?" She kicked him in the chin with her free foot. Michael grunted and leaped onto her. She smashed the heel of her palm into his face and tore at his hair, but in seconds he had a knife at her throat.

"Be nice, little bird," he said. "Or do you want me to slice your throat and let all your pretty blood drain out in the mud?"

"Like you did Tracy's?"

Michael flicked the blade a fraction of an inch. Liz felt a hot stinging as the steel parted her skin and blood oozed from the cut. "Will you be good? Or shall we end it here?"

Part of her wanted to urge him to do it—to stop the madness once and for all. But she wanted to live. "All right."

"All right, what?" He pressed the blade harder.

"I'll be good."

He withdrew the knife and seized a handful of her hair with his other gloved hand. "Come on, then." He yanked hard, and she struggled up, wincing when she tried to put weight on her hurt ankle.

"But why?" she begged. "Why are you doing this to me, Michael? I thought we were friends."

"Shut up! That's not my name." He released her hair and shoved her.

"What is your name?"

He cuffed her hard. "I'll tell you when to speak."

Retracing her steps down the marsh path was a nightmare. And worse, when she reached the edge of the yard, she nearly stumbled over Jack's slumped body. Michael switched on the flashlight. Blood darkened the back of Jack's shirt. Another bullet hole gaped in his left thigh. Liz's revolver lay in the grass a few feet from Jack's pale, still fingers.

"He shouldn't have interfered," Michael said, bending to retrieve the gun and tucking it into his waistband beside a holstered .45. "You were mine. You were always mine."

It was still raining, but the storm was moving on across the bay. The flashes of lightning came less frequently, and the grumble of thunder was less deafening. Otto lay sprawled in a pool of blood and water between Jack's body and the barn. Michael strode past the dog without a glance, but not before Liz saw that the ragged hole in the dog's side was larger than that made by a .22-caliber bullet. Her gun hadn't killed the German shepherd.

"You," she said. "You shot Otto."

"He got in the way."

"Did Heidi get in your way?"

He slapped her, knocking her backwards onto the grass. "I told you to shut up. I won't tell you again." He pointed toward the barn.

Liz bit her lip against the pain and got up. When they reached the open double doors, he gestured toward the car. She hesitated, and he laughed. "Who do you think took your spare?" He reached up on a shelf where her father had kept small tools and produced the missing key.

Michael knew where she kept the key. He'd been the one who'd insisted she keep an extra taped to the car. Liz gritted her teeth and leaned against the wall as he advanced on her. She was acutely aware of the rain drumming on the shingled roof and the scent of Michael's aftershave.

She was going to die.

How could she have been so stupid . . . why hadn't she guessed that it was Michael all along?

"We're going for a ride," he said.

"You said you cared for me. You asked me to marry you."

"You catch more flies with honey than vinegar."

"I'm not an insect!"

"You're not?"

She tried not to flinch as he brushed past her and unlocked the trunk. "No," she protested through bruised lips. "No."

She saw him raise the flashlight. She tried to dodge the blow, but her ankle wouldn't hold her. The heavy flash light smashed into the crown of her head. She felt a jolt of pain . . . and then nothing at all.

Chapter Nineteen

Light flooded Liz's eyes as the trunk swung open. She'd been vaguely aware of the car's movement, but the blow had left her too groggy to think clearly. Her head throbbed. When she touched the lump, she discovered that her hair was sticky with what she could only imagine must be her own blood. She wondered if she'd lost so much blood that she was in a state of shock.

"Get out!"

Rain streamed down Liz's face and arms as she crawled out of the confined space. Her knees felt weak, and it was all she could do not to gag. She knew she had to summon her wits or she'd be as dead as Jack, but, strangely, she was nearly at the point of not caring.

Jack was gone.

Michael wanted to kill her.

One thought was as impossible to comprehend as the other. Shouldn't she feel something deeper than disbelief? "Move!" Michael's voice was harsh.

How could Michael be her stalker? Yet he was. *Not Michael*, Liz thought. He'd warned her not to call him that . . . but if not Michael, then . . . "Who . . . are you?" she managed.

"Your worst fear. The faceless shadow that haunts you in the night. I am the Game Master."

His hand clamped around her upper arm, powerful fingers biting into her flesh. He shoved her forward, and through the pelting rain she could make out the back of his house. "Why?" she asked. "Why are you doing this to me?"

He shook her so hard that a corner of a tooth cut her tongue. "Shut up! I'll tell you when to speak, Professor." He strode toward the back door, dragging her after him.

The kitchen was dark, the only light the dim glow of a coffee maker. Liz clutched the edge of the table, wiping the rain from her eyes, dripping onto the clean floor as waves of nausea washed over her. She was cold, so cold. When she looked down, she saw that her legs were scratched and bleeding, but she couldn't feel the injuries or remember how she'd gotten them.

Her teeth began to chatter. The house seemed large and cavernous, no longer familiar territory. She became acutely aware of the scents of Lysol Disinfectant Cleaner and floor wax. Even the throb of the refrigerator motor and the icemaker's clicking sounded overloud and ominous.

"This way. Do I have to carry you?"

His detached, almost mechanical voice made the hair prickle on the nape of her neck. The thought of his gloved hands touching her made her skin crawl, and she forced herself to obey. As she crossed the spotless kitchen floor, one unsteady step at a time to the walk-in pantry, she looked toward the telephone.

The space was bare. Someone, and she guessed it must have been Michael, had removed the telephone. Obviously, he had planned to bring her here, and he wanted to make certain that she had no way to call for help.

She stopped. "You're walking. How can you walk? Your legs . . ."

His eyes gleamed. "Do you think I'm so weak I'd stay a cripple?" He slapped his right thigh. "I rebuilt my legs—muscle by muscle. Weights. Massage. Water therapy. Electric shock."

"The pain must have been excruciating," she said in an attempt to maintain a thread of rapport between them. When he didn't answer, she added, "You're still in pain, aren't you, Michael?"

His mouth curved in a frightening imitation of a smile, a smile that didn't alter the cold expression in his eyes. "Pain beyond anything you can imagine."

"But why keep up the pretense—"

"Pain can be your friend, if you let it. Pain can give you power."

"Please, don't do this."

"Shhh," he warned, making a slicing motion across his throat. He slid open the handicapped-accessible pantry door, paused to lay his .45 on a shelf behind a box of saltines. He then wiped her revolver dry with a cleaning cloth and checked the remaining ammunition. After discarding the spent shells, he reloaded the revolver with .22-caliber bullets from a carton on an opposite shelf.

"You were a policeman. You spent your life saving people."

"Can you think of a better disguise?"

"Why? Why are you doing this to me?"

Michael raised a finger to his lips. "All in time, all in time." Smiling grimly, he placed her smaller handgun beside his larger .45 and glanced back at her. "Have you forgotten everything I taught you about maintaining your firearm?"

"Please, just let me go. You don't want to hurt me."

"Impatience, impatience." Michael shook his head. "It's your greatest fault. I have something to show you, Professor. Something I've wanted to show you for weeks."

"Why? Haven't we been friends?" Worse than that, she thought. He'd deceived her so completely that she'd considered becoming his wife. "I don't understand how a friend can . . ."

His face twisted into a grotesque mask. "We were never friends!" Abruptly he lashed out, backhanding her, splitting her lip. She staggered back against the shelves of canned goods with blood trickling down her chin. Before she could run, he caught her by both shoulders and yanked her so close that spittle spattered her face. "You're nothing. Less than nothing. Understand?"

"No, that's not true." She refused to flinch from his chilling stare. "I'm Elizabeth, and I care about you."

Michael's eyes narrowed. His brow furrowed. For an instant, she thought he would tighten both hands around her throat and choke the life from her. But his mood shifted, and he laughed. "We'll see," he said harshly. "We'll see who you are." He shoved her away, reached behind a box of Tide, and flipped a switch. Soundlessly, half of the back section of the pantry wall swiveled to reveal a wooden staircase. "Go on." Michael motioned to the hidden doorway.

Liz moved to the top of steep steps. Michael had told her that his house had only a partial cellar, barely high enough to allow a plumber and electrician to crawl under. He'd lied. She held tightly to the raw wooden rail as she descended to a dirt-floored basement. The naked bulb at the top of the stairs cast a small circle of light; beyond that, the cavernous room stretched in utter darkness.

The stench blasted Liz's nostrils, a foul odor so intense that she shrank back. She clamped a hand over her mouth and tried not to vomit as the rank smells of rotting flesh, stagnant water, and decaying wood enveloped her.

"Move!" Michael grabbed a handful of her hair and hurled her ahead of him. She tripped and fell into a heap of half-cured deerskins. "Do what I tell you, Professor. Or pay for your disobedience." A match flared. Michael lit a kerosene lantern, adjusted the wick, and hung the rusty handle from a peg.

Liz gasped at the dozens of commercial crab pots—wire cages containing glistening white bones and wooden floats—heaped one upon another. Behind the traps, newspaper clippings and women's photographs lined the rough concrete block walls. A polished human skull with a neat, round hole in the center of the forehead leered from a spike on a post, and in a far corner of the room, standing on a plastic drop cloth, was a stump with a bloody, gristle-streaked hatchet buried in it.

Liz shut her eyes and drew in a ragged breath. This was a nightmare. A dream too horrible to be real. She'd wake to find herself warm and dry in her own bed.

"You have to die," Michael said as calmly as if he'd announced what he was preparing for the evening meal. "You know why."

Liz's eyelids snapped open. She was going to be sick. "No, I don't know why!" A sour fluid rose in her throat. "Why?"

Michael swept his hand in an arc, his gloved fingers taking in the clippings and the women's pictures. "It's all part of the game," he said. "And so is this." He ripped a curling, fly-specked page from the wall and held it out to her.

She swallowed and focused on a yellowed newspaper article that she hadn't seen in decades, yet she remembered every word by heart. A faded picture showed her father standing on a dock in front of his fishing boat. The front page headline—in bold black letters—read: "LOCAL WATERMAN SHOOTS INTRUDER."

"Buck Juney," she whispered hoarsely.

"Smart girl."

She shuddered. "He's dead."

"Dead because Donald Clarke murdered him."

Her eyes widened in shock as the horror of that long-ago summer afternoon flashed before her. She scrambled to think, to try and reason what and who this man was and what his connection to Buck Juney was. "You don't understand," she argued. "You don't know what happened."

"Your father killed him, but he paid for his crime."

"My father?"

"Did you really believe he fell off that boat and drowned?"

The buzzing in Liz's head grew louder. "No, you're lying to me." Her father had died in a boating accident. She couldn't let Michael pull her into his madness. Everyone knew that her father was a heavy drinker, and . . .

"He was drunk, but not that drunk."

"Stop it. It's a lie, and you know it. You never knew my father."

"Why do you think they never found his body, Professor? Or his anchor?"

A single tear ran down her bruised cheek.

"Are you crying for him or for yourself?"

"He was my father."

"A redneck. A drunk."

"A decent man. A man who would do anything for his family."

"He was a cold-blooded murderer."

"No! It wasn't like that!"

Michael stripped away his glove and touched her cheek. She winced, but he only laughed as he brought his finger to his mouth and licked it. "Salty," he said. "Don't waste your tears, little professor. Save them for when you'll need them."

"You have everything mixed up. I don't understand what you have to do with what happened then. You're sick."

"It's you who are mistaken, Professor. I understand everything." Michael tugged off the hood and his shirt, and then removed the second glove, all the while watching her with dead eyes.

She wanted to scream—to run, but there was nowhere to run, and she wasn't certain her legs could carry her if she tried. "Who are you?"

"You don't question me! You don't question me!"

"Were you ever Michael Hubbard?"

"Michael? Michael? Don't you know? You're so smart. You should have guessed." He turned, and she saw the map of twisted and discolored scars traversing his back, vanishing beneath the waistband of his black pants. "There's more. Lots more." He took off his shoes and, facing the wall, unsnapped his trousers.

Liz choked back a moan and knotted her fingers into tight fists. Michael wasn't wearing briefs or boxers. Instead, he had a length of white cloth twisted around his middle and tucked between his legs. A loincloth? Or . . .

She almost burst into laughter as crazed as his. A diaper? Two large safety pins with yellow duck heads secured the obscenity that could only be a diaper. Ropes of purple scar tissue continued down Michael's thighs to ruined legs that, despite the hollows and deformities, bulged with sinew and muscle. The sight of his poor tortured legs turned her fear to something akin to pity.

"Who hurt you? It wasn't just the accident, was it? Someone hurt you."

For the space of perhaps two minutes he stood there, not answering. And then he whirled on her, teeth bared. "She did! She did! She did!" His words shot out like bursts from a gun barrel, so closely together that it sounded like "*Shedidshedidshedid.*"

"Women steal the power," he crooned. "But no more." His grotesque grin became a chuckle. "The Game Master has a present for you, Professor."

Liz shook her head. "I don't want anything from you. Just let me go. I won't tell anyone."

"Bad girl. Bad, bad girl." He frowned and shook his head. "Your lies won't work here. The Game Master knows everything." He moved forward, quicker than she would have thought possible, and slapped her twice across the face, rocking her head back with the force of the blows. "I told you not to speak. I have the power. I'll tell you when to speak."

She wanted to leap up, to throw herself on him and claw out his eyes, but she knew she would get only one chance—if any. She had to wait, to pretend, to play the game even though she didn't know his rules. "I'm sorry," she said. "I'll be good."

"You will, won't you?" Michael said. "My girls are always good here." He took the lantern, walked to the far end of the cellar, and flicked on a light obviously intended for a child's nursery—a round, yellow, plastic moon painted with eyes and a mouth. Across the top third of the fixture danced the figure of a blue cartoon cow wearing an old-fashioned bonnet.

The moon light illuminated what appeared to be a crude stage set representing a shack built on pilings in a marsh. The hovel was detailed, down to water-stained planks, a sagging window patched with tarpaper, tin and shingle roof, and decking complete with mooring posts set into the dirt floor.

Homemade fishing poles leaned against the

house; rusty muskrat traps hung from the rotting windowsill, and a moth-eaten raccoon hide, complete with grinning head, was nailed to the shack wall.

Liz bit her bottom lip until she tasted blood. This wasn't just any hut, but one that she had seen time and time again in her dreams. This was an exact replica of Buck Juney's shack in the far end of the marsh at Clarke's Purchase when she was a child.

"Do you like it?" Michael asked. "Do you?"

She looked away without answering. None of this made any sense.

"You didn't even know his name, did you? He was a war hero, and you didn't know his name. It was Eugene. Eugene Winston Juney."

She closed her eyes, trying to concentrate—to remember. What had Jack's mother told her? Had Buck had a wife and child?

"Now, tell me who I was."

"Eugene's son?" she guessed.

"Good girl." He clapped. "Excellent. Now, what was my name?"

How the hell was she supposed to know? Gooseflesh rose on her arms. His name? His name? What was it?"

"Cat got your tongue?" he demanded. "Speak up, or I'll cut it off."

She took a wild stab. "Were you Eugene Winston Juney, Jr.?"

"Ding. Ding. Ding. Now, who killed Donald Clarke?"

"You?"

"Ding. Ding. Ding. The professor wins the grand prize." Michael lifted the top of a nail keg, removed a dripping object, and carried it back to her. "Hold out your hand."

God help me, Liz thought.

He dropped a withered human finger onto her palm. She gave a cry, let the awful thing fall onto the deerskins, and stared in horror. The slender digit was obviously a woman's. The nail was long, carefully filed, and painted with dark red nail polish.

"Do you recognize it?"

Liz shook her head.

"Think, Professor."

"I don't know."

"Bad girl," he admonished slyly. "You know. It belonged to the little sophomore. In your office . . ."

"Tracy?"

"Ding. Ding. Ding."

"Why Tracy? She didn't do anything to you."

"For you, Professor. All for you."

"Michael, for the love of God—"

"Not Michael! Don't call me that. I took care of little Michael, and then he didn't need his name anymore. Did he?" He smiled as he picked up the finger and brushed the red polished nail over his bottom lip. "Did you know that any crime a child younger than twelve commits is erased once he turns eighteen? He can become anything or anyone he wants. Even a policeman. Whoosh. All his past childish sins are washed away." He chuckled. "Michael died for his sins, and the sophomore died for your sins."

"And my father? Did he die for my—"

He cuffed her again, hard enough to send her sprawling half onto the dirt floor. "Stupid girl! We won't go there again. I told you why he had to die."

"For . . . for shooting Buck," she managed. Her jaw felt as though he'd cracked the bone, and it was difficult to speak. One eye was swelling so that her view of him was distorted. "But what's my sin? What did I do to you?"

"You know. You know what you did." His voice had dropped to a gravelly rumble. "You stole him. He loved me, and you stole him."

She sat up and drew her knees to her chest, unconsciously falling into a childhood habit, something she'd always done when she was afraid. "Who, Game Master?" she asked. "Who did I steal?"

He nodded. "All right. All right, Professor. Play dumb. I'll play your game, if you'll play mine. And mine is much more fun." He returned to the shack and drew a canvas sack from under the rotting floorboards of the dock. She watched as he removed a bundle and unrolled an old rubber hip boot. "Come here," he said. "Don't make me come and get you."

Liz did as he ordered, stopping out of arm's reach. Blood trickled down her face, and she could feel her strength draining with each passing moment. But if she didn't stay on her feet and keep fighting him, she'd be as dead as Jack. She'd never see her daughter again. And . . . oh, sweet Jesus. Katie would come home. He could do to Katie what he intended to do with her.

"See," Michael said. "See." He held a handful of black-and-white pictures, wrinkled and water-damaged. "Eugene was a good boy. Sometimes he had accidents and wet his bed in the night. That didn't make him stupid. It didn't make him bad."

Liz took the offered photos, but she had only to glance at two to see know how vile and disgusting they were. She let them all slip through her fingers and turned her face away. "How could he? You were his son. How could he?"

The pictures showed a dark-haired boy, no more than six or seven, with a man. The child's naked body was thin and bruised, his eyes large and frightened. And the man—the sick son of a bitch she knew as Buck Juney—was doing what no human being should ever do to a helpless child. The photographer's finger covered one corner of the snapshot.

"Who else was there?" Liz asked. "Who took the pictures?"

"The first mommy. But she didn't like Eugene. She was jealous, because the daddy loved Eugene best. He said Eugene was a good boy. But then you ruined everything. You lured him away. You stole the daddy from Eugene."

"No," she protested. "I didn't. I never—"

"Liar!" Michael dropped to his knees and dug through the photos. "There!" he cried. "Proof!"

She tried to run then, but he dragged her down, rolled her onto her back, and shoved the picture in her face. She clamped her eyes shut.

He leaned close to her ear and whispered, "Look at it, Professor, or I'll gouge your pretty eyes out and pin them to my wall."

She opened her eyes. The photo was out of focus and taken from a distance, but she recognized herself at once. The picture must have been taken the summer that Buck died. It was a shot of the dock at Clarke's Purchase. She and Crystal had been skinny dipping as they did most afternoons. The back of her sister's head was clearly visible above the surface of the water. She, Liz, was laughing and diving off the top of the mooring post. She hadn't reached puberty yet, and her bare chest was as flat as a boy's.

"No more Eugene," Michael said. "He didn't want Eugene. He sent Eugene away. First the mommy tried to steal Eugene's daddy from him, and then you."

"What happened to the first mommy?" Liz asked, afraid to hear the answer. "Where is she?"

"Eugene fixed her." He winked. "Daddy was angry at first, but then he understood why she deserved to die. The daddy was the one who thought of feeding her to the crabs. But then the daddy liked you best. He told Eugene he could never tell his real name or the daddy would come in the night and put him in a crab pot with Mommy. The daddy rowed all the way across the bay and left Eugene. Then the bad foster-home mommy was mean to Eugene. She said he was a stupid piss pants. She made him wear a diaper. Ten is too old for a diaper."

"But Eugene wasn't stupid," Liz said. "He was smart."

"Smart enough to make the fire look like an accident. Smart enough to fix the second mommy and Michael."

"Did you hurt them?"

"Do you think you can trick me? Manage me?" He laughed. "Did you wonder why Tarkington never returned your phone calls? Why no one took your stalker complaints seriously? Why the police treated you like a crackpot?"

He drove a bare foot into her side, and she gasped in pain.

"The Game Master told them that you were a lonely woman who loved the publicity you got when the girl was murdered in your office at the college and didn't want it to end. That you'd left California due to a mental breakdown."

He kicked her again.

"He even told the dean that you'd made sexual advances to Cameron—that you left suggestive messages on his home voice mail at night."

"Why?"

"Do you still think Eugene is stupid?"

"No," she said when she could draw a breath. "I don't. I don't think Eugene was a bad boy. I think the foster mother was bad. Did she hurt Eugene?"

"All the mommies hurt Eugene," Michael said lightly.

"Wasn't there anyone to help him?"

"The Game Master."

She swallowed. "Wait? What about your wife? What about Barbara? She loved you, didn't she? Would she want you to—"

"Michael's wife, not mine. Barbara was an ugly cow. Michael married her to get this property—next door to you."

"I don't believe that. I've seen you tending her grave. I know you—"

"You stupid bitch, you don't know anything."

"Barbara died years ago. I wasn't at Clarke's Purchase. You couldn't have—"

"The Game Master knew you would come. He knew you couldn't stay away from that house. All Michael had to do was get rid of Barbara and wait."

She had to keep him talking. "Where is Michael now?"

"Gone." He smiled. "Like you'll be. And the daughter." He jerked her to her feet and tugged her toward the corner of the room where the chopping block stood. "Will Katie like me best when you're gone?"

"Stop. Please. You're hurting me!"

"Game over, Professor," he said. "This one has gone on too long. You're boring me."

Liz saw the hatchet and knew what was coming. She struggled with every ounce of her remaining strength, attempting to break his grip on her arm. But the contest was unequal—had been unequal from the moment he caught her in the marsh.

He stretched out a hand for the hatchet.

A high-pitched alarm blasted. Red lights blinked from two corners of the cellar. Michael let go of her and turned toward the wooden staircase.

Liz didn't hesitate. She dove past him, seized the hatchet, and wrenched it free from the block. Before Michael could react, she slammed the blade of the hatchet down on his bare foot.

Michael shrieked in pain.

She caught a glimpse of him clutching his bleeding foot as she dodged and raced for the only exit. Michael's scream became a howl of fury. Oblivious to her own injuries, she scrambled up the steep steps without looking back.

Liz heard him on the stairs, no more than seconds behind her. She grabbed the first thing she saw, a can of oven cleaner. Snatching off the cap, she sprayed it full in Michael's face. He fell back howling, clutched at his eyes, and charged after her again. She fled from the pantry as glass shattered on the far side of the kitchen.

"Professor!" Michael bellowed. "I'll hurt you! I'll skin you!"

She was already moving out of the pantry when she remembered the guns. She reached back and snatched both weapons from the shelf. The heavier .45 fell and skidded across the kitchen floor, but she clung to the .22 in desperation.

More glass splintered. Liz glanced toward the kitchen door. Jack's face loomed, white and haggard. One bloody hand reached through the broken door pane to fumble with the lock.

But Michael was already there in the kitchen, huge and terrible, advancing on her with mad, bulging eyes. "Put it down, Elizabeth," he said. His gaze locked with hers, blue eyes once again human and beseeching.

"Stop," she said. "I don't want to kill you."

"Shoot him!" Jack yelled.

Michael's voice was calm, rational. "You won't shoot me." He reached for her. "You don't have the nerve."

"Don't I?" She held the revolver steady with both hands and lifted the barrel.

Donald Clarke's soft advice echoed out of the past. *Always aim for the largest target, Lizzy. Give yourself the advantage.*

"No!" Michael said.

"Shoot him!" Jack urged.

Chapter Twenty

Liz squeezed the trigger. The first and second bullets tore into Michael's chest, slightly to the left of center. He shrieked, but kept coming, eyes flaming with madness, arms wide to grab her. She stood without flinching and placed a third shot cleanly between his eyes.

Michael sagged to his knees, blood bubbling from his nose and mouth. "You can't," he rasped, crawling toward her on hands and knees. "I taught you—"

"You didn't teach me to shoot," Liz said. "My father did."

"Shoot him again!" Jack yelled.

Michael rose and lunged at her. "I'll choke—"

"Game over," Liz said. Without blinking, she emptied the revolver, placing the final three shots in a half-inch circle in the center of the Game Master's temple.

He fell, twitched, and lay still.

"I can because I've done it before, you bastard!"

Her voice dropped to a whisper. "My father didn't kill Buck Juney. I did."

"Lizzy?" Jack's voice seemed to come from far off. "Put the gun down. It's Jack. Don't shoot me, Lizzy."

She turned away from the dead thing on the floor and placed the empty weapon on the counter. "I couldn't," she said. "I couldn't shoot you if I wanted to. I'm out of ammunition." Beginning to tremble, Liz waited for a rush of guilt, but there was none. She felt only relief and joy to be alive.

"Lizzy, look at me."

She turned to see Jack swaying in the open doorway. His face was an alabaster mask, his torn shirt and shorts soaking wet and dark with blood. "I think I'm going to . . ."

"Jack? No!" Liz dashed to catch him in time to keep him from collapsing. "I thought you were dead," she said as she eased him into a kitchen chair.

His eyes lost focus, and his words slurred. "Tarzan . . . suppose . . . to . . . save Jane."

"Right." Liz knelt amid the broken glass to examine the bullet wound in his thigh. Jack had used his belt as a tourniquet, but blood still oozed in a thin stream from the gaping wound. His breathing was harsh and irregular, his lips blue. "I don't know how you walked on this leg," she said.

"Neither do I." He coughed and wiped his mouth with the back of his hand. "Hurts like a bitch."

"How did you get here?" She pushed back the torn and gore-streaked shirt to see the hole in his chest.

"Boat . . . same way I got . . . to your . . . your house. I was worried about you . . . in . . . storm. Your damned . . . damned bridge is out. Again."

"Figures." She took a deep breath and said softly, "I killed him."

Jack tried to chuckle, but the sound came out as more of a whistling moan. "I saw you. I thought . . . for a minute . . . thought you . . . were going to . . . to shoot me, too." He blinked, and his eyes lost focus again. "Damned . . . damned good shooting . . . for . . . for a woman."

"I always was. Daddy said I had a good eye."

"The things I . . . don't know . . . about you."

You or anyone else, she thought. All those hours of practice with Michael . . . when she'd deliberately missed the target . . . not wanting to think about taking another life . . .

"Damned . . . good shot even for . . . for a man," Jack whispered, fighting to remain conscious. "I feel drunk, Lizzy. Am I drunk?"

"No, you idiot. You're shot." She stood up, cradled his head against her breast, and kissed the crown of his head. "When I saw you in my yard, I thought . . . I thought it was you," she said as she stroked his wet hair. "I thought you were trying to kill me."

"Never . . . never hurt a hair on . . ." His head sagged. "Tarzan supposed . . . supposed to save Jane . . . but . . . Jane . . ."

"You did save me. If you hadn't set the alarm off by breaking the window . . ."

"Jane . . ."

"Jane needs to stop this bleeding. Can you move? You'd be better off lying down. I'll try to call 911, but I think the phones are out. Wait." She left him long enough to get Michael's wheelchair from the dining room, helped him into it, and pushed him into one of the bedrooms.

Another telephone sat on the nightstand. She picked up the receiver, and, oddly enough, there was a reassuring dial tone. With trembling fingers, she punched in the emergency number. When the dispatcher answered, Liz told him that she needed medical help immediately. She gave her name, Michael's name and phone number, and the address.

"What is the nature of your emergency?"

"Gunshot wounds. An adult male bleeding heavily from gunshot wounds."

"Are you in danger?"

"No, the only danger is that this man will bleed to death if you don't get a rescue helicopter here in the next half hour. The bridges on Clarke's Purchase Road are out. Do you understand? The bridges are out. There is no way to get here by ambulance. Behind the house, there's a wide driveway and space for a helicopter to safely land."

"Where is the weapon?"

Liz tried to keep her temper under control. "Send the police. No one is in danger of being shot. The assailant is dead."

"Are you certain of that?"

"I should be. I killed the son of a bitch."

"Stay on the line."

"I can't. I told you. I have a man bleeding to death."

"You must stay—"

"Get someone here fast or hire the best lawyer in Delaware. Because if you don't, I'm going to personally sue you." She slammed the phone down.

"That was pleasant talk for a college professor," Jack said.

"Sometimes the best form of communication is the vernacular."

Jack was a big man and heavy. It was all she could do to move him from the chair to the bed. He groaned.

"Hang on, Jack." She slipped a pillow under his injured leg.

"Not . . . not going anywhere. Got a dead . . . dead . . . deadline."

"Sure you do." She found a pair of scissors in a kitchen drawer and scooped up an armload of linens from a hall closet. She hoped that a State Police helicopter was on the way, but she couldn't wait. She couldn't think about Michael or her fears, about the people she'd lost to his madness. Jack was alive, and it was up to her to keep him that way.

It took time to stop the worst of Jack's bleeding, to force several glasses of juice down his throat, and to bandage his wounds. She thought the bullets had passed through him, but probing the injuries was work for a surgeon. That could wait for a hospital. What mattered now was keeping him from losing any more blood and dehydrating.

"Stay awake, Jack," she urged quietly. "Talk to me."

"I told you . . . told you not to trust . . . not trust . . ."

"Listen. What's that?" She threw up one of the bedroom windows and heard the unmistakable *chop-chop-chop* of a helicopter. "It's them," she said. "It's the E.M.T.'s. I've got to go out and warn them about . . . Don't move. I'll be right back."

"Promise?"

"Cross my heart and hope to die."

Four days later, Liz sat beside Jack's hospital bed reading the synopsis of Jack's third novel as he recovered from surgery to repair the damage done by the two bullet wounds. He was propped up, lightly sedated and bandaged, an I.V. running from his left arm, and a small oxygen tube under his nose.

She was still coming to terms with the knowledge that the Jack Rafferty she'd grown up with had written and sold two blockbuster suspense novels under the pseudonym John Marshall. In his more lucid moments, Jack had explained that he'd finished the manuscript of his first novel, *Chilling Habit*, shortly before being charged with attempted murder. He'd sent the proposal to a dozen literary agents, and Gregory McMann had called him a week later with an offer to represent him. McMann had been excited about the project, so much so that he'd generated enough interest in the novel to prompt three major publishing houses to make six-figure bids on the manuscript.

"Gregory has contacts with the legal community and in law enforcement. I trust him explicitly."

"I didn't know a literary agent's duties included arranging counsel for accused murderers."

"You'd be surprised at what writers expect their agents to do for them. Gregory could tell you stories that would curl your hair. But we've become good friends. I've even taken him off-shore tuna fishing. He deposited my advance check three months after I went to prison, and he's kept my identity out of the media."

"And you kept me in the dark about all this because . . . ?"

Jack managed to look sheepish. "Because I was writing this new book about major drug-running operations on the Delaware Bay, and because George was one of my main sources. Information he fed me could have gotten him murdered three times over."

"So all the while your mother and I thought that you were involved in the drug trade," Liz said, "you were really—"

"Doing research for my book," he finished. "I was afraid to tell you the truth, afraid that if I shared my secret with anyone, George, Mom and Pop, or even you would suffer. So long as the local dealers thought I was a typical ex-con, cop-hating waterman, the people I cared most about were safe."

"And now?" Liz asked.

Jack attempted to shrug, grimaced, and groaned. "Instant karma," he said. "I was wrong. I should have been honest with you. I meant to tell you and my parents everything, once George testified and was settled into a new life."

"What if the public finds out the truth?"

"The people I was most afraid of have more worries than hunting me or my family down. One's dead, shot by one of his partners who thought he had ratted them out. Three of the others, including the trigger man, are in prison, awaiting trial. I doubt any of them will live long enough to be a threat to me again."

"What about your brother?"

"George may be in witness protection, but he's not getting away with his crimes. He'll pay for them as long as he lives. And despite what's he's done, I love him. I just couldn't risk . . ." Jack broke off as a chubby nurse entered with a tray.

"Time for your pain medication, Mr. Rafferty." She glanced at Liz. "If you'll give us a moment."

"No need for her to leave," Jack said. "She's seen my bare ass before."

"Oh, is this Mrs. Rafferty?"

"No," Liz said.

Jack's "No" echoed her own. "At least not yet," he added hastily.

Liz smiled, and winced as her swollen lip cracked. "Not anytime soon." One of her eyes was still black and her jaw ached when she spoke, but her worst injury was a cracked rib. That was tightly bandaged and hurt whether she sat or lay down or walked. Knowing how lucky she was, she ignored the pain.

"Ouch!" Jack said as the nurse gave him the injection. "I think you went all the way in to the bone."

"Hardly, Mr. Rafferty. You'll be feeling much better in a few minutes." She took his temperature.

"Not soon enough," Jack mumbled.

The nurse completed her tasks, made several adjustments to the I.V. line, and left the room. Jack rubbed his hip. "Damn, it wasn't so bad until she jabbed that ice pick in me."

Liz sighed. "Poor Jack."

"You could be a little more sympathetic."

"I don't believe Tarzan ever whined about a little prick."

Jack grinned devilishly. "That's not my problem, and you can testify for me in any court in the country."

"Braggart." She laid the folder on the floor beside the folded newspaper.

Only part of the front page showed, but Liz knew

what the headline read: CRAB-POT KILLER SHOT BY KIDNAP VICTIM. There were photos of her, of Michael in his State Police uniform, of his wife Barbara's grave in the walled cemetery near his home—where investigators had dug up the flesh-stripped remains of at least nine unidentified victims—as well as pictures and drawings of the murder house and dock. The authorities had not yet permitted media access to Michael's gruesome cellar, and if Liz had her way, the entire place would be blown up before TV cameras, sleazy tabloids, and reporters had a field day with the contents.

Neither she nor Jack had spoken of Michael, but now Liz felt that it was time. Sliding the straight-backed chair closer to the bed, she took Jack's hand and squeezed it. "Is it my fault?" she asked him. "Did I set this in motion by shooting Buck Juney all those years ago?"

"Hell, Lizzy, how could you think that? How old were you?"

"Eleven."

He gripped her hand. "Are you certain you even did it? You must have been pretty scared. You—"

"Buck came into our house," she replied in a low monotone. "I screamed at him to go away, but he kept coming. He tore off my T-shirt. He was . . ." She stiffened. "He exposed himself. He meant to rape me, Jack. But when he tried to yank my shorts down, I jabbed my finger in his eye and ran. He came after me, but I found Daddy's pistol and . . ."

"Your father took the blame for the shooting to protect you, didn't he?"

She nodded. "He made me swear never to tell. He said I hadn't done anything to be ashamed of, but other people might not see it that way. He said it wasn't right that his little girl should be branded a killer for protecting herself."

"Buck deserved killing. You've got no reason to feel ashamed."

"He was a monster. He did terrible things to Michael . . . to his son. Molested him—twisted him."

"Mom and I talked about Buck, when she was in earlier this morning. She said all the Juneys were stark raving lunatics. It didn't surprise her that Michael turned out the same way. But she said she thought you were right—that the boy was named after his father."

"Eugene Winston Juney. Michael was a name that he must have assumed later. At least, that's what he told me. He rambled on. I didn't understand half of it, but he did say that he killed his mother, and that Buck buried her in the swamp. I know about Tracy and my father, but how many others? Cameron Whitaker seems to have vanished. Did Michael have a part in that, too?"

"Maybe," he said. "Maybe Whitaker's buried out there in the marsh someplace. I don't think we'll ever have all the answers."

"Jack, there were piles of human bones in that cellar. It was hideous." She hesitated. "I think Michael may have murdered Amelia, too."

"It's not your fault," Jack said. "You stopped him from ever hurting anyone again."

"But why did he insist that I learn to shoot? I killed him with the revolver he bought for me. How crazy is that? Did he want to be stopped, or was it all part of his sick game?"

"It's beyond me, honey. Maybe they'll find a tumor the size of a baseball in that skull of his."

"No." She shook her head. "There's nothing there but pure unadulterated evil." She rose and kissed Jack's forehead. "Maybe there's a best-seller in it, Mr. Marshall?"

"I don't need to glorify that bastard by writing about him. It's better that we forget he ever existed." Jack's eyes were growing heavy. "If I never write another word, I don't have to worry about money. My last advance was half a million."

"I'm glad for you. You deserve your success."

"It was never the money. It's nice. Hell, it's great, but I don't write for the money. Books influence people, maybe change some ideas. Who knows? Maybe in time we can even clean up the bay, get rid of the chemicals and the parasites and bring back the fish. Make things the way they used to be."

"You're starting to sound like my father after two six-packs and a pint of Wild Turkey."

"Is that bad?"

"No, it's not. There was a lot of common sense behind his rambling."

"Will you be all right, Lizzy? Can you put the bad stuff behind you and go back to teaching kids? Or will you be afraid to return to the farmhouse? Mom told me that your phone lines were cut, that the police found cameras in your ceiling, and electronic bugs in your walls. Will you ever be able to sleep under that roof again?"

She shrugged. "Do you think I'd let Buck Juney's

crazy kid drive me off my land? Not no, but *hell* no."

A smile tugged at the corners of Jack's mouth, and he looked at her with admiration. "You're a stubborn woman."

"Not stubborn, rational. If Michael couldn't get the best of me, why should I be afraid of anything else life throws at me?"

"Your daddy would be proud."

"Maybe there's more of me in him than I thought."

"You're not telling me anything I didn't know."

She glanced at a mirrored wall. Her face and arms were a mass of bruises, her eyes sunken and bloodshot. "I look like Daddy did after a rough night at Rick's." She touched her swollen cheek gingerly.

"You'll heal, and you clean up good," Jack said. "It's me I'm worried about. Is there any hope for us? Mom keeps telling me she wants to die a grandmother."

"Isn't there a slight problem with that idea? You told me you couldn't father a child."

"We could always figure out something. Mom says that there are plenty of kids out there who need families. Adoption wouldn't be the worst suggestion she's ever come up with. Of course, if you're dead set against any more babies . . ."

Liz settled back in her chair, folded her arms, and scowled at him. "You lie to me, drag me into the middle of a redneck bar fight, and let me believe you're a drug dealer in league with organized crime. No self-respecting, intelligent woman would date an out-of-work commercial fisherman who's just gotten out of prison, let alone let him sweet-talk her into a commitment."

"Lizzy." Jack groaned.

"But then again, as my daddy used to say, 'Where there's life, there's always hope.'"

The Barbarian

Judith E. French

Surrounded by the exotic luxuries of ancient Alexandria, courted by the world's most powerful men, Roxanne is a woman of privilege—and one with no memory of her past. Flashes of recollection bewilder her, images of a tiny baby torn too soon from her loving arms.

Then one starless night a stranger enters her silken chamber, startling her with his dark savagery, seducing her with his sensual mastery. Does he hold the key to the mysteries that plague her? His tales of passion and betrayal seem too fantastic to be true, but her heart tells her one thing is as certain as the rising of the sun: She once gave all her love to this daring warrior, had pledged her hand and her honor to... The Barbarian.

FATAL ERROR

COLLEEN THOMPSON

West Texas gossip paints every story a more interesting shade, especially when a married man goes missing with a small-town banker's wife and a fortune in fraudulent loans. Susan Maddox is tired of feeling like an abandoned woman, and even angrier when the neighbors act as if she's the one getting away with murder. Maybe her handsome-as-sin, bad-boy brother-in-law wasn't the smartest choice of ally, but who else could she trust to recover damning information from her husband's crashed hard drive? Who else is there to pick up the pieces when intruders set fire to her home, a truck runs her off the road, and a trail of dead men stops her cold? Who else can help her uncover a . . . FATAL ERROR.

KATHLEEN NANCE

THE WARRIOR

Callie Gabriel, a fiercely independent vegetarian chef, manages her own restaurant and stars in a cooking show with a devoted following. Though she knows men only lead to heartache, she can't help wanting to break through Armond Marceux's veneer of casual elegance to the primal desires that lurk beneath.

Armond returns from an undercover FBI assignment a broken man, his memories stolen by the criminal he sought to bring in. His mind can't remember Callie or their night of wild lovemaking, but his body can never forget the feel of her curves against him. And even though Callie insists she doesn't need him, Armond needs her—for she is the key to stirring not only his memories, but also his passions.

___ 52417-1 $5.99 US/$6.99 CAN

CHRISTINE FEEHAN
LAIR OF THE LION

Impoverished aristocrat Isabella Vernaducci will defy
death itself to rescue her imprisoned brother. She'll even
brave the haunted, accursed lair of the lion—the
menacing *palazzo* of legendary, lethal *Don* Nicolai
DeMarco. Rumor says the powerful *don* can command the
heavens, that the beasts below do his bidding . . . and that
he is doomed to destroy the woman he takes as his wife.
But Isabella meets a man whose growl is velvet, purring
heat, whose eyes hold dark, all-consuming desire. And
when the *don* commands her to become his bride, she
goes willingly into his muscled arms, praying she'll save
his tortured soul . . . not sacrifice her life.
